Annaliese Fry, MD

Annaliese Fry, MD

Johnny Fry and Jinx ~ Book 3

Skeet Will

Annaliese Fry, MD
Copyright © 2021, 2025 – Skeet Will
ISBN: 979-8-9986565-2-1

JK
Press

JK Press
Oregon, USA

This is a work of fiction. Names, characters, places and incidents are either the product of the author's imagination or are used fictitiously, and any resemblance to any actual persons, living or dead, events, or locales is entirely coincidental.

Dedication

To my daughter Samantha, who constantly amazes me.

Annaliese Fry, MD

Like most towns in the Spanish New World, San Diego grew up around a catholic mission. The first European settlement in California, it was founded in 1769 and was still a small village of mostly Indian inhabitants when it became part of Mexico in 1821.

As a result of the Mexican American War, California became a part of the United States in 1848, but it was still a village of less than five hundred when gold was discovered on the American River in 1848. The Gold Rush brought people from all over the world, and though California was admitted to the Union as a new state in 1850, San Diego remained a small town until the railroads arrived in the late 1880's and then it began to grow.

Chapter One

Doctor Annaliese Fry's father and mentor had studied medicine in Germany under a teacher who believed in the newly developed germ theory of disease transmission. The man was a fanatic believer in washing hands and instruments after each patient. Because her office help had no training in washing instruments, she was bent over a sink doing it herself when her receptionist came into the room and said, "There's a gentleman here who wishes to speak to you."

"A patient?"

"I don't think so. Looks like he just got off the train."

"Seat him in the office and I'll be there in a minute." She finished washing and wrapping each instrument in a clean towel, arranged them in a basin so she could have them when needed, washed her hands and was drying them with a towel when she walked into her office.

She walked past the man sitting at her desk and when she turned to sit down, her face was transformed to a look of wide-eyed, open mouth surprise.

Her father was sitting there smiling at her. She stared at him for a moment and then collapsed into her chair.

"What?" she began, and then she was up and around the desk and they embraced - for a long time.

She stepped back open mouthed and shook her head as though she couldn't believe what she was seeing.

"Hope I didn't shock you too much," he said.

"It did shock me. It was just so unexpected. What are you doing here?"

"Could it be that I just wanted to see my favorite daughter?"

She grinned. "I can understand that, but this is a long way for a busy man to come just for a visit."

"Now that you mention it, I guess it is. But let's talk and I can answer all your questions. Here, or would you rather go somewhere else?"

"I was closing up for the day, so why don't we go to the store? Actually, it's also a house, so we can have coffee and talk all night. You can see Johnny and Lemuel. Wash will probably show up when he hears you're here."

After she locked the door, she turned and embraced him again. "It doesn't matter why you're here. I'm glad you are."

He had rented a buggy and followed her to the store. It was a large building; four levels with attic rooms above that were built around the bookstore which was on the first level. They stopped in the store to say hello. Johnny wasn't there but they talked to Lemuel for a minute, and when they were finally seated in a study overlooking the city she said, "How is everyone at home? The last letter I got was months ago."

"They're all fine. Tommy finally got married and she has a little girl." Her sister's name was Thomasina, hence 'Tommy'. He sipped his coffee and continued. "The reason I'm here will take some explaining. Of course, I wanted to see you but things have changed at home.

"Over the years I've traveled and been exposed more than most people to influences outside the Saints' world. I find that I've changed as the world around me has but they have not so much. So,

I've decided to leave Salt Lake City and seek my way in the 'gentile' world.

"For one thing, I've never liked having three wives. I did it because it was the way of things when I was younger, and the practice became more prevalent as I got older." He shook his head and took a deep breath. "I can see all the advantages of it from their point of view, but I don't want to carry it with me into a new life.

"When I began to move toward this separation, I found it was a little more of an undertaking than I had originally thought. Finally, I went to the Elders, and we worked out a plan."

He looked at her over his cup when he took a sip. "I decided I wanted to come here because you were here and from your letters were doing well and liked the place.

"After much thought I presented my plan to them, and they agreed. So, I've come here to open a clinic for the faithful similar to ones we've opened before. This one will be a little different." He paused and looked at her steadily. "I would like to join it to your practice."

He stopped and continued looking at her to see her reaction to this, but her expression didn't change. She sat listening expectantly. When he didn't continue, she said, "Knowing you, I'll bet you had a plan for that too."

"Yes, I did, and they seemed to like it. Before we talk about that, I want you to understand something. You're a doctor in practice now and I will treat you as a colleague. If you accept my idea, I believe it will benefit us both. If for some reason you don't, I will still open the clinic. After all, I've had a lot of practice with that over the years."

"I'm all ears," she said. "Tell me how it looks to you."

"Why don't you tell me what your practice is? Then I'll tell you how I see it."

She had been leaning forward listening to him intently. Now she sat back, gathered her thoughts a moment and finally said, "Probably three out of four of my patients are Mexican women and children. Some men, especially with wounds and injuries. They had been Dr. Clark's people for many years, but they seem to have accepted me mainly because he spoke for me.

"He was a shipwrecked sailor who had been an assistant to the surgeon on board and, with no other trade set up as a doctor back in the early 40's. Since most of the people here at that time were Mexicans and Indians, they became his patients. He told me many of his patients now are the grandchildren of his first ones.

"Since we opened the store last year I've met some of the Anglos in town, and some are now my patients, but not many. I think that will change over time. It seems to me I remember you spoke some Spanish, so you could help me there. Mine is still rudimentary."

She paused. "That's about it. I'm not getting rich, but I pay my bills, and they feed me. We're getting used to a new diet. A lot of Mexican food." She grinned at him. "Payment in kind. I never give them a bill, but they always pay me. So how do you see your idea and my life coming together?"

"Pretty simple, really. The clinic will take Mormon patients as needed, and if they can't pay, several times a year we'll send a bill to Salt Lake for their treatment. I'll share new patients with you, help you when you need help and you do the same for me."

"What about the family? Will they be coming?"

"Once I get settled and we know where we are Cinthia and two of the younger children will likely come out. They will remain in the flock. There are a few of the faith here and Cinthia 's a good organizer and a good speaker. She can spread the faith for the church while she organizes the faithful."

He smiled at her. "You have to give the Elders credit. They always seem to be able to use events to their benefit. The others of my family I will support from a distance. I'll probably go back now and again but I'll live here."

"Are you still a Saint?"

"No, I don't think so. There are too many places I find our

thoughts don't line up anymore. I love many of them and believe they are good people but..." he shook his head. "I feel like we're moving in different directions, away from each other and I don't feel I'm a part of things there anymore."

"Do you love Molly or Agatha or even Cinthia for that matter?" she asked.

"Love has not been in my life much since you left," he said. "I love my children, though I don't know them very well, but their mothers? No, I don't think so. Their focus has been on raising the children and on the faith, so we don't really have much in common anymore." He sat for a moment looking out at the city and the bay in the distance.

"It may be that I have a certain amount of love in me, but not enough to spread to three women." He shrugged. "Maybe when I try to spread it around that much it's not there anymore.

"To get back to my idea for us, we would treat each other's patients as needed and work out some kind of arrangement on who comes in the door. Your last letter said you were moving the practice here to the house."

She looked around and said, "This is my new office. When we finish here, I'll show you the other rooms. This whole place was built with the idea that it would be a home, a doctor's office, and a bookstore."

"Well, that's my plan," he said. "Any part of it is subject to adjustment or compromise and, if we can't come to common ground on things I will still live here and open the clinic."

"I can tell you right now I know it will work," she said. "In fact, I think it's a wonderful idea and I can't imagine there would be a problem. There are times when I could sure use the help. There's enough room for you to stay here and when the family comes out we can likely squeeze them in until you can get them settled elsewhere."

She took him into the clinical rooms and showed him the equipment already installed. "Can we arrange to expand if necessary?" he asked.

"Yes. We own the building where the office is now, and if need be, we can improve it and make it into a separate office plus we have enough land around here to grow as much as we need. We could have moved over here last year but I didn't want to disrupt the lives of my patients so soon after Doctor Clark left.

"I don't pay any attention to the business end of The BookSeller, but between this store and the one in San Francisco, it more than supports us, so what I make is mine to use as I need or want, not that there's ever that much. We can grow as much as we can afford."

"Well, I've got some money I can bring to the venture. I believe the closest hospital is Los Angeles so we might begin to plan one here. Surely there's a need?"

"There's a hospital of sorts that's joined to the poor farm, but it's not much in terms of services, and most of the patients are indigent. Most times if someone needs a hospital, we put them on a train to Los Angeles.

"There were three other doctors when I got here, and we've added three more. Things have slowed down lately as far as people moving here to live. When we got here it was booming. Not so much now.

"Still, I believe you're right. I think there's enough need that we can probably find the support we'd need for a hospital. There are several wealthy businessmen here who underwrite civic projects. I imagine it will be a matter of soliciting their support."

"Well, I'd say that's down the road a little but until then we can work with what we have." He took her hands. "When Johnny gets here let me take us all to dinner. Is there a ferry over to Coronado? I hear the hotel over there is quite spectacular. If we can get there and back, we can sightsee, eat, and talk about the future."

She embraced him again. "I'm so glad you're here Papa."

The first thing Will Crawford noticed about his son-in-law was that he'd grown several inches. He'd first met Johnny as an unconscious accident victim with a broken right arm and left leg suffered when he was thrown from a horse. He and Annaliese had doctored and nursed Johnny through his injuries and a bout with pneumonia. Since they'd been married he hadn't seen him much, and now he was a good three inches taller than his wife. They had left Salt Lake City five years before the same height.

Lemuel, Johnny's partner in the bookstore, joined them on the deck of the ferry. They all leaned on the rail and looked at the city behind them and around at the bay.

"It's a pretty place, though still a little rough around the edges but that's just newness. It looks a little like a desert." said Will. He and Johnny had decided his given name was easier than Dr. Crawford. "How many people are here?"

The question was right up Johnny's alley. He had taken it upon himself to learn all about the city that was his new home and he knew enough people at City Hall to help him. He also spent time at the library and, in addition to learning things there, he was working with the staff to help them enlarge their collection. Sometimes he spent entire days looking through back issues of the San Diego Union.

"Last I heard we had a little over 16,000, maybe 30,000 when you include the county. The railroads coming in a couple of years ago started a boom, and the two of them got into a rate war that lowered the cost of a ticket to about twenty cents on the dollar. So, with cheap fares and developers who wanted to sell land, lots of people came to look around. Some stayed though lately it's slowed down a bit."

"Why has it slowed down? If the weather's all that I've heard, in the winter they should be standing in line."

"The biggest reason is probably water. Many new businesses need good water supplies. Without enough municipal water sources we can't attract them, which means few jobs for new residents. We've had some companies that have built two dams back in the hills, which has helped, and I understand there are plans for three more.”

Annaliese turned to him and said, “It looks strange to see you without that cat on your shoulder. Where is he?” To everyone else he was Jinx, but to her, Johnny’s little black buddy was ‘that cat’. The rivalry between them was a running joke and Johnny grinned at her.

“Where *is* Jinx?” asked Will.

“He’s back at the store. I didn’t know hotel policy on cats in the dining room, and I didn’t want to get there and have them tell me ‘No’, then what do I do with him?”

This was one meal Jinx, usually his constant companion at mealtime would miss. In the year long trip on horseback from Kansas to San Francisco six years before they had shared meals in hotels and restaurants, and no one cared. Though a little clown at times, he was well-behaved and knew when to sit quietly or slip under the table and take a nap.

When he looked at the hotel as a place to have dinner Johnny was sure cats weren’t allowed. The first time anyone saw the Hotel del Coronado, or the Del as everyone called it, they usually stood with their mouths open staring, trying to take it all in.

The center of the hotel, the Rotunda, had a round, tent-like roof that rose to a peak some seventy feet high. From there the place spread out into a rambling, many storied, impressively ornate building that eventually resolved itself around a courtyard that could be viewed from five stories up. The hotel had been open just two years, but with 757 rooms, an abundance of luxury appointments and the San Diego weather had quickly become a resort destination of the first rank especially in the winter.

Twice they had been to celebrations there, so they knew the quiet yet extravagant elegance of the place, but this was the first time they had eaten a meal in the dining room. When seated by two stewards the first thing they did was look up. Electric chandeliers swung from beams centered in a grid of window skylights framed by smaller beams. The combination of natural and artificial light made for a pleasant atmosphere, day or night.

"I'll bet the man who designed this place wanted everyone to look up when they sat here for the first time," said Lemuel, eyes sweeping around the room.

"I wouldn't take that bet," said Johnny, also looking around. The others just nodded.

The Crown Room, where they were sitting, was at least two hundred feet long, and the domed ceiling was a good forty feet high in the center. Plants were spaced around the perimeter with statuary interspersed between them and stained glass and paintings were abundant. Slowly revolving fans constantly moved air around the diners.

This was only one of several dining rooms in the hotel. A string orchestra was playing on a small stage near where they sat, loud enough to be heard but low enough to allow for conversation. Ordering their meal was a combination of efficiency and performance by the waiters, then they were free to talk.

The conversation had just gotten around to the Doctor's proposed clinic when a steward hurried up.

"Are either of you doctors?" he asked hurriedly. "We need a doctor! Please, can you come with me? And hurry. Please."

Annaliese was up and following him immediately, but Will looked at Johnny meaningfully for a moment. "I think I'll just go along and watch," he said and followed them out of the big room.

"Well, that pretty much takes care of the idea of dinner," said Johnny. "At least for a while. I think I'll tag along and watch too. Maybe I can help." He stopped and looked back at Lemuel. "Did you see the look he gave me? I wonder what that was all about."

"I have no idea," replied Lemuel, shaking his head, "but I'll bet if you ask him, he'll tell you." He picked up his cane. "You go on ahead. I'll get there as best I can."

Johnny was up and moving. There was a swirl of excitement along the way to a porch fronting on the water where a crowd of people were milling around something on the ground. Johnny worked his way through the crowd to a place where he could see Annaliese kneeling with her hand pressed against a blood-soaked rag applied to a woman's arm.

She looked up at one of the men leaning over her and snapped, "Give me your shirt!"

The man was taken aback but quickly realized her need. He unbuttoned his shirt frantically and handed it to her.

She looked up at him again. "Come here. I need you to hold this tight." She moved out of his way, continuing to hold the cloth tightly in place until he was in position to take it from her. Once he was there, she held the shirt by the sleeves and spun it into the shape she needed. Then she bandaged the wound, winding the sleeves around the arm to form a dressing that pressed tightly against it then she tied it in place.

She stood and looked around. "Johnny, can you get me some warm water to clean things up with?" He nodded and turned away without a word. A maid provided several basins and three of them were filled and carried back to where Annaliese was on her knees, looking at the dressing intently for traces of bleeding.

The maid came forward, knelt and gently began to wash the patient's face while Annaliese cleaned the blood from her arm as much as she could. The woman opened her eyes and struggled to sit up. Annaliese laid a hand on her shoulder, leaned forward, and said, "You must lie still. I've stopped the bleeding for now, but if you move around it may start again."

Her father stood to one side watching her, a faint smile on his face. She looked up at him.

"Good job, Doctor Fry," he said quietly.

Chapter Two

"What was that look you gave me all about?" asked Johnny.

Will smiled. "It's very important to me that she," here he inclined his head to Johnny, "and you, realize that I understand she's a doctor now, and that I respect that and would never do anything to make her feel we are less than equals."

While Johnny was pondering this, the man whose shirt she had requisitioned had found a stretcher and the woman was carefully lifted onto it and carried to a room close at hand that had been prepared for her. From a supply of medical items present at the hotel, Annaliese redressed the wound.

By the time she finished, a woman in uniform was standing by the bed and Annaliese took her to be the hotel nurse. She introduced herself and gave instructions for care for the night.

Once she felt the patient was safe and the nurse had the situation in hand, she washed her hands and arms and joined Johnny and the others by an open window in the Rotunda. She stood for a moment, eyes closed, breathing deeply of the cool ocean air.

"Let me lean on you for a minute," she said to Johnny. "That was exhausting after a long day." She stood with his arms around her for a minute, looking over his shoulder at her father and Lemuel talking. They turned to greet the man whose shirt she'd used to stop the lady's bleeding.

He'd found another shirt and was now talking to Lemuel and her father. After a moment he looked up, and when he saw her came forward with his hand outstretched.

"I can't thank you enough for what you did," he said, taking her hand in both of his. "I think she would have bled to death if you hadn't been there. Your father tells me your name is Annaliese. Mine is John, and my wife is Lille. I'm so glad to know you and that you were here when we needed you."

She smiled wearily. "I'm just curious. How did you know we were doctors?"

"Henry, the steward who seated you, heard you talking," he said with a smile. "I sent someone for help, and he remembered. I need to give that fellow a raise."

"A raise?" asked Lemuel. "Does he work for you?"

"Yes, he does. I'm John Spreckels. This is my hotel."

Annaliese had a habit she'd begun in childhood. Every night she brushed her long red hair a hundred strokes before bed. Johnny loved to watch her and many nights when she finished, he would take her to bed and mess it up.

At thirty-two, she was ten years his senior and sometimes he was a little too frisky for her when she'd had a hard day. They had met when his horse was spooked by a rattlesnake, and he had fallen off the side of a hill outside Salt Lake City. Her father had patched him up and set the broken bones. She had healed his other hurts and nursed him back to health.

In the process they had fallen in love. One night she came to his bed and taught him what she had learned from another. He was an eager pupil, over-eager sometimes, especially when she'd had a day like this one.

That night though, she wanted to talk, and their conversation was about her father and his idea for the clinic and about John D. Spreckels.

Though they had never met him until that night, they knew who he was. Spreckels was a millionaire several times over who owned nearly half the land in and around San Diego and the surrounding county.

He had invested as a minor partner with the men who conceived and built the hotel. When the local land boom suddenly collapsed and they ran short of money he stepped in and saved them by paying the bills and let them retire gracefully with a little money in their pockets. From 1890 on he counted himself the sole owner of the largest hotel in California, indeed the largest west of the Mississippi River.

"Are you going to be caring for his wife going forward?" asked Johnny.

"Well, I'll see her tomorrow and I guess we'll talk about that. I suppose she has a regular doctor here in town.

"We didn't get to talk much about the Doctor's idea for the clinic tonight. How do you feel about it?" she continued turning away from the mirror to look at him. When she was talking about her father to someone else, she always called him "the Doctor".

"It sounds like a good idea. I remember when we first talked to Dr. Clark about you taking over his practice, I thought it would be like his clinics only with Mexicans instead of Mormons."

"He's also talking about looking into the idea of building a hospital here," she said. "If we do that our lives could become much more complicated a few years down the road. If we move in that direction, it will make my life much busier, probably frantic at times.

"Of course, with him in the practice it will likely raise our visibility in the Anglo community too, but I don't want to lose sight of the patients I have now. They're important to me and I did promise Dr. Clark to care for them."

She stood, walked toward him, shrugged her dressing gown off her shoulders and let it fall to the floor. "I need something to help me to sleep," she said. He sat quiet looking at her and she finally said, "Well? Aren't you going to do something?"

He put his finger to his lips. "Shh," he said. "I just want to look at you. You know how much I like looking at you."

She moved forward until they were almost touching and bent to kiss him. He grabbed her and they tumbled into the bed together laughing, with him on top. "How long do you reckon it would take for me to count all your freckles with my tongue?" he asked, beginning with one on her chin.

"Too long," she said. She had a lot of freckles, and she wasn't in the mood to wait. It turned out she wasn't really as tired as she thought.

The next morning Johnny rode with her to the ferry, and when she was embarked, turned his horse and rode south out of the city about ten miles to the cabin where Wash lived with his partner, a woman named Woman.

She was sitting on the porch shelling peas. He joined her and she nodded to him but didn't speak. That didn't surprise him as she was not much for just chatting.

"Is Wash here?" he said looking around.

She shook her head. "He's working."

"I thought he was off today."

"Kate needed him to do a delivery this morning, something special that came in on the train. She wanted to get it out to a customer right away."

"Well, when he gets here, tell him I'm out at the rock."

The rock was a place where he and Wash liked to sit and think and talk. It was a large flat stone, and by some trick of acoustics, there were times of day when the ocean sounded like it was right in their lap, though it was a hundred yards away and down a cliff where the creek that ran past the cabin dropped off and wandered out to join it.

Johnny had some thinking to do and he liked to have Wash

nearby when he was thinking so they could talk about things. Wash was a man who always thought before he spoke and Johnny had come to value the way he looked at things when there was an idea being considered.

Wash's full name was George Washington Moore. He had been born a slave on a South Carolina rice plantation and had joined the Union Army in New Orleans after he was freed. For the next three years he fought through the War with Sherman and Sheridan and became a Buffalo Soldier afterward. He took his discharge in the middle seventies and spent years roaming the mountains and deserts of the west with different groups of men, enjoying the freedom he never tired of.

At loose ends in Casper, Wyoming one night, he went into a café for a meal, and the only open seat was at a table with two young white men. When a Southron at the next table objected to him eating with 'white folks' he left rather than provoke a problem, but he somehow felt the two young men would have taken his part if he had.

The next night he rode into their camp and had been with them ever since. Woman once asked him why he stayed with Johnny and his friend Handy. "Because I can trust them," he had said. "Really trust them; with anything." She understood. She always seemed to understand.

She was as unusual as her name. Short, stocky, with long dark hair, an aquiline nose and piercing dark eyes, she was in her middle fifties, older than Wash by a few years. She had come to San Francisco from Australia with her father and two brothers in 1849 during the Gold Rush. After they were murdered by claim jumpers, she had survived in a gold camp by carrying a long, sharp Bowie knife that she was inclined to use when she felt the need.

She was known as 'the Woman' in the camps and she kept the name when she moved to San Francisco in the early fifties. She dressed in men's clothes, wore miners boots, a wide-brimmed gray felt hat and still carried the Bowie in a sheath on the back of her belt.

One night in San Francisco a few years later she had intervened in an attempted robbery and later had gone to work for one of the women she had rescued. The woman was a former bawdy house operator, and Woman was hired as a bodyguard. Just like that her life changed and for the first time her future was secure.

Her benefactor, Mrs. Hannah Grimes, was known as Madame (accent on the second syllable). When in her forties and very successful in her own business, she had married a very wealthy man and with his death suddenly found herself one of the few rich widows in a city with more than a few rich men.

Woman became her bodyguard then her companion, finally her friend, and then more than her friend. One night they had been drinking wine, sitting together in Madame's dressing room looking out at the city. When Madame leaned over and kissed her on the lips, Woman realized she very much wanted her to.

The time they spent together was special to them because it was so different from being with a man. Once they became lovers their relationship was as unique as they were. They both still enjoyed men in bed, but only certain men. Madame preferred ship captains because they were usually here and gone and demanded nothing but what she wanted to give. Woman chose her men but would not let herself be chosen.

Fortunately, Wash was a man who could let himself be chosen. He had been amazed when they first met that she was attracted to him at all.

He was very black, and though only in his mid-forties, his hair was completely white. He had been born with a slightly twisted spine that gave him an unusual gait. He was short, less than five and half feet tall, with broad shoulders, a large chest, and very bowed legs.

His face was deeply wrinkled and bore a large, cream-colored scar that ran from below his left eye across his lips to the middle of his jaw on the right side of his face. He had once heard a man call him grotesque looking. He wasn't sure what that meant but he knew it wasn't handsome.

From the beginning they were compatible in bed. She could be insatiable and had worn men out, but he loved trying to keep up with her. When she invited him to join her in Madame's bed one night he was a little reluctant at first. He soon came to know the wonder of having two women share with him the special something they had with each other.

Over time he came to love Woman but realized her independence made her different so how they were with each other was different. As a couple they were unique, and Johnny appreciated that and appreciated what they brought to his life.

The events of the night before were on his mind, but he pushed them aside and focused on what he wanted to talk to his friend about. On the trip from Salt Lake City across the deserts of Utah and Nevada, Wash had taught Johnny much about deserts and they had talked about finding new deserts to see together. In the interim, life had intervened.

Wash moved quietly in the woods, so Johnny didn't know he was there until he sat down on the rock beside him.

"I think you need to talk," his friend said.

Johnny looked at him grinning. "How can you tell?" he asked.

"I'm good at reading sign," Wash replied.

"You are at that," said Johnny. "You're right." After a moment's silence he continued. "You ever think about deserts, maybe taking a trip east? How long would it take to get to El Paso from here? Or maybe Santa Fe?"

Wash thought for a moment. "Are you planning on a 'lookin around' kind of trip?" When Johnny nodded, he continued. "We could wander around for a couple of months, see some things. Almost as far from here to El Paso or Santa Fe as from Kansas to California, and it's desert a lot of the way. Why? You thinkin' about going?"

"I've been thinking about deserts a lot these days. Thinking maybe it's time to take another trip."

"Hot out there this time of year."

"I'm not talking about leaving tomorrow. But what about the middle of September?"

Wash looked out toward the ocean. "That'd be better. Maybe early October."

"You up for it?"

"I'll have to talk to Woman. She might want to go along."

"That'd be fine. I know she'll pull her weight."

"What's Annaliese going to say?"

"I'll let you know when I find out."

While he and Annaliese were falling in love they had talked about the life he could expect married to a medical student, and after, a doctor. Because he loved her, he followed her and she had led him to this place for her to begin her practice.

He believed he was the tail on her kite, that her being a doctor and the responsibilities she had assumed because of it gave his life its shape. So far, he felt comfortable with that shape.

The plan they had made for their future was for each to live their lives and live them together when they could. He had taken that to mean that because he helped and supported what she saw as her future, he was free to look for the kind of things that would make him happy within the life they had. This idea of a trip across the desert was one of those things.

Lemuel Waters was Johnny's friend and business partner in the bookstore. After his wife died in Kansas City, Lemuel had built a special wagon that he and his blind daughter had traveled west in, selling books as they went. When he and Johnny met, some of their early conversations had been about creating a special kind of bookstore somewhere west of where they were.

While Annaliese was in medical school, he and Lemuel had opened The BookSeller in San Francisco, and in the three years before she graduated, it had become the special place they envisioned. When Annaliese finished school the plan was for her to begin her practice in Los Angeles, but a trip to San Diego had changed her mind.

While she finished her schooling Johnny, Lemuel, and Wash had taken a two-month sojourn south in the great central valley of California selling books from Lemuel's wagon any time and any place they could. When they got to San Diego, they set up to begin selling from the wagon until they could build the store they wanted. Then they waited for Annaliese to join them.

Now, two years later, this store was the same kind of special place they had before. Though Johnny loved what he was doing, lately he had begun thinking about the desert and had decided to ask Wash how he felt about seeing it again.

The three years Wash had spent in San Diego were the longest he had been anywhere since he was freed, but Johnny knew his friend's restless spirit, like his, was probably still there. Now he was seeing an adventure across a desert landscape in his daydreams, and he was glad the idea seemed perfectly normal to his friend.

When the ferry docked on the Coronado side of the bay, Annaliese saw a surrey from the hotel waiting. She had told them when she would arrive, and someone paid attention. At the hotel the driver dropped her at a different door with the comment, "His office is through that one."

Apparently, John Spreckels had seen her arrive and met her at the door. In answer to her query he said, "She seems better this morning. She slept most of the night and there was no new bleeding I could see. She's had nurses with her all night."

He led her into his wife's room. She was lying with her head propped up on pillows, sipping water. A plate of what looked like buttered bread was in her lap and she had apparently been eating some of it. She put it aside and smiled weakly at Annaliese.

"I remember seeing you last night, but I don't remember much," she said in a low voice.

"I'm not surprised. I'm Dr. Annaliese Fry. We happened to be eating dinner in the dining room when the accident happened. Exactly what did happen?"

"The children were playing. One of them accidently ran into me and I fell against the window. I guess I put my arm out to catch myself and it went right through the glass. I think the problem came when I tried to pull it out."

"Yes, I'd say you're right. From what I could see, when you pulled it out, the glass cut into an artery in your arm and by the time I got there you were bleeding badly. But, thanks to your husband's shirt, we were able to get it stopped."

"Thanks to you, you mean," said John.

"Well, the important thing is we got the bleeding stopped."

"Dr. Fry, my name is Lillie. So tell me, what happens now?"

"Well Lillie, the dressing needs to stay in place at least until tomorrow and then it can likely be changed. The second wound especially needs to begin healing. I worry if we loosen the dressing too soon it may undo our work, and you may start bleeding again. Once the edges begin to knit together it should be fine. Unfortunately, I had no way to suture the wound last night so you will probably have a bad scar."

"When can I go home.?"

"Where is home?"

"It's just down the street."

"Why don't you wait until your doctor can assess the situation and you can make that decision together."

Lillie looked enquiringly at her husband then back at Annaliese. "But you are my doctor, isn't that right John?"

He stepped forward, smiling and took her hand. "As far as I'm concerned, she is." He turned to Annaliese. "Is that alright with you?"

Annaliese nodded. "If that's the case, I would rather you didn't move for now. You've lost a lot of blood and you're probably weaker than you realize. If you tried to stand now you would probably be very dizzy and a fall could be bad. You could be carried, but unless there's a reason for you to be at home, I don't see the need."

"The only thing is the children, but I guess they can visit me here."

"We need to make sure you don't use that arm, so I'm going to put it in a sling. That will help hold it in position and protect it and also remind you not to use it. Make sure you protect it from the children. They might hurt you or reopen the wound unless they're careful."

Lillie nodded and her husband put his arm around her. "I'll make sure they behave," he said.

"Fine. I'll be by to check on you in the morning and we can talk about going home then, and other things."

John walked out with her.

"I know this was a serious wound, but she will be alright, won't she?" he asked. She could see the concern in his eyes.

"It looks like she will, but she'll need to be careful with that arm until it heals. An infection would make things difficult. I didn't have the things I needed to suture the wound closed last night so the healing might take longer than normal. Once I can change that dressing, I'll know where we stand and what we'll have to do. Make sure she stays in bed."

On the ferry ride back across the bay, she pondered how this new patient would affect her life. What would these people think when they found out that she was the 'Mexican doctor'? She knew many in the Anglo community avoided her practice for that reason. Well, she thought, she'd just have to cross that bridge when she came to it.

Chapter Three

Wash enjoyed sitting on the front porch in the cool of an evening, rocking, smoking his pipe and talking to Woman about the day or about tomorrow. On this night, however, he was remembering and thinking how his life had changed the last few years. Though trains ran regularly now, they had ridden into town on a horse and a mule.

It was just 500 miles from San Francisco, but they had taken three months to get here. As he was inclined, their path had wandered. They took side trips to visit a lake he heard about or to stand and gaze at a peak he'd never seen before, to visit a small town and have a good meal or spend a few days in a quiet place where the trees grew so tall the sun seemed like an afterthought.

Since he'd left the Army, he had loved the feeling of choosing; to go or stay, to turn on a new path or stay on this one. For most of his life his choices had either been taken away, as in slavery, or restricted, as in the military. After he left the Army, he had roamed the mountains for ten years, always having the freedom to choose, to come and go as he wished, with someone or by himself.

With Johnny he still had that freedom. Which is probably why he stayed with him. The three years he had been in San Diego were the longest he'd stayed in one place since they struck the shackles off his legs twenty-five years before.

He had been next up on the block when Union soldiers came into the square that day in New Orleans. The lieutenant in charge, who he later learned was from Massachusetts, halted the sale and suddenly, after twenty years of being owned he was free. That freedom was something he never got tired of feeling.

Woman joined him, took his hand, and for a while they rocked in silence. Since neither was inclined to talk much there were a lot of silences in their time together.

"What did Johnny want?" she finally asked.

"Thinking about takin a trip," he said. Because she knew he'd tell her more she sat quiet, waiting.

After a moment he did. "On our trip across Utah and Nevada, we talked about seeing some new deserts together. He's thinkin east across the Sonoran into Arizona, maybe New Mexico. There's a canyon over that way I'd like to see, and I haven't seen Santa Fe for years. Like to see how it's changed."

"When are you thinking of leaving?"

"Maybe early October sometime. It begins to get cool about then."

She didn't ask so he continued. "Would you like to go along?"

She sat thinking about it and he let her.

Finally, she said, "Yes, I think so."

Her first time out of San Francisco had been their trip south along the ocean to San Diego and he had wondered whether it had given her the same kind of itch he had felt for years.

"It'll be hot and dry and dusty not like the trip along the coast." He was still holding her hand.

"Sounds like it would be."

He turned his head and smiled at her. "I was pretty sure you'd want to go along." She smiled back at him.

The thing Johnny liked to do in the bedroom at night, besides mess up her hair, was to talk to his wife. Because they were both busy, they seldom saw each other in daylight, and many times even when she had a day off, she would be called to help a patient in need or deal with an emergency such as the night at the Del.

Before marriage they had vowed never to decide anything without talking to the other and watching her brush her hair at night was their time to decide things.

"Did you go out to the cabin today?" she asked.

"Yeah," he answered. "I had something I wanted to talk to Wash about."

He waited for her to turn around and face him. "Tell me," she said.

"Since Greta and Roy are moving down here, Lemuel won't need me at the store as much. In fact, he won't really need me at all."

Greta was Lemuel's daughter, and she and her husband were moving to town so Lemuel could be part of his grandchildren's lives. Greta was blind, and because they had anticipated this move, the bookstore here had been designed and built as a copy of the one in San Francisco so she would be able to come in and right away know where everything was.

"Wash and I are talking about taking a trip for a while."

Her eyes opened wide and her mouth fell open.

He went on hurriedly. "Things are pretty much stable with your practice and with the Doctor here you don't really need me either, so we thought maybe it would be a good time for it. We're thinking about east through the desert, maybe as far as El Paso or even Santa Fe."

He flinched a little and waited for her reaction.

"You mean just go?" she asked. When he nodded, she continued "For how long?"

"Maybe a couple months. Wash thinks to Santa Fe and back would be a couple of months, three at the most."

She sat looking at him in silence for a long moment, trying to digest what he'd said.

"What about his job? He can't just walk away. It wouldn't be fair to Kate." Kate Sessions owned the plant nursery where Wash and Woman had worked since they came to town three years before.

"He told her when he started there he would probably come and go and apparently she likes having them around so much she'll welcome them when they come back."

"Them? Is Woman going too?"

"Probably. He's going to bring it up to her tonight. I get the feeling she'll be going along."

She turned back to the mirror and began absent-mindedly brushing her hair, forgetting she'd already done so.

"Well, I must say you've taken me by surprise."

He stood and put his hands on her shoulders. "When we talked about you becoming a doctor and what it meant for our lives you agreed I could do things like this."

"I know, but I guess since we hadn't talked about it much since, I thought maybe you'd forgotten about the idea." She was quiet for a moment. "Isn't it dangerous out there? I've read about problems with renegade Indians. Apache, if I remember right."

"With Wash, Woman and Jinx, I should be safe enough, and we'll talk to the Army before we go and take their advice if it comes to it."

"When will you leave?"

"We're thinking about October, maybe the first week." He moved her over and sat on the bench beside her. They looked at each other in the mirror.

"You'll have the Doctor here and you'll be busy setting up the clinic and I have a feeling this new patient will become an important part of your practice in one way or another. You'll probably be so busy you won't even know I'm gone."

"I'll miss you," she said. She turned and he could see tears on her cheeks. "And worry about you. This won't be like selling books in the Valley. It's still a wild place, and dangerous too."

"That's one of the reasons we want to go. There aren't many wild places around anymore. Besides, we won't be just in the desert. Wash told me about a canyon up near the Utah border he's always wanted to see, and I've read about and heard about Santa Fe all my life, and there's Tucson and El Paso. It will be exciting.

"Probably hot and dusty and dirty too, but that's what'll be fascinating about it. The kind of creatures and plants that can survive in a place like that are worth seeing and learning about and Wash is a good teacher."

She smiled at him through her tears. "You'll probably be doing things like this when you're an old man and Wash isn't around anymore."

"Probably," he agreed, "but you knew that when you married me."

Lemuel was smiling when he and Johnny watched the train bringing his daughter and grandchildren back into his life come into the station, brakes squealing, blowing steam.

Greta was standing at the top of the steps with Roy holding her arm. Behind them were Mrs. Keane and the children. When the conductor put down the stool, Roy stepped off. He turned to help his wife and guide her down the steps and to one side so he could swing the twins down one at a time, then help the housekeeper.

Lemuel embraced his daughter, kissed her and shook hands with Roy. "Welcome to San Diego," he said to the children. He bent to kiss his granddaughter, Mary, then his grandson and namesake.

Johnny led them to a waiting wagon, and when everyone was seated and luggage loaded, started the horses and said over his shoulder, "Annaliese is working, or she'd have been here."

When they stopped in front of the store, he gestured up at the sign painted in gold leaf above the front window.

"'The BookSeller at San Diego'" he read. "Your Papa got a fellow to come down here from Los Angeles especially to paint that.

Couldn't find anybody good enough around here to suit him."

Roy leaned over and murmured something in Greta's ear, then said to Lemuel. "I didn't know you named it that."

"It just seemed like the right thing to do," said Lemuel. To his daughter he said, "And the inside is laid out just like The BookSeller back home, so you should be able to find your way around easy enough."

He handed her down and led them through the front door. As everyone came through the door, he introduced them to a young woman behind the counter and another putting books up on shelves. Johnny stopped to talk to them, and Lemuel led his family into their new home where they followed their noses to where two Mexican women were putting steaming dishes on a long table.

"If you want to wash up, there's a water closet through there." He pointed and Roy guided Greta in that direction while Johnny led Mrs. Keane and the children into the kitchen where there was a water tap and sink.

When everyone was seated at the table, Lemuel tapped his water glass and said, "It makes me very happy you're all here. Now, for the first time, this house will really feel like home."

He smiled around the table at them. "The ladies in the kitchen are Maria the cook and Consuelo the housekeeper. We don't really need a housekeeper, but she's one of Annaliese's patients and this is how she pays for care for her family.

"I'm afraid you'll have to get used to different foods. Most of what we eat now is Mexican. That's how Annaliese's people, as she calls them, pay her when they don't have cash, which for some of them is most of the time. But the more I eat it, the better I like it. If you don't know what something is, ask. That's what we do."

After dinner they all went into the study. The twins were chasing Jinx, and he seemed smart enough to stay just out of their reach.

"When do you want us to go to work?" asked Greta. "I want to begin to work on the inventory right away. It will likely take me a few weeks to get it all in my head."

After Greta had lost her sight as a child, he had sought ways to help her deal with her new life by helping her strengthen her other senses and her memory. During their meandering, three-year long trip west in the wagon, he had read to her most every night, then challenged her the next day to remember and talk about what she'd heard. Many long, lazy days traveling from town to town they had played games to exercise her memory and her grasp of what he had read her the night before or even the week before.

As a result, she had developed an amazing memory. She held the entire stock of books in the San Francisco store in her head and as one was sold, could adjust the inventory accordingly. Shortly after she became pregnant with the twins, Jed, her young husband, had been murdered by an assassin's bullet and the shock of it had driven all she had learned out of her mind.

It took her time to move from under that shadow, but eventually she had and gradually worked herself back to where she had been. Now she would have to learn the stock here as part of her new job, but he had no doubt she could.

Before the twins were born, she and Annaliese had worked hard using information they'd found to help her learn what she needed to know to care for them safely and successfully. She had learned so well that Lemuel no longer had any fear about the safety of his grandchildren even though their mother couldn't see.

"Let's get you settled in and used to the place and then we can talk about going to work."

Chapter Four

It was early the next morning when Annaliese and the Doctor stopped in front of the hotel, but John was already standing on a porch smoking a cigar and looking out at the ocean. He saw them, waved and met them at the door.

"How's she feeling this morning?" asked Annaliese while John shook hands with the Doctor. He led them around to the side door where she had entered the day before. On a lawn that led down to the beach a woman stood by a baby carriage watching some children play.

"She's been staying in bed, and we've been very careful with the arm. I haven't seen any new bleeding but she's having some problems with pain, especially when she moves."

"The nurse should be giving her medication for that."

"She has been." He knocked lightly on the door, then opened it and said, "Lillie, the doctor's here."

Lillie looked up and started to smile but it became a grimace when she turned her head.

"Looks like it hurts a bit." When Lillie nodded, Annaliese said, "Your husband says you've been a good patient." She said this while she was listening to her heart and lungs and taking her pulse. "Are you having any trouble breathing?"

"No, I just feel a little weak and it hurts some. Do you think I might go home today?"

Annaliese looked up at John and said, "Before we talk about that I'd like to talk to you about a treatment for your arm."

When they were all seated at bedside she began. "With an injury like you had the first thing is to stop the bleeding, and we were able to do that. The problem is suturing the wound. I didn't have the tools for it then, but even so if I'd tried it immediately you would have lost too much blood. If we just keep it clean and watch it closely, the wound should heal all right, but there will likely be a rather large scar and probably a certain amount of damage to the muscle of the arm. That could restrict movement of your arm somewhat. We could reduce all that by suturing the wound now, but to do so we would have to give you what we call a local anesthetic.

"I'm not familiar with the use of cocaine hydrochloride, but my father is and has used it many times in his practice. If we do this, he will administer the drug and monitor your reaction, and I will suture the arm."

John reached out and took his wife's uninjured hand and squeezed it gently.

"Would it hurt?" he asked.

"The idea is to inject enough of the drug so it won't. It will numb the arm. We will also give you laudanum which will make you drowsy. Then I will suture the wound. When the drug wears off there will be pain, but we can medicate you for that.

"Also, I want you to understand I will be working inside the skin. I'll be using material that's very clean, sterile in fact, but infection and all the problems that go with it is still a possibility. In addition, there may be side effects with the drug."

"Side effects?" she asked. "What do you mean?"

"Things like dizziness, problems breathing, nervousness. You also may have a feeling of wellbeing somewhat like you've had too much wine. There are other side effects that can be more serious so one of us will want to stay here in the hotel for a day or two so we can check on you until we feel you're ok."

Lillie looked at her husband. "What do you think, dear?"

"What if we decided to just let it heal up and not do the stitches? You said a large scar, how large?"

"The scar would probably be a large check mark shaped thing. From what I could see the short side of it will be about three inches long, the long side maybe five or longer. The skin that forms over a scar is not as flexible as other tissue. Just allowing it to heal might mean you'd have a certain loss of flexibility in the arm."

"How much loss?" John was leaning forward now, forearms on his knees.

Annaliese shook her head. "It's difficult for me to say."

"Is it something we need to decide right away?" he asked.

"The longer we wait the longer it will take to heal. If new skin has begun to form, the sutures will damage it. Then it has to heal again."

He sat back and took his wife's hand again. "Tell me the ups and downs of the whole thing again," he said to Annaliese. "Then we can talk about it and decide."

She explained again and left them to talk while she and the Doctor sat over coffee in one of the dining rooms.

"If they decide to go forward with it, I suggest we work from a plan," she said. "You have more experience with clean areas. If you could handle that, I will gather the equipment and supplies I'll need. Then we can check each other."

He nodded. "Rather than try to clean that room I think we should set up another room and have her brought to it. How long do you think it will take you on her arm?"

She thought for a moment," I'd say forty-five minutes to an hour at least. I'll have to clean the wound and get all the blood and damaged tissue out first, and I'll want to keep the stitches close to reduce scarring. Before I begin, I'll put a tourniquet above the wound to retard the bleeding. The wound is shaped like a check mark and the main area I need to work on is the short side of it, three or four inches, if I remember right. The other side is more superficial, and I don't think I will need suturing as much."

"If they decide to do it, when would you want to begin?"

She glanced down at the watch pinned to her dress. "It's just nine now. We should be able to have things ready by early afternoon."

A steward summoned them back to Lillie's room. When they were seated John said. "Several questions. One, how long will it take?"

"The whole thing will probably be an hour, maybe less," answered Annaliese." But it will take several hours to get the room ready. All the furniture must be removed and replaced with a rigid bed of some kind raised to about waist height. The room will have to be cleaned with soap and water and then with carbolic acid. Once it's clean and the patient is there, no one can enter for any reason until we finish, and the wound is dressed."

She could see the questions on their faces.

"This is necessary to counter the risk of infection. Our practice is the cleaner it is the safer it is. Next question?"

"What is the risk of infection? I've heard that wounds that have these stitches are more likely to get infections."

"This is why we take these precautions. The equipment and supplies will be sterile so the chance of introducing infectious material into the wound will not be likely. Not only that, but we will wash our hands carefully and our instruments have been disinfected to avoid introducing any germs."

"Then I can't be in the room with her, can I?" he asked. Annaliese shook her head, and he sighed deeply and looked at his wife. "I'll be back as soon as they'll let me." He leaned to kiss her and stood up. "Well, if we're going to do it, let's get started."

Lillie nodded and looked at Annaliese and the Doctor.

"After we're through you'll need to stay here for a couple of days," she said. "We need to have someone watching to make sure it's healing well, and everything is as it should be. Then you can go home."

With plenty of help from the hotel staff, the operating room was ready shortly after lunch. The hotel had two tall trunks at hand, so they were covered with clean cloth, and a stretcher was placed between them. By the time the patient was moved into position the laudanum was beginning to take effect, and she was drowsy. The wound was washed, the tourniquet placed, local anesthetic administered, and Annaliese went to work.

She began by cleaning the wound and removing any tissue that had formed since the injury. Then, using catgut thread and the smallest needle she had available, she tried to make the sutures as close together as she could. Lillie's arm was effectively numb and the nurse working with them held it in position, so she was able to work rapidly.

Even so, by the time she finished, her face was dripping with sweat, and the top of her smock was damp with it. She had to resist the reflex to wipe her face with a hand and was surprised to feel she was panting slightly. She realized she had been holding her breath each time she punctured the skin and smiled to herself. A lesson learned.

Lillie slept through the ordeal and didn't awaken until the dressing was being applied. Her eyelids fluttered, then closed again.

"Is it over?" she whispered.

"Yes," said Annaliese. "When I finish this dressing, we'll take you back to your room and you can sleep 'til you wake up."

"Can I see John and the children?" she murmured drowsily.

"He'll be right beside you as soon as we get you in bed."

When it was all over, she stood on the porch again, eyes closed, breathing deeply. She had never realized how therapeutic ocean air could be.

The Doctor came up behind and put his arm around her shoulder. "You did very well, Dr. Fry. I tried to stay out of your way." He paused for a moment. "It would be easy for me to fall back into our old relationship. If you notice me doing so tweak my nose a bit. I think you're pretty good at what you do. We will work well together."

She leaned against him. "Of that, I have no doubt," she said.

Greta had been in San Diego ten days before she and Annaliese had a chance to sit down and talk. Annaliese had been a mother substitute of sorts for the girl during her courtship and first marriage and had helped her climb out of the emotional pit she had fallen into when her first husband was murdered. Jed had died from an assassin's bullet intended for Lemuel the day after Greta had told him he was to be a father.

Annaliese had found books and magazine articles about raising a child safely when blind and together she and Greta, blind from a childhood accident, had learned to care for the twins.

Greta and Roy had worked together in The BookSeller for a year before she got the courage to write him a letter asking him how he felt about her.

They had been married a year later and, from what Anneliese had seen were a good pair. He seemed to love the children and had accepted that responsibility to Greta was a part of his life. He was always there when she needed him. They worked well together in the store, and she could tell he enjoyed the job and the surroundings.

"I've been so busy the last little while, we haven't talked much since you've been here," said Annaliese. "How are things going in the store?"

"We're getting used to the differences. Roy is good at working with me on the inventory and the ordering, and it helps that the store is arranged so much like back home."

"Lemuel was adamant about that. I think he wanted you here from the first and was determined to do all he could to make it come about."

"I have it all in my mind now and we just need to get the others to make sure they record the titles of sales so I can keep track."

Greta was quiet for a minute then said, "Something I wanted to ask you. Can we figure out a way for me to learn Spanish? Do you know someone who could help me learn?"

"Why?"

"We have some books in Spanish, and some of the customers don't speak English very well, so I have trouble helping them. And since so many more of our customers speak it, I think it would help if I could talk to them."

"That's a good idea. Let me think about it and see what I can put together." She sat back in the chair and thought for a moment. "You know, my Spanish is still pretty bad. Most of what I've learned has to do with medical things. Maybe I could learn with you. We could help each other. I can probably give better care if I could talk to my patients about something besides their medical problems. A lot of that now is in sign language or grunts." She laughed. "Let me see if I can find someone to help us learn what we need to know."

She sat for a moment, thinking. "I'm glad you thought of that. I've been saying since I got here, I need to do it but with one thing or another I just never got around to it."

"There's another thing I want to talk about," said Greta. "It has to do with being married."

Annaliese sat quiet, waiting for the girl to speak.

"Remember when I got pregnant, and I believed I could tell the night it happened?"

Annaliese smiled. "How could I forget? You seemed so sure at the time, and when the twins were born, I counted backwards. I've always believed you were right."

"Since we've been married, I've made Roy let me tell him when it was safe to make love. I seem to be able to feel when I can get pregnant and when I can't. Maybe that's the same kind of thing? Is that possible?"

"With you I'm not sure what's possible and what's not." Annaliese looked out the window for a minute while she thought about the question. "If it's worked so far I guess it must be," she said with a shrug, "although I've never heard of anything like it before."

"I've been thinking about having another baby and I wanted to hear how you feel about it."

"Greta, it seems to me that's something for you and Roy to decide. Why are you asking me?"

"I understand that, but I wanted to talk to you and make a plan, like we did before. The twins are still a handful but they're growing and Roy is a big help. Besides, Mrs. Keane has told me she doesn't want to go back to San Francisco, so I'll have her and Consuelo will help with them too. I probably won't need all that help but it will be nice to have it around just in case, until the baby's out of nappies."

"Why now? Why not wait a little and when the twins are older it wouldn't be as hard?"

"I'd like to give Roy a child of his own. He loves the twins and helps with them but if he's like most men, he wants children of his own."

"Have you talked to him about this?"

"Not yet, I wanted to see what you thought about it."

"Well, I'd say the first thing to do is talk to him and if you decide to go ahead then we can make a plan."

"Do you think I can do it? Care for another baby, I mean."

"Greta, with all the things I've seen you do I have no doubt about it."

"Thank you," said Greta, standing up. Annaliese embraced her.

"When you get ready, I'll give you an examination and then we'll see." As Greta was leaving, Annaliese continued. "What will we do if you have twins again?"

"I think Roy would probably faint. Of course, I might too."

Chapter Five

Handy Josephson was sitting on the porch reading Johnny's letter when his wife came to the front door.

"Lunch is ready," she said. She walked to a metal triangle hanging from the eaves and rattled an iron rod around inside it.

He was still sitting there tapping the letter on his leg looking pensive when his partner and several ranch hands came up on the porch in response to the triangle.

Gray, his partner, held the door for the hands and said to Handy, "You going to join us or sit there thinking?"

Handy stood up, tucked the letter in his pocket and joined the others at the table. He was quiet while they ate and after the rest were gone helped his wife clear the table all the while seeming preoccupied. This was not like him.

Handy—his name was Hansford Robert Josephson, and as a child was known as Handy Bob—was a gregarious, open-faced fellow, the indulged youngest of five who grew up on a farm in Minnesota where he was petted and pampered by older sisters. He smiled, grinned, and laughed much of the time and was a trusting soul, always ready to give someone a hand and the benefit of the doubt.

He was visiting his uncle in Nebraska when Johnny Fry rode into his life. At age twenty-three, Handy was away from the farm for the first time and here was a young fellow, five years his junior, who was off on the adventure of a lifetime. Two days later they rode out of town together.

Wash had joined them in Casper, Wyoming Territory and, in June a year later they arrived in Sacramento with some more new friends having completed a 1900-mile trip across the country on the Pony Express Trail.

Along the Sweetwater River in southwest Wyoming, they stopped at a wilderness store run by a friend of Wash's and Handy saw Rebecca for the first time. She was Sioux Indian on her father's side and beautiful, with coal black hair and deep brown eyes that were full of mischief and fun. Two days later he proposed, and she accepted.

For the next couple of weeks Handy was, as Johnny put it, "not good for much, not even conversation." In October her mother closed the store, and the family moved to Salt Lake City to winter with some friends and there the couple was married.

Earlier on the trip they had stopped in North Platte, Nebraska and were eating in the hotel dining room when Buffalo Bill Cody walked by took one look at Handy and offered him a job in his Wild West Extravaganza. It was easy to see why.

Handy was built like a lumberjack, six feet eight inches tall with broad shoulders, muscular arms and a chest that strained the buttons on his shirt. His shoulder length silver blond hair, deep tan and sparkling blue eyes made him look just like Cody's idea of a perfect cowboy and he offered Handy the moon and stars to join the show.

Handy had turned him down rather than leave Johnny and Jinx, but the idea had lingered, and in Sacramento he sent a telegram. With the answer the young couple was off on a train to St. Louis to join Buffalo Bill and his Congress of Rough Riders.

It didn't take them long to find out they didn't really like it, and after six months joined their friends in San Francisco so Rebecca could have their child with her mother there to help.

A few months later he and a new friend shook hands as partners and together bought a horse farm near Mill Valley, a small village a little north of the Golden Gate. Just that quick he was a farmer again though raising horses instead of wheat. When he finally brought his wife and newborn son home to the ranch, Handy was a happy man.

He was sitting on the porch staring into nowhere when she stood before him, hands on hips and said, "Alright, Handy Josephson. What's the matter? Are you sick or something?"

He looked at her, startled out of his reverie. "No," he said and then grinned at her. "What did you think it was?"

"I knew it sure wasn't you," she said. "What are you grinning about?"

"If I tell you, you'll hit me," he replied. He reached out and unbuttoned the top button on her shirt. When his hand dropped to the next one, she slapped it away, then sat in his lap and stared into his eyes.

"You were thinking about something in that letter you got from Johnny, weren't you?"

"How'd you know about that?"

"I saw it on the desk in the office last night."

He sat quiet for a moment, looking at her. "Yeah, that's it. He and Wash and Woman are going to take a trip across the desert east of there. He said Wash called it a 'looking around kind of trip'. Be gone about three months."

"And you want to go along?" She was still looking into his eyes.

He took a deep breath. "Yes." He took a deep breath. "No. Maybe," he said with a wry smile. "I admit it's the first thing that came to mind. I know I can't, but it sure sounds like it'd be fun, especially with the four of us. Well, five if you count Jinx.

"But there's things that need doing around here and it wouldn't be fair to you and Bobby, or Gray for that matter, for me to go off traipsing about the country like that, not to mention I might get scalped or something."

He reached for the button again. "And besides, there's things I'd miss around here." She didn't slap his hand this time and he picked her up and carried her into the bedroom.

Afterwards she lay with her head on his chest, listening to his heartbeat. "Why don't you talk to Gray, and we'll think about it for a while and then we'll decide?" She kissed him on the lips and sprang out of bed. He tried to grab her but missed. "Our son needs me," she said, tossing her head saucily. "Besides, you've got what you wanted." She stuck her tongue out at him and fled the room.

He lay back on the bed and began to think about the desert.

Early on at the ranch Handy, remembering his mother's isolation during long winters on the farm when he was growing up, encouraged Rebecca to visit her mother in San Francisco whenever she felt the need. Before long they had settled into a routine where she would spend a week with her mother and a week at the ranch.

This morning, she was getting ready to leave and came into the office to say goodbye. In the carriage at the front door Handy could see his son sitting with Dut Mowbray, one of the hands who usually drove Rebecca to the rail stop.

"Wendy will be here in time to get lunch," she said, and bent to kiss him. He swept her into his arms, carried her down the steps and deposited her in the carriage.

"I'm going to have to quit doing this," he said, stretching, hand on his back. "Either I'm getting old or you're getting fat." He stepped back quickly but she just grinned at him.

"Are you coming to town this week?"

"Not planning on it."

"Well, I'll see you when I get back then," and they drove off, little Bobby waving at his Papa.

As they were leaving Gray drove into the yard. He and his wife, Maxine, lived in a small house Handy could see in the distance. It was small but sat on a ridge overlooking an arm of the bay. Though it had been built as a summer cottage, Gray was gradually working on it as their family grew, and he had plans to make it something special.

They always began their day by sitting on the porch, drinking coffee and talking about what they had done the day before and about things they wanted to do today and tomorrow.

"Heard anything from Hank lately?" asked Gray. Hank Rose was a third partner who bought Johnny's share of the ranch when he left for San Diego. Every couple of months he joined them for a few days and the three of them would go over the books and talk about plans.

"No. As far as I know, he'll be up the end of this month just like always." Handy was quiet for a moment. "Something I wanted to talk to you about though."

Gray looked at him, a question on his face.

"What would you think about me taking a little trip?"

"How little?"

"Maybe three months."

Gray stared, open mouthed. "Three months? What are you talking about?"

By the time Handy finished explaining, Gray was trying hard to keep from smiling.

"And what does Rebecca say about this?"

"Well, I caught her in a good mood, and she said to talk to you about it and then we could think about it and decide."

"She must have been in a really good mood. Maxine would throw me out if I tried something like that."

"She's got her mother and Wendy to help her with Bobby, and you don't really need me around here so much you couldn't get along without me for a few months."

"Hell man," said Gray, "you don't need to ask me. You do more than your share around here and if we get in a pinch, Hank could send someone up from his place. I am a little jealous though. That sounds like something I'd like to do. O'course you might get scalped. I hear there are still some renegades out in that country."

"That's what Johnny said in the letter." He leaned back in the rocker. "I don't know. It's a mighty big desert. We might could get across without running into something like that."

As usual, her mother was sitting with Madame over morning coffee, talking and reading the newspaper.

Madame looked up and said, "Look it's Sarah's daughter. What's her name again? Oh, that's right, Becky."

Rebecca grinned. Her dislike of the diminutive was a running joke between them. She bent to kiss her mother.

"Good morning, Rebecca dear. Where's my grandson?"

"He's playing with Geppetto. I left him in the kitchen."

"So, what are you up to today?"

"I've got some errands to run and I'm going to have lunch with Sun Li, and then we're going to wash each other's hair."

She flopped into a chair. Though twenty-two and a wife and mother, she sometimes acted like she was still a saucy young girl. "Handy got a letter from Johnny and now he wants to go off on a trip in the desert with them."

"What? When?"

"He said October. They'd be gone for three months."

"Who all's going?"

"Johnny, Wash and Woman, I guess. And Jinx, of course."

"Did he ask you if he could go?"

"No, but I know he wants to. He's told me before how much he loved coming across the desert with Johnny and them on the way out here." She looked at Madame. "Did Woman say anything about it to you in your last letter?"

"What last letter? I haven't heard from her in three months." At that point a maid came in with several letters and handed them to her.

"Well, speak of the devil! Here's a letter from her." She opened it and began to read. "Yes, she says they're planning to leave at the end of the first week in October. Be back when they get back. Typical letter from her. Doesn't say much." She smiled, thinking of her friend, and handed the letter to Sarah.

Madame was a still beautiful woman at sixty. She had come to San Francisco before it was San Francisco. The little town of Yerba Buena grew up around an army stronghold built by the Spanish to guard the entrance to San Francisco Bay. She was the wife of a young Mexican army officer who died suddenly of a fever in 1845 and left her alone and penniless among strangers.

With few choices, she turned to earning a living on her back for a few years, and a young Mexican, her first customer, gave her a place out back to practice her trade. Then gold was discovered and suddenly she was inundated with men, far from home and lonely. Within three months, she bought a house and was able to set herself up as a madame where judicious management and a select clientele soon made her well to do and then wealthy.

She eventually married a wealthy man, and on his death was suddenly very wealthy. During all this time she remembered her old friends, and over the years many of them had come to the mansion on the hill to work for her and live their lives.

Jose, her first customer, was the stable man and had been for years and some of the maids were daughters of friends she had in the old days. She really didn't need most of the people working there, but she had the money so why not?

She lived in only a small part of the mansion, as it was known, surrounded by people devoted to her and used her money to help the city become what she felt it could be.

Her friendship with Woman had brought Wash into her circle and through him she became a regular customer and later a partner in the new bookstore.

She had joined Johnny and Lemuel to lead a movement to clean out a corrupt city hall and when Sarah came to town with Handy and Rebecca, she had offered them a place to stay. Eventually, what was a temporary thing became permanent. Now she usually began her day at breakfast with Sarah, talking and reading the newspaper and soon came to feel Sarah's family was her own.

"She wants to know if we can come to visit before they leave," she said. "What say, Sarah? Want to go to San Diego for a visit? I hear they've got a wonderful new hotel and it's time I looked it over." She looked up at Sarah. "And by the way, I know the fellow who owns it. Met him and his wife at a soiree here in town and he invited me to come and stay."

Before she left, Rebecca asked her mother, "What do you think I should tell him about the trip?"

"I'd say think about it, make up your mind and tell him. Be fair about it but if you don't want him to go, tell him. He's not going to leave you over it."

When she closed the door, Sarah turned to Madame. "Do you really want to go down there?"

"Yes, and I can't think of one good reason not to. In addition to seeing them, I've read about 'The Del'. It must really be something. So, we can stay for a while." She grinned impishly at Sarah. "Besides, we can make it a honeymoon of sorts. We never get to spend a whole night together around here. Too many long noses."

They stood and came together in a long romantic kiss. "It will be nice not to have to sneak back to my room when we're finished," Sarah whispered. Their love affair wasn't an exciting, every night kind of thing, but more a 'whenever they looked in each other's eyes and nodded' kind of thing. Usually once a month or so they would meet in lingerie in one or the other's bedroom, slowly make love and enjoy the things two women can do to one another that are exciting and feel good.

It was something Madame had done occasionally over the years, and with someone special she enjoyed it. She and Woman were lovers and Sarah knew of it. One day she asked Madame what she got out of it. That night a demonstration was arranged with gratifying results.

Sarah had an ongoing relationship with a man, and it seemed to add spice to her time in the bedroom with him. Although he didn't know about it, she thought Jonas wouldn't see it as a problem. It just wasn't something the ladies wanted to share quite yet.

"I know, Let's get a compartment on the train and see what it feels like to make love at forty miles an hour," said Madame.

Sarah kissed her again. "I don't know how you come up with some of these ideas," she said. "But I'm glad you do. Maybe we could take a train somewhere once a month or so." They were both giggling now. "And invite Woman along."

Madame snorted. "If we did she'd be naked on the bed before we had one shoe off. That girl likes to play."

"Are you ever going to tell her about us?"

"Tell you the truth, I hadn't thought about it. I don't believe it would be a problem, but who knows? Of course, I haven't seen her much to tell her since we began..." She paused and drew Sarah close again. "What did we begin?" she whispered. "A love affair? A relationship? Occasional sex?" She kissed her again. "I think we're friends who happen to be lovers. How's that?"

"Hmmmm," said Sarah. "That's me purring,".

Chapter Six

Johnny was doing bookwork in the office when Roy came to the door.

"Gentleman to see you," he said. Things had settled into an arrangement where Roy and Greta managed the store, leaving Lemuel and Johnny to operate the business. In conjunction with opening the new store, Lemuel had begun to wholesale books to stores up and down the state and had acquired a warehouse near the station as a place of business. With that and operating the two bookstores, they stayed pretty busy.

When he saw the man standing at the counter, he thought, "Where do I know him from?"

When he stuck out his hand Johnny realized who he was. "John Spreckels?"

The man nodded. Johnny hadn't seen him since the night of his wife's accident and that night he was not dressed in the business suit he wore now.

"You're Dr. Fry's husband, is that right?" When Johnny nodded, Spreckels went on. "Can we talk for a few minutes?"

Soon they were seated across Johnny's desk from one another.

Spreckels offered Johnny a cigar. Johnny shook his head, and he took one for himself when Johnny said, "We don't usually smoke in the store. We have many women and children who come in and we try to keep it nice for them. Would you like to sit where you can smoke?"

"No, it's not necessary. Lillie's always after me to quit smoking them anyway. I would like to look around the store though when we're through talking."

He looked at Johnny keenly for a moment and said, "People around town tell me you have an interesting hobby."

Johnny looked puzzled.

"You're learning all you can about the town and its history." It was a statement not a question, so Johnny waited for him to go on. "Had a fellow doing that kind of thing for me for a while, but he's gone back up north, and I need someone to fill his place."

"I'm pretty busy around here and I'm not really interested in a job."

"This would fit right into what you've been doing. I would just like you to share what you find out about the city with me."

Johnny sat back in his chair and looked thoughtful.

"I have many interests in San Diego," said John, "and like to know as much as I can about the city and the county too, for that matter. Problem is I don't have time to look. If we could sit and talk every week or so for a little while it would help me, and you'd be getting paid for doing something you like to do anyway."

Johnny shook his head. "I would like to help you and maybe sometime in the future I could, but I'm planning to leave with some friends on a trip across the desert. The plan is to be gone for probably three months."

Spreckels was staring at Johnny with his mouth open. "Really? You're really going to just take off and ride around deserts and mountains and such for three months?"

"Yep. I won't be alone, though. A friend and his wife are going with me, and maybe someone else if he can talk his wife into it."

"His wife? You're going to take a woman on a trip like that?"

"She's not like other women."

"She must not be."

"Mr. Spreckels," Johnny began but Spreckels raised his hand.

"Please call me John. After all, your wife did save my wife's life."

"OK, John," he smiled, "but that sounds funny to me. That was my Pa's name. I might be able to find someone to help you. I have a friend in San Francisco who does that kind of thing for a living." When John looked a question at him, he continued. "His name is Herschel Grieve. He's a newspaper reporter and what you want is right up his alley."

"That would be great. I own a newspaper, and he could go to work for me and do this on the side. He'd have a lot of freedom and the pay's pretty good, but he wouldn't know much about the city, would he?"

"I'll fill him in on what he needs to know and introduce him around. He's used to finding out the kind of things you want to know. He's been talking about coming down to see me, so I'll send him a wire and maybe you can work something out with him."

"Let's get back to this trip you're taking. When are you leaving?

"Wash wants to go around the end of the first week in October. He wants to be in Yuma by the middle of the month."

"Wash?"

"George Washington Moore. He's a special friend who keeps me out of trouble."

"I'd like to have you sit with me and talk about this some more. Could the three of you come to dinner one evening at the Del? I'd like you to bring your wife and Lillie should be able to join us by then as well."

Johnny shook his head. "They wouldn't come."

"Why not?"

"He was a slave for many years, and she is...," he paused. "Well, she's unusual, some call her strange. They don't talk to other people very much."

"Really? But they talk to you?" John was quiet for a while, digesting this. "Hmm." He looked at Johnny for a moment, then continued. "Well, I'd like to meet them. I've traveled widely and I've seen strange. It usually teaches me something."

"We might go out to their place, but I'd need to ask."

He stood up. "Do that. I must go but anyway I'd like for you and your wife to come to dine with us. Give us a day and time and we'll do our best to make it."

They shook hands and John held Johnny's grip a moment longer than necessary. "Let me know about your friend."

Kate Sessions was watering the plants in front of her nursery when Johnny rode up. It seemed like every time he saw her she was watering plants, but the plants were beautiful so she must know what she was about.

"Hi Kate," he asked. "Wash around?"

She nodded toward the side door. "Hi Johnny. They're in there washing up, I think. They'll be out in a minute." She put the can down and wiped her hands on her smock. "I heard about Annaliese saving that lady down at the hotel."

"Yeah, we were having dinner, and they came to get her. I guess it's part of being a doctor. Do you know John Spreckels?"

"Oh yes. I do all the landscaping at the Del, and we talk a lot whenever they're here. They travel quite often, kids and all."

"He came into the store today and we had quite a talk. He's really fascinated by this trip we're planning and invited the three of us to dine at the hotel. I want to talk to them about it."

Kate shook her head. "They won't go," she said. She looked at Johnny, her lips pursed.

"That's what I told him, but he wants to meet them. I imagine it will be at the cabin if at all."

"What will be at the cabin?" asked Wash as he came out the door.

Woman hopped off the porch and started toward the stable

inside the fence.

Johnny explained and Wash asked, "Why does he want to talk to us?"

"You know, I'm not really sure," said Johnny. "Tell you the truth, I think maybe he's just the kind of person who likes to know things and people."

Kate raised a finger. "That's probably true. You know, I never thought about John that way but that sounds about right." She looked up at Woman who had stopped beside her leading Wash's mule. She reached out to slap her friend's leg. "Are you really going to leave me and go run around the country with that fellow?" she said with a smile.

Woman smiled down at her. "Not for a while," she said.

Johnny watched them ride off down the road and when he turned Black to leave, Kate said, "If you have some time, come in and have a cup of tea. There's something I want to talk to you about."

Like Kate, her office was no nonsense. Her success was such that she could live where she wanted but she spent most of her waking hours in this utilitarian, cluttered, almost spartan room or working with her plants and trees, up to her elbows in dirt.

"Looks like life is bringing you into more than casual contact with John Spreckels. What do you think about that?"

Johnny gave her a puzzled look over his teacup. "Hadn't thought much about it. I guess it's true."

"I say this, not just because he's rich, but because he's someone who seems to be invested in the future of this town. He and I are a lot alike in that way. We think this is a special place. If we can get enough water, we know it will grow anything we plant and we can turn it into a beautiful city.

"He feels we can shape what we want it to be instead of letting it grow wild like San Francisco or Los Angeles. I agree with him and most of the contact we have is over what you'd call 'civic improvements'.

"I've come to understand that you and Annaliese and Lemuel came here because you want to grow up with the city it becomes. You'll never have a better chance to help that happen than to reach out to him with ideas or improvements. I believe a working relationship between John D. Spreckels and Doctor and Mister Annaliese Fry will be good for the future of San Diego."

He burst out laughing and looked at her with a wide grin on his face. "You know, that's the way I look at my marriage. I think you're the first person that's noticed."

"It's an unusual one and I noticed that."

"What should I do about Spreckels now that you've pointed it out?"

"I know doctors well enough to know that Annaliese and her Papa have already talked about needing a hospital here. I think you ought to talk to her and suggest she should talk to the other doctors in the city and create a committee to move that idea forward and make sure to bring it to John D.'s attention."

Johnny was sitting on the bed watching Annaliese brush her hair.

"Ninety-nine, a hundred," she said. She put the brush down and turned to face him. Her breasts were showing enough that he could see the nipples peeking out. He knew she was doing it on purpose, but he didn't take the bait.

"I want to talk to you about something serious," he said walking toward her. "So put those away."

"Put what away?" she asked demurely.

He scooted her over and sat beside her.

"You know what," he replied. "Kate and I had a talk today and I want you to pay attention to what I'm saying."

He told her and then watched her face closely to see how she took it. She turned around and began absent-mindedly to brush her hair again, looking at him in the mirror.

"I don't know Johnny. It's a good idea but I'm their doctor. I can't ask him for money, other than my fees that is. I'm not even sure it would be ethical."

"Kate and I talked about that. She thinks you need to get all the doctors together, form a committee dedicated to building a hospital and then approach John for his support."

She thought about that, continuing to brush her hair. He reached over her shoulders and cupped her breasts.

She slapped his hand. "Oh no. You're not going to get me thinking about something like that and then want to play. Oh no."

"We can talk about it while we're doing it," he whined. She looked at him askance, trying to suppress a smile.

"I don't think that would work. Let's talk about this and then, if you're a good boy, we'll see."

When he was back on the bed and at a safe distance she asked, "What do you think about the idea?"

"I think Kate's right. But she doesn't just mean the hospital. It's like she wants to organize a civic improvement movement. Sit down with some people who can make decisions that will improve the city and help it grow in a way that will benefit everyone who lives here.

"For her that means parks and trees, for us it might be good schools and a better library, for John it might mean an improved water system or good streets. He owns one of the newspapers in town so he could be helpful in a lot of ways in addition to any money he would put toward the venture.

"Remember what I told you Lemuel said when we were thinking about where to put the store? 'Make it worth the trip'. She thinks that's what we should try to do. We're tucked away in the corner of the state, so we need to make San Diego a place where people come because it's worth the trip."

"The Doctor said something about a hospital in the first talk we had when he got here," she said. "He'd be a big part of any hospital we'd have. With all the clinics he's opened he'll know a lot about the process and what to do when. He was also a part of starting the hospitals in Salt Lake. I'd say the next step would be to talk to him about it tomorrow."

He took the brush from her hand. "Now can we do it?" he asked, cupping her breasts again.

"I guess," she said. "If it will put you to sleep."

It did.

Wash was sitting on the rock. Woman was sitting on the ground between his legs, and he was stroking her hair. They were listening to the ocean and talking about their day.

"What do you think about that man wanting to meet us and talk?" asked Woman.

He was quiet for a long time. "Normally I'd say no, but he isn't a normal man. I don't like being looked at just 'cause someone's curious, but I've heard Kate talk about him. It seems he's one of our best customers and he's helped her do some things she wanted to get done around town. I've delivered out at The Del quite a bit and he is right involved with things.

"With him and Kate being friends and all and also, if Annaliese did save her life like he says and now he asked Johnny to go to work for him, I'd say he's going to be in our life whether we want it or not. It seems maybe the best thing is to meet him halfway so if he wants to talk, I would say yes. What do you think?"

"I hadn't thought about it that way, but I can see what you mean. If he's important to them he'll probably end up being important to us."

"It sounds like Johnny's going to see if Herschel wants to go to work for Spreckels' newspaper, too. That means he'd end up down here."

"It's funny, I looked at him so long as one of the bad guys, I have trouble liking him. He's strange."

Herschel Grieve had been the enforcer for a corrupt politician in San Francisco. After a good government group threw the rascal out, Herschel stayed in the city to work as a newspaper man and somehow became a friend of Johnny's. Most of Johnny's friends were still on the fence as to his trustworthiness but Johnny seemed to have accepted his friendship unreservedly.

"I feel pretty much the same but maybe Johnny's right. He might be among us again, so we'll have time to find out if he's real or not. Johnny's different that way. Sometimes he seems to see things in people others don't, both good and bad."

One afternoon, a few days later, Johnny and his new friend rode into the yard at the cabin. Wash had put glass in some new windows he built looking over the porch and was painting the sills and frames. Johnny made the introductions, and they all sat around the kitchen table with coffee and talked.

"Johnny's been telling me about this trip you're going to take," said John. "I'm fascinated by the whole thing. If I weren't a husband and father, I'd want to go along."

"I just got a letter from a friend in San Francisco and he's going to go along," said Johnny. "That will be four of us plus Jinx."

John looked around at the cat who was drinking from a bowl of water Woman had put on the porch. "Won't that be dangerous? Lots of things out there that can get him."

"He stays pretty close to me. He came out here with us on the trip from Kansas."

"And you?" He looked at Woman. "It's not the kind of trip most women would fancy."

"I'm not most women," Woman said with a smile.

Wash and Johnny laughed. "Amen to that," said Wash.

Their coffee grew cold as they sat talking for an hour, but no one seemed to notice. They talked about the route they planned to take, the supplies they would need, the desert itself and the wild animals and wild men they would meet.

"Have you ever been out in that desert before?" John asked Wash.

"Been around the edges several times but never gone across from this side. I have talked to people that have, and I've been across other deserts. Nice thing about doing something like this is learning new things." He looked at Johnny who nodded in agreement.

"Annaliese asked me why we'd want to go out there when it could be dangerous," said Johnny. "That's one of the reasons to go. Every year there are fewer and fewer places that are wild and dangerous. Like to see some of them before they all disappear."

"I think places like the Sonoran will always be wild," said Wash. "Take too much to tame it."

John turned to Woman. "You haven't had much to say."

"Learn more by listening. Not much sense in talking when you don't know anything about what folks are talking about."

"You could ask questions."

"If I wait and listen, I probably won't have to."

When they were leaving, John said, "I have a special dining room at The Del just for the family. I'd like it if you could join us for dinner some evening. My wife and children will be there." He looked at Johnny. "I hope you and Annaliese will come too."

On the way back to the city Johnny asked, "You said you usually learned something when you met strangers. Did you learn anything?"

"Let's say it reminded me of something I already knew."

"What's that?"

"There's more than one kind of lady."

Chapter Seven

When Johnny had worked with her at the store in San Francisco, Greta had been a part of things from the beginning, and he didn't especially notice her that much. Now, having been here for two years without her around, he found himself watching her move around the shelves and do her work. Several times a day a question came into his mind: How did she do that?

She was shelving a book and as he watched she counted down three shelves with her hand, ran her fingers along the books counting them as she went to the place on the shelf where she felt it belonged, and that was that. Her hands and fingers were constantly moving, and it dawned on him that this was how she 'saw' things. Her fingers told her mind what was there, and somehow her mind made a picture she understood.

He had seen her run her fingers over a friend's face and remembered feeling an emotional surge for some reason as though the fingers were touching his face instead. Now as she moved toward the counter, she stopped suddenly and opened her mouth with a look of wonder on her face.

"Sarah? Madame?" she gasped. "How are you here?"

"We just got off the train and thought we'd surprise you. We were wondering if you could tell it was us but you always can," said Sarah laughing. Neither woman had spoken and yet she recognized them. *'How does she do that?'* thought Johnny and then he smiled at himself and at his friends from back home.

They greeted Lemuel and he joined them. Johnny led the group into the house and to the office where they sat over coffee and talked while Sarah went off to find her grandchildren.

"How long are you gonna be with us?" asked Johnny.

"We have a room at the Del for a month, so at least that and then we'll see," said Madame. "I've heard a lot about your winters down here so we may stay a while."

"Who all's with you?"

"Just Carlotta right now. Tony and Geppetto will be down in a few days."

"You take the servants' children on vacation with you?" asked Johnny in amazement.

"He's such a little dear and if I wanted her, I had to have him. I'm not like Sarah, with grandchildren all over the place. To him I'm 'Auntie Mad' and to me he's something I've never had."

They talked about friends back home and how things were and about friends here and how things are.

"So, you're really going to take my Woman out in the desert for three months?"

Sarah had returned and was curled up in the Doctor's favorite chair.

"The plan is to leave here the end of the first week of next month. We'll probably be back before the first of the year."

"Why so long?" asked Sarah. "Aren't there things closer to see?"

"It's what's out there," answered Johnny. "I got a taste of it when we were coming out here from Salt Lake and Wash promised to show me more when I was ready. I'm ready and Woman's a big girl and she wants to go.

"The plan is to go east to Tucson, then Las Cruces. When we get there, we decide to go north to Santa Fe or east to El Paso. I have a feeling we'll end up in Santa Fe. It's a place I've heard of all my life and want to see.

"We'll come back by Grand Canyon. Wash has always wanted to see that then across the Mojave to Los Angeles and home. All in all, I'd say we'll cover a lot of ground, maybe two thousand miles. If I don't do it now, I may never get another chance."

"Rebecca says Handy wants to go," said Sarah, "and I suppose Jinx is going with you?"

"Oh yes," replied Johnny, reaching out to put the cat in his lap. "Where I go, he goes. Had a letter from Handy and he'll be down first of the month."

"I was a little surprised she let him go." Sarah shook her head. "I'm not sure I would've, but she says he'd pine away if he got left behind. And she says it's fair. He lets her come down to the city every other week. Not many husbands would be OK with that."

Madame stood and began to put on her hat. "We want to get checked in and settled. We expect y'all to meet us for dinner this evening and then we can all talk to our hearts content.

"Also, we're going to stop at the nursery first. We want to say hello to Wash and Woman and meet their boss. From what we've heard, she sounds like someone special."

"Kate's definitely someone special," said Johnny. I think you'll get along famously with her. She feels about this place like you do about San Francisco. Wants to 'make it what it can be', is the way she puts it."

"Sounds like a kindred spirit."

A taxi took them to the nursery, and when they entered Kate was behind the counter.

"Now, off the top of my head, you don't look like most of my customers," she said. "How can I help you?"

Sarah smiled at her and said, "We're not customers, but we think you have something we want. Are Woman and Wash here?"

Woman was totaling some figures when she heard a familiar noise but couldn't relate it to where she was. When she looked up, Madame was standing in the doorway chirping in a way she did sometimes when they saw each other. Suddenly all her teeth were showing. She slowly got to her feet, and they embraced.

"I've missed you so much," Madame whispered in her ear and their kiss was long and ardent.

From the doorway, Kate tried unsuccessfully to hide a smile and said, "I'm not sure I'm supposed to be seeing this."

Beside her Sarah, smiling herself, said, "Too late," and then whispered. "Too late."

Kate took her hand and gently pulled her away. When they were on the front porch she said, "I think that's what you call a private moment." She motioned to some chairs. "So, let's sit and talk. I'm sure they won't be long."

"I assume you're Sarah," said Kate when they were seated. Sarah nodded. "When did you get here?"

"We came in on the noon train. I don't recommend it. Very sooty and hot. We stopped at the store and talked to Johnny first and here we are."

Kate looked at her for a moment before she nodded her head toward the office and said, "Did that surprise you?"

"Not even a little. You?"

"No, not really. I didn't know it, but I might have guessed if the question had ever come up. It never has."

Sarah smiled. "She and I have breakfast together every morning, read the newspaper and talk for hours. Been doing it for the better part of three years. There aren't many secrets between us."

"Woman is a special person. She has become an important part of my life since she's been here." Kate let a ladybug crawl to the tip of her finger then threw it into the air. "I hope she comes back from this trip in one piece."

"Yes, this trip!" said Sarah, shaking her head. "My son-in-law is going on this trip. He'll be down next month, the week before they leave."

"Normally I wouldn't think of a woman going on a trip like that, but she..." Kate paused and shook her head. "Let's say it doesn't surprise me that she'd want to go."

"I'm not sure how Handy talked my daughter into it, but she says it's fair. He lets her come down to the mansion every other week. But from what I've heard there might be some danger to the whole affair and he's a father as well as a husband."

Madame came out of the store holding Woman's hand and trying to straighten her hat with the other.

"Like I thought, she won't come to dinner with the rest of us," she said. "We better get going if we're going to change out of our travel clothes in time for dinner." She turned to Woman. "We'll be out at your place tomorrow afternoon." She kissed her on the cheek and turned back to Kate. "We'd love to have you join us tonight at the Del. We have a table in the Crown Room at eight. Annaliese, Johnny, Lemuel and Greta and Roy will all be there, and I understand Will is also coming."

"Now there's a man I'd liked to talk to," said Kate.

Johnny missed the dinner because at eight o'clock he was sitting in John Spreckels' outer office with Herschel Grieve, waiting for a meeting with John.

"Sorry I'm a little late, gentlemen," said John as he came through the office door. He led them into his office and when they were seated facing him across a huge, cluttered desk, opened the conversation.

"Mr. Grieve, is it?" John shook hands with Herschel. "Glad to meet you," he said, and turned to Johnny. "This is the fellow from San Francisco you told me about?" Johnny nodded.

"You're sure he can get what I need even though this is his first day in the city and he knows nothing about it?"

"I believe he can. I can show him around, tell him much of what he needs to know, and introduce him to people who can help him get what you want. In addition, he has several years' experience on how to go about finding those kinds of things. He's a reporter, and he worked as an assistant to several of the city supervisors a few years back. In other words, he knows how to find out what you want to know."

John turned to Herschel. "I understand you worked for Smiling Jim O'Hanlon for a while."

"That's right. I was his assistant in charge of dirty tricks," Herschel replied with a straight face.

"That's what I heard. But now you've reformed and are working for the good guys?"

Herschel nodded.

John laced his fingers, leaned his chin on them and looked at Herschel for a long moment. Finally, he nodded his head and said, "When can you begin work?"

"I'll need a couple of days to get settled and then some time with Johnny. I'd say give me a week and I think I'll be ready."

"You'll be on the payroll at the Union as a city reporter as of tomorrow, but whenever we get together and talk, it will be on the sly. Much of what you learn will be in the paper, but some of it will be for my ears only.

"For some reason I believe you'll know the difference. I think our game will be most effective the fewer people know about it. We can work out a schedule of when and where we meet to talk so people won't connect us so much."

He opened a drawer and took out several sheets of paper. "Now let's talk about your salary and how you'll collect it. What you do for me is outside your work at the paper, and even there I hope we can keep it under our hats."

Johnny stood. "I'm going to slip out at this point." He looked at Herschel. "I'll meet you in the bar when you're through."

"Well, what do you think?" Johnny asked later when Herschel sat down and ordered a beer. Johnny had taken advantage of the free food and was eating a sandwich.

"It seems like a good situation, and I can surely handle the job."

Herschel looked thoughtful. "If you fellows survive the trip you're talking about, you'll probably want the job back when you get home, won't you?"

"Can't imagine," replied Johnny. "Don't want the job and don't need the job, though I'll be a good source for you when we get back. I'll go right back into digging in the library and newspaper files again, just like before.

"Might even sit down and do some writing about the trip, so I could maybe use you to read over that when the time comes. Also, when I get back, you'll be able to fill me in on what's happened while I've been gone."

They sat quiet for a minute, then Johnny asked, "Are you going to take it?"

"Can't see any reason not to. I've been in San Francisco a long time. I'd say it's time to try someplace new. This looks like a nice place."

"Where are you staying? Did you get a room yet?"

"No. I wanted to wait and see how things turned out with him, and I wanted to talk to you before I did. I left all my dunnage at the station."

"Annaliese's father is staying with us, and Greta and Roy and the twins, but we've got a couple of rooms up under the eaves if you don't mind climbing three floors. You can stay there until you decide what you want to do, or I can drop you at the Horton Hotel. That's a good place and it's downtown."

"I'd like to see what you have in the store about the city, so I'll take you up on the offer to stay at your place until I find something."

Carlotta opened the door to the room at the Del and invited them in while Madame and Sarah finished getting ready. In a few minutes the ladies emerged from the bedroom and off they went to the Crown Room to eat and talk.

As they were seated Kate arrived, and they all began to talk to one another. By the time dessert was over they had covered most topics of interest and were conducted to a parlor on the third floor where they could sit and look at the ocean, talk and drink coffee. When they were all seated, Kate turned to Will and said, "I've been wanting to talk to you since you got here. I've heard tell you expressed interest in building a hospital in our fair city."

"That's right, though with all we've had to do getting things set up for the clinic," he replied, "I must admit it was just a passing thought."

"Well let's pass it again," Kate replied with a laugh. She looked at Annaliese. "How much contact have you had with our present hospital?"

"Not much," replied Annaliese. "It's not so much a hospital is it, as just an adjunct to the poor farm? Most of the patients are residents of the farm who need care and can't afford it. It's sort of a holding pen until they die."

"So, you don't send your patients there?"

"Not unless I have to. We have several rooms we use for temporary residential treatment, but patients who need hospital care usually go to Los Angeles."

She turned to Will again. "What types of services do you intend to provide at the clinic once it's open?"

"Mostly people who walk in and can walk out," replied Will. "We will have some residential care for new mothers and some emergency wound care and illness treatment, but we'll be limited. We surely won't provide hospital services to the people of the city, if that's what you're asking."

"Do you have any idea of what it would cost to build a hospital here that would meet the needs of the city now and for the foreseeable future?"

"To get the answer to that would require a committee of professionals well versed in the costs of goods and services and operational requirements. I could serve on such a committee and could help them with some of what was needed, but I would defer to others on what it would all cost. There would be many questions to be answered before you could even begin that calculation.”

“My mother used to tell me, ‘You can’t finish something you don’t start’,” said Kate. “I think we need to start the process, and in the near future.” She looked at the people sitting around her, stopping at Will. “What would be the steps necessary to get it all started?”

“First thing, we’d need to put a steering committee together to decide where we need to go and lay out a map showing us how to get there.”

“Would you need funding to begin the process you’ve described?” asked Madame.

“Yes. To answer the questions that arise and to assemble the calculations necessary for decision making will take time and someone has to be able to put in the time. That takes money, but how much would be a guess. Generally, the people who have the money don’t have the time, or if they do, would rather have a professional do the job.”

“Tell you what,” said Madame. “You put together your committee and I’ll put up the money to get the ball rolling. Then present the map of where you want to go, and I’ll help you along. I’m sure you’ll be able to find some of the funding you need locally?” She addressed the question to Kate.

“I think there are several people in the area who see the need and recognize the benefit of such a project.” Kate held out her hand and Madame took it, and so the idea for a hospital in San Diego was born.

Chapter Eight

Johnny was watching his wife brush her hair again. "So what did you talk about with everyone there tonight?" he asked.

She turned and looked at him, still brushing and counting. When she finished, she put the brush down and said, "Kate brought up the hospital idea and we ran with it."

"What do you mean, ran with it?"

"The Doctor told her what we need to do and how to get started, and Madame wrote a check to cover getting things rolling.

"Tomorrow, we begin looking for whoever is willing to serve on a steering committee probably among the doctors of the community for a start. Then we decide the next steps and take them one at a time going forward."

They looked at each other in silence for a moment. "How did Madame get into it? She lives five hundred miles from here. She wouldn't be using a hospital down here very much."

"I pointed that out to her as we were leaving. She said she's a Californian and figures what's good for one part of the state is good for the rest of it."

"What's next?"

"The Doctor said the committee will have to create a map of where we need to go and find out what it will cost then try to find the funding we need to get there."

"Where are you in the middle of all this?"

"Truth be told, I don't know. I think the Doctor will be one of the leaders, if not the leader of the whole thing but where I fit in I have no idea at this point. Eventually, it may tie him up so tight I'll have to handle the majority of the practice until they get it on the road and running. I don't think that will be a problem by which I mean I believe I can do it. One of us needs to focus on what's in front of us while the other works toward the future."

She sat quiet for a moment.

"What about the clinic? What's going to happen with that?"

"I don't think this whole thing will come together that soon. We should still have time to get the clinic going before this becomes a consuming process. I believe eventually it will become consuming, and we need to be ready when it does."

"What about Kate and the other non-professionals who will surely become involved? What'll be their part in it?"

"That seems to be one of those things we'll find out as we go along. I have a feeling they'll be in the fund-raising end of it and drumming up support in the community which is an important part of the whole process. I'm sure we'll find a few stumps in the road as we go forward. We'll just have to pull them if we can and go around them when we can't.

"Johnny, like everyone who was there tonight, I have many more questions than answers about the whole thing. But we got started toward something tonight, something important for the city and very likely for us too. Now all we can do is do what we can and get someone to help us when we find something we can't."

She sat down on the bed next to him. "Johnny, I'm going to have a hard time sleeping tonight if you don't do your husbandly duty," she said.

His mouth fell open again and he gaped at her. "Wait a minute,

I thought it was a wifely duty."

"Whatever," she said, and kissed him and kept kissing him until they fell over on the bed. "Now get to work," she murmured.

And he did. After all, if it was his duty he supposed he must.

Downstairs about that time, Will and Lemuel were discussing the evening over brandy and cigars. They were seated in an alcove that jutted out toward the city below and gave them a fine view of the lights of Coronado and the Del in the distance.

"That's some place for a small city like this," said Will.

"It is that," replied Lemuel. "I wonder if he'll be able to make it pay. He's got a lot of money in it and people have crawled out on limbs like that before only to have them break."

"It looks like your business is thriving," Will said, changing the subject.

"Yes, it is. We learned a lot from the store in San Francisco, and we used what we learned in making decisions when we opened here.

"What do you think about what we talked about tonight?" he continued. "Sounds like that could be the kind of thing that could keep you busy all by itself. Can you get involved in that and still run the clinic and the practice with Annaliese?"

"That's one of those questions you can't answer 'til you're in the middle of it. Back in Salt Lake I was constantly trying to juggle more than a few things at once. The Saints were good at keeping you busy and moving forward so I have some experience at keeping a few balls in the air. I don't know as much as I should about costs and such because most of the time, I didn't even get the bills back there. Everything went to the Saints, and they paid.

"This thing will take a while to get moving forward, so I think we can get the clinic started and working before the hospital gets too far along. There will come a time however, when it will take up most of my time for a while if I'm selected to lead the effort."

"Do you think you will be?"

"I can't answer that, but I think I got one vote tonight." He smiled.

"You mean Kate?"

"I think so. She strikes me as a woman who decides where she wants to go and moves ahead come hell or high water."

"From what I know of her I'd say you're right. She sure is leaving her mark around here. She's planted over three hundred trees all over this town, especially in City Park. She's determined to make that park something special, kind of a centerpiece of the city."

"Sounds good to me," said Will, rising to his feet and draining his glass. "Well sir, I believe tomorrow is the first of many busy days for me, so I bid you goodnight."

"Good night, Will. It's nice to have someone my age to talk to around here."

Will grinned. "Do I look that old?"

"Good night, Will."

When Lemuel had laid out the plans for the house, he had drawn Johnny a small office on the top floor with an alcove facing west so he could sit and look over the city to the bay beyond. This evening he was sitting in the alcove looking out toward the setting sun and at the lights beginning to come on around the city in the dusk. Behind him he heard someone come in, then Handy was moving a chair into position beside him.

He would always remember the first time he ever saw his friend. He was sitting in the Sheriff's office in Kearny, Nebraska and looked up to see a man who completely filled the doorway and had to bend his head to get into the office. A little conversation over coffee, and Handy asked if he could join him and Jinx on their ride across the country on the Pony Express Trail. Handy, and later Wash were the first two real friends he'd ever had besides his cat and his Pa, and he was glad he would have them with him on the trip.

They sat quiet for a while, then Handy said, "Do you sit up here every night?"

"Pretty much. Lemuel built it for me specially and it's where I come to sit and think."

"You thinking about tomorrow?"

"Oh yeah. Haven't been thinking of much else for a while now."

They were quiet again, and then Johnny asked, "When you think about the trip on the Pony what do you remember most?"

Handy chuckled. "Mostly about Rebecca, I guess, and the gunfight we had in Carson City. First one for me and I hope the last. Mostly about Rebecca, though."

"I could have guessed that," said Johnny with a laugh. "I guess the moon and some of the things we saw in moonlight are what I remember most. Remember what it looked like when we were on the prairie with the wind blowing through grass as far as you could see in the moonlight? And what about the full moon over the desert, or it coming up over the mountains in Salt Lake? I remember when we were in the desert. We used to ride for hours without saying a thing, just looking around at all that and thinking."

Johnny shook his head as though to clear it. "We're going to see things like that again. Remember how nice it was to sit around the fire and talk about the next day and the one just over? And other things? Wash told me once he wished he could remember all the things he learned sitting around a campfire. We had some good talks those nights."

"That we did. I guess that's one of the reasons I wanted to go as soon as I heard about it. I think about some of those nights."

Herschel Grieve was coming to love San Diego. Though he hadn't spent one of the wonderful winters there yet, he had heard tales and was looking forward to seventy-degree days in December. He liked the people at the paper, and his boss gave him free reign as long as he met his deadlines. Johnny had introduced him around and shown him the places where he could gather the information he needed both for the paper and for John D.

Even though it was a different town, the basic job was the same: gathering information and distilling it so people could make sense of it. He was enjoying meeting new people and seeing new things. He felt a little strange keeping his life in separate compartments, but since John D. seemed to think it was important, then he would too.

The BookSeller was crowded when he went in. Apparently, there were many people who wanted to say goodbye to Johnny before he left. He roamed the shelves, spotted Johnny, and waited until they made eye contact, then slipped into the back room to await his friend.

Johnny stopped in the doorway and heaved a big sigh.

Herschel grinned at him. "Nervous about tomorrow?"

"Not so much tomorrow. I'll bet by the time we get to Yuma I'll be tight as a fiddle string."

"You've been across deserts before, right?"

"Yes, but Wash tells me this one is different. I tell myself that's what I want to see, the difference, but I'm still nervous. Of course, with Handy and Wash along, we can likely handle anything that comes up."

"Does it bother you that she's going along?"

"No. I know her well enough to know she can take care of herself. And she won't need any pampering. Jinx will get all of that."

"You do like having him around."

Johnny grinned. "He's my little buddy. Can't go anywhere without him." He stood and extended his hand to his friend. "Keep an eye on things for me. The first town of any size we'll come to after we leave Yuma will be Tucson, and Wash figures about two weeks to get there. I'll check the telegraph office when we get in town, so if you need to contact me that'll be the place."

"I'll try to help them keep the lid on 'til you get back. Around Christmas?"

"See you about then. Wish me luck."

Annaliese lay with her eyes open in the darkness beside her husband. Tomorrow he was leaving for three months, and it was one of those strange things she knew but didn't yet realize. She could feel him lying beside her after lovemaking and couldn't imagine him not being there.

"You still awake?" she whispered. He squeezed her hand and turned toward her.

"I'm here," he replied, and after a minute, "Want some more?" He nuzzled her hair and began to stroke it.

"You are going to come back, aren't you?" she whispered. "I mean, even if you find some beautiful senorita in Santa Fe to have fun with, don't tell me about it, just make sure you come home, OK?"

He lay still for a long moment, then said, "Everything I could possibly want in a woman and a wife I have in you. I'll always come home because I could never find another one like you." He kissed her lightly and sweetly on the tip of her nose and lay down again holding her hand.

"Anywhere," he said after a moment.

She smiled and was smiling when she fell asleep, still holding his hand.

Chapter Nine

Johnny stood on a precipice looking out over the shadowed landscape that lay beyond the Colorado River. The full moon, halfway to the top of the sky, was reflected brilliantly off the river below. Beyond, the desert stretched to the horizon, with shadows reaching back toward him. North a few miles the lights of Yuma sparkled and across the river there were lights that indicated the presence of the territorial prison.

It was a silent world, yet his mind comfortably filled the void. He was thinking about what might be out there in all that vast space, what he might see and hear and feel. He knew there was danger but there would also be beauty and peace and a calming quiet.

Johnny had seen enough of the Sonoran since they left home to realize it was different from the desert they had crossed earlier. On the maps it was huge, covering 100,000 square miles in California, the Arizona Territory and three states in Northern Mexico. The ground was different, with more loose sand and mountain ranges that ran in random directions instead of the long straight ridges that separated the multiple valleys across the Great Basin.

There was more vegetation here and more water, but the rains were a month gone and it was dry and very hot, though like deserts everywhere, it was chilly at night. It seemed like every plant had thorns of some kind, either for protection or propagation, but other than birds he had seen almost none of the teaming life he knew existed out of his sight.

"You sure you want to go out there?" He hadn't heard Wash come up behind him.

"I'm standing here thinking that same question." They stood quiet for a moment looking out at a different world.

"I'm excited about heading out into it but standing here I'm thinking about all the people who died out there whose bones were never found. It seems to me dying's a part of living in the desert. If that's where we're going, we need to keep our minds on the job if we're going to get home safe."

Wash was quiet a moment. "We won't be going into the worst of it. If we were to take the most direct route to Tucson, it would take us along the Camino del Diablo, the Devil's Road. Our road won't be so hot or dry. The rivers are low this time of year, but we should have some water following them. "Out there," he swept his arm around the horizon, "there's not much water and you have to know where to find it. When it's 120 degrees and there's no shade, you don't have much time to look before you're dead."

Johnny reached up to where Jinx was sitting on his shoulder and scratched the cat's ears. "What do ya think, little Buddy? Want to go?" He looked at Wash. "You know, every time my gut feels like this, I never know whether I'm excited or scared to death."

"Maybe, you're just hungry and smelling dinner cooking," Wash said. "Let's see if it's ready."

They walked back to the campfire, Jinx running ahead of them. He was already talking to Woman and Handy about getting fed when they got there. Johnny was amazed how well Woman got along with the cat. She moved like a cat herself and when she looked at you her eyes were more like a cat's than anyone he'd ever seen.

Apparently, Jinx thought so too. He spent part of every evening around the fire rubbing against her, being petted in return and snoozing in her lap. Jinx had always liked Handy and between him and Woman, Johnny was seeing a lot less of his cat.

Johnny, Handy and Woman had agreed to share the cooking, and he was glad it was her week because she was much better at it than the rest of them. When they were settled, plates in hand, he said to Wash, "I was thinking earlier, I never see you cooking when we're on a trip. Why is that?"

Woman snorted and Wash grinned. "Found out years ago since I was a bad cook people would rather do it themselves, so I let 'em."

Johnny grinned. "Makes sense," he said. He looked at Woman. "Sure do like it when it's your turn. Where'd you learn to be so good at it?"

"When I was alone in the gold camps I didn't have much to do at night." She looked up at the stars, remembering. "No books around and I didn't trust anyone enough to talk so I began to work on making my food taste better. Since the food was pretty bad to start with it took a long time to learn how."

"Makes it a little hard on the waistline," said Wash, patting his belt.

"Let's talk about the route again just so I got it straight in my head," said Handy. He was bending over a map with his finger following the river. "Tomorrow when we leave the fort, we cross the Colorado then east along the Gila to the big bend then south and east to Tucson, is that right?" When Wash nodded, he continued. "So, how much extra distance are we going north out of the way to get there?"

"Probably adding sixty miles, maybe less, but we're a lot more likely to make it going that way. I've never been the other way, but people have told me. There's not much room for mistakes along that road. In the desert water's mostly in natural tanks of stone that fill up when it rains. They're usually in the shade so they last, but if they're dry or bad, things can get rough in a hurry.

"What do you mean, bad?"

"A dead animal floating in the middle of it, for instance, would probably mean it was bad," replied Wash.

"And you need to know where they are. If you miss one it's liable to be thirty miles to the next water, and even this time of year, out there that's a long, long way. The way we're going means we won't ever be far from water, but we'll see as much of the desert as we want. There's a place where the Gila turns north in a big bend, and there we'll head south and east a little to cut the Santa Cruz. The cutoff will be all desert but there's only about twenty-five or thirty miles of it."

"Is the Sonoran that bad?" asked Handy.

Wash nodded. "Parts of it. I've been told it's so dry and hot south of the border in the summer that a man walking can live one day without water but not a second. I've also heard about a bad stretch of dunes south of here in Mexico you have to cross to get to the Gulf of California. Hard going.

"On the way back we'll cross the Mojave, which is also bad but by that time we'll have had time to get used to desert travel and should have learned enough to make it across OK. Also, it will be later in the year and not so hot. Or so we hope." He smiled.

"Tomorrow we'll be stopping by the fort at Yuma. It's not really a fort anymore, but there's a fellow there we can talk to. He knows what's out east of here. He can tell us a lot of what we need to know, so if you got any questions make sure you ask. Not much about this desert he don't know."

The fort at Yuma hadn't been an army installation for about five years, but an enterprising old soldier invalided out from a wound suffered in the Apache wars had turned it into a store for outfitting people traveling across the desert. He even ran a bit of a hotel and a restaurant of sorts.

After tying the animals to the hitch rail under a shade porch, Wash walked across to the trading post while the others sat on a veranda to wait for him. Not surprisingly, the old soldier had served with him in the Army, and it wasn't long before they were crossing the yard to where the others sat, talking as they came.

His name was Terrance Donnelly. He had been the only one in his family to escape Ireland during the great famine of the 1840's. The rest had starved to death. Unable to find work in the new county, he joined the army to get fed and found a home. He came out of the War a sergeant and served on frontier posts for twenty years until an Apache arrow took his right arm. In spite of all this, he was a cheery soul who loved to talk, especially about the deserts of the southwest.

"It's a hell of a place to cross in summer, especially going due east. Shouldn't be too bad the way you're going this time of year. How long do you figure to take?" They had all decided a cool beer would be better than hot coffee and were already deep into the first one.

"We figure a week to ten days to get to Tucson. Not in a hurry. Want to look around a bit."

"The way you're going makes sense cause due east of here there ain't much room for mistakes. Heading up the Gila you'll likely find water without much trouble, though you might have some stretches where it's dry or almost dry for a while. Wash tells me you're going to take the cut off at Gila Bend. That's a dry stretch, but it's not long, so it isn't hard to carry enough water to make it across. I'd rinse your bags good here and fill with fresh. No guarantee there'll be water in the Santa Cruz. Might be able to dig and find some in the bed if you run short.

"Make sure you keep the water spread around on your mounts. Don't want to lose one horse and lose all your water. You'll be traveling with mountains on either side and they look like barren piles of rock, but there's water above the trail in a few springs and tanks if you know where to look. I can give you a map, but don't count on it. They can be dry or fouled. Don't leave one source of water with any space in your water bags. The source you're counting on may be dry."

"We'll take a couple of those maps. Anything else you

recommend?" asked Johnny.

"I think Wash will have you supplied up. He knows what's out there. You interested in traveling with anyone? There's another party headed the same way, about the same time."

They looked at each other. "People you know?" asked Wash.

Donnelly shrugged. "I know one of them. There's four others." He hesitated then said, "I'm bound to ask." He looked at Wash and shook his head slightly.

"Good enough," said Wash. "Any renegades out there you know about?"

"Haven't heard about any lately but keep your eyes open. You never know. Renegades will kill for anything you have, or for nothing, for that matter. Think about them like you would a big cat or a grizzly. Mercy's not in their souls."

They sat and talked for a while and then went over the horses, checking supplies, filling water bags, and making sure the load was spread among them.

Finally, Donnelly said, "Looks like you're in good shape. Recommend you hang around until late afternoon or a little later and drink your fill of water before you leave. Inside you is a good place to store it. Keep your horses in whatever shade you find as much as you can out there." He shook hands with Wash and slapped him on the back. "Glad to see you're still alive and kickin." After he left, they sat in the shade and talked.

"Are we going to wait or leave now?" asked Handy. "Might be best to get out ahead of that other bunch."

"Probably best to stay in front of them, but we don't want to leave too soon. They say only mad dogs and Englishmen travel in the noonday sun," said Wash. "Remember, we're in the desert. Always take the sun into account. Shade is precious so use it when it's there."

After looking over the trading post they returned to the café for dinner then sat and watched the shadows lengthen until Wash finally said, "Let's head out." He smiled around at them. "Have to make a start before you can get where you're going."

As Johnny was mounting, several men came out to stand on the porch across the yard. He caught a glimpse of one in the middle of the bunch and a memory told him he'd seen him somewhere but couldn't place him. When he looked again the man had turned away.

They crossed the Colorado on a ferry at Yuma, rode north along the river, and after a few miles turned off east on the south side of the incoming Gila River. The trail was wide enough to ride two abreast and Johnny and Handy fell in behind the others. Jinx was sitting on Handy's shoulders which gave him more room to move around than on Johnny's and he was looking around at everything just like a tourist.

An hour plus a little and the sun was getting low enough to give some relief from the heat. The trail had turned away from the river and they passed a crude sign that read "Quicksand".

Wash said back over his shoulder, "I've heard there are a few places like that along this stretch and there's probably not any more signs, so we need to pay attention to the ground close to the river. Don't want to be looking at the water and ride into trouble."

To the south, some rocky hills rose suddenly from the surrounding country. Wash pointed to them and said, "Most of the mountains we see on this trip jump out of the flat like that, sudden like. You want to get used to looking at them up-close. When there's a tank or spring up above you can usually see some sign of a trail, so it's good to look for it."

The lower the sun got the more they could feel the swift cool as heat on the ground dissipated and the chilly desert night began. The stars appeared gradually, incredibly bright, and so close it looked like they could be touched.

"Wow," said Handy looking up. "You forget how big and bright they look out here. I wonder how far away they are?"

"I don't think anybody knows," said Johnny. "They're building some pretty big telescopes these days to look at them, but I haven't heard any distances. Maybe one day they'll figure it out."

"This should be the place to look at them," said Handy. "They sure look different back home."

"Where's home?"

"Mill Valley, of course. That's where Rebecca and Bobby are."

They rode in silence for a while, then Handy asked, "You reckon we'll regret coming on this trip before we get home?"

"Might. Never know what tomorrow brings."

Ahead of them Wash pulled up, turned to them and said, "Let's have some dinner and give the horses a break and some water." He pointed at some rocks a few yards off the trail. "Looks like a good spot. Then we can decide whether to go further this evening."

They found a small open area among the rocks and soon had fire going and coffee on while Woman got dinner ready.

"I'm getting used to beans and bacon again," said Handy. He had just come back from picketing the horses.

Wash came back into the circle carrying some green stuff. "We all have to get used to new stuff." He showed them some cactus he had cut. "This is prickly pear. Knock these spines off and the horses will eat it. Got a lot of juice in it. My old mule has eaten a lot of this stuff over the years. After dinner I'll show you how to cut and clean it. It'll probably be around most places we camp."

They were sitting around the fire with plates in laps when Johnny suddenly snapped his fingers. "Now I know where I've seen that fellow before." He looked at Handy. "Remember Zack Grayson?

Handy narrowed his eyes. "Isn't that Gray's older brother?"

"Yes," replied Johnny. Wash and Woman were looking at him.

"Who's Zack Grayson?" asked Wash.

"He and another brother tried to muscle into the ranch one time. They tried to force Gray to let them and another fellow stay at his place. We decided we didn't want them around and ran 'em off. They ended up in San Francisco and were making threats, so I braced 'em. The younger one drew on me and he's dead. Zack decided leaving town was the better option."

Wash's jaw dropped. "You killed Gray's brother?"

"Not like I had much choice. He thought he was a gunfighter. He was trying to kill me."

"And Zack's the one you saw on the porch back there? Part of the group that's probably behind us?"

"Looks like it."

"You reckon he saw you?"

"Maybe, maybe not. I just got a glimpse of him. He may have gotten a better look at me."

"Jesus," said Wash, and ran his hand through his hair. "That might just make this whole trip a little different for a while, at least until we find out a little more about this fellow and his friends." He sat thinking for a minute while they all watched him.

Finally, he looked at Johnny. "Let's us take a climb up this rock behind us and look back."

About a hundred feet above the camp, Wash stopped and pointed west. "See anything out there?"

Johnny looked. A three-quarters moon had risen over their shoulders and the desert night stretched out before them. In the distance they could see the occasional flicker of a fire. They stood looking at it for a while then Johnny asked, "How far you reckon?"

"Hard to say. It looks closer than it is. The desert will fool you about distance." They stood quiet, each thinking about what the fire could mean. "Tell me what this fellow looks like."

"A little shy of six feet if I remember right. Stocky. About half bald. I'd say he's about fifty."

Wash led the way back to camp. When he got there, he went to his mule and got some clothes out.

"Is that your dark suit?" asked Handy.

Wash nodded. He turned to Johnny. "I'm going to take a look and see if it's him. When I get back, we can talk about how to deal with the situation."

Wash's dark suit from his days as a scout with Sherman with his very black skin and a black cloth cap covering his white hair rendered him almost invisible in the dark. Before long he disappeared into the desert night, and they sat and waited 'til he returned.

Johnny was sitting looking out at the night when he heard, "Johnny, I'm coming in," and he watched his friend suddenly materialize as though from thin air.

"Well?" asked Johnny as they walked into the circle of the campfire.

Wash nodded. "It's him. Heard 'em talking and one called him Zack. He saw you at the fort and they were talking about it. Sounded like he'd told them what happened, and they were deciding how to deal with it."

"Any Idea what they decided?"

"He wants to get even but he's leery. Seems like they're worried about Donnelly knowing they left behind us. If they jump us, even out here, they're worried he'll send the law after them."

"From what I remember of him, it's likely the law's after them anyway."

When they were all seated with coffee in hand Handy said, "So what do we do now? I'm guessing this changes our plans a bit."

"It's going to need some thinkin', that's for sure," replied Wash.

Johnny shook his head. "It looks like whenever you two get tied up with me we find out someone wants to shoot me."

"Maybe not," said Wash. "They saw us at the fort, and they'd have to have seen the firepower we carry. And he's seen you handle a six-gun, so he probably wants no part of that. If we do have a problem with them, it will probably be an ambush of some kind. That gives us an advantage."

Johnny looked a question at him. Wash shrugged. "I imagine I'm better at watching them than they are at watching us. I don't think they could set an ambush I won't know about."

"Humm," said Handy. "I'll bet."

"We don't know anything about the rest of them," said Johnny, "but if they're anything like him they're probably half-drunk most of the time."

"They were drinking tonight while I was watchin'."

Handy looked around the circle. "So do we want to camp here for tonight, or put some distance between us and them?"

Johnny looked at Wash. "Been listening to you for a while about things like that," he said. "You decide and we'll do it."

Chapter Ten

There was a surrey waiting for Annaliese and her friends when the ferry docked in Coronado. She was nervous about the coming meeting with John Spreckels. The people with her were Kate Sessions, the Doctor and two of the other doctors in town. They were the newly created hospital steering committee and were meeting with the hotelier to sound him out on his support for the hospital.

Though she was glad the people around her were there, she missed her husband. Not that he knew much about hospitals, but he was the one she always talked to when moving forward with anything. Now, for the first time in a while, she was alone at night instead of having him there watching her brush her hair and talking with her about things going on in their life.

She was seated and they were waiting for John when she heard a commotion at the door.

"Please let me in. I need the doctor. The lady doctor." The voice was loud and familiar, with a strong accent. There was a murmur and then, "They are sick. Please! We need the lady doctor."

Her bag was beside her and she picked it up and opened the door. Federico, husband to Consuelo, their housekeeper, was trying to get past a steward.

"What is it, Federico?" Who's sick?"

"You must come, Senora," he said. "The children, three are sick. Also, next door."

She turned to John who had just come in. "I must go. The Doctor will fill me in later on what's been said."

She followed Federico out the front door to a wagon and within a few minutes they were embarked on the ferry. Her Spanish wasn't good enough for talking over the noise of a loud wagon, so she waited until they were on the ferry to ask.

"How are they sick?" she asked. He mimed vomiting and patted his backside.

"Bad, not stop."

Back in the wagon he whipped up the horses and they raced through town to the old town neighborhood. Consuelo had been with her for a year. Annaliese knew all her children as patients and had been to the house many times.

As she hastened up the path, she could hear children crying inside. Juan, the oldest, opened the door and the sounds told her that she had at least three sick with whatever it was.

It took her less than five minutes to diagnose cholera. She turned to Consuelo. "We need hot water. Everyone must wash their hands whenever they touch one of the children."

"Two of the children next door also are sick," said Consuelo.

"We need to try to give them water. Is the water here good? They need to drink as much as they can."

She closed her eyes and stood for a moment organizing her thoughts.

"I need to talk to Estela. Send Federico to bring her. Right away." Estela's children were next door and apparently sick the same way. To Consuelo she said, "We need to bring the ones next door here so they will all be together. Also, we'll need all the towels and rags you have to keep the children clean. Put a large kettle on for hot water to wash the towels."

The odors in the room were overpowering. She recognized the rice-water stool as much from its smell as how it looked, and between that and the vomiting children, the sick room was noisy and foul smelling. All three children were wailing their misery, and it was hard to keep her thoughts straight.

When the neighbor arrived, she sat the two mothers down and quickly outlined what they needed to do to keep the rest of their families safe.

"This disease comes from dirty water. The germs are in the stool, stool gets in the water and if you drink it, you get sick. Do you know where they drank water that was not at home? It might be well water or in a pond. Where the water is still."

The women looked at one another. One of the older boys said, "They were playing in a ditch yesterday. Maybe they drank some of the water there."

"How many of them were there?" his mother asked.

"All of them." That meant five of them from one house and four from the other. She looked at the neighbor. "How many are sick at your house?" She held up two fingers. That meant the others could get sick too. They just had to watch and wait.

Annaliese knew that at least the ones not sick should eat and drink as much as they could hold. That seemed to have an effect on the severity of the symptoms if they did get sick. She turned to the neighbor and explained the precautions and the need for water, as much as they could drink.

For the rest of the night Annaliese worked beside the mothers trying to keep the children clean and encouraging them to drink water when they could. Other women from the village came and went with food and water, helping to wash clothes, clean the room and the house and caring for the other children.

The Doctor joined her, and they worked together doing what they could. The problem was that the children needed fluid but some of them were too sick to drink it. They added a little sugar or salt to the water, and it seemed to help. Men gathered in the yards to talk and smoke and help when needed.

The sun was just coming up when Annaliese came out into the yard and sat in a swing. She couldn't recall when fresh air smelled better, more invigorating.

She closed her eyes for a moment and opened them when she heard the door open. Will came out and sat next to her.

"I'm going to have to try to do this whenever I have a hard night," she said. "It feels so good out here after being in that closed room all night."

"I'd say we're holding our own," he said. "They don't look any worse. Their skin turgor is still good. I don't get much of a tent when I pinch. Little Pablo looks the worst." He shook his head. "He might not make it."

"It's hard to get him to drink." She shook her head. "The most important thing is to keep it from spreading. If we keep it clean in there, we'll probably make it through. Everyone is washing their hands good and the whole village seems to be washing bedclothes." She pointed down the street where every house had things drying on clotheslines or porches.

"Why don't you go home, clean up and have breakfast?" she said. "Then you can come back, and I'll do the same. You know, if this hangs on for a while or spreads, we'll need some help from the other doctors in town."

After he left, she was sitting with her eyes closed when she heard someone pull up by the front gate. A minute later she heard footfalls coming up the path, and when she opened her eyes her face suddenly split into a grin.

"Is this where Doctor Annaliese Fry is working?" asked Maggie, her friend and classmate from med school. They started to embrace but at the last minute, Annaliese demurred. "Don't know if that's a good idea," she said, "but I sure am glad to see you."

"Looks like you could use a little help," said Maggie. "I've got my bag in the buggy if I need it."

"I don't know how much you know, but it's cholera. Got five

children down with it. Not much surgery in that." Maggie had just finished working with surgeons in Chicago and Annaliese knew she was ready to open her own practice.

"Well, I can help wash sheets while we talk, if nothing else," said Maggie and she sat beside her friend.

Pablo, the youngest of Consuelo's children, died that evening, but the rest of the children seemed to be recovering. Maggie and Annaliese sat on the porch talking after the little boy passed.

"I see you're still wearing pants," said Annaliese, "which with all the stuff on the floor in there I should probably be doing myself." During school, Maggie had preached the idea that the long dresses and heavy undergarments fashionable at the time were unsanitary and dangerous in situations where floors dirty with one thing or another could soil skirts and carry blood and other things out of sick rooms and into homes.

"Oh yes," said Maggie. "I haven't changed much, except that I know a lot more now and realize how much I don't know about what we do for a living. Besides the surgery I was supposed to learn, I remembered Dr. Rose and worked with some researchers trying to learn more about the physiology of the body."

"I envy you," said Annaliese. "That was my ambition in school but keeping people alive and healthy has kept me pretty busy these last two years."

"Today's the first time I've ever been around many Mexicans since I finished school. I really like the women in there. Not many in Chicago. Seems like they're good people."

"We had some as patients in Salt Lake. Enough that the Doctor learned some Spanish. When we moved here I was like you, but it's easy to love these people." She stopped for a moment, looked down the street at all the sheets and linens billowing on clotheslines, then continued.

"I took on old Doctor Clark's practice. He'd been taking care of them for forty years. I remember him sitting with me and looking me right in the eye and asking, 'Will you take care of my people?'"

She smiled. "He sold me his practice for a dollar and a handshake because I promised to take care of his people." She shook her head. "I do my best."

Maggie sat silent.

"Sometimes I wish he'd come back so I could thank him."

Annaliese was sitting at her desk for the first time in three days. Across the room Will sat smiling at her. They had just come from the funeral of little Pablo, and the kitchen was overflowing with food brought by Dr. Clark's people.

"So, this was your first experience with something like this. Was this what you thought it would be like?" he asked.

"This is the first time I've had to deal with anything like this," she agreed. "It could have been much worse."

"Well, I'm glad it's over," he said. "That's the first night's sleep you had in a while. How do you feel?"

"I'm alright. I'm so glad Maggie's here. Things are always better when she's around. So, what happened at the meeting I missed? Are we going to build a hospital?"

"If it's up to Kate Sessions I believe we will. She's like a locomotive; she pulls us along behind her." They laughed.

"So, what does John say about it?"

"He's on-board. Says he'll help put in part of the beginning cost and have the paper focus on getting the town involved." He looked at her for a moment. "It was a strange meeting."

"How so?"

"His wife was there."

"Really? What did she have to say?"

"Asked a lot of questions. He introduced her and said she was interested in the hospital. I got the impression they're like you and Johnny. They'll talk about it later. Kate said that's not unusual. He likes for her to get involved in things she's interested in."

There was noise on the steps and Annaliese stood and said, "We're having a few guests for breakfast if you'd like to join us."

When she opened the door Maggie was there and Madame, Sarah and Lemuel were behind her.

Soon they were sitting at the long table talking while Maria and her daughter Katrina put platters on the table and filled cups and glasses with drink. Consuelo was still at home with her children.

"How much longer are you going to stay?" Lemuel asked Madame.

"We'll be leaving the first of next week. I've bought a cottage in Coronado and Tony and Carlotta are staying for a while to get it ready to live in so when we come down next time we'll have a place to stay." She grinned at her friend. "Sarah wants to get home and see Rebecca and Bobby."

"Got to spread Grandma around," said Sarah. "Keep everyone happy."

"We should hear from the travelers by then," said Annaliese. "They are supposed to be in Tucson pretty soon. Johnny said he'd write to me from there."

"How are your patients?" asked Sarah.

"Consuelo is with them, and she knows what to do from here. We lost the littlest one and should feel grateful there were no more."

"With the cottage here we'll be down every once in a while, so Sarah can keep track of her kinfolks," said Madame. "When do you expect Johnny back?"

"They're not even halfway to Santa Fe by now. The plan was to be back by the first of the year, but I wouldn't be surprised if they don't get back a little early. I know he misses me the way I miss him." She paused. "He better anyhow." Everyone laughed.

He did. He was sitting outside the circle of firelight looking out at the desert night wondering what she was doing. When he thought of her, he always thought first of the hair, her brushing that long, beautiful red hair. He knew he probably wouldn't see her for a couple months but that didn't seem real to him yet. He knew it but didn't realize it. He'd heard Annaliese say that and it fit perfectly with what he was thinking.

Around him the sounds of the desert night were the constant hum and whir of insects. Wash had told him when they were quiet you needed to wonder why. From the top of the sky, the last quarter moon spread a dim light on everything that wasn't in shadow

When he thought about it, he realized that he loved the difference in his life when he was in a place like this. Sitting cross-legged round a fire with your plate in your lap was very different from being served in the dining room back home while waking up in the cold dawn from birdsong so loud you couldn't sleep anyway was much more memorable, if not as comfortable as waking on your innerspring mattress beside your wife's warm body.

He glanced back at the fire and saw a shadow pass before it. It had been three days since Wash had heard the men who were following them talking. That night they had moved off the trail and up into a hollow among some rocks on a hillside looking out on the country toward the Bend of the Gila. Wash wiped out any sign of their camp, and they had watched the pursuers ride by the next day without seeming to notice.

They stayed in place the next two days and let the men get ahead of them. As Handy pointed out, "they weren't in a hurry." The first night they could see a distant campfire but the last two nights, nothing. Wash was out and around, and when he came back they would make plans.

Tomorrow they would likely be back on the trail with Wash scouting out ahead looking for any signs of the men. If they held a steady pace they could count on getting to Tucson a few days after them and hopefully they would have moved on. If not, they might have to force the issue. It was not the kind of thing Johnny liked having on his mind.

Handy called from the fire, "Wash is back. Come on in and we'll talk."

Jinx was in Woman's lap and Wash was lighting his pipe when Johnny sat down.

"Well, they've turned into the cutoff to Tucson and they're holding a steady pace. If we lollygag a little, we can hope they get impatient and move on before we get there."

"Lollygag?" asked Handy.

"Means take our time and look around," said Johnny.

"You've heard them talking," Handy said. "What do you think the chances are of that?"

"I'm not sure. I don't think Zack's the leader of that bunch. Didn't hear anyone giving orders, so they might not have one. Could be they're just traveling together."

"Any sign of them thinkin' about an ambush?" asked Johnny.

Wash shook his head. "It could be that some of them don't want any part of it. It could also be they'll realize they've lost our trail and are just going to wait in Tucson to see if we show up. Course, it might be we're imagining the whole thing, and they don't give a damn one way or another."

He sat smoking for a minute and then said, "We're going to be passing through a cut with mountains close on either side not long after we make the turn. If they're planning anything on the trail, that's where it'll be."

"We're lucky," said Johnny. "With five horses and a mule on watch, we shouldn't have to worry about anyone sneaking up on us at night, but from what you say, once we get back on the road we need to pay attention to things."

Chapter Eleven

Wash and Johnny were checking the horses before bedding down when Johnny asked, "Do you ever see that fellow who shot Jed?"

Wash looked at him for a moment. "You mean Schweder?" When Johnny nodded, he asked, "Why do you want to know?"

"Just curious. I've avoided going out by his place since I've been in town. I guess I just wondered, that's all."

"I see him now and again. He comes into the store once in a while, but not as often as he used to. I deliver out there occasionally. He's not still in the business of shooting people for money if that's what you were wondering."

The bullet that killed Jed had been fired from a window down the street from the bookstore in San Francisco. Johnny's return fire had scored, raking the right side of the killer's face and leaving a distinctive wound.

When Wash and Woman stumbled on the man when they first got to San Diego, Wash had puzzled for a while on what to do about him, and whether to tell Johnny. What kept running through his mind was fear that the man might get a telegram and set out on another job before he made up his mind.

Ultimately, he decided he needed to stop the man from practicing his trade as a paid killer and put a .50 caliber Sharps bullet through his knees. Now the stealth necessary in his chosen profession was impossible for him to practice.

An infection had taken one of his legs and now, instead of a paid assassin, he was a one-legged farmer, who spent much of his time sitting on his porch in a rocking chair watching oranges and lemons grow. Wash wondered if, when he was sitting there, he ever thought about the people he'd killed, the lives he'd ruined.

They stood quiet for a while, feeling the desert night. "What do you reckon you'd say to him if you saw him?"

Johnny thought for a long moment before he answered. "Probably nothing. I'd have so many things going through my mind I wouldn't be able to pick out any one of them. How do you feel when you see him?"

Wash was quiet so long, Johnny thought he wasn't going to answer. Finally, he shook his head. "I don't feel bad about it if that's what you think. I guess I feel sorry for the man, though I realize that doesn't make any sense when you think of how much suffering he's caused. You'd think someone like that would be a pretty poor excuse for a man, but that doesn't seem to be the case. He's a good farmer and a good employer. Never heard anyone speak ill of him.

"At the time I had enough proof and felt it was a way to handle it without becoming an assassin myself." He was quiet for a minute. "It would be interesting to be inside that fellow's head for a while."

The next two days were hot and dusty, but with the evening breeze and the cooling with the coming of night, the desert became a magical place again. Always after they camped, one or another of them would sit outside the fire light alone and listen to the quiet emptiness that was all around them; look at the shadows cast by a beautiful moon, all the while thinking of the life out there they would never see. Even with the threat the desert posed Johnny felt a peace and calm seeping into his soul right down to his toes and he reveled in it.

Two mornings later Jinx was sitting on a rock watching Woman brush her hair. She dipped the brush in the pool of water at her knees and slowly worked the dust and knots out. The tank was a little above and several yards outside the circle around their campfire. Wash was adamant about not camping close to a tank or spring and shutting animals off from needed water.

Suddenly Jinx turned his head and growled, a strange sound Woman had never heard before. As she turned, her hand went to the Bowie, and it was out and poised before she finished her turn.

Coming toward her, a knife held low in his right hand, was an Apache. Naked except for a breechclout, he was small and wiry with scars across his chest and face that showed light against his dark skin. His eyes glowed like blown-on coals, and he made no sound as he approached.

He came toward her in a crouch circling away from her knife and toward Jinx. Suddenly the cat leaped. The Indian, startled, raised his knife hand and the back of it struck Jinx and knocked him flying.

That was all the opening Woman needed. The Bowie flashed across his body as she leaped aside to avoid his rush, and when he turned toward her there was a steady flow of blood from a gash opened across his belly. His knife hand drooped and he tottered on his feet, but when she moved to strike again, he lashed out suddenly, his knife hitting her belt and knocking her off balance. She fell, rolled away from him, and came up with the blade waist high, poised to strike.

There was no need. He had fallen to his knees, bent forward, long hair reaching almost to the ground. As she watched, he lurched to his feet and staggered back the way he had come leaving blood on the ground behind him. When he was out of sight in the rocks and underbrush, she checked that Jinx was OK and called to Wash. Before she could get to camp, he was beside her.

"There's Indians about," she said, a little breathless. "You'd best look to the horses."

"What happened?" asked Wash, his glance taking in the blood in spots on the ground and her disheveled state. Behind him Handy was moving toward the horses and Johnny had picked up the Henry rifle and slipped into the rocks away from the fire.

"Is that your blood?"

"No, I guess it's his." She took a deep breath. "Come help me track him. I don't think he'll make it too far."

He hadn't. They found him a few feet from where his horse was tied. He was sitting against a rock in a patch of bloodstained dust, head hanging to one side, and he was dead. At his side was a US Army carbine; from its shiny stock and well-oiled appearance, not long out of the hands of a soldier who had been proud of it. A fresh scalp was hanging from his horse's bridle.

While Wash was securing the horse, she leaned against a rock and let her fingers probe the place on her belt where the Indian's knife had struck. The blade hadn't gone through the heavy leather, but there was a bright gash across it, and she realized if it hadn't absorbed the blow, she could have suffered much the same wound that killed her attacker. The thought made her a little dizzy and she was sitting on the rock when Wash came up leading the horse and carrying the rifle.

"Are you all right?" he asked, peering at her intently.

She nodded and turned to show him the belt where the knife had struck.

"Jinx jumped at him and that's when I got him. I never heard him and if Jinx hadn't growled, I never would have seen him," she said.

She stood, a little shakily, and he put his arm around her. "It looks like he was alone. Don't see any other tracks around, but we best be careful the next little while. I've heard an Apache can steal your horse while you're holding the reins."

When they got back to camp, Woman came to where Johnny

was standing with Jinx on his shoulder. She took the cat, hugged him gently and kissed him between the ears. "Thank you, little Buddy," she whispered.

A few minutes later Wash came back into camp. "Don't see sign anywhere so it seems like he was a lone wolf. No guarantee of that though. San Carlos is east of here about fifty miles and I've heard they have problems with young ones who get restless and go off the reservation looking for scalps and loot."

"What do you think?" asked Johnny. "Do we keep going or not?" He looked around the circle. "Nothing says we have to go to Tucson. We could go elsewhere. Hell, we could go back to Yuma."

"It don't make much sense to change our route," said Handy. "We don't know where they are, how many there are, what their plans are, or even if they're really out there." He waited for someone to say something, then continued. "No matter which way we go we could run into them. Might be best to just go about our business and keep our eyes open."

"From what I've heard," said Wash, "the renegades around here have trouble getting their hands on rifles, so that's what they'll be looking for. We'd be a treasure trove for them.

"With them on the loose, I'd say we got more important things to worry about than those other fellows." Wash looked around the circle. "We all have to be alert and keep our minds on what we're doing. Don't do any good to look if you don't see."

Everyone agreed, and before long they were on the trail again.

That night they camped at a tank a few yards above the trail. Handy had taken over cooking, and Wash and Woman were sitting on a rock a little way off, looking out at the desert night.

"Are you OK?" he asked.

"Yes," she replied, and then after a bit asked, "Why do you ask?"

"You haven't said much today."

"For me that's not unusual."

"Have you been thinking about the Indian?"

"Yes, a little. Every once in a while I run my fingers across my belt where his knife hit me, and it reminds me. I was lucky."

He looked at her for a moment. "No, I'd say he was unlucky. Because you're a woman he thought he had you. You were much more than he bargained for."

"If Jinx hadn't been there, he might have gotten me."

He smiled. "Maybe. Maybe not." He kissed her on the forehead. "You're more than most men can handle."

She was quiet for a minute. "But you think you can?" she said, a smile playing around her lips.

"Not in a thousand years," he said, grinning at her.

Over the next two days they stayed along the Gila and then turned southeast toward Tucson when the river bent north. The next day they saw buzzards circling far ahead, and near evening they found the bodies.

Wash was scouting ahead when he saw buzzards landing and hopping around on the ground. Suddenly he held up his hand.

"Let me go have a look around," he called. "Probably get a good idea of what happened." He rode ahead, found a place to tie his mule, and as he approached the rocks he stopped suddenly, and they could hear him say something. After a moment he waved them forward and disappeared behind some foliage.

When they got into the circle of rocks he was squatting beside someone lying against a rock giving him a drink of water. When he moved to one side, they could see the shaft of an arrow sticking out of the man's thigh, a little above the knee. Beyond them were two bodies, and as they came closer, they could see they'd been scalped and mutilated.

Woman went to the pack horse, unslung a bag, and carried it to Wash's side. She rummaged in it and handed Wash a cloth then took a few herself, poured water on them, and began to sponge the man's face and neck.

Handy and Johnny gathered wood for a fire, and by the time

they had it burning Wash had water in a pot ready to heat.

"He told me they came two nights ago. Apache likely. Probably from San Carlos. Killed one of their bunch right off and he got this arrow. He got back in the brush, and they had left him alone. Maybe they thought he was dead. He thinks he passed out, and when he came to, there were two bodies and the other two had gone."

"Since I don't see his body, I supposed he means Grayson and someone else."

"I guess. He wasn't too specific."

Woman came to the fire. "I think we need to get that arrow out before long," she said. "He sure can't ride with it in his leg like that. It's good it went through. We can cut the head and the feather off, and it shouldn't do too much more damage when we push it through. We've got enough bandages to stop the bleeding."

Wash looked at Johnny. "Why don't you and Handy get the camp set up and keep an eye out. They probably won't come back but we don't know that so you might want to make it easier to defend this place if they do. Woman and I will get that arrow out and see where we are." He looked at Handy. "Might need your help. I'll call you when we're ready. From the look of it, we might be here a few days."

When the water was hot, he stood and said, "Handy, we'll likely need you to hold him while I push it through."

Handy looked at Johnny. "Something new every day. I swear, Johnny, I'd probably get bored to death if you two weren't around." He followed Wash back to where the man was lying and crouched by his head. "Do we know his name yet?"

"I think he said Ollie, but he's just mumbling so it's hard to tell. I have to break the head off the arrow first so whenever you're ready."

No matter how careful Wash was, getting the head and feather off the arrow caused the man to writhe and cry out in pain. When it was finally cut through, they repositioned him. Wash nodded at Handy again, poured some whiskey on the wound and began to work the arrow loose so he could push it out the back of the leg.

The screams and convulsive spasms continued, and Handy and Wash were running sweat before it was out and the man finally fainted. Woman washed the wound as best she could. The passage of the arrow through the leg had started the bleeding again. She poured some more whiskey on the wound and bandaged it quickly, pulling the dressing tight around the leg to stop the bleeding.

"It looks like you're doing better," said Johnny. It was the evening cool on the second day, and he was crouching beside the wounded man. He had been unconscious or delirious the day before, but now he smiled weakly. "I'm Johnny and this is Jinx. The big fellow there is Handy."

The man nodded his head. "My name is Ollie," he said weakly, his voice husky with pain.

"I'm sorry we don't have anything for your pain, but there's not much whiskey left."

Ollie nodded. "I understand. I'm just glad to be alive. If you hadn't shown up, I wouldn't be."

He closed his eyes, breathing heavily. "You reckon I'm going to make it?"

"We'll do our best. Wash seems to think you might if we can get you into Tucson."

"I might could make it if you could get me on a horse."

"You'd probably bleed to death in a few miles."

"Kinda puts you all in a spot, don't it?"

"Yeah, it does. We're pretty well supplied, but things are getting a little short. With these renegades out, it doesn't seem like a good idea to send anyone for help, and we haven't seen anyone else on the road but you and your friends."

"They weren't my friends. They left me here to die, didn't they?" His eyes were closed, and his voice trailed off at the end. Johnny didn't know if he'd passed out or just fallen asleep, but he moved quietly back to the others around the fire.

They heard nothing or no one on the road until late that day when they heard what sounded like a wagon and someone called out, "Hello the fire! Can I come in?"

"Come ahead," said Wash, repositioning his Sharps.

A wagon came almost into the campsite and a big man sitting on the seat said, "Howdy. I was just looking for a place to stop for the night when I saw your tracks. Mind if I get down and have some of that coffee?"

When they assented, he climbed laboriously down, stretching his back and grinning, holding out his hand.

"Tom Wise. Sure am glad to see you." He accepted the cup of coffee Johnny handed him and took a drink. "Where y'all headed?"

After introductions, Handy said, "We were headed to Tucson, but we got sidetracked. What are you doing out here in a wagon all by yourself?"

Wise was a big, jolly fat man with a happy, open face. "I had it made brand-new for me up in the capital," he indicated the wagon, "and this was the only way to get it back to Tucson."

"Had any problems on the way?" asked Wash.

"No, this is my third day on the road and you're the first people I've seen."

His eye fell on the wounded man. "What happened to him?"

"Long story," said Johnny. "We came on the scene a few days ago. Two dead men, scalped, and him with an arrow in his leg. Buried the other two, and we're waiting to see if he dies or gets better so we can put him on a horse and get him out of here. I'd say you've been lucky. There's Apache about. "

"Well, I can probably help with moving him. You can lay him in the back of the wagon. It's not sprung so I'll take it easy on the road. Even so, we can probably get to Tucson day after tomorrow if it don't rain." He laughed at his own joke. "Seems like he's getting better?"

"He comes and goes," said Johnny. "Today he's been talking some and seems to be improving. If we get him to a doctor soon he might keep his leg."

"Can we start tomorrow morning? I could use a night's sleep. We can be on the road early as you want."

"Best offer we've had since we got here," said Handy and the others agreed.

Ollie was awake when Johnny and Handy sat down next to him. "I heard," he said. "Seems like I might make it after all."

"Looks like it."

He looked at Johnny. "Your name's Fry, isn't it?" When Johnny nodded, he continued. "Grayson was talking about you. Says you killed his brother."

"He drew on me. I had no choice."

"He wanted to jump y'all, but the rest of us wouldn't buy in. He was a little put out. If you ever come across him, be careful. He's carrying a grudge."

"From what I've heard, that's a lifelong habit where he comes from," said Johnny.

"Where are you from?" asked Handy.

"I was born and grew up just the other side of the Mississippi in Minnesota."

Handy smiled at him. "Thought you sounded familiar. I grew up on a farm on the west side of the river in Minnesota, the nearest town was Slayton."

"What's your last name?"

"Josephson."

"Lots of them around there."

"I'm one of them. Try to get some sleep. We'll probably be on the road early."

Chapter Twelve

They were up, and on the road as the sun came up. Ollie was lying in the bed of the wagon, surrounded by all their supplies and gear. In addition to allowing the horses to be free to move faster, if necessary, the bags and packs were arranged to provide protection and cushioning for the patient. Woman was riding with him in the back and Tom Wise was driving and taking up most of the seat in front.

In addition to taking care of Ollie, Woman was watching their back trail, Wash was scouting ahead, and Johnny and Handy were riding on either flank.

Between the horses tied to the back of the wagon and the need to avoid jarring the patient too much, Tom held a slow, steady pace. Other than some dust in the distance, they saw or heard nothing that day and the sun was nearly down when Wash directed them to a place to set up a small camp.

The clearing was defensible, and they set about making it more so. Their meal was dried meat, cheese, and bread and with a small, smokeless fire they heated coffee and some water to bathe Ollie's wound when Wash changed the bandage.

"I heard somewhere that Apache don't like to fight at night," said Handy. "Something about having to wander in darkness ever after."

"Don't you believe it," said Tom. "If they think they got an edge, them young bucks will try it." He pulled at his chin. "Fact is, over the years I've killed a few at night myself."

"I agree with Tom," said Wash. "We got the animals close in and they'll likely warn us if anyone comes around, but we still need to watch. Let's set a watch with two people on for two hours at a time. We can be up, and on the road early again." He looked at Tom. "How far you reckon to Tucson?

"Four or five hours. Once we cross the river, we should be safe."

Johnny was on watch, and it wasn't a good time to talk so he and Tom didn't. When you were talking, you weren't listening, and listening was what you were supposed to be doing on watch at night because you couldn't see much in the dark. He thought back to stories his Pa had told about his experiences in the war. He didn't know if Apache were out there or not, but the fact they could be, put him in the same kind of situation. Waiting for someone coming to try to kill you might cause you to be a little edgy.

He was trying to concentrate on what Wash had told him about hearing when you listen and seeing when you look. The best thing was to listen for anything from the horses. They could hear and smell much better than he could, so if they became restless or snorted, it probably meant something. On the other hand, the Apache were good at moving silently and making sure they were downwind from the camp when they attacked.

What was it Wash said about the insects.? When they stopped their constant chatter there was a reason. The only reason was that a predator animal or human was out there.

Johnny spoke close to Wash's ear. "It's too quiet out there. No bug or animal noises. I think we might have visitors." Handy was awake and listening. "Handy you keep that ten-gage handy. Cut loose at the first thing you see coming toward you. One barrel at a time. Who knows, the noise that thing makes might make 'em change their mind."

"Johnny, don't worry about wasting ammo," said Wash. "We got plenty. Just hose the bullets at them. If it's not a big bunch we could cripple them at the start. Maybe they'll decide it's not worth it."

Tom had two new Winchesters with plenty of ammo he'd bought in Phoenix, and a twelve-gauge double barrel with plenty of loads. Wash's Sharp's was a single shot, but Johnny had seen how fast he could reload, and the .50 caliber slug it fired would knock a man backward off his feet if it hit him in the shoulder. Woman was good with the Winchester too, so they had enough firepower and ammo to fight for a long time.

It was just getting light when suddenly they heard the horses moving restlessly and the Indians came in a rush, seven or eight, maybe more, screaming and shooting as they came. The blast of the two shoguns and the crack of the Henry were loud and suddenly there were screams of pain and the attack broke as quickly as it began.

Johnny looked around. Wash was sitting, holding his left shoulder where blood was seeping through his fingers and Handy was down.

When Johnny turned him over, he saw blood running down his face. His fingers felt for the wound and found a shallow groove that ran several inches along the top of the skull. A bit more than a graze, but he would likely have a bad headache for a few days. While Johnny was parting his hair to get a better look, Handy said, "Wow, what happened?" He shook his head and moaned.

"Hold still. Let me see how bad it is."

Johnny searched through the thick blonde hair, now tinged with blood, and felt a rising knot but found no more bleeding. The blood was coming from where the bullet first struck and laid the scalp open for an inch or so. The wound was jagged and looked like it might have come from a ricochet.

"Looks like that hard head of yours helped. You're probably going to have a headache to beat all headaches, but it doesn't look bad. Sit here for a bit and I'll go watch. They may come back."

Tom was still watching, rifle ready. Woman had unbuttoned Wash's shirt and was pressing a cloth against the wound to stop the bleeding. She looked up and said, "The bullet went through, but I need to stop the bleeding before I can bandage it."

"Woman, I need to keep an eye out in case they try again. Can you handle that?" When she nodded, he found a place among the rocks and began to scan the area. Taking Wash's advice, he slid a new tube into the Henry and began a rapid searching fire into the rocks and foliage across their front, and after a moment Tom joined him. Changing positions between them, they poured shot after shot toward an enemy they couldn't see. After a while they paused, smelling dust, and in the distance, heard the sound of horses running.

"One thing about Apache," said Tom as he was reloading one of the Winchesters. They don't believe in this 'fight to the last man' thing. If they don't like the odds, they figure there'll be another day."

Inside the circle there were three bodies, two of them torn by buckshot from Tom's and Handy's shotguns. The other had two bullet holes in his chest. Buckshot from the ten-gage had cut one of them almost in half.

Tom was experienced at treating gunshot wounds and helped Woman get Handy and Wash cleaned up and bandaged.

"Might be you have something broken in there," said Tom to Wash. "I think you need to be in the back of the wagon today. The less you move it the better, so let's make a sling."

Johnny crouched down before Wash and Woman. "It looks like they're gone. With all the shooting we did, they must have figured there was an army in here." He had given Ollie a pistol and the wounded man had kept his place in the wagon, but things happened so fast he hadn't had a chance to use it.

Wash nodded and grimaced at Johnny when he crouched next

to him. "Well, what do you think?" he asked. "Is this trip a little more than we bargained for?" Johnny could tell he was in pain from the way he winced with any movement.

Johnny took a deep breath and said, "Maybe, but all these shenanigans sure make you know you're alive, don't they?" He stood up. "From what Tom says, we should be in Tucson around noon today if nothing happens."

When the wagon pulled back on the road a short time later Wash was sitting in the back with Ollie and Woman. Handy was riding alongside sporting a blood-stained turban and a very bad headache. He seemed to be a little dizzy, so Johnny rode close beside him, ready to grab him if need be. After a few miles he stopped and tied his friend to the saddle. What with keeping an eye out for more trouble and keeping the horses from tangling one another behind the wagon, he had enough to worry about without having Handy fall off his horse.

Chapter Thirteen

"You seem to be settling in all right." John Spreckels' desk was big, and though he was not a small man, he looked small behind it.

Herschel took a seat. Their meetings had already developed a routine. He removed some papers from a folder, handed them to John and sat while he read them. Herschel waited and as he sat there, thought about his new life.

His job at the newspaper was a job. That's all he could say about it. in a city less than one-twentieth the size of San Francisco, he couldn't expect to find the same interesting and challenging situations to deal with.

He loved his new home, though. Everything about it was good and he felt its size and the distance from his past in San Francisco made for a new start in life one where he could make some changes. He thought maybe he could be the person he wanted to be. In San Francisco life seemed to be forcing him into a mold he never felt good about. Here maybe he could make a new mold, try new things, meet different kinds of people.

The work he did for John was interesting yet not much different from the job at the paper. Johnny had given him a good start on learning where to go and who to know and he was developing a system to organize and catalogue the bits and pieces of information he accumulated over a week. For every meeting he wrote a summary for John to peruse before they talked.

"Not much new this week," said Herschel.

"No, it's been a little slow around here too."

They sat and chatted for a few minutes until John leaned back in his chair and asked, "Have you heard anything from your friend Johnny?"

"No, not yet. I'm not surprised though," he answered. "Desert travel can be tricky. They weren't on a schedule, so I figure I'll hear from him when I do."

"I take it you know him well?"

He was not surprised by John's questions. For some reason he could tell John and Johnny were moving toward one another. Now John Spreckels wanted information about Johnny Fry. He shrugged to himself. He couldn't see where it would hurt Johnny, and since information was his job, he couldn't believe giving it to John was a problem.

"Probably better than most. After Sunny Jim left, I got to know him and found out he's a different breed of cat. He lost his mother when he was young, and his father never remarried. Together they ran a livery stable in Kansas. They lived above the stable and every night they read and talked. Old newspapers, magazines, books, whatever his father could get ahold of they read and talked about. He knows more about more things than anyone I ever met.

"After his father died, he left Kansas with Jinx to ride the old Pony Express Trail to Sacramento and made some friends along the way." Herschel paused for a moment. "Did you know he was a gunfighter?"

John's eyes widened and his mouth dropped open. "Why do you say that?"

"I've seen him work," said Herschel. "In San Francisco a couple of brothers threatened him. I was in the saloon. He braced them and told them to leave or fight. One of them drew on him, I should say tried to draw on him. Wasn't much of a contest.

"When I was running around with some bad guys a few years ago I heard about a gunnie, Glenwood Coe, supposed to be pretty good. Johnny killed him in Carson City. Same thing. He drew on Johnny. I'd say that's not a good thing to do if you want to live a long time."

"He doesn't carry a gun."

"No, he hung it up for his wife a couple of years ago. But you can bet he's got it on now, out there in the desert."

They sat quiet for a spell. Finally, John said, "He'd have to have had a lot of practice to be that good."

"Among other things, his Pa was a gunsmith. They shot together testing guns he worked on. He told me he'd been drawing and shooting a gun since he was eight years old. I've heard his friend Wash call him a magician with a six gun."

John shook his head. "That's something else. Have you ever talked to Wash? Or his lady, Woman?"

"I know them, but we don't talk. They talk to certain people. I've never been one of them."

"She's fascinating."

"You know she carries a ten-inch Bowie behind her belt, don't you?"

"Really!?" John grinned in amazement. "Didn't know it, but it doesn't surprise me now that I think on it. How many women would go on a trip like that? And I'll bet she'll pull her weight too."

"She's Madame's best friend. Started out as her bodyguard."

"Madame? Oh, you mean Hannah Grimes."

Hershel nodded. "Woman stepped in one night and saved her from a robbery. They've been friends ever since."

"You know his wife, I take it?"

"Annaliese? Oh yes. I'm usually in the bookstore every day. I start my day with the paper there. We talk, but I don't know much about her. I know my wife loves her, and from what I've heard the people in Old Town love her too. She seems to be special."

John sat quiet for a minute. "Thanks for the information. I have a feeling we're going to be glad to have these people around. They're good for the city."

Herschel was talking to Lemuel when Annaliese knocked on the door jamb at the office. "Hello Herschel," she said, then to Lemuel, "Did Roy get the mail yet this morning?"

"Nothing from Johnny," Lemuel replied.

"Hmm," she said, almost to herself. "They should be in Tucson already. Wonder why we haven't heard?"

She turned to Herschel. "Have you heard anything?"

He looked at her for a moment and with a straight face said, "Even I, little as I know about wives, know enough not to admit I got a letter from your husband before you did."

Lemuel burst out laughing and she was trying not to, but gave in. When she recovered, she said, "OK, OK, I won't ask you again."

"Thank you," he said as she left the room.

Maggie was waiting for her in her office. Her friend had been staying in one of the spare rooms in the house and they usually had breakfast together before they went their separate ways for the day. Today, however, they were going to lunch at the Del, so they skipped their morning meal and talked instead.

"When is Charlie coming?" asked Annaliese.

"He's going to meet me in Los Angeles. I miss him. This is the first time we've been apart. At first it was fun, but not so much now."

"How did he like it in Chicago? Was he still working in a bank?"

"Yes, but he's decided he doesn't like being a banker. He got a job at one of the banks in Los Angeles, but it's just to pay the bills until he decides what he wants to do instead. We need to save a little more and see how much I can make."

"Does he have any ideas?"

"Not that he's told me about. He's moody sometimes, and when he's in one of those moods he's like a sphinx. It's probably because he doesn't know where he's going or what he wants to do."

"We should go. I want to show you a little of that place before we sit down to eat."

A harsh jangling noise startled them both.

"That's the new telephone. It always makes me jump when I hear it. Let me see if that's for me before we leave. We put it in the hall so everyone can get to it, and they usually answer it in the store." They heard a voice and then conversation, but when no one called to her, Annaliese picked up her bag and led Maggie out to the carriage.

When they debarked in Coronado, Maggie stopped and swept her gaze around the bay and the city beyond. "It's so pretty here. I'd love living here, but I can't see a surgeon making a living."

"You could have a general practice, but I think you're right. You'd probably starve as a surgeon."

"Speaking of starving, let's eat first and then you can show me things. I'm hungry, and from the size of the place it will take a while to show me around."

Maggie and Annaliese were just finishing lunch when Lillie Spreckels and her oldest daughter entered the dining room. She saw them, waved and came to the table.

"Hello Dr. Fry. Have you met my daughter, Grace?" said Lillie. "We're just going to have lunch.

Annaliese nodded at the girl and introduced Maggie. "We're almost finished but we'd love to have you join us."

After she ordered, Lillie turned to Annaliese. "Grace and I have been talking the last week about something I think we need to get your ideas on. Can we talk here, or do you have something to do?"

"Nothing that I know of. Of course, as you know, that's subject to change. Maggie is one of my classmates from medical school. She's a surgeon hoping to begin a practice, but she hasn't figured out where. She will likely find something funny to say, regardless of the topic, but that's just the way she is."

"I'm glad she's here," said Lillie. "It's a question about medicine. Grace thinks maybe she'd like to become a doctor, and we want to learn more about it, not just about medical things, but about your life. What it's like being a doctor and how you feel about it."

Annaliese looked at Maggie and raised her eyebrows, then looked at Grace. "What caused you to start thinking about it?"

Grace looked to be thirteen or so. She had blonde pigtails and bright blue eyes with a sprinkle of freckles across her nose she'd probably outgrow in a few years. "When Mama was in bed after she cut her arm, I sat with her, and we talked about what you had done. I thought how wonderful it would be to be able to help people like that. Mama thinks we should find out about it and then discuss it with Papa to see if it's something I'd like to do."

"Thank you, Grace. Feeling I may have some influence on how you will spend your life is quite a compliment." She sat for a moment looking at the girl.

"Recently we had a little outbreak of cholera among some of the children in Old Town. Maggie showed up just in time to help me with it. It's a disease that's spread in human stool. It's very contagious and to keep it in that house Maggie and I helped the children's mothers scrub it off the floors, change and washed sheets covered with it and were constantly cleaning it off the children who couldn't help themselves. For three days we smelled it and after we left it took a while to stop smelling it."

She stopped and looked steadily at Grace. "I tell you this to make sure you have a real idea about what it means to be a doctor. There are things you see and do that other people don't, and it's all part of the life. Being a doctor means there are times when nothing else matters but your patient and that can lead you into some strange situations, especially if you're married."

She sat thinking for a moment, then said to Lillie, "I think this is a conversation I need to think about before we go any further with it. Why don't you pick an evening next week and come to the office.

I'll show you around and we can talk about being a doctor. Would that be OK?"

"That will be fine. Tomorrow at seven?"

"Sounds like someone's impatient," Maggie said with a laugh.

At the door, Annaliese looked back. Mother and daughter were talking earnestly and seemed excited.

"A rich man's daughter? What do you think?" asked Maggie. "Will she be willing to work that hard?"

"I guess we'll start finding out tomorrow night."

Annaliese put down her pencil and stared out the window. It was a cloudy, drizzly evening, so unusual in the city she was almost tempted to go outside and see how it felt. Since she put Maggie on the train earlier in the day she had been thinking about her impending conversation with Grace Spreckels and her mother.

Other than the fact she was the oldest daughter of a very wealthy man she knew nothing about Grace. Annaliese and Lillie had become friendly during her recovery from the arm wound but she hadn't had any of the children as patients and had only seen Grace occasionally when she attended to her mother.

She was in the bookstore to greet them just before seven and led them to her office. After a short tour of the treatment and clinic rooms, they sat in the office with tea.

"Why don't you ask any questions you have to start with?"

"You seem to have blended the bookstore and your office together," said Lillie.

"And the house too. We live upstairs. The building that came with the practice is now the clinic. I moved over here this year."

"The clinic is in Old Town?"

"Yes. The practice I acquired was from Dr. Clark. He had been treating the Mexicans in town for years, so most of my patients live in Old Town. We've made some improvements, and it works well enough for us. The Doctor and I rotate between the office and the clinic."

"You've been here two years?"

"Yes. I didn't start out to be a pediatrician, but most of my practice right now is treating the children of Old Town. The parents seem to be pretty healthy, but the kids keep me pretty busy."

Grace raised her hand and Annaliese laughed. "No need to raise your hand."

"Do you ever get sick from your patients?"

"I guess an occasional cold but nothing else, so far anyway. My father taught me to wash my hands and keep everything clean, and I think that helps. If a patient has something contagious, I wear a mask. I did get the measles from a patient when I was working with him back home."

"I heard you worked with your father for years as a nurse before you went to medical school," said Lillie. "Is that the reason you became a doctor?"

"I worked with the Doctor for seventeen years. I started by running errands and cleaning up, but the more I asked the more he taught me."

"Did that help when you went to medical school."

"Oh yes. He had all sorts of medical books. I read them and he would answer any questions I had. I was treating bullet wounds and helping him deliver babies by the time I was eighteen."

"What's it like being a doctor?" asked Grace.

"That's an interesting question. I'd begin by saying once you become a doctor, you're always a doctor. Every minute of every day. When someone's in need, you ask no questions about who they are or what they are, you just try to help them. No matter how much you learn and how much time you spend studying, you'll never know it all, but you're always trying to learn more.

"Doctor Rose, my anatomy professor, used to tell us to always ask questions and always look for answers, and I think that's a big part of the job; asking questions and looking for answers."

"Do you like it?" asked Grace.

"It's my life's work. I love it. I can't imagine doing anything else."

"What does your husband think about it and what if you have children?" asked Lillie.

"When I first met Maggie, she asked me if I'd had the 'being married to a doctor' talk with Johnny." She laughed. "Once you begin on this path, then every man who is interested must hear the 'being married to a doctor' talk. There are times when my husband is not the most important person in my life, and he knows it.

"If you marry it will have to be different than most. Your husband must understand that and accept it. Some try and find they can't do it. So, you need to realize it can be a problem before you jump.

"As far as children goes apparently, I can't have children so it's not a problem for me. There are women doctors who do have children, so it's conceivable. I can see where it would be difficult though."

"If you don't want to answer this one, I'll understand," said Lillie. "How have you and your husband managed? You've been married for five years, is that right?"

"Yes, we talked about it before we got married and he agreed that there were certain choices in our life that were a part of my future which means they were part of our future. Supposedly we each live our lives and, when we can, we live them together.

"That's what this trip to the desert was. But I must admit it's the first time he's taken advantage of the idea, and it took me by surprise. So, I guess we'll find out if it works out the way we planned."

"When is he supposed to be back?"

"Around Christmas or New Year, but if the trip so far is any indication, it may be later. The plan was for him to be in Tucson by now, but we haven't heard from him yet, so I have no idea how things are with them."

"I think if it weren't for me and the children, I think John would love to have gone with them."

"His friend Handy somehow talked his wife into it. You know Madame, don't you?"

When Lillie looked puzzled, Annaliese said, "Hannah Grimes."

"Oh yes, we had dinner with her and her friend one evening."

"Her friend Sarah is Handy's mother-in-law. She thinks her daughter is crazy for letting him go, and at this point I'm inclined to agree with her."

Chapter Fourteen

Johnny awoke when Jinx crawled onto his chest and began to purr. He opened his eyes and for a moment was puzzled. Then he remembered he was in a hotel in Tucson and lay thinking about the last few days. The doctor had cleaned the wound in Wash's shoulder and ordered bed rest for a few days. Woman was next door with him making sure he behaved.

Handy had a concussion and was lying in the back room of the doctor's office not allowed out of bed. "He'll have that headache for a couple of days," the doctor had said, "and he might get dizzy and fall, or even pass out if he tries to do too much. He needs to take it easy for a while. Let me keep him here a few days so I can see what happens. I've got a lady who will sit with them at night if they need anything, and we'll see how he feels in the morning."

"So little Buddy, looks like we'll be here a few days." He lay scratching the cat's ears, looking at the ceiling and thinking about his wife.

He needed to write to her today and he had to be careful what he put on paper. There was no profit in telling her about the Indians and Handy's and Wash's wounds. She couldn't do anything about them, and he knew it would cause her to worry. On the other hand, he knew he'd feel bad if he didn't tell her, because they always shared everything. He needed to talk to Wash and Woman about it.

With that thought he threw back the sheet and got out of bed. Standing at the window he could already feel the heat of the day and was surprised he had slept this late. He was exhausted last night. He remembered getting his boots off before lying down and then nothing.

He splashed water on his face, changed his shirt, ran a wet comb through his hair and, with Jinx on his shoulder, found his way to the dining room.

Woman was there waiting for her breakfast. "How's Wash this morning?"

"Stiff and sore. I think he's a little weak. He's going to stay in bed today. I told him I'd feed him breakfast in bed if he didn't cause any trouble." She smiled. "He said that will be a first for him."

As she was leaving carrying a plate for Wash the doctor came in, saw Johnny, and came to sit with him.

"How are the patients this morning?"

"The big fellow was still sleeping when I left. That happens with a head injury like that. He should be fine before long. I'd say three days, and he should be ready to go."

"How about the other man? Is he going to lose that leg?"

The doctor shook his head. "I'd say it's touch and go right now. He's getting blood to his foot, and I don't smell anything like gangrene, but it's early. I'll watch him and see."

"What do you mean, 'you don't smell anything'?"

"That's how you'd know if gangrene is in the leg. If you ever smell it, you don't forget it. At this point I'd say he's got a good chance, but there may be some damage. We'll have to see once he gets on his feet, which will be awhile."

After breakfast he sat in the shade on the hotel porch and looked around the main street of the town. The clerk had told him there were around 5,000 people here. It was a pretty place, a lot like Old Town at home. Adobe buildings, bright colors everywhere against a tan background, lots of places to sit in the shade and talk or doze or just look around.

Tucson was founded in the late 1700's and was part of Mexico until 1854. In a deal known as the Gadsden Purchase, the United States acquired it as necessary for a proposed southern route for a transcontinental railroad.

Almost 30,000 square miles, it had cost the country ten million dollars. Since they left Yuma, they had been traveling in the Purchase, and so far, there wasn't much to see but desert, cactus, and rugged, mostly bare mountains. It sure didn't look like it was worth ten million dollars.

Unlike most historically Mexican towns in the country, Tucson hadn't grown up around a mission. Instead, it was about seven miles south of one, but the mission influence could still be seen in the wide streets and orderly arrangement of buildings. He could hear a guitar then another across the street in a cantina.

With Jinx exploring the landscape, they walked two blocks to the doctor's office. Handy was lying on a bed much too small for him and appeared to be asleep. Johnny sat by the bed petting the cat and watched his friend for a minute, and when he quietly got up to leave, Handy opened his eyes and smiled.

"I'm awake," he said in a low voice. When Johnny looked a question at him, he continued. "Makes my head hurt to talk loud."

"I talked to the doc at breakfast. He said he'd keep you in bed for a couple of days and see how you do."

"What's a concussion?"

"Annaliese told me it's when your brain gets jarred inside your skull. It can cause pressure to build up from swelling. I guess the best thing you can do is be patient and take it easy until the doc says OK."

"How long is that going to be?"

Johnny shrugged. "As long as it takes. We're not going anywhere until you're alright.

"Where's Wash?"

"He's in bed at the hotel. Woman's with him."

"What's he doing in bed?"

Johnny looked at him for a moment, taken aback. "You don't remember Wash getting shot?"

"Wash got shot!?" Handy's mouth was open, and his eyes were wide.

"In the shoulder. Same time you got shot. He's OK though." Johnny heard someone come into the office and a minute later the doctor came into the room.

Handy's exclamation had awakened his roommate, and the doctor checked him and then turned to Johnny. "I didn't mention the memory being gone to you. It's probably temporary. Not unusual with something like this."

"How much does he remember?"

"I think the question should be, 'what doesn't he remember'? That's kind of hard for me to say since I don't know anything about what happened to him. I think you can probably help him more than I can with that."

He pulled a chair up to the bed and sat down. "Maybe if you sit and talk to him, you can help him remember what happened and find out how far back he does remember."

"Do you want me to do it now?"

"No. I think it would be best to let him rest today. Tomorrow will be soon enough."

Johnny patted his friend's knee in farewell and stopped to say hello to Ollie, then headed for Wash's room in the hotel. When Woman opened the door Johnny was standing there with a thoughtful look on his face. Wash was sitting up in bed and looked fine except for the bandage around his shoulder and upper arm and a sling to keep it from moving too much.

In answer to his question Wash said, "He said there was no break. He gave me some medicine for the pain. It hurts some but I was able to sleep last night. It hurts when I cough but the doc says I have to cough to keep pneumonia away."

"It seems Handy can't remember you being shot or anything about the fight." They both looked at him open mouthed.

"What? He doesn't remember I got shot?"

"The doctor said it's not uncommon for someone to have trouble remembering things after they get a rap on the noggin like that. We don't know what he remembers. Doc wants him to rest today, and I'll talk to him tomorrow and see what he does remember."

"So, we have no idea how long we'll be here?" asked Woman.

"No, we don't," replied Johnny, "and that's something I need to talk about. I'm getting ready to write to Annaliese. What do I tell her about why we're going to be here longer than we planned? And what do I tell her about Handy? Should we write to Rebecca? How much do we tell them? Doesn't seem to be the kind of thing you'd put in a telegram."

He looked hopefully at them expecting something, but they just stared at him. After a long silence Wash said, "You might just try the truth."

Johnny shook his head. "That's liable to scare her so much she'll climb on the first train headed east and show up here. Same with Rebecca. It looks like the doc's got things under control. If I tell her about Handy, she'll want to know how it happened. Do I tell her about the renegades and the fight? She might just want me to come straight home."

"You'll have to wait and see how Handy is in a couple of days, then write to her," said Wash.

"I can't do that. We were late getting here. I don't want to put off writing. She'll worry herself sick."

Wash grinned at him and shook his head. "Well, I'm glad it's you and not me who has to write that letter."

Johnny felt the same way. He wished someone else was writing the letter, instead of him.

October 30, 1891

Dear Lillie.

You and I need to talk without Grace around.

I can come to the Del any morning this week. Let me know which is best for you.

Also, please call me Annaliese. I think we're friends enough for that.   Annaliese.

Two days later Annaliese asked at the front desk at the Del and was shown to a small office with a large window looking out on the bay. Lille soon appeared and led her to a private porch where they could see the bay and the city in the distance.

When they were seated Lillie asked, "Have you heard from Johnny yet?"

"Not yet but I'm not worried. What I wanted to talk to you about has to do with Grace and her idea about becoming a doctor."

"I thought that might be it," said Lillie.

"Your children don't go to school, do they?"

"No, they don't. Until we moved here, we traveled a lot, and John always wanted the family with him so we decided they would do better with tutors, and he hired a couple. Grace is their star pupil. They live here and travel with us. They also work as John's secretaries. We try to set a normal schedule of learning. So far, it's worked out," she smiled ruefully, "though better for some of the children than others."

"If she's serious about finding out what it's like to be a doctor, I'd like to propose she spend two or three days a week with me for a while, say six months. She'd work with my patients, and I have enough material for her to read and study so that at the end of that time she'd know enough to decide for herself if it's what she wants to do."

"How many hours a day?"

"If she wanted to stay with me she'd work pretty much what I do. We have room for her to stay at the house. She could come home the other days and live her normal life."

"You said two or three days, which do you prefer?"

"I'd prefer three days. If we decide on Tuesday, Wednesday, and Thursday, she could come to me at 8:00 Tuesday morning and she'd be home Thursday evening."

"What would she be doing?"

"Pretty much what I do. Between working with patients and studying and discussing things, she'll probably be pretty tired when she gets home every week."

"I'll need to discuss it with John, but I think it would be a wonderful chance for her."

"How do you think she'd feel about it?"

"I think she'd be very excited. We would pay you like we pay the tutor, of course."

Annaliese smiled. "I'd have a chance to do for someone what the Doctor did for me, and you want to pay me for it? No, I'm just repaying him for all the years he put up with me and my questions.

"No money would be involved. It's as much of an opportunity for me as it is for her. I believe teaching her will help me be a better doctor and it might lead someone special into the profession. That's all the payment I need."

Two days later Grace was in her office at eight AM sharp to begin seeing whether or not she'd like being a doctor. Annaliese was reading the letter from Johnny when the girl knocked on the door jamb.

"Come in Grace. You'll have to excuse me a minute. I just got a letter from my wandering husband. I'll be with you in a minute."

When she finished the letter, she laid it on the desk and looked at it for a long time then picked it up and read it again. When she finally turned to Grace she had a thoughtful expression on her face.

"Hmm," she murmured, then shook her head.

"Before we start, let's talk and I'll see if I can answer any questions you have. The idea I have is to have you with me whenever I see a patient. In the beginning you just watch and don't say much. We can talk after they're gone, and you can ask questions.

"Today I'm going to show you the rooms and equipment we have and give you some reading assignments that you can work on when we can squeeze them in around here, or you can take the books home and study there if you like. If we have time, I'd rather do it here so I can answer any questions you have. After that I want to take you to the clinic so you can meet the Doctor and look around over there. Any questions?"

Grace shook her head.

"OK. Let's begin." For the next hour she showed the girl what equipment they had, how it was used and for what. In the room set aside for childbirth and recovery she asked questions, but as for the rest of it she just looked on.

When they were seated in the office again Annaliese said, "You know most of my patients are from Old Town. When I came here Dr. Clark had been caring for some of these people for forty years. He called them 'my people' and I promised him I'd take care of them. Now they're my people too. I think you'll feel the same way before long.

"I'm also going to show you the record keeping system I use. Dr. Clark wasn't very good at keeping records, but in school they taught us having a good record of a patient and their history is an important part of providing good care.

"And there are other things to learn. All the things you need to do to keep the office going, like ordering supplies, billing, and records of income and expenses. Some of these things don't seem to have much to do with being a doctor, but if you go into practice they're things you'll need to know.

"Any questions?"

Grace shook her head. "I'll probably think of some as we go along."

"The first thing we'll do before we go to the clinic is go out to Consuelo's house. She's my housekeeper. She has five children and three of them were sick last week. I want to check on them and see how they are, and also, I want to talk to her about having a telephone put in her house for everyone in Old Town to use if they need a doctor. I want to make sure it's alright with her and arrange to have it installed as soon as we can."

When they were in the carriage Annaliese said, "It will probably take me a while to get used to having you along. But I'm glad you're here, don't ever think I'm not."

Chapter Fifteen

The next morning Grace was waiting when the clerk arrived to open the store. She introduced herself and was sitting in the waiting room when Annaliese came in. Grace had spent the previous night at home, and after gathering up all the things she would need living away three days a week, felt she was ready to begin her new adventure.

"Sorry I'm a little late. Had trouble getting to sleep," said Annaliese. She sat down and was quiet for a moment, thinking.

"First off, I want to get you some clothes and shoes to wear while we're working. You can leave them here and Consuelo will wash them every week when she does mine. My friend Maggie made me realize there were certain clothes that were not a good idea when you're working with all sorts of things on the floor. How do you feel about wearing pants?"

Grace grinned and answered. "I never have but if it's a part of what I do for you then I will."

"After that we're going to Consuelo's house to meet the fellow installing the telephone. Then we'll pay a visit to a lady I know who can make your new clothes."

"I'll pay for them, OK?"

"If you wish. I was thinking it was something I could give you, sort of a 'welcome aboard' gift."

Grace looked a little puzzled and then smiled, "OK," she said.

"Since we're going to be spending a lot of time together, I'll talk to you about things, and you can ask me questions if you want to learn more. When I look back, I'm amazed at how patient the Doctor was with all my questions.

"The one thing I don't want you to have at the end of a week is an unanswered question. When you don't know something, the only way to learn it is to ask. When you open any of my books, you're asking questions and looking for answers. Between me and the books, we'll try our best to find answers for you."

Later that day they had lunch at the Horton Hotel centered in New Town and sat talking for a while.

"As a doctor, one thing about any day is, chances are it's not going to work out the way you planned. For a doctor, your practice is the thing that interrupts your plans. Today the plan is for the Doctor to take care of our patients so I can get to know you and talk about what we'll be doing. On the other hand, if there's another outbreak of cholera or a little boy falls and breaks his arm, then suddenly our plans for the day don't matter.

"Remember the night your mother fell?" When the girl nodded, she continued. "I never got to finish my dinner that night. As far as I know the food was thrown out. If you stay on this path, there will be many meals you don't finish, things you don't do with your husband or children, or your mother and father because you're a doctor.

"I'm sitting here telling you this and you think you understand it, but you don't. Not yet. You won't understand it until you've spent some time doing what we'll be doing three days a week. I want you to learn things you can't learn in a classroom or from a book. When we work with patients and talk about it, you'll understand. Then you can see if it's what you want to do with your life."

That night as she was brushing her hair, she was thinking about the letter she got. The idea that they had been in a fight with renegade Indians and Wash and Handy had been wounded made her wonder if she'd be able to sleep. Johnny had said everything was alright, but that was while they were in Tucson. What about when they left and were in the desert again?

Were the Indians still a threat? Two men killed and three wounded. Would he make it home? She wondered if Wash knew enough to get them back in one piece. And what about that other fellow, Zack Grayson? Would Johnny be forced into another gunfight? She realized she had stopped counting and had no idea how many strokes she had done.

She looked at herself in the mirror. "There's nothing you can do about it one way or another, so you're foolish if you let it upset you," she said to herself. Easy to say, but could she do it? She couldn't even write to him. They would probably leave before a letter got there and what could she say? No matter how much she wanted to, she couldn't ask him to come home.

For the first time she looked back on the deal they had made in Salt Lake and wondered if she could live up to it. What if next year he wanted to take off to Oregon or even Alaska? What would she do then?

She sighed deeply and shook her head. She started to turn off the light and then stopped and got up to check on Grace before she went to bed. Though she hadn't considered it at the time, having Grace with her might just help her keep her mind off Johnny and on other things.

As she lay in the dark bedroom a few minutes later, looking at moonlight and shadows on the wall, she realized she didn't want to keep her mind off Johnny. She knew she wouldn't be happy again until he was lying beside her where he belonged. She smiled to herself and thought, "And no, that's not the only reason."

Johnny was looking out the window of the hotel room when he

saw Zack Grayson and another man come out of the saloon and stand on the porch smoking.

He closed his eyes and shook his head. "I don't need all this happening right now," he said. One of his friends in bed with a bullet through his shoulder and another with a knock on the head and no memory, he was five hundred miles from home in the middle of a desert peopled by renegade Indians who wanted his scalp, and now here was a man with a grudge against him who might just want to settle an old score. For some reason he already had a bad feeling about the day.

Woman was in the dining room when he and Jinx came in.

"How's he doing this morning?"

"I think he's getting to like me waiting on him hand and foot too much," she replied. "After tomorrow he can come down here like the rest of us." She smiled. "It is kind of fun at that. How's Handy doing?"

"I'm hoping we can get him back to normal today. The doc said it's usually a temporary thing, so we'll see."

Handy was sitting up in bed talking to Ollie when Johnny and the doctor walked in. To Handy, the doctor said, "I want you to stay in bed for another day and then tomorrow we'll get you up and see how you do." He turned to Johnny. "Just talk to him. I can't really tell you much about the problem, not having dealt with it myself. Just know what I've read. Maybe if you start a couple days before the fight and bring it forward, he can get back on track again. If you need anything there's usually someone out front."

When he closed the door Johnny sat looking at Handy. Finally he said, "Let's start at Yuma. Tell me what you remember about the trip."

He listened and asked questions but Handy seemed to remember everything until suddenly he didn't.

"I remember Tom showing up and we talked, and then nothing until I woke up here day before yesterday."

Johnny sat pondering that for a long minute. Finally, he said,

"Let me tell you what happened and let's see if it triggers anything."

He talked about everything until he got to where Handy didn't remember the fight. Handy's eyes never left his face. "I don't remember any of it. You say I killed an Indian?"

Johnny nodded. "We found one of them almost cut in half. The only thing that could have done that was the ten-gage at close range and that's what you were using."

Handy already looked a little strange with some of his hair cut off so the doctor could get to the wound, but now the look of bewilderment on his face was something Johnny had never seen.

"I've been wondering why my shoulder's been sore. Whenever I fire that thing my shoulder hurts for a couple days."

From the other bed Ollie said, "Beats anything I ever heard. Did the doc say you'd get it back?"

"He said he didn't know a hell of a lot about it. He's just guessing like we are," replied Handy. "I guess it really doesn't matter, but it does feel strange. Two whole days gone." He snapped his fingers. "Just like that."

He shook his head. "Well, I guess the next thing is to get out of bed and see how I feel."

"Not today. Doc hasn't had a case of amnesia before, but he's seen a few concussions. He says another day in bed and then we'll see." Johnny laid his hand on Handy's. "We're not going anywhere until he says so, so don't you worry about it. It will be a few days before Wash can ride, so we got time. Won't do any good to have you fall off your horse out there in the middle of nowhere."

As he closed the door behind him, he heard Ollie say, "I'd say your friends are a better lot than that bunch I was with. They ain't gonna ride off and leave you."

That reminded him of Zack Grayson, and he stopped on the boardwalk outside the doctor's office, loosened the Colt in the holster, and let his gaze sweep the street before he stepped down and crossed to where Wash and Woman were sitting on the hotel porch. Jinx was already in Woman's lap when he climbed the steps and sat down in a rocker beside them.

"You look better today," he said. "How's it feel?"

"I've had worse. How's Handy?"

Johnny shook his head. "I don't know. Doc says another day, and he should be up. Then we'll see. He still doesn't remember anything."

They sat quiet for a while.

"I saw Grayson again. What am I going to do about him?"

"We still don't know if he's a problem, do we?"

"I sure don't like the idea of waiting for him to make up his mind. He had a fellow with him today. I don't like the idea of bracing him without one of you two backing me."

"I don't know about Handy, but it'll be a day or two before I'm up to it."

"I'm going to be fidgety until I find out what he's about. I hate to let someone like that get the jump on me. Don't know if I can wait. I may just have to ask him what's on his mind."

Wash looked at Woman. She nodded. "I'll take the Henry and cover you if you want to go talk to him now."

Johnny looked at her for a minute, saying nothing. Finally, he said, "OK. I won't be looking for a fight, but I don't know who and how many he's got with him, so it's best to be ready."

"I'll be ready, and I've used a Henry before. I know what I'm about."

"I'd say he's probably in the saloon. I think that's where he spends a lot of his time."

"I've been in saloons before too. If we're going to do it, let's do it."

"I'll get the Henry from next door and I'm ready,'' said Johnny.

They stopped outside the batwing doors and surveyed the inside of the saloon. Johnny could see Zack sitting with two others at a table in the rear near the bar.

"It feels strange not having Jinx with me," he muttered. He had left the cat with Wash. He checked the Colt, settled it into the canted holster on his left hip, took a deep breath and stepped into the dim smoky room. Woman followed him in, moved out of the doorway and stood with her back to the wall, rifle at port arms, ready. There was a general scraping of chairs as men became aware of her and decided they had business elsewhere.

Grayson looked up and started to rise then sank back and muttered something to the two men sitting with him. Johnny stopped a few feet from the table.

"Hello Zack." When the man nodded, Johnny continued. "I've got some things going on right now and I want to be free to deal with them, so I wanted to talk to you to see if we're going to have a problem. If so, let's get it over with. I don't want to be looking over my shoulder the whole time I'm in Tucson."

Behind him Johnny heard Woman lever a round into the Henry. The saloon was deathly quiet.

"You gonna run me out of town again?"

"That's up to you, Zack. I don't want any trouble, but I figure that's your call so let me know what you're going to do."

One of the other men had been looking down at the table but now he raised his head and said, "Sounds like you're looking for a fight."

"I'm not but I thought he might be. That why I'm here. One thing you should know. She's not here for decoration so do what you're gonna do."

The man looked at Grayson and when he looked back at Johnny he was startled. He was looking down the barrel of the Colt. His hand dropped to the butt of his gun, but he decided not to be foolish, sat back in his chair, and put his hands flat on the table. Zack's were already there.

"I don't have any quarrel with you Fry," Grayson said. No one in the room believed him.

"Let's keep it that way, Zack." Johnny released the hammer and slowly holstered the Colt. "But I want you to know if anyone pulls a gun on me while I'm in town and I survive, I'm going to come looking for you. Is that clear?"

He looked at the other man, then turned and walked out of the saloon. Woman backed out the door behind him, lowered the hammer on the Henry and ran her hand across her forehead. It came away wet.

Johnny smiled at her ruefully. "Me too," he said. "Every time."

Chapter Sixteen

John Spreckels looked up from some papers he was reading and smiled at his daughter. "How was your first week in the new school?"

"It's not a school, Papa," Grace said.

"Oh, I think it is. As good as any you'll ever attend."

Grace nodded determinedly. "I want to try my best to do what she gives me to do and then see if being a doctor is what I want for my life."

"Your mother and I will help you anyway we can, and anytime you want to talk we'll be ready to listen."

"Thank you, Papa." He came around the desk and hugged her.

"I expect you're tired. I know it's different from anything you've done before." He held her at arm's length. "You're growing up before my eyes, young lady. Now run along and I'll see you at dinner."

Lillie came in after she was gone. "Are we doing the right thing with this?" she asked as she settled herself in a chair.

"If we're not, she'll probably let us know before long. You know, when she saw you bleeding that night, it was probably the first time in her life she ever saw blood other than a cut finger." He was quiet for a moment then continued. "If she wants to pursue this I'm all for it and I'll do everything I can to help."

"As will I."

"From what I read and hear being a doctor is changing. They're learning new things every day and our daughter might decide she wants to be a part of that. That makes me proud," he paused, "and a little nervous."

She stood and came around the desk. "Give me a hug, old man. I've got some things to do."

While they embraced, she murmured in his ear. "Thank you for being nervous too. I didn't want to think it was just me."

Even with a bullet hole in his shoulder, Wash was still up with the sun. He was eating breakfast with Woman when Johnny and Jinx came into the hotel dining room.

"How are you feeling?" asked Johnny. He pulled out a chair and sat.

"Stiff and sore. Doc says it will be a couple more days before I'm out of this sling. Not using the arm for a while yet. It's healing and itching to beat the band. Fortunately, it's my left."

"How do you like being a nurse?" he asked Woman.

"Other than thinking I might have to sit on him to keep him in bed, it's not too bad. I've done it a few times over the years."

"What's the news with Handy?" asked Wash.

"I'm going over there when I finish breakfast. You coming?"

Wash looked at Woman. "I guess it's OK. What do you think, nurse lady?"

"I think I'd have to tie you to the bed to keep you from going."

Over coffee Wash said, "I'm assuming you wrote that letter."

Johnny sighed. "Yes, I decided it was best to tell her everything and hope she won't do anything but wait 'til we get back."

"I'd say you best check the telegraph office every day until we leave," said Wash. "And you might want to send her another letter with a revised timetable, so she knows when we expect to get to Santa Fe."

"How long you reckon?" asked Johnny.

"Probably a week to Las Cruces and another week to Santa Fe. If we spend an extra day in both places, figure seventeen, maybe eighteen days."

"I'll just tell her three weeks, and she'll be happy if it's less." He scratched his head then shook it. "I wonder if she'll let me in the house when we get back."

Handy was just finishing breakfast when they walked in.

"Morning," he said. "I'm feeling fine today."

They looked at the doctor. "He was up for a few minutes a little while ago. Looked steady on his feet. Heart sounded normal. Wasn't dizzy, and the pain seems to have gotten better. Let's try it several more times today and if he has no problems then I'll let him go tomorrow. If something doesn't feel right to you now, let someone know. Anything. It seems like you're doing fine but concussions can be strange," he paused, "and dangerous."

They arranged things so one of them would be with the patient all the time the next day to watch and listen and try to enforce the limits set by the doctor.

With Wash out of action, Woman and Johnny set up a schedule and when he wasn't sitting by the bed, Johnny was spending time at various newspaper offices reading about Tucson in back issues. He had borrowed a stack to bring back and read while he sat with the patient.

"This place used to be pretty wild, and Tombstone's not far south of here," he said. "Hear that was the same. Silver mining town. But I guess it was like some of the 'end of track' towns we saw in Nebraska and Wyoming. Either they grow out of it, or they don't grow. Remember Julesburg? Fortunately, there seems to be enough good people around to keep the rowdies in check most places."

He was sitting at Handy's bedside reading to him from local papers. This was his third two-hour tour, and he had noticed nothing other than Handy wanting to do more than the doctor allowed. Johnny knew his friend was more likely to try things with him than with Woman. Handy didn't know her as well as Johnny did, and she made him a little nervous sometimes, which was not unusual. She seemed to make everyone a little nervous.

The doctor knocked on the door jamb. "From what I hear you're doing fine, so you can leave in the morning. But take it easy in the heat, especially in the middle of the day."

When he had gone Johnny said, "Well I guess after tomorrow we can talk about moving on. We'll never get to Santa Fe if we don't leave Tucson."

"I'm ready," said Handy. "Wasn't in bed this long with a bullet hole in my leg that time."

"Why don't you come to breakfast in the morning? We can decide some things and make some plans. I'll walk over and get you."

"I'm gonna miss my roommate," said Ollie. "We talked some about home. Haven't done that with anyone for a while." He stuck out his hand. "If it wasn't for this leg I'd like to go with you, but I got a feeling it's going to be awhile before I can ride."

"We'll stop and see you before we go," said Johnny, shaking his hand. He began to gather up the newspapers.

"You can leave those. We need something to read."

"They're old copies. I'll leave them if you remind me to take them back. I just borrowed them."

Johnny felt the tension drain out of him the next morning when he looked around the table at his friends. Wash would be out of the sling by morning, and they could probably get away late afternoon the following day. Handy seemed to be fine, so the only fly in the ointment seemed to be Zack Grayson.

He had heard and seen nothing of the man since his visit to the saloon, but he was still cautious. Now he pushed that out of his mind and joined the conversation.

"Doc says I'll be able to ride by tomorrow if we take it easy," said Wash, "but I need to be careful of lifting and carrying too much. You want to aim for late afternoon?"

"You must be reading my mind," said Handy.

"I was thinking along the same lines," said Johnny. "Why don't Handy and I take a ride this evening and see how he does? After dinner tomorrow we can pack up and go."

The desert was cooling when they mounted up and rode south out of town. The landscape was stark, not much but cactus and rock, but still fascinating. From the top of a hill several miles out they sat and listened to the silence. In the distance, they could see nighttime Tucson waking up.

"I've actually enjoyed my time here. It's a nice place and I've learned a lot about it. Where we sit, we're about forty miles from the border. You know, when I'm looking through old newspapers I can forget about the rest of the world. This afternoon sitting upstairs at the Citizen I felt like I was home."

"I liked reading those newspapers you had today. Lot of stories about Indians just a few years ago." Handy shook his head. "I'm so glad to get out of that bed," he said. "Wash tells me for the next month we're going to be riding a big circle around San Carlos. He said we'd be within fifty miles of it the whole time. If something stirs that place up while we're out there, we could be in the wrong place to live a long and happy life."

"From what I've heard and read, when they leave there, they usually go south," said Johnny. "Once we get to Las Cruces we should be pretty much out of their path. Since they live off the land they tend to split up into small groups and head for the border.

"That's probably what hit us. A small band headed for the border trying to pick up loot and guns on the way. It seems like they'd rather deal with the Federales down there than the U.S. Army up here. Also, I hear the mountains down there are more remote and rugged, so they don't rub up against people so much."

After they stabled the horses for the night they gathered in Wash and Woman's room and made plans for leaving.

"Let's plan on five thirty tomorrow evening," said Wash. "Then we can ride 'til the moon sets and get a good start. Just like before, we'll spread the water and supplies around and keep an eye out for hostiles. We aren't in a rush but don't need to lollygag."

Handy looked at him. "You said that word before. I remember. And Johnny said it meant to take our time and look around."

Johnny looked at him sharply, "Are you remembering anything about the fight?"

Handy thought for a minute, then shook his head. "No, nothing. You know, I can't think why those lost days should bother me but they do. Why can't I just let it lie? It's like when you lose a tooth, you can't keep your tongue out of the hole. I can't quit thinking about it, trying to remember."

"Maybe it's like any other injury," said Johnny. "Maybe it takes time for the mind to heal just like it does the body."

When she came in the door of the clinic, Annaliese could hear the Doctor talking to Grace in the treatment room. Every once in a while, she needed to catch up and organize her paperwork, so her young intern had spent the afternoon at the clinic with him. She slipped into the office and was sitting at the desk when they came in.

"Hello there, you two." She looked at Grace. "So tell me. What have you learned today?"

Grace removed her smock and sat in a chair by the desk. "I learned how to clean and dress a cut on a boy's leg. And we had three men that ate some meat that had gone over and were pretty sick for a while. It was right much of a mess."

The Doctor said, "We weren't very busy this afternoon, so she got some studying done."

When they arrived at the store Grace stopped to talk to Greta while Annaliese and the Doctor sat in her office waiting for dinner.

"How do you like having a new Annaliese?" she asked.

He grinned. "Does bring back some memories, doesn't it?

How's she doing?"

"Well, she's bright as a new penny and I haven't asked anything of her that she didn't give it her best. You've seen the notebook she keeps with her. She writes questions and answers down, and anytime we aren't busy she's got her nose in a book. Her father suggested she keep a diary, so she got one and usually writes in it every night before bed."

"She sure seemed to take your teaching about cleaning up between patients to heart. I like working with her so anytime you're busy with something send her over."

Maria called them to dinner and Grace joined the family at table. She was already friendly with Greta and the twins so there was lots of conversation.

"Hear anything from Johnny today?" asked Lemuel.

"He said they were leaving Tucson, so I guess Handy and Wash are alright. He said it would probably take them about three weeks to get to Santa Fe. That's where they turn to come home."

Lemuel asked how the hospital committee was doing and the Doctor explained how things were organized and what progress they'd made.

Annaliese was listening to the men talk out of the corner of her mind, but she was watching Grace. The girl had fit right into her new living situation and already seemed comfortable with it. Maybe it was because of the unusual nature of her education or being first born, but something had given the girl confidence and maturity beyond her years.

Having Grace with her most of the day and quite a bit of the night was constantly bringing back memories of her childhood.

Annaliese was a survivor of the infamous Mountain Meadows Massacre. In 1854 a wagon train from southern Missouri was ambushed in southwest Utah by Mormons disguised as Indians. Everyone in the train over the age of seven was murdered, shot to death under a flag of truce.

She was just six months old when the Doctor had come and

taken her into his home. Though she grew up in the Doctor's house, she never really felt she belonged. When she was eight years old her brother George, also a survivor, had told her the story of the Massacre. From then on, she had seen herself as different from the people around her.

Though he was a Mormon and there were three wives and many children in the house, the Doctor always made her feel special. Over the years she became closer to him than his own daughters and was his right hand as she grew and learned the things it took to care for people who came to them needing help.

She heard echoes of her youth in some of the questions she was hearing now. She had asked the same questions of the Doctor, and he was always there with the answers. Now it was her turn to be there with the answers, and she wanted to give to Grace all she'd been given. She seemed to feel she was repaying her father for giving it to her.

The telephone she had installed at Consuelo's house was proving to be a godsend. It helped her respond much more quickly to emergencies and also allowed her to talk to someone without having to be in Old Town to do it.

With three of the new devices, one in Old Town, one in the office and one in the clinic, she felt like she was living in the future. Indeed, in the last decade of the Nineteenth Century new gadgets of many kinds were becoming more and more common, each changing lives just enough that there always seemed to be new possibilities just around the corner. If ten years from now Johnny took another trip, they could probably talk to each other from places as far away as Tucson or Santa Fe and no one would think anything about it.

"What do you think about that?" The Doctor was looking at her quizzically. "Annaliese are you listening?"

"No, I wasn't really. What did you say?"

"I asked if you were going to be available to attend the next meeting of the steering committee."

"I hope so, but we'll see." She knew, as he did, in their

profession there was little hope of a regular schedule, and everything promised was subject to cancellation at the last minute.

"We need to talk about how we're going to blend the needs of the practice with those of the hospital," he said.

"Papa," she said, "I hope you know I support the aim of building the hospital, but I don't know how much time I'm going to be able to devote to it."

"I understand that and it's not something to worry about. We do need to decide how we're going to arrange things so when I need to focus on the hospital we still care for our people."

She grinned at him.

"What are you grinning about?"

"That's the first time you called them 'our people'. I'm glad you're beginning to feel that way."

He shrugged. "I see why you feel that way and agree with you. We're a part of their families in many ways, so they're our people. Not much different from back home, really."

Chapter Seventeen

Kate Sessions stood at the front door of the nursery and watched the rain pouring down. In the time she'd lived in San Diego she had never seen it rain like this, and she and her people were trying their best to protect her plants and trees from the unceasing downpour. She was also worried about the newly built dams back in the hills.

Their ability to withstand something like this had never been tested. There were two of them now, plus an old one the Spanish had built years before, and there were plans for at least three more. The future growth of the area was dependent on the water they collected from the winter rains being sufficient to carry the city through the rest of the year. In addition, the dams helped contain the runoff, so damage downstream wasn't as much of a problem as it had been during years past when they had the occasional cloudburst.

If any two dams, or even one of them, were to fail the damage could be catastrophic.

She missed Woman. One thing about her friend, she was a good listener, and when she finally said something, it was usually worth listening to. For some reason, she felt Woman would have had something to say today that would make her feel better. Now she was alone in the store because all her employees were working frantically in the nursery digging ditches to carry the water away from her precious plants.

She had come inside to the bathroom and there was no use in changing her clothes. She wouldn't stay dry anyway so she headed back into the rain to direct the work that would help protect and salvage her business, indeed, her life.

There was little wind when she went out the back door again carrying several tools. The rain was coming straight down, and it was cold. In a few steps water was pouring off the brim of her hat. She splashed her way to where three men were digging steadily, diverting the rising water into a ditch that would carry it to the canal about fifty yards away.

The problem they faced was that the canal was almost out of its banks, and the usually slow-moving water was rushing to the bay in a torrent filled with a flotsam of things from upstream. There were no signs the rain would let up anytime soon, and before long it would be over its banks. Other men were working to pile sandbags in a line forming a wall against the time the water would come for them and carry much of her life away with it.

Annaliese was watching it rain out the front window of the store. Though they seemed safe on their hill away from the water, she still was afraid. It was as though a pet, a gentle loving animal, had suddenly grown savage and turned on her. The weather here had always been so beautiful and suddenly it was raining hard and it wouldn't stop, and she could see damage being done in the city below her.

Consuelo and Maria had told her of winter floods in years past and how bad they had been. This seemed headed in that direction. They both had gone home to be with their families as had the clerks in the store. Greta and Mrs. Keane were upstairs with the twins while Roy was at the warehouse helping Lemuel try to keep water from getting at his beloved books. She turned to Grace who had joined her to look out at the gray, gloomy picture. "I'd send you home but I'm not sure you could get there," she said.

"That's alright. I think they're probably all safe so I'm just as well off here."

The store was on the crest of a small hill above the reach of the water, but in the years since the last bad flood many people had unwisely built in some areas that would mean destruction if it flooded again.

The lights flickered and went off, and suddenly all was the gloomy gray they'd been seeing through the window.

"Let's go sit in the house. I keep lamps and kerosine in case we lose the electrics." They groped their way through the hallway and at the top of the stairs she stopped, lifted the earpiece of the telephone, and turned the handle. Nothing.

"Well, that's no surprise. I'd have been shocked if it was working."

When they were settled in the office, she decided there was something to be said for lamplight. It made for a cozy place to sit and talk on a rainy day.

"Any questions you've been dying to ask?"

Grace laughed. "You've already answered all I have."

"Tell me a little about yourself," said Annaliese. "I know you've traveled a lot but don't know where all you've been."

"Papa likes to have us with him when he goes somewhere, and he travels a lot. I've been to England, Germany, Switzerland and Italy in Europe, and we lived in Hawaii for a while." She smiled. "I really loved it there. I've been to Japan and China." She thought for a minute. "Papa owns a steamship line and we go on his ships. I've been to Tahiti and some other islands, and we were in Singapore for a month while Papa did some business there."

"How does your mother like all that traveling?"

"She's used to it. She says sometimes he comes in the door and says we're going somewhere and off we go. She enjoys it. We've usually got someone to help with everything so it's like an adventure for us.

"I like it best when we're on a ship or a train. Papa and Mama talk to us and play games with us and plan things we'll do when we get where we're going."

"Sounds like a fun way to do things. How about school? I know you've been well taught, but how do you go about it?"

"We have two men as tutors and they take turns. They teach different things and when we're in one place for a while we're in school most days. Usually, three or four days a week. They're also secretaries. They help Papa with his work.

"When we're on a ship or traveling they try to find out about where we're going and then teach us about it so when we get there it's not so strange for us."

"I've wondered how you can be so grown up at your age. Now I can see how."

They sat quiet for a minute.

"Have you thought about what you'll do if he leaves again?"

The girl was quiet, thoughtful for a minute. "I'd want to stay here. Papa said this was the most important school I'd ever go to. I think he's right."

"Well, this weather may give us a busy spell when it stops raining. If there's flooding, there will likely be injuries and illness. Things may get frantic around here."

"I can stay over if you need help," said Grace quickly. "Mama will understand, and it will be a good time to learn new things."

"I haven't told you, but your mother and I had a talk yesterday evening. You've been coming here three weeks now and I wanted to let her know how you were progressing."

"We talk when I'm home, so she knows all about what I've been doing."

"I thought maybe she'd like to hear it from my point of view."

"So, what did you say?"

"That if you continue the way you've begun, you'll make us all proud."

Grace blushed a deep red. "Do you really think so?"

"No, I just said that to see you glow like one of those new light bulbs," Annaliese replied with a laugh. "Of course I think so. There's a lot to know, but I can't think of anything you need to know you're not capable of learning."

"How long will it be before I can go to medical school?"

"That's hard to say. I don't think it will be long until you know what you'll need to do well in school, but that's not the only thing to think about. Let's say you go to school next year and finish by the time you're seventeen. At seventeen, how many mothers would trust you to care for their children? Or their parents? How many patients would feel comfortable with you as their doctor?

"The people I cared for in Salt Lake City trusted me because they trusted my father, and I'd known many of them all my life. But by that time, I was in my twenties. If he said I could do it they accepted that. Without him looking over my shoulder, would they have? I doubt it.

"Trust is an important part of medical practice. Faith in you as a doctor is not something you're given. Most people will have a hard time accepting you until you're a little older or prove yourself."

They were quiet for a minute, looking out at the rain and listening to it drumming on the roof.

"So, I'll have to be more grown up to be a doctor?"

When Annaliese nodded, she continued, "Mama always tells me I want things to happen too fast, but I guess I may have to learn to be patient."

"I think that impatience is a part of being young. You need to learn to walk before you can run. I saw myself as a nurse for ten years before I became a doctor, learning all the time."

"So maybe I'll be like you and be a nurse before I become a doctor."

"There are worse ways to become a doctor, but Grace, I don't want you to be like me. I want you to be what you want to be. There are so many new things happening in medicine right now, so look around and think about where you'd like to be in ten years, or twenty years, for that matter."

By the next morning it finally stopped raining, but water still rushed to the sea and there was much damage to be seen everywhere. All sorts of things were scattered around, and all electricity and telephone services were out for the foreseeable future. It seemed even if this kind of storm was only an occasional happening, some of these newfangled things might need to be a little stouter.

Fortunately, most of the things swept away were not fastened down or not fastened down enough. No buildings were lost, there were only minor injuries, and no one died. After two days of sunshine, things were almost back to normal, and people had forgotten their fears.

Roy came out of the back room with an armful of books and stacked them by where one of the girls could begin putting them on the shelves. He stopped at the counter where Greta was talking to another of the clerks.

"Why don't you go tell the children good-bye and I'll go get the buggy out." He patted her backside and kissed her on the ear. On the way out the door he heard her say, "You need to improve your aim."

He turned and smiled at her, then retraced his steps and kissed her on the lips. "There, is that better?"

"Much better," she said, smiling through the kiss. "What's it feel like out there?"

"You should have a sweater," he said on the way out again.

She finished what she was doing and went through the office to their apartment where she found her sweater, said 'goodbye' to the children and Mrs. Keane, and was waiting for Roy when he drove out of the stable.

The weather was so nice for a moment she almost forgot it was November, though the sweater did feel nice when the buggy was moving. It hadn't taken long after the move to begin to feel comfortable in her new home, and the nice winter weather was a big part of that.

"How long will it take to get there?"

"Wash said it's about an hour's drive in good weather and it's nice today."

He was in the habit of describing the scene they were passing through to her and today, after all the rain, it was particularly beautiful. With the light breeze it was altogether a perfect day.

"We are going to find that rock they talk about, aren't we? The one where they go to think about things."

"Yes, but I told Wash I'd watch the place for him, and I want to see if there was any damage from the storm. That won't take too long then we can look for the rock."

When they pulled into the yard he left her sitting in the sun while he walked around the cabin. Before long he was back, handed her down and led her out the path toward the rock.

"Can you see the ocean?" she asked. "It sounds like it's right here."

"I can see it through the trees but it's a ways away." They had been seated for a few minutes listening to the ocean and the creek rushing toward it, when he leaned over and whispered, "Wash told me to look around inside, so I think it would be fun to get the key, go inside, look around to see if everything is ok, then find the bedroom, take off all your clothes so I can look at you and make love before we go back. What do you think about that idea?"

She didn't answer but pulled him to her, slipped her hand between the buttons of his shirt and began to run her fingers across his chest while she kissed him ardently.

"I was going to suggest it," she whispered back. "So what are we waiting for?"

Later, in the dim light coming between shuttered windows, she lay on her side and let her fingers wander over his body. When she touched him like this a thrill ran through him. They hadn't been together long before he had realized this was her way of looking at him, making a picture of him in her mind. The idea excited him, and it showed.

"Again?" she murmured. "Do we have time?"

He answered through a kiss. "Let's make time."

Kate was sitting in her office when a man from down the street rushed in.

"Kate, we need two wagons. Do you have two here? A section of the road has collapsed and dumped a wagon and a buggy into the hole. There are people down there underneath and I think they might be hurt."

Two wagons were waiting to be loaded and in less than a minute both were on their way to the accident. They could only get the wagons so close to the hole because the sides were liable to crumble, so men were carefully lowering ropes to let themselves down to the wreckage. Two of her men removed the tailgates from their wagons and worked to rig them as stretchers to lower the men working to free people trapped beneath the overturned vehicles.

Ultimately there were three people, and she recognized them all. One was a boy who worked at a feed store where she traded; the other two were Roy and Greta Carver.

Annaliese and Grace were on their way back from tending a man who had broken his arm when he fell from a hayloft while he was drunk. The bone was through the skin and setting it had been a long and painful process with much swearing and screaming. They were talking about it when a horseman rode up shouting.

"Dr. Fry. You're needed at your office. There's been an accident."

"Hang on," she said to Grace and whipped up the horse. When they arrived, a wagon was pulling away from a back entrance leading to two treatment rooms. When she rushed into the room the first thing she saw was Roy, bruised and bleeding, lying on one of the beds. Her father and their nurse from the clinic were working over a patient on the other one.

With Grace at her side, she examined Roy and could see the most immediate problem was a swelling on his head. Her fingers told her the skull was likely fractured, and the swelling was serious. It didn't take her long to gather the instruments necessary to pierce the skull to try to relieve the pressure before it damaged the brain. Without being told, Grace examined his other injuries and found they were mostly just cuts and bruises.

When Annaliese was finished and had dressed the head wound, she moved to her father's side and saw Greta lying unconscious on the pillow. Suddenly her knees felt weak, and she grasped her father's shoulder for support.

"How bad is it?" she asked, her voice shaky.

"She's unconscious right now which is fortunate because I think she has several broken ribs. When she wakes up she's going to be in extreme pain with every breath. I think the buggy turned over on them. The other injuries look worse than they are, mostly scrapes and bruises. The rib fractures will interfere with her breathing. That could be the most dangerous thing going forward. We'll just have to see. How's Roy?"

She was stunned by what she saw, and it took her a minute to answer. She shook her head to clear it.

"I've pierced the skull to relieve pressure on the brain and dressed the wound and the incision. Grace has cleaned him up but he's still unconscious. All we can do now is watch and wait..." she paused and took a deep breath... "with both of them. What happened?"

"It appears the road was undermined by all the rain. They were just driving over it when it collapsed onto a hole and turned the buggy over on them."

"Does Lemuel know?"

"He's been working in the warehouse. I haven't seen him to tell him."

She closed her eyes and shook her head. And the tears came.

Chapter Eighteen

A loud crash from outside the room startled Johnny out of a sound sleep. It took him a moment to realize where he was and then to notice that the bed was empty. Handy had been lying there when he went to sleep. He shook his head to clear it, put his feet on the floor and felt his way to the window of the hotel room.

Below him and across the street he could see the front window of the saloon was gone, and the reason looked to be a body lying half off the boardwalk in the street, not moving. The size of the figure he saw in the light streaming from the saloon told him where his friend had gone.

He lit the lamp and hastily began to pull on his clothes. He was buckling his gun belt when Wash knocked and entered, Woman close behind. She picked up Jinx. He glanced at the bed and said, "Where's Handy?"

Johnny gestured at the window. "I think he just threw someone through the front window of that saloon across the street."

Wash's mouth dropped and he seemed struck mute. Woman moved from behind him and looked out the window.

"Someone's kicking up a ruckus over there yet," she said. "We better go see."

Several people were standing on the porch of the hotel when they came out the front door and others were standing around where the window had been and looking under and over the batwing doors of the saloon.

The man on the ground began to groan and stir feebly as Johnny led them through the crowd carefully stepping through the glass. Looking over the swinging doors he could see Handy backed against the bar with three men in a half circle around him, two of them with drawn guns.

"Handy!" Johnny spoke loudly and pushed his way in. Handy never took his eyes off the men in front of him.

"I was hoping you'd show up," he said. "Could use a little help here."

One of the men asked, "Do you know this man?" without taking his eyes off of Handy. Johnny could see a badge of sorts pinned to his chest.

Johnny nodded, "Yes sir, he's our friend. What happened?" Jinx had jumped onto the bar and was sitting watching everything.

"I've been trying to find that out myself. We just got here. One body out front and two more in here." He gestured at a man sprawled across a table and another lying on the floor with his head through the legs of a chair who was beginning to stir.

"Handy, are you OK?"

"I'm alright, Johnny and with you here we can talk." He said to the marshal, "I came in here for a drink and this guy," he gestured at the body draped over the table, "started giving me guff. He was drunk. I tried to ignore him, but he got right nasty, and I popped him one. His friends got upset and wanted to cause more trouble. They were pretty drunk too, so it wasn't much trouble." He shook his head and smiled wryly. "Sorry about the window, but at the time I didn't stop to think about where he'd land."

The marshal looked at the barkeep. "Is that right?"

"That's what I saw." There were murmurs of agreement from

others in the crowd. "They were asking for it, Marshal. He just gave them a little more than they could handle." The speaker was an older man well dressed and smoking a cigar.

"What about damages, Van?" the Marshal asked.

"Looks like this fellow was just defending himself. Of course, it don't look like the three of them got a dollar between them so I guess it's my loss. Do you know these three?"

"They're hands out at the Double B Bar, that place of Bixby's out in the canyon. You can probably get him to hold their pay for you. Figure out what it'll be, and I'll take the bill out to him." His deputies got the men on their feet, and he followed them out the door.

The man offered his hand to Handy. "I'm sorry about all this. You're not from around here, are you?" asked Van, who appeared to be the owner.

"No. Been here a few days while I've been over at the Doc's. We're planning to leave this morning.

"Will you join me for a drink? Or maybe to sit and talk a bit?"

"No drinks," said Johnny. "We're leaving in a little while. A drink might make us feel a little rough and we got some things that need doing before we go."

They sat around a table drinking coffee instead and watched the barkeep and a helper clean up the broken glass. Jinx joined them and the man smiled and reached to pet him.

"Never seen anyone travel with a cat before. Where y'all headed?"

"Las Cruces."

"Not much between here and there. Couple of small towns. I think Bowie and Maley are the biggest, and that ain't saying much. Although they don't call it Maley anymore. It's Wilcox now. Problem is to get to Las Cruces you have to go through Apache Pass. Never know what you're going to find up there."

"We've been warned about the Pass," said Wash. "From what I hear it's the only reliable water between here and Las Cruces."

"Yes, and everyone knows that especially the Apache. Sometimes people stop at Fort Bowie and wait to join others going through. Might want to think about that."

"It's that dangerous?" asked Johnny.

"Any young ones who leave San Carlos are usually headed for Mexico and they need the water at Apache Springs to get there. That means the chances of running into them in the Pass or at the Springs are more likely than anywhere else around."

"We ran into a bunch north of Tucson," said Wash.

"Really? Get into a scrap?" When Wash nodded, he continued. "You know the Mexicans call that pass El Puerta del Dado. It means the Pass of the Die, like in a game of dice. It's the Pass of the Chance. What they're saying is you have a chance to make it through."

"That was the strangest thing in there last night," said Handy. They had just finished breakfast and were getting ready to leave the café later that morning.

"What do you mean?" asked Johnny.

"When that fellow put his hand on my shoulder I just sort of went crazy. I got so mad I didn't think about being the stranger in the place or that he had a gun. All I wanted to do was to get my hands on him." They were all quiet for a moment, waiting for him to go on. "I didn't have to do that. I could have just walked out the door. It felt like I was glad when the other two came at me. Like I wanted them to, so I could get hold of 'em."

"Why were you even in there?" asked Johnny.

"I couldn't get to sleep. My head hurt and I thought maybe a drink or two would help."

"Did it?"

Handy looked at him with a wry smile, shook his head and chuckled. "I don't know. I guess. At least it don't hurt now."

Johnny looked at Wash and was surprised at the way he was looking at Handy.

"You ever felt like that before?" asked Wash. "I mean that crazy mad?"

"No, never," replied Handy. "That's why it felt so strange."

They sat quiet for a while.

Finally Handy said, "So what do we think about this pass we have to go through?"

They all looked at Wash. "We got some choices. We carry enough water so we could go around it to the north along the railroad line, but that would take us right across the Apache's route to the pass and Mexico. We could wait at the fort for reinforcements like he said. Or we can catch the cars at Wilcox and go around the pass, get off on the other side and continue on our way." He sat back in his chair and looked around the table. "Or we can go ahead and go through the pass and deal with it. What do you think?" he said to Johnny.

"Or we could get on a train at Wilcox and go back home," answered Johnny.

"Yes, we could do that," said Wash. "What do you think, Handy? Or you?" He looked at Woman.

"I wonder if Handy is OK," she said. "If his head is hurting from the ride yesterday maybe we better stay put for a few days and let him take it easy. You heard what the doctor said about concussions being dangerous."

"Or we could get a train back home," repeated Johnny.

"Are you really thinking about going back?" asked Wash.

"I don't like the idea of that pass but what bothers me more is his headache and what it might mean. He's never before done anything like he did last night. It's not like him. He goes into a saloon and suddenly someone comes flying out the window. What if he has some problem when we're out there fifty miles from nowhere? This isn't something we have to do, you know."

"I don't want to cut the trip short because of me," said Handy, his face reddening.

"I'll tell you what," said Wash. "Let's see how he does from here to Wilcox. We can take it easy, and we can make up our minds when we get there. It's about twenty miles. We can think about it while we ride and decide."

What passed for a hotel in Wilcox was two shacks behind the saloon next to an outhouse, and after a vote they decided to find a place to set up camp outside of town. While the others were settling in Johnny rode into the town marshal's office. The marshal was reading something and talking to another man when he entered.

"Howdy, how can I help you?" He looked to be middle aged with a bushy mustache and a visible paunch.

"Just got into town and would like to find out a little about it. Name's Fry. My friends and I are just traveling around and I like to learn about the places we pass through."

"Well, I'd say you got here at the best time. We've had a little rain lately so it's not as dry as it could be. Where you headed?"

"We're in the process of deciding that. Tell me about Apache Pass. Any problems lately?"

"Why would you want to go through the Pass? You can catch a train to Bowie about noon tomorrow. They'll have a car for your horses." He leaned forward and said intensely. "Mister you'd either have to be crazy or part of a detachment of cavalry to try that pass right now."

Johnny sat pondering this for a bit.

"This time of year, when we've had some rain around here, some of the Apache at San Carlos like to head down to Mexico. There's a permanent spring in the pass that's right in the middle of their preferred route. The odds of running into a bunch of them are pretty high."

"Sounds like good advice. Another thing, is there a doctor here?"

"No, the closest one I know of is in Tucson. Or Las Cruces if you're going the other way. What do you need a doctor for?"

"One of my friends was shot in a scrap on the other side of

Tucson. I'd like to talk to a doctor about it."

"We have a bartender who handles things if someone gets shot or cut up, but no doctor."

He got back to camp just in time for dinner, and when he was seated with a plate in his lap he said, "Not much here. Maybe a hundred people. A few ranches around, some mining."

"That's about what I thought. What did the marshal say?" asked Wash.

"He said stay out of Apache Pass and we'll live longer."

"Seems like everyone feels the same way about that place."

"So, what's the alternative?" asked Handy. "I mean, we're out here in the middle of nowhere and we got to go somewhere."

"With the route we have planned, the time of year and what's going on right now, the odds of another scrap are pretty high, so maybe we'd be better off if we think about cashing in our chips and heading home." Johnny looked around at his friends. "This whole thing was my idea and I'm beginning to wonder if it makes sense to keep on."

Johnny was looking at Handy and could see his friend's face redden.

"This is because of me, isn't it? I feel fine, OK? And I don't want us to give up the trip because I have some headaches." He didn't sound like Handy, and as Johnny watched he threw his plate aside and got to his feet.

"You're angry, aren't you?" asked Johnny. "Why? I just want to talk about it and when you're making a decision you put everything on the table."

"I don't want us to cut and run just because I got shot in the head that's all. I feel fine." He was almost shouting.

"You didn't answer me. Why are you angry?"

Handy stood looking at him for a long moment, then sat on a rock and put his head in his hands.

"I don't know," he muttered.

"You've changed since that fight. Something's going on inside your head that causes you to act differently, and it makes me nervous, especially this far from anywhere. What if whatever's going on in there has to do with that knock on the noggin?"

He looked at Wash and Woman. "What do you think?"

"There's something to what you say," said Wash. "We can look at the odds or look at what could happen. When the odds get too high it changes things." He looked at Woman. "What do you think?"

"I think we need to talk about it and make a good choice," said Woman. She picked up Jinx who was sitting in her lap. "What do you think?" she asked. She lowered her ear to him, then looked up and said, "He says he's just along for the ride, pretty much the same as me."

They all laughed.

"The idea for this trip was to enjoy ourselves and learn some things," said Johnny. "It wasn't to put us in danger of losing our hair. Think about what could happen and what it would do to the lives of people back home if we don't make it back."

He looked at Handy. "You have a beautiful young wife and a baby boy." He looked at the others. "We all have lives that mean something to us, things we want to do and I for one don't want my hair to end up hanging on some Apache buck's bridle because I was trying to prove a point."

He looked at Wash. "I know you've been thinking about this, so what do you have to say?"

He was used to Wash taking his time with a question, but this time he sat silent for a long time. Finally, he said, "From what all you've said, I think you've decided you want to go home. Or if not that, at least change the plan for the trip. I think the reasons you give are sound but are those the only options?"

He let the question hang in the air for a moment, then said, "What if we change how we cover the ground? Keep the same route but use the cars to get around the places where we're liable to run into trouble with Apache."

"What do you think, Handy?"

"I'm surprised you asked me, seeing as how I'm the reason we're changing things around." Again, Johnny could hear things in Handy's voice that sounded different.

"We've been traveling together for a while," said Johnny. "Do you remember a time I haven't asked you about a plan or change in plans?"

Handy looked at him in silence. Finally, he shook his head. "No. Never," he said. "I'm sorry Johnny. I don't know what's the matter with me. It's like I'm looking for reasons to get angry."

Wash got to his feet and pulled Woman up beside him. "We're going to take a walk and let you talk about things. We'll be back before long."

Johnny watched them disappear toward the spring outside the camp circle then picked up Jinx and handed him to Handy.

"Here, I usually feel better when I'm petting him."

Handy smiled and reached up to take the cat. "Me too," he said. "Think better too."

Johnny looked at him with a straight face. "That's why I handed him to you, pardner."

Chapter Nineteen

Annaliese had no idea how long she'd been staring out the window when Grace knocked on the door jamb. Almost startled, she gestured for the girl to sit down and looked down at the paper in front of her. It was Greta's record of treatment, and it was blank. Every time she sat down to write on it she seemed to end up staring out the window. She covered her face with her hands, took a deep breath and shook her head.

She knew what she wanted to write. Greta had three broken ribs, maybe more. Her other injuries were easily treated and healing, but this one could very well kill her.

Each breath she took triggered a stabbing pain in her chest so she wasn't breathing the way she normally would, and she couldn't cough as much as she needed to. With no treatment available, the chances were, she would die from pneumonia. On the other hand, if she was medicated for pain, the laudanum would suppress her cough and slow her breathing which meant her lungs would be kept from working the way they should, and chances were she'd die of pneumonia.

In either case she felt helpless to keep the girl alive. Greta was like a daughter to her. She had stepped in when Greta came to her with questions mothers usually answer, had answered them and helped the girl grow into the woman she had become. Now she was slipping away and Annaliese felt powerless to stop it.

She could feel the tears coming again and then Grace was there, arms around her, and she knew that's what she needed but Johnny wasn't here to give it to her.

As she was wiping her eyes she said, "There are times when this is part of the job and even when you know that it doesn't seem to help much."

"Have you told her father?"

Annaliese nodded. "Yes, and I'm sure he understands. He's been close to the same situation, and we talked about it then."

"I can't imagine having to tell someone something like that," said Grace, "but if I go through with my plan to be a doctor there'll come a day when I'll have to, won't there?"

Annaliese nodded and looked out the window again. "When I was your age, the Doctor told me about the war and what it was like with so many young men dying or crippled for life and how many of the doctors he worked with stayed drunk when they were off duty, and sometimes even when they were working.

"At the time I didn't understand how a doctor could do something like that, but after three years in practice I can see why they could. Dying's part of living but knowing that doesn't help when you're faced with it. Drinking's a way to help forget. To put off thinking about today until tomorrow, hoping the problem will solve itself. There are times when I wish I could forget like that, but I can't. We don't see this kind of thing enough to drive us to drink but now I understand how it might."

They heard Lemuel on the steps and Grace quietly slipped out. He tapped on her door, came in and took a seat. They sat in silence for a while.

"She's going to die, isn't she?" It was a statement, not a question.

She closed her eyes and after a moment said, "I'm afraid so, Lemuel. You've been there yourself and you know what she's facing. I don't see how she comes out the other side."

He ran his hands through his hair. "A man shouldn't have to bury his children, but I guess sometimes 'shouldn't have to' don't matter."

She could hear tears in his voice and when she looked at him could see them running down his cheeks. She stood, pulled him to his feet and embraced him. They stood like that for a while.

"How's Roy doing?" he asked.

"He woke up today but didn't say anything. We're just going to have to wait and see. I'm keeping the hole open to drain anything that needs draining. Eventually that will heal and if we can keep infection out of it, he may be all right. Time will tell. It may have affected his speech, or he may lose some ability to function. At this point I can't tell. In a few days I'll begin to see where he is. Then maybe we can figure out where he has to go."

"Mrs. Keane is with the children, and she'll be with us as long as need be," said Lemuel. "Maria and Consuelo help her and between the three everything's OK upstairs."

They sat quiet for a while, probably both thinking about the same thing.

"When Mary died it happened so suddenly and the same when Jed was shot. It was like being thrown into deep, cold water. It took my breath away. Now I have to watch her die before my eyes, see her slowly slip away from me like she was floating down a stream and I can do nothing to rescue her."

The silence stretched out again for a while. Finally, Annaliese said, "One of the great things humans have is their ability to learn from experience. I know this is easier to say than to do, but Lemuel, you helped your daughter climb out of an emotional pit when Jed was killed. You'll be in that pit yourself before long so try to remember what you told her when her whole world had crashed around her, when she could see and feel nothing outside the hole she was in.

"Greta told me what you said about remembering the good times and getting your face used to smiling again. When you lost your wife, you realized Greta needed you, and you were there for her. You need to be here for the twins now. You need to let them make you smile again.

"The choices you made when Mary died helped your daughter become who she is. The choices you make now will do the same thing for your grandchildren. That's what you should keep in your heart as you watch your daughter slip away. Her children will need you the same way she needed you."

Lemuel took off his glasses and rubbed his eyes. "You're right about it being easier to say than to do but that's what I need to be reminded of. That is really the last thing I can give her; a promise to be for them what I was for her." He looked at Annaliese. "Remind me of that when I seem to forget it, will you?" he said.

He got to his feet. "I'm going to get a bite to eat. I'll see you a little later." He put his hand on her shoulder, squeezed gently and left through the store.

Rebecca missed her husband. Handy had been gone over a month, and she missed him every day. She was looking out the window of the ferry as it drifted into its berth in the terminal. She was thinking about how long 'til his return and how she didn't want him to do something like this again. Her trip was routine now, and Jose was waiting to take her to the mansion.

She sat Bobby down in the kitchen with his friend Geppetto and climbed the stairs to Madame's dressing room. She found the ladies sitting over coffee, but she could tell when she walked in that something wasn't right.

Her mother handed her a telegram. She read it and stared open-mouthed at them.

"What can we do? Can we go down there?" she asked.

"It came last night," said Sarah. "Apparently It happened two days ago. We're already packed and ready and we'll catch the noon train. I packed your things. Is there anything at the ranch you need?"

Rebecca's mind seemed paralyzed. She finally stammered, "No. No, nothing,"

Sarah was watching the scenery pass the window of the train and thinking about Greta and Lemuel. "I don't know what we can do once we get there," she said, "but with Johnny and them in the desert I'm sure there'll be something. Annaliese will have her hands full. She not only has these two on her hands, but her practice too. We'll just have to find things that need doing that she doesn't have time to do.

"It seems Roy was hurt too but she doesn't say how bad and nothing about the children, so I guess they're all right."

She looked over Rebecca's shoulder and could see her grandson and his friend listening to Carlotta read them a story. "It's nice we can bring them along. Give them an adventure."

"I like to have Carlotta and Tony travel with us," said Madame. "So, we bring Geppetto along and everyone's happy. It's nice he has Bobby to play with."

"If it's alright with you, I'll stay with Annaliese at the store," said Rebecca. "That way Bobby can play with the twins, and I can see Greta and help if they need me."

"Have you heard anything more from Handy?" asked Madame.

"Just the one letter from Tucson. Everything's alright so far and they'll be home around Christmas."

"It's not going to be a happy homecoming," said Madame. "I wonder if Annaliese will let them know or just wait 'til they get home?"

"It sounds like it wouldn't make any difference if they were here," said Sarah. "From what that telegram said, she's probably not going to make it, and Annaliese has enough help. They're out in the middle of the desert and getting in touch with them is a problem and besides, what could they do if they came rushing home?"

She looked at Madame. "I know Annaliese will have all the help she needs taking care of Greta and Roy. I wonder if it might be best if we were helping Lemuel deal with it?"

"That sounds about right," Madame replied. "He had a rough time before they moved down here, and everything's been going wonderfully since. And then, out of the blue, this happens. It will shatter him."

"Well, Annaliese and Lemuel brought Greta back to life after Jed's death. I just hope they remember how they did it."

After they all were settled in the next day, they gathered in Annaliese's office, and she gave them a summary of what had happened and where they were.

"Greta is beginning to show signs of pneumonia. It will gradually get worse, and she will probably die from it in the next week. We decided to give her laudanum for the pain, so she will probably just go to sleep one time and not wake up."

"Can we talk to her?" ask Rebecca. "Will she know who we are?"

"Oh yes, she's drowsy from the medicine but she'll be able to talk to you. Her breathing is so altered from the pain, we thought under the circumstances it would be much easier for her this way."

Sarah shook her head. "How's Roy?"

"He sleeps most of the time and hasn't spoken since he came in. We'll just have to wait and see what happens with him. I think he'll heal up alright, but I don't know if any damage was done with the fracture. He took a pretty hard blow. It's hard to say for sure but he may have a good-sized dent in his head when it's over. What it means for his future I couldn't tell you right now."

When Annaliese stuck her head in the door to Greta's room she couldn't decide if she was asleep or not, so she stood and watched her for a moment. Her breathing was shallow and more rapid than she had expected. Usually laudanum slowed the breathing, but the injury meant she was taking shallow breaths anyway and needed more of them to get the air she needed to make her system work. Twenty-eight times a minute. That was way too fast, and meant the lungs were not keeping up the way they should.

Under normal conditions the lungs produced fluid when injured, and coughing removed it. In this case coughing would aggravate the pain and the lack of it allowed the fluid to fill up the lungs until the minimum of air needed to sustain life could not be reached. At that point the patient usually just went to sleep and didn't wake up.

She stepped on something and at the sound Greta opened her eyes. A weak smile acknowledged her presence. They closed again and she whispered. "I'm awake."

"How's the pain?"

After a moment she replied. "It hurts."

"Can you cough at all?"

A weak cough, a grimace and she shook her head. "Not very well." After a moment she continued. "That's bad, isn't it?" She opened her eyes.

"Yes," replied Annaliese, nodding.

Her eyes closed again and then opened. "I remember when Papa was recovering, you told him he needed to cough, or he'd get pneumonia. Am I going to get pneumonia?"

"That wheezing tells me you likely already have." She unlimbered her stethoscope and listened for a few breaths.

"Will I die?"

"Every day that goes by with you coughing like that, the chances go up that you will," Annaliese replied after a moment.

Greta was silent for a while then spoke clearly. "I need to talk to Roy and Papa."

Annaliese shook her head. "Roy is in the next room, but he hasn't spoken since he woke up. Your Papa will be here in a little while. Madame and Sarah are here, and he went with them to get a bite. When he gets back, I'll keep everyone else out while you talk."

"Is Rebecca with them?"

"Yes, and so is Bobby. They'll be over to see you this evening."

Annaliese and her father were sitting in the office talking when someone knocked on the door. When she opened it she was surprised to see Maggie standing there.

"If you're busy I can come back."

"No, no, come in. It's just me and the Doctor. What are you doing back so soon?"

When she was seated, she took a deep breath and said, "Charlie's gone."

Annaliese stared at her, mouth open.

"I found a letter in our room when I got back to Los Angeles. He said he didn't want to be a banker and didn't want to be married to a doctor anymore." Her eyes were red and swollen and her nose sounded stuffy. "I didn't know what to do but I thought of you and decided I'd come here before I went home."

They looked at each other in silence for a long moment. "And you didn't have any inkling this was going to happen?" asked Annaliese. When her friend shook her head, she stood and pulled her into an embrace. "I don't know what to say. You can stay here as long as you like and we can talk," she said. "Maybe I can help you decide what to do."

"Thank you. I've just been in a daze since I read that letter. I feel I want to sit and cry but don't see how that will help."

The Doctor rose and said, "This sounds like you need to be alone to talk so I'll head home."

When he had gone Maggie asked, "Doesn't he live here?"

"No. Not anymore. We did some renovations to the building and now he lives upstairs over the clinic. Part of his family from back home is coming this week and they'll be staying with him until they decide what to do."

She looked at her friend. "I can use your help if you want to stay." She told Maggie about the accident, and they talked about it for a while.

"Well, have you thought about what the next step is? Will you go back to Carson City or San Francisco?"

"Since you might need my help for a while, maybe I won't think about that right now. I can help with your practice while you deal with the family crisis and then we'll see. If that's alright with you, that is."

"Maggie, whenever you're around things are usually better. Stay as long as you like and we'll see what the future looks like, for both of us."

Chapter Twenty

Sarah and Madame were eating dinner at the Del when a strange thing happened. A stocky man who looked familiar came to the table and spoke to them. "Mrs. Grimes, Mrs. Travers my name is Herschel Grieve. I met you in San Francisco at The BookSeller. I'm a friend of Johnny's. I heard about the accident and wanted to let you know if I can help you in any way while you're in town please contact me at the Union newspaper, city desk." He nodded and walked away.

That evening while they were talking to Annaliese and Lemuel at the store Sarah brought it up. "Have you ever figured out this friendship of Johnny's with Herschel?"

Annaliese shook her head. "I don't really know the man and the funny thing is I don't think anybody else does either. I remember Wash saying he doesn't seem to have any friends, but for some reason Johnny trusts him the same way he trusts Wash or Handy or you, Lemuel."

Lemuel shook his head. "I can't explain it, but I remember something Handy said one time. He said, 'Johnny's got more in his head than anyone I ever knew, and I like the way it comes out'. I think that might be the attraction between them. Johnny once told me that Herschel said he needs to have interesting people to talk to and I think that's the basis of the relationship. They like talking to each other, which means he has something in common with us all. We all like talking to Johnny." He looked around the circle and they were all nodding.

Annaliese looked up when Grace came into the room. The girl nodded at her, and she said to the rest of them, "You can all go in to see her now, but I'm going to have to ask you to keep it short this time. She gets tired easily and she needs to talk to Lemuel and Roy, and I think it's best if they're alone. So just say hello and talk for a minute and then we can visit upstairs while they talk. You can see her again tomorrow."

She was in the kitchen arranging refreshments when they began to join her. When they were all seated Annaliese said, "Thanks for understanding. They need to talk and it's important they have the time."

"She looks weak," said Rebecca. "It looks so strange to see her like that."

"We made the decision to use the laudanum, and it makes her drowsy, but the pain is still what's wearing her out. Every breath is hard work, and when she tries to cough it's like a knife in her chest. But if I give her enough to get rid of the pain completely, she'd probably be unconscious. The laudanum also keeps her from coughing, as well as helping her with the pain and that's a problem."

"Are you going to let Johnny know?" asked Madame.

"I haven't thought much about it. I don't know where he is or how long it would take him to get here if I did."

Sarah sat forward on her seat. "We talked about it on the way down here and we're thinking we might try to help Lemuel come to grips with this. I know you'll be busy with her and Roy and your other patients, so maybe we could take that off your shoulders."

"Thank you, I've been wondering how I was going to cover it all. That takes a lot off my mind."

A few minutes later Lemuel and Roy appeared.

"Anything you want to talk about?" she asked Lemuel.

He shook his head. "First, I want to think about it. I need to lie down. We can talk tomorrow."

After he had closed the door they sat in silence for a while. Annaliese looked at Roy and said, "You know, though there's no blood tie between us we're all family," said Annaliese. "And I can't tell you how good that feels at a time like this. If you need us for anything we'll be here."

Roy looked at her for a long time, then nodded and left.

Annaliese was sitting at her desk doing some paperwork when she heard footsteps on the stairs and Maggie came into the office.

"Why don't you turn on the electrics? I could smell the lamp upstairs."

Annaliese smiled wearily. "I like the lamplight sometimes. It's softer and makes the room feel warmer."

Her friend's eyes were still a little red and puffy from the crying, but she seemed determined to put this problem behind her and get on with her life. They had decided she would help at the clinic for a while and, once she felt able to would begin seeing patients herself.

"Where's Grace?"

"She's only with me three days a week. She just left. I won't see her again until Tuesday morning."

"She seems to be learning fast and I can see she's helping you already."

"She is. I remember the things the Doctor taught me when I was her age and that's what I'm aiming at for her. She's a little older than I was when I started but she's a quick study and you only have to tell her something once. And, of course, she spends time with him at the clinic which will help her too."

They were quiet for a moment then Maggie said, "I know this thing with Greta is very personal to you, but life has suddenly pulled the rug out from under me. I need to talk to someone and you're it."

Annaliese turned her chair to face her friend. "It looks strange to see your face like that. You were always smiling and laughing in school, but I can see it would be hard to make light of what's happening to you right now."

"I guess the first thing I need to think about is Charlie. What do I do about him? What if he shows up and wants to be taken back? Do I want that again?" She shook her head slowly. "No, I don't think so. We were both unhappy and he's just the one who did something about it. So, I guess I'm going to move forward with my life." She smiled weakly at her friend then suddenly her face lit up. "What now? If I don't starve it might be fun. Something new every day."

Annaliese laughed and suddenly realized it felt good. Greta's accident and where it was leading was always on her mind. The fact that the whole thing was both personal and professional magnified it but until she laughed, she hadn't realized how much it was weighing on her soul.

"Maggie, I love you and right now you're better medicine for me than any I could prescribe." She hugged her friend, then pulled her hair into a ponytail and tied it up with a band.

"I need to see Greta and give her some medicine. Lemuel is having dinner with Sarah and Madame, but he should be back soon and I want to see how he's doing. Then I want to see Roy and begin making a plan for him. He still hasn't spoken." She stood to leave and said, "Maggie, you know you can live here as long as you like, don't you? When I come back, we can sit and talk for a while. Welcome to the family."

"Do you want to talk about it?" asked Sarah.

Lemuel took a deep breath and said, "Not really, but I guess I should." He put his head in his hands and looked at the table for a moment. "Since we left Kansas City I've always tried to help her deal with the life she's been given. That's what I need to do now. Deal with the life I've been given. The problem is, all I can think about is 'why me'? There's no answer to that. What I can do is live the best life I can with the time I'm given and now that life must center around Greta's children. And," he said after a moment, "her husband."

"Annaliese told me I'd soon be in the same pit Greta fell into when Jed was killed. That's coming and I know it. But I have to keep my feet make sure I give the twins the best chance in life I can."

He took off his glasses and rubbed his eyes. "The problem is I know that's easier said than done. My old Pappy, God rest his soul, used to say, 'nothing's real until it happens' and I know this is going to happen. It won't be long before it's real."

He looked around at them. "I'm glad you're all here."

Roy was sitting at Greta's bedside holding her hand. His head still had a small bandage on it and the hair was shaved around the incision, but he seemed to be alert and understand what was going on around him. He still hadn't spoken and the day before Annaliese had realized he couldn't, at least not yet.

Because there were several people in the room, they had opened the door to allow the breeze in and as she and Grace walked down the hall Annaliese could hear Greta's rapid, shallow, rasping breaths.

She paused in the doorway. Rebecca was on one side of the bed holding Greta's hand. On the other side Roy's eyes were closed and he sat with his head bowed, hand resting on his bandaged forehead. Madame and Sarah sat along one wall. Lemuel stood at the foot of the bed gazing at his daughter and listening to her breathing. He raised his head and smiled weakly at her and moved to the empty chair.

Annaliese listened to lung and heart sounds for a while. No one was expecting good news, but she had to assess the patient occasionally. The rasping noise made it difficult to hear, but Greta's breathing was shallow and very rapid, her heart sounds were getting harder and harder to hear and her pulse weaker.

She stepped away and said quietly, "Can I get anything for anyone?" They all shook their heads.

Suddenly Greta said very clearly, "Mama, is that you?" Annaliese closed her eyes and after a pause heard, more quietly, "hold my hand," and then nothing else. She stepped to the side of the bed and unlimbered her stethoscope, but there was nothing to hear. Greta was gone.

When John came into the library he was surprised to see someone sitting by the fireplace in an otherwise dark room.

"Is that you, Gracie?"

"Oh, hello Papa." She sniffed and dabbed at her eyes.

He sat in the chair on the other side of the fire. "Have you been crying?" she nodded. "What's wrong?" he asked. "Did something happen at work?" She nodded again. "Can you talk about it? If you can't, I understand."

"Greta died today," she said and began crying again. "She just went to sleep, and she'll never wake up. I didn't think about this part of it when I thought about being a doctor. I guess I thought we'd help everybody get better."

"I met Greta when I was first at the store," he said. "Johnny introduced me, and she always recognized my voice after that whenever she heard it. I watched her work around the store and couldn't believe some of the things she could do. She was a special person."

They sat quiet for a while, both staring into the fire.

"This is the first time someone you've known has died, isn't it?" She nodded and he continued. "Your mother and I have been lucky enough to be able to shield you and your brothers and sister from things like that so far in your life but it's something everyone has to learn how to get through. It's a part of growing up.

"We had hoped to keep it from you until you were a little older, but when you decided to work with Annaliese, we knew this would happen. The fact that she was a family member someone you ate your meals with and talked to when you were there makes it even harder."

"I don't understand why it would happen to someone like her, someone so special."

"Grace dear, if you ever figure that out make sure you let me know because I've never been able to." He leaned forward with his elbows on his knees. "It's the kind of thing where you have to look to God to find the answers you want. But I can tell you this. We have little power over what happens around us. All we can do is to keep moving forward, get to the other side of whatever happens and live our lives.

"The time you spend with Annaliese will force you to face things you wouldn't have if you weren't there. If you ever reach a place where you don't want to carry on with it, we'll understand."

She looked up suddenly. "No Papa, I don't want to stop. There's so much to learn and so much to do." She wiped her eyes and blew her nose. "No, this is just the beginning and it's something I want to keep doing because of how it makes me feel like I'm important to them, to 'our people', that's what Annaliese calls them; our people."

He stood, took her in his arms, and they stood that way for a long time.

Johnny felt a tap on his nose and opened his eyes to see Jinx lying on his chest, eyes closed, purring. This was about all of him Johnny got these days. Usually, Jinx would be out on the porch of the hotel watching the town of Las Cruces wake up while Johnny washed and got dressed. Instead, this morning he had been curled up on the pillow next to Handy's ear. Since Johnny had handed the cat to Handy five days before Jinx seemed to understand Handy needed him and Johnny almost felt he had lost his little Buddy.

When Handy was petting him or Jinx was riding on his shoulder or in his lap, Handy was himself again, and Jinx seemed to realize he needed to be there. Johnny knew it was something he could do for his friend, and that was all fine and good, but what did it mean for Johnny? He wondered if he would change because Jinx wasn't with him so much now. Maybe he'd find out just what Jinx did for him now that he wasn't there to do it, where Johnny could see and feel him, pet him and hear him purr.

He also wondered if Handy was getting better, recovering from the injury or if he'd go back to being the touchy, moody introvert he had become since he was wounded if the cat wasn't there.

He and Handy were eating breakfast and talking about leaving on the noon train when the hotel manager came in. "Good morning, sir. This just came for you," he said and handed Johnny a telegram.

"Thanks," said Johnny. He took the envelope, tore it open and unfolded it. "Oh my God!" he said. He looked at Handy, his face a study in shock then at the flimsy paper again as though it must be a mistake. In an unsteady voice he read. "Greta died yesterday. Need you as soon as you can get here. Annaliese."

Wash and Woman had been getting the horses ready to leave and now they came in and sat down. Johnny handed Wash the telegram.

He read it, handed it to Woman and said, "I'll check the schedule to see the fastest way to get there," he said and got up to leave.

"Hold on," said Johnny. "Let's talk about it a minute. Do we retrace our steps or go on to Albuquerque and see if we can catch an express? If it's only a matter of a few hours let's stay on the route we planned, just ride the train the whole way. What do you think?" He looked at them in turn and got an assent.

"That gives us a couple hours to get ready," said Johnny. He stood. "Let's get the horses over to the station and make arrangements."

Since they were already packed, their duffel was soon deposited at the station, and they decided to wait at the hotel which was only a few blocks from the station. When the train came in, everyone in town could hear the whistle.

Las Cruces, the name means 'the crosses', was originally part of the Mexican Session after the Mexican War and, like many places in the west it grew up when the railroad came. In their case that was truer than most.

Founded in 1849, it was a small village not far from Mesilla which was on the original proposed route of the Santa Fe RR. When the people of Mesilla wanted more money for the right of way than the railroad was willing to pay, a local rancher from Las Cruces stepped up and offered them a route sans cost. They took it, and Mesilla is now a small village not far from Las Cruces.

"We were lucky," said Johnny. "We'd probably have left within the hour and wouldn't have known about the telegram."

"Bet you a dollar she sent one to more than just this one place," said Handy.

"You're probably right," said Johnny.

"Wonder what happened to Greta?" asked Handy.

"You'd be trying to make bricks without straw on that one," replied Wash. "We don't know enough about it to even speculate."

Chapter Twenty-One

Handy sat with Jinx in his lap and looked out the window as the train slowly climbed a grade into some desert mountains. Johnny sat down across from him and Handy said, "Remember that dollar I bet you on the telegram?" When Johnny nodded, he continued. "Bet you another one Rebecca and Bobby are in San Diego."

"What makes you think that?" asked Woman, who had joined them.

"Sarah would have jumped on a train when she heard the news and Rebecca is sure to be along, probably Madame too."

"You're getting to be a pretty smart fellow," said Johnny. "What else does your crystal ball tell you?"

"That you're going to be wanting your cat back when we get home."

Johnny grinned at him. "I've been thinking about that. How are you feeling?"

"Head still hurts once in a while, but I feel pretty much back to normal. You reckon he had anything to do with that?"

"It looks like he might have, but the question is, will you need to keep him around to keep on feeling normal?"

"I guess the only way to find out is to put him back on your shoulder and see what happens."

Johnny ran his hand over his bristly jaw. "You know, he's a pretty smart cat and if he still stays with you there may be a reason we can't see. Why don't we just let it ride for a bit and see how things are when we get home?"

"Your home or mine?"

"Mine. If it turns out you still need him, we'll try to find you a kitten to raise. If you get a new one used to hanging around with you and riding with you, you could have your own Jinx." He grinned. "I'd love to see you with a little black kitten in those big hands."

He looked up to see Wash coming down the aisle. "Everything alright?"

"The conductor says we're on time so far. If that holds we should be home sometime tomorrow evening." He sat down. "Looking out the window is not the same but we're still seeing the desert. I was standing back there in the door of the horse car. Sure feels strange to move that fast. But there's still a lot you can see when we're running slow like this."

They had been lucky to get seats two cars back from the locomotive. As a result, when they were moving fast there weren't many cinders, or much smoke and the breeze kept the heat down. But on long, slow stretches like this, with the sun beating down on the car, the air coming in the open windows was like a furnace and smoky to boot.

"So, tell me Wash, what do you think about our trip?" asked Johnny. "With the problems we've run into, would you do it again?"

Wash looked out at the desert moving slowly by.

"I guess I'd have to put it into a ledger. Good things in one column, not so good in another then see how it totes up."

"Hadn't thought about it that way," said Handy. "Makes sense. And I guess it also depends on where you're standing. I doubt Rebecca will see much good about it. What about Annaliese?"

Johnny chuckled dryly. "Probably not. Of course, if she'd seen some of these desert nights and sunsets she might." He sat quiet for a moment. "Even the bad parts were good in a way. Can't go through a fight like we had and feel the same about life again. You look at things a little differently. Maybe it makes you value it a little more."

He looked at Woman. "You had the most memorable moment of the trip. What do you think about it?"

She looked back at him with her usual straight face and nodded. "I'd do it again," she said without hesitation.

Annaliese was sitting in a lamplight reading a telegram she'd already read five times. "In Las Cruces. Coming straight home. Johnny!" She could hear people through the open door leading down to the store, and someone running water somewhere in the house.

The funeral that morning had left her limp and she had been that way most of the day even while she tried to help everyone else in their grief. Now that she was alone, she could work on her own grief. She thought about Greta's last words and the rush of emotion that had surged through her when she heard them, and it helped.

She had no firm ideas about life after death, but if anyone she'd ever known deserved a heaven, it was Greta; and the idea that her mother was there to hold her hand somehow made it all more bearable.

And yet she couldn't just stop and face the loss of her friend - more than a friend really; she had too much to do. Not only her patients, but she needed to help Maggie get accustomed to the routines of care at the clinic and to find her way around town when she needed to go on a call. She also had a responsibility to Grace. She had accepted the task of mentoring the girl, and she needed not to lose sight of that important part of her life.

Fortunately, the Doctor could help with both of them. His wife and two children had arrived the day before and he would have to get them settled in. She also had to do some reading to see if she could find some ideas for treating Roy. He still hadn't spoken, and she had been so involved with other things she hadn't been able to find any answers that would guide him on a path back to some kind of life.

And then there was Lemuel. Sarah and Madame had taken that off her shoulders for now, but that was only temporary. She had a feeling Lemuel, and the twins were going to be an important part of their life as long as any of them lived.

She heard the noise of someone coming up the steps from the store and knew right away it was Johnny. She covered her face with her hands and cried. He came into the room quietly, ran his hand across her hair and then kissed her on the top of her head.

"Let's not do this again," he said quietly. "OK?"

She stood and they embraced tightly for a long time. "OK," she whispered, and kissed him.

They were still kissing when Handy, Wash and Woman joined them.

"All right, all right, we gave you some time but that's enough," said Handy. "Where are you hiding my wife and kid? I bet Johnny a dollar they were here."

"They're at Madame's cottage in Coronado," replied Annaliese. "If you give us some more time I'll show you where it is."

"I know where it is, thank you, so you just go ahead with what you're doing."

"Welcome back, Handy." She looked at him strangely. "Why is that cat on your shoulder?"

"Johnny will explain," he said as he went back down the steps.

Wash and Woman said hello and took off to home, leaving Annaliese staring at her husband with a question on her face. He kissed her again and said, "I'll tell you later," and kissed her again. "Unless you want to talk now instead of later," he said through another kiss.

She ran her hand across his cheek. "You need to shave first, or people will take one look at me and know what I've been doing."

"They'll know what you've been doing anyway," he said, his voice muffled because his face was in her hair. "I've been thinking about this since I left.”

“What? Smelling my hair?”

“Yes,” he said, “and other things.” He took her hand and led her to the bedroom.

Afterward, he was lying beside her in the dark, propped up on his hand. “Now tell me all that’s happened since I left.”

She sighed deeply. “It’ll take a while,” she said.

“You didn’t see Handy with his hat off, did you?”

They were sitting up in bed cross-legged, facing each other.

“No. I’m afraid I wasn’t looking at much beside you,” she said.

He smiled. “His hair is trimmed in front, and he has a scar here.” He put his finger high on his forehead, right in the middle. “It looks like a ricochet hit him. Lot of blood but it wasn't too deep and it’s healing alright. The problem is, he doesn’t remember anything of the two days right after the fight. The doctor said he’d had a concussion and while it’s not uncommon to have some memory loss, it’s usually temporary.

“It’s been ten days, and he still doesn’t remember the two days after the fight.” He paused, then told her about the fight in the saloon, Handy’s sudden hair-trigger temper and sullen disposition. She sat, eyes wide, open-mouthed, and heard him out.

“The other day we were discussing what to do about the rest of the trip. He got angry and threw his plate and when he stood up I could see his fists were balled.

“We talked about it and he calmed down, so when Wash and Woman took a walk, I put Jinx in Handy’s lap. He’s been with him ever since.

“Suddenly he’s Handy again. Says his head hurts once in a while but other than that, back to normal.”

She sat for a minute, a puzzled expression on her face, waiting for him to go on. “You’re saying you think Jinx made the difference?”

“Sure looks like it. I just wonder if he’s healed and back to normal, or if we take the cat away will he become Mr. Hyde again?"

"Mr. Hyde?"

"Remember that book I told you about? About the fellow who drank something he brewed up and turned into the evil Mr. Hyde?" He looked at her meaningfully.

"Johnny, that's just a story."

"You didn't see Handy when he was like that. *Annaliese, he threw a man through a saloon window!*" He got off the bed and stood looking at her. "What's the chance Jinx senses some need in him and stays with him because of it?"

"I've never heard of anything like that," she answered slowly. "Of course, that doesn't mean it doesn't exist."

"Well, the fact is Jinx is with Handy and not me, and I believe there's a reason for that."

He dropped on to the bed and she put her hand on his cheek. "I sure have missed you," she said.

"Show me how much."

So, she did.

When Rebecca woke up, Handy was lying on his side watching her sleep. She looked up at him with a serious face and said, "You do realize I won't say yes the next time Johnny and Wash go somewhere and you want to go along?"

He grinned at her. "Is that right?"

"That's right," she answered. "Now tell me again why Jinx is in our bed? I had something else on my mind last night when you told me about it."

He pulled his hair back and she saw the almost healed wound on his forehead. "I got this in that fight with the Indians I told you about. From that time 'til this I don't remember anything that happened for the two days afterward.

"I was in bed in the doctor's office for three days in Tucson and the first night I was at the hotel with Johnny and them I woke up and my head hurt so I went across the street to a saloon for a drink."

Her mouth fell open. "You went into a saloon to have a drink?" she said in amazement.

"Well, it was the only place open, and my head hurt. Thought maybe a drink would help."

"What does that have to do with Jinx being here?"

Handy reached out and pulled the cat in next to his stomach and began to pet him. "We'll get to that in a minute.

"I got my drink and was standing at the bar when a drunk came up to me and grabbed me by the shoulder. Almost before I knew what was happening, I had cold-cocked him and when his friends tried to mix in, I threw one through the front window and knocked the other one clear across the saloon.

"Johnny and them heard the noise and came to see. By the time they got there, three deputies had me surrounded with their guns out, and things were getting serious. There were plenty of witnesses, so we got out of that OK, but Johnny noticed over the next couple of days that I'd changed. It's like I was looking for things to get mad about.

"We talked about it, and Johnny put Jinx in my lap one evening after supper. Woke up the next morning feeling back to normal. Since then, I've been fine."

She sat looking at him in silence, waiting for him to go on. Finally, she shook her head a little and said, "Wait a minute. You're telling me the cat made you better? Solved your problem?"

"Looks like it. But of course, now the question is, what if Jinx goes back to Johnny and suddenly, I'm upset with the world again?"

He shook his head. "I don't think you'd like being around me when I'm like that. For that matter, I don't think anyone would. I'm too damn big to be mad at the world all the time."

Hershel was sitting quietly across the desk from John like he did every Thursday morning waiting for his boss to finish reading his weekly report.

John looked up. "So, you think we might have some trouble

with some of this new bunch from up north?"

"They got run out of Santa Barbara, a little place up the coast from LA. Never been there but people tell me it used to be a rowdy town. Lots of places like that have been cleaned up in the last few years and I guess the rats gotta go somewhere. Some of them had gotten into the city and county government up there. Squeezing people. Not much different than the way it was up on the Bay."

"Well, no sense in letting 'em get their foot in the door here," said John. "Keep an eye on them and let the Sheriff know about it."

He looked up with a smile. "Your friend Johnny is back in town and they're all coming to breakfast this morning so we can hear about their adventures. Would you like to join us?"

"Thanks for the invite but I don't think I will. With my history, some of his friends and family don't quite know what to make of me just yet so I think I'll pass. Tell Johnny I'll see him later in the store."

Chapter Twenty-Two

Lillie and Grace were waiting when the others began to arrive. While they were waiting for the food to be served, Johnny talked to Grace and her mother, and John when he joined them. They were seated at a large round table that allowed everyone to talk to and hear each other. After the meal they sat and talked some more, Johnny and Handy telling of the trip and the others of things that had happened at home while they were gone.

"You said there were three Indians killed in the fight?" asked John. "How many were there?"

"Tell you the truth, it all happened so fast I couldn't tell you," answered Johnny. "Maybe seven or eight, but that's a guess."

He looked at Handy. "We found three bodies, but I've heard they carry off the dead and wounded, so it could have been more. Handy cut one of them almost in two with the ten gauge."

Handy was sitting with Jinx in his lap. He looked sheepish. "Don't remember a thing about it," he said. "I woke up in a doctor's office two days later with a sore shoulder and a headache, wondering why. Didn't even know Wash had been shot."

"Actually, Woman killed one a couple of days before," said

Johnny. "She was at a spring a few yards out of camp when an Apache jumped her. Jinx saw him sneaking up on her and growled. She turned around and there he was. I didn't see the body, but Wash told me he bled to death. She keeps that Bowie sharp. They found him near his horse, fresh scalp on his bridle. Those people play rough and for keeps."

"Woman!" said Lillie. "John's told me about her. I'd like to meet her, but he says they don't talk much and keep to themselves."

John looked thoughtful, then turned to Kate Sessions. "They work for you, don't they?"

"Oh yes, and I love it when they're around," said Kate. "The problem is they like to roam. On the other hand, when they come back, I'm always glad to see them. I think Madame knows them better than anyone."

"It took a while for me to get to know her," said Madame. "She doesn't talk much and he's not much better."

She ran her tongue across her lips and smiled at a memory. "I was out with some friends late one night in San Francisco. We were in a part of town where we had no business being and these two men were in the process of robbing us.

"Suddenly, out of nowhere, this person came to our rescue and when she turned around to clean the blood off her knife, I saw it was a woman. Took me a few days, but I found out who she was and offered her a job. She started out as my bodyguard, then became my companion, and now she's a friend. I pity anyone who tried to hurt me when she was around.

"Wash knew her before that and when he came to town with Johnny and them, she introduced him and now he's part of the family. Hell, we all are when you come right down to it."

John looked at Johnny thoughtfully. "So, Woman doesn't talk much, but she talks to you. Wash doesn't talk much, but he talks to you, and I know Herschel doesn't have many friends he talks to, but he talks to you." He looked thoughtful. "Wonder why?"

Johnny shook his head. "Couldn't tell you."

"Hell," said Lemuel. "Like I've said before, we all like to talk to Johnny. I think that's mostly what we have in common."

Johnny turned to Grace and Lillie with a smile. "So, enough about that, tell me how you like working for the clinic. Do you think you'll end up being a doctor?"

"I love it," said Grace, "though sometimes it's a little hard to handle."

"She's learning a lot," said Will. "I keep waiting for her to say 'uncle' but she just keeps on going. Annaliese was like that. The more she learned the more she wanted to learn." He reached out and patted Grace on the shoulder. "Having this one around brings back a lot of memories."

Johnny turned to John and said, "How about Herschel - how is he doing? Has it worked out OK for you?"

"Oh yes, I'm really happy with him. He picks up things as quick as can be, and he already knows a lot of people in town. I asked him to join us this morning, but he said he'd see you at the store later. Strange fellow. But handy to have around. He said you might write something about this trip. Is that right?"

"I've thought about it. Never written anything before, but I've read a fair amount. Thought I might try my hand at telling a story and see how it comes out."

"I'd like to read it if you do. In fact, if I like it, I'll put it in the Union."

Johnny looked at his wife. "You think that will keep me out of trouble for a while?"

A slow smile spread across her face. "You're no trouble, Johnny, as long as I keep you on a short leash."

When they were getting ready to leave, John accosted Johnny and said, "Later this week Herschel and I are going to take a ride up to begin looking at the dams they're building up east of here. We'll be going up every couple of weeks until we see them all. Care to ride along?"

Johnny looked at his wife and shrugged. "Don't see any reason why not. Let's see what comes up between now and then."

Grace was studying a thick book at the desk in the office when Annaliese came in.

"When you get to a place to stop you can put that away," she said. "I've some things to discuss with Maggie and the Doctor. I want you to sit in and listen. If you have any questions we can talk about them later."

By the time Grace had everything put away, everyone was seated. Maria brought them coffee and Annaliese began. "Roy's head is healing nicely, and if that was his only problem he wouldn't really need to be here anymore.

"Unfortunately, there's another issue. I need help deciding what's the best way forward for him. He hasn't spoken since he regained consciousness. This appears to be a result of the fracture impacting the brain in some way during the accident. Whether it's permanent or not I have no idea, but I'm not sure anything we do will help. I believe either he'll regain speech, or he won't. Regardless, I think we need to assess his abilities or lack thereof and see what this means for his future."

Maggie shook her head. "I don't know much more than you. We studied brain function in Chicago, but nothing about treating that kind of injury."

"Over the years I've had to deal with it to some extent," said Will. "It amounts to seeing what he can and can't do, then helping him with what he can."

Annaliese spoke to Grace and Maggie. "You two are not that familiar with these people around us, but we all feel we're part of a close family relationship, and as Lemuel's son-in-law, Roy's a part of that. That means as a group we feel a personal connection to this patient, though I'm not sure how professional that is.

"I'm going to work out a plan for treating Roy and I'll share it with all of you. I'd like you to talk to me about any ideas you have. I'm working in the dark here, and any light you can throw on the problem will help."

"What about sign language?" asked Maggie. "I've heard there are schools that teach sign language back east; in fact, I think I've heard of one in San Francisco."

"I guess I'll have to look into that. The way I see it, Roy's not the only one who would need to learn sign. For him to communicate with someone else they would need to know it too. He can hear us, but it wouldn't do him any good unless the person he's signing to knows the language too. Those schools teach deaf-mutes, and his hearing doesn't appear to be affected. I'll talk to him and see how he feels about it."

She looked around the circle. "Now let's talk about Maggie." She looked at her friend. "What ideas do you have about your future?"

Maggie took a deep breath. "I'm OK as long as I stay busy and don't think about it," she said, "but at night when I'm trying to sleep it bothers me. I don't really miss Charlie that much, so I guess the problem is I had all these plans and suddenly I don't know where my life is going. That bothers me."

Annaliese looked at her father. "I'm going to say a couple of things here and if you have something to say, jump in." She turned back to Maggie. "If you want to remain here we can put you to good use. You can work with the Doctor until you feel you're ready, and then we can work out how to share the responsibilities of the practice.

"It seems he's going to be involved with the hospital idea for a while, and it may become his primary focus at some point. Which would leave the majority of the practice in our hands. If that future appeals to you that's great. You can live here as long as you like. As I said, we tend to behave like a family toward each other and, if you want to, you'd be part of that."

"I won't say much," said Will, "except I think it would be a good thing for all involved. Welcome to the practice. I look forward to working with you."

"One other thing before we break up," said Annaliese. "Tell me about the hospital."

He ran his hand over his shiny bald head and closed his eyes for a moment. "We're moving forward. The committee meets weekly and each of us has tasks to accomplish which, if all goes well, will lead to a hospital. When we finish these tasks, we will have more tasks and more again until we get where we want to be.

"Doctor Bone has returned from the East, and we've asked him to serve on the committee. He's the senior physician in the city. Doctor Place is also a member, and his wife has volunteered to become our recording secretary. She's a nurse and it seems she learned a shorthand writing system when she was in school. She's pregnant, so we may lose her after a while, but for now she's a godsend."

"I like Gen. She was the first person to welcome us when we got here. Who else is on the committee?"

"One of the new doctors has made an interesting suggestion, and we're devoting some time and energy to examine its possibilities. Have you met Doctor Dowd?"

"I've met him once, but I don't know him."

"He suggested we look into contacting religious groups about some kind of a partnership in the ownership in return for financial support. His point is that it would allow us money to create a hospital aimed, not just at filling our present needs, but at the future. By trying to arrange such an association we're betting the city will grow and we're giving it a push in that direction."

"It sounds like time and energy are producing ideas. You've got some experience with having a church involved in medicine. What do you think about it?"

He sat back in his chair and took a sip of coffee. "It's something we should explore, but we will need to be alert and cautious. One thing I learned about religious leaders. They're just like most leaders, they enjoy power. Of course, they cloak it as 'for the glory of God', but if we begin to consider associating with a religious group, we should always keep the power thing in mind. Ultimately, they might seek to control things for the glory of God and if we don't agree, we could have problems. I'd say if we can do it without them, we'd probably be better off."

"Sounds like things are moving right along. Any idea when they might begin construction?"

"It's too early to even think about a target. Too many things we need to find out. Something we need to remember. In Salt Lake, the Saints took care of things we will have to do here, like hiring an architect or a contractor, paying bills and creating the business side of things. These are all things I know nothing about because they took care of all that."

Annaliese looked at Maggie. "You can see why we can use you. The further he gets into this thing, the more it will demand of him."

"Well, I like the idea." Maggie smiled. "And I like the idea of being part of a family. I miss my family, especially my father, but I don't think there's a future for me back home. Having all of you here makes it seem safer. The hell with Charlie. Who needs him anyway?"

When they were unpacked, the first thing they did was walk down to the rock. They sat quiet for a while listening, his hand stroking her hair. At certain stages of the tide the waves sounded almost on top of them, as though they were going to come crashing out of the trees and engulf them.

"This feels like home," said Woman.

After a moment he responded. "For me too."

They were quiet for a while, then she asked, "Do you think we'll ever do something like that again?"

Again, the pause. "I'd have to think about it for a while. I don't know if I'd want to risk what we have here." He was quiet for a long moment. "I've never said that about a place before."

"I know."

He resumed stroking her hair. "You always know," he said after a while.

The next morning, he was sweeping out a wagon at the nursery when Kate came up behind him.

"Wash, Ger Schweder is over at the wagon shop. Seems he came into town to get a wagon fixed and it's going to take longer than he thought, so he and his men need a ride home. Can you pick them up?"

He looked at her for a moment, shook his head to clear it and replied. "Sure, let me wash up a bit."

"Toss a few bags of manure in the wagon and use them to prop his wheelchair so he won't roll around. Just leave them out there and I'll bill him for it."

By the time he drove the wagon out of the yard, his heart had slowed, and his nerves had calmed enough that he could help load the invalid. His nurse, a big strapping Mexican, laid some boards up to the end of the wagon, pushed the wheeled chair into the back and they choked it with the bags, so he was facing to the rear while they were traveling.

For some reason this made Wash feel better. He knew it would have bothered him to have Schweder looking at him from behind all the way to the grove. He closed his eyes for a moment as they passed under the tree where he had lain to put a bullet through the knees of the crippled man riding behind him.

Chapter Twenty-Three

"So, when are you two going home?" Lemuel was sitting in the dining room of Madame's cottage in Coronado. They had just finished breakfast and were talking over coffee.

"We haven't talked about it much," answered Sarah. She looked at Madame. "Any thoughts about that?"

"Probably in a week or so. Nothing really needs doing back home. Why? You trying to get rid of us?"

"No, of course not." He paused then continued, looking at Sarah. "In all that's gone on since you got here, I hadn't thought to talk to you about the twins. They're as much a part of your life as mine, and I think we should talk about what you see as their future."

"I wondered when we'd get around to that."

"I guess I just thought they'd stay with me because Greta lived with me all these years. But I forgot you might have something to say about their future. So, let's talk about it."

"Lemuel, the way I see it, it would be best all-around if they stay with you. I have Rebecca and Bobby up there, and it looks like we'll be spending time down here, so I see no reason to change things."

"Well, anytime you want them to come up and spend time with you, just say so. It seems like Mrs. Keane will be staying with me to help with the children, and with Maria and Consuelo we should be fine. It's Roy we don't know about right now."

He paused and shook his head. "Annaliese will let me know what she learns, and we'll just have to take it a step at a time and see where it leads."

"I know this has been hard on you, Lemuel. I remember what it was like when Jed was murdered. But life goes on. We have to keep going for others, even if we don't want to for ourselves."

"I try to keep thinking that their life is more important than my grief, which is how I dealt with Mary's death and Greta's life." He closed his eyes and shook his head. "Though I must admit for the last couple of weeks I've just wanted to lie down and die. Close my eyes and have it all go away."

He opened his eyes. "But I promised, and I never broke a promise to her."

Annaliese turned off the light above the examination table and pushed it away.

"Well Roy, your head looks fine, so now we're going to begin to get you back on your feet and see what you can do and what you can't."

She looked into his eyes, covered one eye and then the other to see how the pupils reacted. They seemed normal. She asked him some questions, and he was alert and moved his head in response.

Moving her face close to his, she said slowly. "It seems the injury has caused some damage to your brain. The problem now is that we don't know a lot about how the brain works, so I'm having to make this up as I go along. The idea is to get you back to as much of your life as you can as soon as you can."

He looked at her, his eyes pools of mystery, and slowly nodded his head.

"His eyes." Annaliese looked at Johnny in the mirror and shook her head. "They look so strange. When I ask him something I can see in his eyes that he knows the answer, but he can't speak." She was brushing her hair but suddenly put the brush down and turned to face him. "He makes some noises, but he seems to know he can't talk, and he may quit trying. But he knows. He could answer if his brain would let him."

"Can he write at all?" asked Johnny.

"He tried a little today, but his hand was shaking and he's still weak, so it was pretty bad. Tomorrow that's what we're going to work on. I told him to keep the pencil and pad and see if practice would help. He nodded. He understands."

Johnny looked at her without speaking for a long moment. "Wow," he finally said. "I got a feeling this one is going to help you learn some things."

She resumed brushing her hair. "I'm going to meet with Maggie and the Doctor tomorrow and see what their ideas are. And you are too. Think about this and let me know if anything pops up in that brain of yours."

He thought about it a lot the next day. How would he feel if he couldn't speak, if his brain worked but he couldn't say the words? How would he get his emotions out? He rolled his eyes. He'd probably explode. He could imagine anger and frustration beyond belief.

It seemed the most important thing was to give him a way to let off the pressure that would build up. The only way would be for him to write what he wanted to say. But could he?

"That's what she needs to find out. If he could write, then he could blow off some of the steam he's probably got building up inside." He didn't realize he was speaking out loud until Handy said from behind him, "Who needs to blow off steam?"

"Oh, hi Handy," he answered. "I was just thinking out loud. Annaliese is working with Roy, and she asked me to think about it and see if I had any ideas." Jinx hopped up on the desk and Johnny stroked him and put him in his lap where the cat settled down and began to take a bath.

"Do you?" Handy dropped into the other chair.

"I don't know. It seems to me they have to find some way to talk with him. With Greta's death and his own injuries, he has to have a lot to say and no way to say it. I would think the most important thing is to find out how much he can write. If he can ask questions and get answers, it would seem to be a step in the right direction."

"Sounds about right," Handy paused. "Rebecca and Bobby and I will be leaving tomorrow on the morning train, so what are we going to do about your cat?"

"Well, I'd like to have him back if we can work it out."

Jinx was sitting on the desk licking Johnny's hand and trying to get his head underneath it. Johnny lifted him onto his shoulder and began to rub his thumb under the cat's chin.

"Seems like that's what he wants too. "How are you feeling?"

Handy thought for a moment, then nodded his head. "Right now, I feel fine. If I get home and it's still a problem, I'll get me a kitten and name him Jinx, Jr."

"I don't think we need two Jinxes, but he appreciates the thought."

He followed Handy down the steps into the store where Jinx hopped up on the counter and settled into his bed looking like he'd never left it.

After Handy left, Johnny stood and watched Amy and Laverne welcome the cat back and thought about how he'd felt while his little Buddy wasn't around. Of course there was a lot going on in his life, but there had definitely been a hole somewhere inside him.

Jinx was the runt of a litter born in the loft of their livery stable in Kansas. His mama pushed him off, so Johnny fed him with a cloth dipped in milk. Most of the time from then on, where Johnny was, Jinx was, either on his shoulder or somewhere close. He had saved Johnny's life more than once on their trip across the country and was best man at Johnny's wedding.

Every morning, he woke Johnny up by tapping him on the nose. Not feeling those taps seemed to make a difference on most of Johnny's days and he was glad they were back.

He knew he'd never really understand what had happened between Handy and Jinx, but he also knew he didn't have to. Because of the concussion, Handy was different and when Jinx was with him, he wasn't. Lots of things in life you don't understand but still accept.

Of course, the question was still how Handy would react to Jinx not being with him. Would he revert to his 'Mister Hyde' personality or continue to be the Handy they all knew and loved? He wouldn't bet against a cat or two at the Mill Valley Horse Ranch in the near future.

Will and Lemuel enjoyed spending time together. On this day they had met by appointment at Sessions Nursery to discuss planting some new trees and shrubs around The BookSeller and the Clinic. After they had chosen and purchased a few trees and other plants and arranged for delivery and planting, Kate invited them to join her for a cup of tea on a small, covered gazebo she had built in the midst of her nursery.

"This is nice," said Lemuel, sitting looking around at all the different flora. "We might look into doing something like this at the store."

"I just got tired of sitting in that office," said Kate, and she swept her arm around at the view, "when I had all this around me. I come out here in the evenings just to sit and feel the breeze and smell everything."

She turned to Will. "Now that we seem to have gotten this hospital thing on the road, how long before it's up and running?"

"Oh boy," he replied, taking off his hat and running a hand over his head. "You must be the fiftieth person to ask me that this week."

He looked at her for a long moment and shook his head. "I've been thinking about that a lot lately, and how much it will cost and who will build it and who will run it."

"I know you have, that's why I asked you," she said. "I know it would be a guess and could be off by quite a bit. But who could give me a better idea?"

"The best estimate I can give you is a year and a half to two years, and there are a lot of ifs in that guess."

"Hmm," she said. "I plan to make my donation to the hospital by landscaping it at my expense. John's going to pay for the labor, and I'll donate the plants. Since they'll likely come from some different places, I'll need to decide when to order them."

"Well Kate, I'm glad to hear you say that, because we were going to give the contract to a fellow from Los Angeles."

He and Lemuel laughed at the startled look on her face.

"What's so funny?"

Grace looked up, startled, and realized she'd been grinning. She hadn't heard her mother come out on the porch.

"Oh, nothing," she replied.

"What's funny about nothing?"

"It's just something that happened at the clinic." She paused. "I'm not supposed to talk about things that happen when I'm there." Her face wrinkled as she tried to keep from grinning again. "I guess if I don't use names, it's OK, but you can't tell anyone else. Promise?"

"Promise!" Lillie leaned forward and Grace spoke in a low voice. "A lady came into the clinic with a rash between her legs. Annaliese said it was poison ivy and gave her some lotion for it, and the lady said, "You might as well give me a bottle for Bill too. I'll bet you can guess where he's got it."

They were still laughing when John walked into the room.

"What's so funny?"

They looked at him and then at each other. Finally, Lillie said, "No I can't. A promise is a promise. Besides, there are some things men just don't need to know."

John looked at her in silence for a moment, and recognizing defeat, smiled a wry smile and said, "Whatever you say, dear."

He bent over to kiss her. "Herschel, Johnny and I are going to ride up to the Sweetwater Dam. They're waiting for me now. I don't know what time I'll be home. I'm not sure how long it will take."

"How far is it?"

"I think maybe it's a few hours each way. So don't worry because we may be overnight."

She got up. "I'll walk out with you."

Johnny sat on Black and looked out at the still, smooth surface of the lake before him. Ahead of him John and Herschel were examining a locked gate that barred access to the top of the dam. Johnny dismounted and tied the horse to the back of their wagon.

"Looks like they don't want any wagons out there," he said. "You reckon it's OK to walk on?"

John was tying the horses to a hitching post. "I want to see the spillway at the other end and get an idea how the whole thing works. That storm must have put quite a load of water behind this thing. If it collapsed, we probably wouldn't have much of a town left. Sort of like having a sword hanging over your head, wondering if it will let go when you least expect it."

"You know, I never thought much about where it comes from," said Johnny. "I just know when I turn on the tap or pull the chain the water's there. There are three of these things now aren't there?" Johnny was at the edge looking down. He could feel Jinx's claws tighten on his shoulder. Below he could see what looked like rocks, boulders really, that appeared to be stuck together with concrete. Stretching across the canyon, the concrete dam filled the center, and beyond that, more fill and concrete. In the distance the Sweetwater River ran away through the hills.

Herschel answered. "One that's finished, that's this one built in 1888, one that's about half done ten miles north of here, and a third to the east they're beginning next month. The original was started by the Spanish back in about 1810. It's about ten miles north and west of here. They built it and some aqueducts to carry the water down to the city. The Mexicans kept it all working while they were here. It's been repaired, and they've added some to it since the war and it works ok, but there have been some problems with leakage as the city's grown. I think eventually they plan on six."

Johnny looked at John. "Why are we here?"

John unlocked the gate, beckoned to Johnny and they followed him along the top of the dam to a place where they could look down at the spillway. In front of them a door holding the water back was standing partially open. They could see where it was connected to the machinery needed to open and close it as necessary.

"They just replaced those gears," he said, pointing. "There's a crew who work up here from time to time, and I just want to keep an eye on them occasionally. This stuff was in pretty bad shape before they re-worked it. Lots of rust on the machinery." He pointed at several trees lying by a pool that received the outflow below where they stood. "See that stuff? When there's any logging going on upstream, trees and other stuff can get caught crossways in the gate and block the flow. Then the water can build up behind the dam and they could have what they call an overflow. This puts extra pressure on the dam and eventually it could collapse. Probably wouldn't take long for all that water to get to the city, and you can imagine what that would mean.

"The crew up here keeps the gate clear and watches things to keep it safe." They stood watching while he looked around and then followed him to a shady spot where they could sit and talk.

"Water's the key to this city's future," he began. "Without it, no growth. Whoever controls it has the city's heart in their hands. With the investment I have in San Diego's future, I don't like the idea of not having some say in how it's handled.

"There aren't any natural lakes in the county. The two that are here are because dams are holding the flow from winter runoff. In addition to storing water needed for the city and county, they control runoff from rains that feed rivers and creeks all winter long. Without that control much of the city could well be washed away every year."

"So, you're thinking of buying all this?" Johnny swept his hand around.

"Not necessarily, but I would like to see if I can offer them some investment capital. If they accept it that will give me some leverage in their councils. Decisions made about water affect how I run the hotel and also impact the value of land. Since I already own a good bit of the city and the county that's a big issue with me too."

"Do you think there might be a problem over control of it?"

"I know people who would see this as an opportunity for profit with no thought of the city, its welfare or future. It's one of the things I have Herschel around for. To see if he hears anyone talking about water."

They both looked at Herschel who looked back solemnly.

After a minute with them staring down into the spillway, Johnny asked, "So, what have you heard?"

"I've talked to the two men who're building the new dams and all I've heard makes me feel they're on the up and up. They may have problems with money now things have slowed down but they seem to know what they're doing. From what I hear they're not flush with cash and this storm cost them some money, so an opportunity to invest in improvements may present itself before long.

"Also, I hear it mentioned around city hall sometimes. Right now, everyone seems to be waiting to see if Vernon and Howard Construction can do what they say they can."

"So, it's just a waiting game now," said Johnny. "You may decide to step in but not unless you have to, is that it?"

John nodded. "So, I answered your question, now I'll ask you one. I notice you're wearing your gun. How come?"

Johnny had been asked that more than a few times over the years, and taking a page from Wash's book, had learned to take his time answering.

"It makes my wife happy if I don't carry it in town."

"Herschel told me you got into a gunfight a few years ago in San Francisco."

"Yes, I used to carry it all the time. For some reason or another I saw it as a talisman. A couple of fellows were heard threatening me. I braced them, told them to leave town or fight. One of them drew on me. His brother had more sense and left town. It scared my wife and rather than have a problem at home, I hung it up." He looked at Herschel. "How long's it been? A couple years now?"

"Yeah," said Herschel nodding. "Closer to three, I think."

"You still practice?"

"Mostly just drill. I only use ammo every month or so. Usually go down to Wash's cabin for that. There's a path down to the ocean there and usually no one is around. I wore it today because I thought I might need it out here in the hills."

"I'd like to see you shoot, if you don't mind."

"Now?"

John nodded. "If you don't mind," he said again.

Johnny turned, scanned the landscape, and chose a bank that would absorb the bullets. He spread his feet to shoulder width, let his hands hang loosely and suddenly the gun was in his hand. He triggered three shots so close together there was just one rolling sound. Splinters flew from a tree fallen halfway down the slope.

The sound of the shots echoed and he stood still for a moment, crouched, gun hand extended like a finger pointing, then straightened up, opened the loading gate and dropped three brass casings into his palm, then into his pocket. Using bullets from his belt he reloaded, slid the Colt into the canted holster, and turned to face his friends.

"Huh," said John after a moment. He looked at Herschel, lips pursed, eyebrows raised. "You weren't kidding, were you?"

"No, I wasn't kidding."

Even though Roy was her patient, Annaliese liked to talk to the others about him to see if they could help shine some light into the darkness of his problem.

"Is this really a medical problem now?" She looked around at them. "We've healed his hurts, he's up moving around with no problems, maybe it's nothing we can help him with. Maybe he should just get on with his life."

"We could look at it as something for his family to deal with," said Will. He paused for a moment. "But that's not a solution because it seems he's part of our family."

"Have you talked to Lemuel about it?" asked Maggie. "If Roy could go back to work the problem might work itself out in his day-to-day life."

"When he's ready to go to work he'll have a job, either at the store or at the warehouse, if that's what he wants," said Annaliese.

"Is his writing getting better?" asked Will. "The big issue would seem to be communication. We need to know what he thinks about what's going on in his life. He just lost his wife and maybe his whole family. Does he have anyone back in San Francisco who needs to know anything about what's happened?"

"I sent his mother a note about the whole thing, but that's been several weeks, and I've heard nothing," replied Annaliese. "He's been working on his writing and it's getting better."

She looked at Grace. "What do you think? You've been around him as much as I have."

"Maybe we should just ask him what he thinks."

The others looked at her.

"Out of the mouths of babes," said Will and rolled his eyes.

Annaliese was getting used to seeing Roy around the store again. He had decided to return to the store to work instead of the warehouse. His head had finally healed, and the knee was improved to the point where the limp was almost gone. He was spending more time in the store and had gradually worked his way back into his old job. This morning, he was making some entries on a sales sheet as

Annaliese walked through the store. She stopped and stared at him with her mouth open.

The pencil was in his left hand. She watched him write the numbers with a smooth, natural motion.

When he looked up she said, "It just dawned on me. You're right-handed, aren't you?"

He looked at her, a strange level gaze, his face puzzled. He pulled a pad of paper to him and began to write, smoothly and rapidly, with his left hand. When he handed her the pad she read, *"I couldn't seem to get the knack of it the other way. It just seems like I can do it better this way."*

She looked at the paper for a moment then at him, a thoughtful expression on her face. Finally, she gave her head a little shake, said, "I've got someone waiting on me," and resumed her way to the front door.

At the door she stopped and looked back at Roy still standing and writing left-handed. She knew she was not mistaken. She had seen him write before. She knew he was right-handed and suddenly he was writing left-handed like he'd been doing it all his life.

Chapter Twenty-Four

The breeze coming in the window didn't feel like November. Sarah smiled to herself. "That's why you come to San Diego in the winter, dummy," she murmured. It looked like they would be spending winters here and the rest of the year in San Francisco, which suited her fine. She heard her grandson in the hall and Rebecca knocked lightly on the door.

Beside her she felt Madame stir. She swung her feet out of bed and opened the door a crack.

"We're going over to the store to help Annaliese get ready, so I guess we'll see you there," said Rebecca. Handy was behind her and Bobby was trying to get through the door, but Sarah kissed him and held him off.

"Go way," she said to Bobby. She kissed him again and said to her daughter, "We'll be over after breakfast. Tell Annaliese to telephone if she needs us to bring anything."

She closed the door and turned back to Madame. Her friend was tying her robe and looking a little mussed and drowsy. Sarah stood and watched her step into her slippers, stretch comfortably and give out with a big yawn during which her robe came open.

"Oh my, don't you look fetching," said Sarah. She sighed deeply, stepped closer, kissed Madame and ran her hands around inside the robe. "You know," she murmured, "the first night we're here is always more exciting for some reason."

"Yes, it is. Ain't it grand?" Madame returned the kiss and the embrace, and they stood gazing at each other, smiling.

"MMM, we need to quit this." Sarah purred. "We got to be somewhere before long. Too bad we can't stay in bed all day. Have Carlota bring us lunch and dinner."

Madame leaned back and smiled. "You know I think the older you get the more you seem to like it."

Sarah laughed. "Well, I went without for a long time. Maybe I'm just catching up." She turned away, poured water on a cloth and began to wash her face. Though the house had running water, for some reason they still kept a pitcher and basin on the dresser. "I've heard it makes you feel younger." She smiled again and kissed Madame on the cheek. "Whatever it is, I like it."

Carlota knocked on the door and they began to get ready for the big day. "So, you'll be sitting up with the bigwigs today," Sarah said in a teasing tone. "I guess you did your part to make it happen."

"When a city gets a new hospital it's important, and since we seemed to have an attachment to this place, I figured it was only right and fitting we chip in." She always noticed Madame said 'we' when she was the one with all the money. More and more it seemed like they were a couple now, and after five years together she guessed it was accepted by all, though she never took it for granted.

Their usually lazy and relaxed breakfast was a bit rushed this morning and soon they were in the carriage on the way to The BookSeller. When they walked in the front door, Roy nodded and smiled, then pointed to the steps leading to the office where they found Annaliese discussing the day with Maggie.

"Ready for today?" Madame asked Annaliese.

"I hope so," she answered. "I'm not used to speaking to a lot of people like this. I hope I don't forget what I want to say."

Maggie snorted. "Never seen anything you couldn't do if you wanted to, but I promise not to do anything to make you laugh 'til it's over."

"I'll probably be alright as long as I don't look at you."

"How's Roy doing at the store?" asked Sarah.

"He's doing great. He is the manager now. He gets all his work done and then he reads."

"So, he's not working with Lemuel anymore?"

"No, he wanted to come back to the store and work, so Lemuel's got a couple of other fellows to help him."

"What do you mean, he reads?" asked Madame.

"I swear, I believe he wants to read every book in the place. I don't know if it's possible, but he's trying. The other day I looked over his shoulder and he was reading about gardening."

"Is he able to talk at all?" asked Rebecca.

"He sometimes makes little grunts, but no, he doesn't talk at all. He writes well enough when he has questions, but he doesn't seem to want normal interaction with others. Strangest thing: he writes left-handed now. Before the accident he was right-handed. He has a good memory and writes well enough to communicate if he wants to, but he doesn't seem to want to. He's polite and he's good with the customers and employees but only as much as needed."

"He fascinates us," she motioned at Maggie, "and we spend some of our free time just watching him, trying to figure out what makes him tick. He's different since he was hurt, since Greta died. I know this won't surprise you but the only one he seems to communicate with much is Johnny."

Madame rolled her eyes. "I could see that coming."

"Well, they work together so he probably spends more time with Johnny than anyone else, and they need to communicate about a lot of different things because they're running a business together."

Sarah laughed. "And of course, it could also be just because he's Johnny."

"You know they went up to Los Angeles for a while to learn typewriting. We keep one up front and one in the office at the store. Roy types very fast now and Johnny's learned with the same system, so they type messages to each other a lot."

"If Roy can hear, why does Johnny need to type messages to him?" asked Sarah.

"I asked him about that. He says it helps him think about what he's going to say, and it puts him and Roy in the same place. He doesn't do it all the time, but I think it's that he wants Roy to feel like they're on the same level and it helps."

Handy came in with Bobby, who immediately ran to his grandmother and crawled into her lap. "What time are we supposed to be there?" Handy asked.

"The ceremony starts at two. I need to meet the Doctor a little beforehand, so I'll be leaving in a few minutes," said Annaliese. She put her fingers on her wrist for a minute and shook her head. *"I'm nervous as a young girl on her wedding night,"* she thought.

John Spreckels grinned when Jinx hopped up on his desk to sit and survey the office like he owned the place. Johnny and Herschel had taken their seats, and Johnny reached to take the cat into his lap.

"Leave him be," said John. "He's fine. Just curious."

The weekly meeting with Herschel in John's office had become a regular thing for Johnny. Because he spent so much time in the library reading old newspapers, and in city and country offices and meetings just listening, he was able to contribute to the conversations and learned even more listening to them. When Herschel invited him to join them, he jumped at the chance.

The meetings helped all three of them. They came into the room with points of view about the information they brought and many times left with another point of view because they had shared and discussed that information. Seeing how it related to things a little differently than they thought, moved them around the circle a bit, so to speak. John was good at blending it all together.

"This will be a short meeting for me," said Johnny. "I want to hear my wife's speech cause I know she'll ask me questions about it tonight."

John grinned at him. "And if you can't answer them, it might have an effect on how much you'll enjoy the rest of the night?"

"That's probably right," replied Johnny, grinning back at him.

"I have to be there early too. Lillie and the children will be there. They want to hear my speech." He looked at Herschel. "Anything that can't wait 'til next week?"

"Not much going on this week. Nothing new about Monroe or that crowd, nothing new about anything really. There's a couple people in town I knew up north that could be trouble. I'll keep an eye on them and let you know if they're going to be a problem here.

"The big story is the dedication this morning, so I guess since I'll have to write a story about it, I'd better go now too. Don't want to be late. Besides, there won't be anyone here to talk to."

Johnny put his arms around his wife and looked into her green eyes. "You'll do fine. You know most of the people here so just pretend you're talking to your friends."

"I think I'll be fine as long as I don't look at Maggie."

He tried to keep a straight face. "Yes, I can see where that could be a problem." They all loved Maggie, but sometimes she could be inappropriate on serious occasions.

He watched her climb the steps to the speakers' stand and make her way to a seat by her father. Roy came to stand beside him as he turned to view the crowd gathered for the dedication of the new San Diego Community Hospital. Johnny swept his gaze around and suddenly his mouth fell open in surprise. Wash was standing beside Woman near the carriage park in the back of the crowd.

This was unusual. Wash didn't like crowds and generally stayed out of sight, happy to live his life free of other people and their problems. It was one of the things that drew him and Woman together. They both were the kinds of people who got stared at and didn't like it much. With Roy trailing behind him, he worked his way around the crowd until he reached them, nodded a greeting, and stood silently beside them, watching the dedication ceremony begin.

Annaliese finished her speech and introduction of her father without even glancing Maggie's way. On the way to her seat in the crowd, she looked out to where Johnny was standing with Wash and Woman. Like him, she was amazed that their friends had come, and it made her feel good they were there.

She turned to watch her father and heard him speak the lines they had labored over for a week.

"This is a community hospital because the community has come together to make it so. San Diego Community Hospital and the doctors, nurses and others who work here will do their best to justify your faith in them by providing you, our fellow citizens, with the best health care and education they can offer.

"This hospital exists as a testament to our faith in the future of San Diego, a place we believe will become special, a place that will grow and thrive because of the people who have chosen to live here."

When he was through and the crowd was applauding, John and Madame cut the ribbon, and the place was in business.

For the next couple of hours, they were serving refreshments and helping people find things and view all the things a modern, up to date hospital embodied. When Johnny looked around, Wash and Woman had disappeared. He and Roy joined the others from their circle of friends who had congregated near the carriage park, and they all left for the store. Kate had joined them, and it was quite late before everyone had gone and Johnny sat watching his wife brush her hair.

"So, how much will this change our life?" he asked her. "A whole lot?"

She finished brushing, put the brush down and looked at him in the mirror. "I don't really know," she answered. She turned to face him and was shaking her head. "It will change the way we deal with some of our patients. We won't have to send as many to hospitals in Los Angeles. All the doctors in town will be working on call in turn, so that might mean we have more time off, but who knows?

"All we can do is take it a step at a time, deal with what comes up and adjust as we need to. Only a few of the doctors in town have ever worked at any kind of large hospital, so it's new to most of us. I know we all have suggestions and ideas, but I think for a while it will be just making it up as we go along until we come up with a system that fills our needs and solves our problems. Anyone who thinks differently is kidding themselves. I think this fellow we have as administrator will help. He's worked in a few hospitals back east."

She had turned back to face the mirror, and he came up behind her and kissed her on top of her head. "Want to talk some more or are you ready for bed?"

"I'll never be able to sleep with all this stuff going around in my head."

"Are you asking for my help?"

"Well, you could at least offer."

He looked at her, rubbed his chin and said, "I need a shave. You might get a beard rash."

She put her arms around his neck and kissed him. "I'll risk it," she mumbled through the kiss.

Lemuel had developed the habit of coming home and joining the twins at dinner with whomever of the family might be there. Many times, he just sat and watched the children interact with others around the table. He was proud of the way they seemed to be comfortable with anyone they were talking to and had noticed they especially liked talking with Grace. He'd had the table made to order. It had seats for fourteen, and many nights was full.

This extended family they had developed over the last few years was a warm, convivial place for the twins to grow up. He remembered how they were somewhat late beginning to talk, but Greta had believed it was because they had their own language and didn't need to talk to anyone else.

Now they talked to whomever was sitting near them and he could see them soaking up new ideas like damp sponges and learning new words in the process.

"Lemuel?"

He started a little, came out of his reverie and saw Sarah smiling at him.

"I'm sorry, I was woolgathering. What did you say?"

"I asked if the twins had started school yet."

"Probably next year. Mrs. Keane and Consuelo are teaching them their letters and numbers already and they're doing well. There's a new academy for youngsters opening soon not too far from us and I think they'll be going there."

"So, are you a doting grandpapa?"

"I try to be. Mary looks so much like her grandmother. I love looking at her when she's writing or playing."

"I was up in their room a little while ago and I had to smile at all the books."

"Did you expect anything different?"

"Rebecca wants them to come up next summer for a visit. Maybe a couple of weeks. They can stay with us at the mansion and spend some time up at the ranch with Bobby. Maybe Mrs. Keane can bring them up."

Lemuel looked at her for a moment, then shook his head. "It will feel strange not having them around. On the other hand, they would have fun, so I guess I'll have to give them up for a while."

"You could come too. We have plenty of room and there are a lot of people who would be glad to see you."

"I might do it. Johnny and Roy could keep an eye on the business." He thought for a minute and then grinned. "Done," he said. "I'll let you know when we're coming."

"Wonderful. Handy will probably have them on a horse before

they unpack."

Grace was sitting on the porch looking out over the ocean again thinking about going back to work the next morning when her mother sat down beside her.

"So how will having the hospital open affect your work with Annaliese?" she asked.

"We've all talked about it, and no one seems to be able to answer that question. Will is the only one who has much experience working in a hospital. For Annaliese and Maggie, it's going to be just as new to them as it is to me. They did some hospital work while they were in school, but not very much. I think we've decided when Annaliese is at the hospital, I'll be working with her, and the rest of the time will work with Will or Maggie. Of course we'll probably switch around some."

Grace sat quiet for a moment then said, "Usually we all sit and talk when I get there on Tuesdays so I'm guessing that will be one thing we'll talk about tomorrow."

Her mother rocked quietly for a while. "I think I know you well enough that I can see you plan to make medicine the focus of your life so where do you go from here? I mean you've been working with Annaliese and Maggie for long enough to begin to think about where you want to go and how to get there."

"Mama, there's so much new stuff to learn every year, and so many new treatments and ways to think about things. Annaliese says I should give it two more years before I apply to medical school. So that will be when I'm eighteen, and then three years of school. After that I have to decide what kind of practice and where to begin it.

"I think I'd like to come back home and practice here, but five years from now what will it be like? I can't expect them to hold a place for three years. What if they don't need me, or what if I want to study some more, or maybe go somewhere else and open a practice? What will medicine be like in five years, and if I want to learn more, where will I go to learn?"

"Sounds like the best thing to do is keep doing what you're doing and see what choices you'll have when the time comes," said her mother.

"I guess the one thing I can't do is get impatient. When the time comes, the way forward may be as clear as day."

Annaliese was sitting in her office writing in a patient's chart when Consuelo knocked on the door jamb and asked, "Are you busy?"

"No, what can I do for you?"

The housekeeper came in and seated herself in a chair by the desk. She sat stiffly erect, smoothed her apron down, took a deep breath and said, "My oldest daughter, Estelida, has been wondering whether she could ever become a doctor. She admires you and has seen how Grace works with you and wonders if maybe she can do the same thing. I told her I would talk to you and see what you said and what was the best way to go about it. I know there are many doctors in Mexico, but I don't know of any Mexican doctors in this country. Maybe she could be the first and a woman too."

Annaliese sat back in her chair. "Come to think of it, I don't know of any either. A few midwives and some old woman healers, but no doctors." She thought for a minute and asked, "How old is she?"

"She will be fourteen next month."

"That's the same age Grace was when she started with me." She sat quiet with her brow knotted in thought again then asked, "Is she going to school now?"

"Yes, she is, and she is a good student. She loves to read and writes a fair hand. She is also good with her sums."

"One thing that made it possible for Grace to work with me is that she was being tutored at home instead of going to class. We'd have to see what kind of arrangements we could make for her. Also, I'd need to talk to my partners to get their thoughts on it." She made a few notes on a pad and said, "Tell you what. Grace comes back tomorrow morning, and we usually have a meeting then. So let me talk to Maggie and the Doctor and see what they think. Would she be able to work with me three days a week?"

More questions and answers followed. When Consuelo left, she sat thinking, gazing out the window at nothing. She had never thought about working with another student, but she supposed it was possible. She knew the girl and had always thought of her as quiet and a little shy.

Estelita was a twin. Her brother Juan, a tall, husky youth, was already working with his father, helping keep up the grounds around the store and the clinic. Where Juan was as tall as his father, she was small, almost petite, with long black hair and usually had a solemn expression on her face, though she could light up a room when she did smile.

They had covered everything else in the meeting the next morning when Annaliese brought up her conversation with Consuelo. "So, what does everyone think about the idea of having another student working with us?" she said after she had explained what Consuelo had in mind.

She looked at her father first. He sat thinking for a moment, then responded. "I'm for it. I've never felt a bright, eager young student was anything but a plus for me and my patients."

Annaliese nodded and looked at Maggie. Her friend shrugged. "I agree," she said. "There definitely are times when an extra pair of hands is valuable, and if she's anything like Grace it will be a positive for all of us, now and in the future."

Grace was grinning when Annaliese turned to her.

"How do you feel about it? We'd have to work out a schedule and I'm sure it would take a bit of thought on how to go about it."

"When would she work?" Grace asked. "Would it be like my shift? Three days a week and stay over?"

"We have plenty of room so staying over isn't a problem," replied Annaliese, "but we'd have to decide which days were best, and there's also the question of school. She would need to continue in school but how would that work? I guess we'll have to put our heads together and see if we can come up with a plan. Think about it, and any ideas you have, bring them to me."

The more she thought about it the more she liked the idea. Now if they could just work it out.

Chapter Twenty-Five

Johnny was sitting in his office up under the eaves, looking out at the morning, when he heard Roy coming up the steps. He spent so much time there now, he could usually tell by the sounds on the stairs who his visitor was before they came through the door. As usual, Roy had a folder of papers related to the store, and on top, personal messages, which was the way he 'talked' to Johnny.

"Morning Roy," he said, and reached for the papers. He read the first message and looked up. "Yes, I'm going to meet with John and Herschel this morning and no we're not supposed to go up to look at a dam today."

The second page was another question. "Yes, I plan to go to the cabin and shoot today, and you can go along. What time is best for you? I don't have anything I need to do later, just so it's not too late."

Having grown up in the city, Roy had never handled weapons much but was slowly gaining the smooth, practiced movements necessary to draw and fire a weapon from the hip and hit what he wanted to hit. Johnny found the boy had good hand to eye coordination and was learning fast. They both enjoyed the camaraderie of their sessions, and Roy was improving each time they practiced.

Later, on the ferry over to The Del and his meeting with John and Herschel, Johnny thought about Roy and how the boy's life had changed since Greta's death. Since Annaliese had asked him to think about ways to help Roy communicate, he had thought about it a lot, and the results had been gratifying.

Their trip to Los Angeles to learn a method of touch typing had been productive and enjoyable. Coming home with textbooks, practice soon added a new dimension to their lives. They also spent a week seeing what the city to the north had to offer curious visitors and came home to four new typewriters Johnny had ordered before they left: one in Johnny's office up under the eaves, one on each of their desks in the store office, and one behind the front counter in the store. Beside each machine was a stack of paper and an eraser. From that point on they learned to communicate differently because they had to.

Some days as many as twenty-five or thirty typewritten messages passed between them: details on managing the store, questions about what to order, and ideas about promotion. More and more as they became familiar and comfortable with the machines, the conversations became practical; what to get at the grocery store, trips to the post office or the bank, and personal; about the future and the past, and later about hopes and dreams.

It didn't replace the spoken word, but it was as good as they could arrange. This tunnel of words, hidden from the rest of the world, became a mark of their friendship and soon, a hallmark that others in the family recognized, respected, and wondered at.

Annaliese had pointed out that since Roy could hear, she didn't see the need for Johnny to learn how to type.

"It puts us on the same level and makes him more comfortable," he said. "Also, I like the way I think about what I'm going to say more when I'm typing than I do when I'm talking."

John was waiting in his office but Herschel, usually the first one there, wasn't.

"He doing anything special for you?" asked Johnny.

"No. Maybe he just overslept. I don't think he's ever been late before."

"Anything special we need to talk about? If not I'll stop by his place and see if he's there and what the problem is."

"You know," said John, "I don't even know where he lives. Or anything else about his private life, for that matter. He's a strange duck, that's for sure."

"I've never been there, but he showed me where it is. I'll let you know what I find out."

As he was leaving, he heard John say, "You always do."

One day when they had been walking around town Herschel had pointed out his dwelling - a two-story house, older than most in New Town and in need of some repairs and a paint job. A roomer, he had a private entrance on the side. When Johnny opened the door after knocking and receiving no answer, it was dark in the hall inside.

When his eyes adjusted, he could see stairs leading up to a dim landing. A switch on the wall lit a single bulb hanging in the hall at the top of the steps, and he climbed to a door he could see was slightly open where they ended. Jinx, who usually led the way up steps, was hanging back, low, moving cautiously.

Looking through the door at the top of the steps he could see a man's leg, naked, stretched out on the floor beyond a bed. He pushed the door open and grimaced. Jinx had hopped on the bed and was looking down at Herschel's body before Johnny saw it.

His friend was naked, lying face-down in a wide pool of drying blood. Johnny stood still for a long moment, mouth open, staring. When he finally moved it was to step carefully around the body and squat by the outstretched hand.

There was no question Herschel was dead. His skin was a sickly purple shade of white and, when Johnny reached to touch his hand, it was cold, and he could feel stiffness. The blood was dry in places and damp in others. It looked like he'd been lying there for a while, probably since sometime after midnight the night before.

Johnny had read about rigor mortis and remembered it usually began three to four hours after death. He took out his watch and glanced at it. Ten o'clock. He moved to the foot of the bed and watched Jinx begin his inevitable assessment of the room. Johnny watched him stop in places, lower his nose, sniff, and after a moment, move on. Johnny moved slowly behind him, looking as intently as the cat. After a good ten minutes Jinx hopped back on the bed and began to take a bath. Johnny felt like he needed to sit down and think, but he also needed to notify the Sheriff as soon as he could.

There was no telephone in the house and on the ride to the courthouse to report what had happened, he thought about what he'd learned in the room.

Herschel didn't smoke and cigar butts in the ashtray on the table told him another person had been there and had spent some time. There were glasses on the table that smelled of whiskey, so it appeared he had shared a drink with his visitor. A glass on the bedside table had half of a cigar butt in it. The bed looked as though two people had occupied it at least for a while. There was no trace of perfume in the air, but it seemed maybe he had entertained a lover. A woman? He didn't ever recall Herschel talking about a woman and had never seen him with one.

The body had some bruises on the neck and on the back. It looked like he had been attacked from behind and stabbed in the throat several times. Herschel was short and stocky and not in the best of condition, but he couldn't picture a woman who could have attacked and killed him in the manner things seemed to indicate.

Herschel's clothes were hanging on a chair. Johnny found a hundred dollars in cash in his coat, as well as a pocket watch, a ring, and a necklace on the dresser, so it didn't look like robbery was the motive.

At the courthouse, the sheriff and two deputies listened to his account, and before long he was leading them up the steps and into the room where his friend's body lay.

He stepped aside, and sitting in a chair by the door, watched the three men deal with the scene before them. Many things he had seen they seemed to gloss over if they noticed them at all and after a few minutes the Sheriff left, leaving one man to secure the room.

Johnny followed the two men down the steps and stopped at the bottom where the Sheriff turned to the deputy and said, "We need to get the doc over here as soon as we can. You stay here and don't let anyone in until he finishes up there."

He turned to Johnny and said, "Can you come back to the office? I'll need to talk to you a bit about what you saw when you first walked in and saw the body."

When Johnny sat down across the desk from the sheriff he asked, "Can I use your telephone to call someone about this?" The man nodded and pushed the instrument across the desk where Johnny lifted the receiver, jiggled the handle and when the operator answered said, "Can you connect me with John Spreckels at The Del, please?"

At the name, the sheriff's eyebrows went up. After a short wait he said, "John, this is Johnny. Heschel was murdered sometime last night, and we just found his body." John's cry of amazement was clearly audible, and the Sheriff smiled slightly. "I'll stop by and give you all the particulars when the sheriff is through with me," he said. He listened for a moment and said, "OK, I'll be at the store when you get back."

He hung up the phone, pushed the unit back across the desk and sat back in his chair.

"So, what did you want to ask me?"

"I know Herschel worked at the Union, but what connection did he have with Spreckels?" Johnny explained the connection and the sheriff made a note and then said, "Johnny, you know about how we operate around here and the things we do. I'm new in the office and

I've never investigated a murder before. Furthermore, I'll bet no one else here has either. Hell, we mostly serve papers, sit in court or arrest drunks. Even when someone is killed in a fight, there are usually enough witnesses that we can figure things out pretty quick."

He looked at Johnny significantly. "I know there are things in that room that might tell me what happened. I plan to go back up there with the Medical Examiner so anything you see you think I should know, I'd appreciate it if you just come right out with it."

"I have no more experience than you do at this kind of thing," said Johnny, "but I can tell you what I saw, and we can talk about what it means."

Johnny was watching Annaliese brush her hair again. He had told her about the murder and what happened that day, what everyone had said. Now he was thinking about what he and the sheriff had talked about after, and how to go about bringing it up.

She finished, laid down the brush and turned to face him. "So, are you going to tell me the rest of it?"

He grinned at her and tried to look innocent. "Why, whatever do you mean, my dear?"

She looked at him over the top of the new glasses she had begun wearing the previous week. "Johnny Fry, long ago I learned how you think and how you act when you've got something to say but don't quite know how to say it. So what's going on in that brain of yours that you don't know how to tell me?"

He smiled ruefully, breathed deep and took the plunge. "How would you feel if I became a deputy sheriff?"

Her mouth fell open and she gaped at him. "What?"

He came over to sit beside her and kissed her on the cheek. "I like looking at you when you look like that. Looks like every one of your freckles is going to jump off your face."

"What are you talking about?"

"OK! I talked to Sheriff Baker about Herschel's murder. Ed hasn't been sheriff very long and has never had to deal with a murder, and neither have any of his deputies. He wanted to know if I would help him out in trying to find out who did it and why.

"We went up to the room with Jim Baldwin, and while he examined the body, Ed and I went over the room to see what we could find that might give us clues as to what happened. When we got back to the office, we all sat around and talked about it, and finally he asked me if I would come on board as a special deputy just to handle this one case."

"And what did you say?"

The tone of her voice warned him to be careful how he answered.

"I told him I'd need to talk to you about it before I gave him an answer."

She sat and looked at him for a long moment, a frown on her face. He watched as her face went through several expressions and finally, she said, "What about the store?"

"Annaliese, I don't think this will be a full-time job. It seems to amount to gathering as many pieces of information as I can, organizing them and then trying to put together a puzzle. Herschel was my friend, and I want to help find the person who did this. I found the body, and before I went for the sheriff, Jinx and I looked the room over carefully. Besides that, I know more about him and his life than anyone else. I think I'm the best one for the job."

"Jinx and you?" Her mouth twisted into a smile of sorts.

"Well, when he found something interesting, I looked at it pretty close."

"And if you find the murderer, what then? Will he try to murder you?"

"If I decide to do it, I'm going to start wearing the Colt again."

She sat quiet for a moment, then took a deep breath and shook her head. She had just gotten used to seeing it hanging on a peg on the wall in his office again. He had stopped wearing it in San Francisco, then worn it across the desert. He knew she was afraid of what might happen when he did wear it, so he had taken it off when he returned.

"This is something you want to do, isn't it?"

He nodded and she stared at him, remembering how she felt when she first saw the gun belt hanging in the office the day he took it off.

"I can see you want to do it, and I can see why, so I want you to carry the gun if it will keep you safe." She sat up straighter and asked, "Do you think this will become permanent, or when it's over, do you go back to being a bookseller?"

He pulled her to her feet and into a hug. "I'll always be a bookseller," he said, "but this is something I have to do for a special friend."

Chapter Twenty-Six

"Do you know what the word 'unique' means?"

Grace looked up from the sink, where she was cleaning some equipment, with a thoughtful expression. "It means 'one of a kind', doesn't it?"

"That's right," said Annaliese. "So, do you know how the word applies to you?"

"I never thought about it. How?"

"I doubt if there is another girl your age working with a doctor the way you do with me in the entire country, much less in California."

"Hmm," said Grace. "I'll bet that's probably true. I never thought about it before."

"If Estelida comes to work here you won't be unique anymore. How do you feel about that?"

Grace stood quiet for a moment, a puzzled expression on her face. "I don't know. I haven't talked to her much, only when we have gone to the house. She seems nice. She's really quiet."

"Consuelo tells me she'll get over it. At home she isn't like that."

"So, when is she going to start?"

"We've got some problems to work out before we move forward with the idea. The biggest one is school. She's still in school and arranging a schedule that will work around her attendance at school is proving to be a problem.

"Also, we have to coordinate the two of you. She'll have to learn what you already know. You'll have to continue to learn at the level you're at while she'll be learning at a different level, so we have to decide how to arrange it so it's best for you both."

"Would she stay here, like I do?"

"That's what we hope. It would be a little crowded, but we should be able to squeeze her in." She looked at Grace for a minute. "You never did answer my question."

Grace looked at her for a moment, puzzled. "Oh, you mean how would I feel about her working here like I do?"

When Annaliese nodded, she said, "I'd like it fine. I can help her, and while I'm doing that it will help me review what I've learned already."

"I was hoping you'd say that."

John and Lillie were enjoying a late afternoon breeze on an ocean view terrace when Grace joined them.

"Thought you wouldn't be here until tomorrow," said her mother. "Anything the matter?"

"No, Annaliese had a meeting at the hospital, so she gave me the day off." She sipped a glass of iced tea then said, "It looks like Estelita might not be able to come to work with us after all."

"Why's that?" John asked. "Thought it was all arranged."

"They can't work it in with her schoolwork. Her mother and Annaliese both think she needs to continue with that."

"I can see where having a tutor would be an advantage," said Lillie. "It will be a shame if she can't. It would be a wonderful thing for the Mexicans in town if she could do this. I imagine they'd all be proud of her." She looked at her husband with a speculative look on her face.

"How much trouble would it be to have her work with Henry and Jess?"

John looked thoughtful. "I'm sure they could work it out. I can give them a raise, and they'll be happy. They'd have to talk to the girl's teachers to find out what level she's at, but I don't keep them that busy, so they'd have the time." He thought for a minute. "As far as the cost, I'll just make it something I can do for the Mexican people of the city. If she comes back here as a doctor, we all benefit."

"Thank you," said Grace. She kissed her parents and went off to telephone Annaliese with the news.

When she was gone, Lille turned to her husband. "She's really good at getting you to do what she wants you to do and making you think it was your idea, isn't she?"

Trying to keep from smiling he replied, "Takes after her mother."

Climbing the steps of the old three-story building, Johnny stopped and read the sign on the face of it. 'San Francisco Morning Call.' He'd spent time in the archives of the place but didn't remember ever having a conversation with anyone while he was there - just "hello", "goodbye", and "thank you".

Well, he hoped he'd have one today. He'd told his wife the investigation would be a part-time thing, but it was turning out to be a lot more work than he'd thought. He'd spent three days trying to find and talk to people who might have seen something the morning of the murder. Two people might have seen someone, but it was first thing in the morning, and they didn't pay much attention to the man so couldn't really help him much, though both remembered he was big and seemed to be in a hurry.

He'd spent time with the medical examiner and the sheriff talking about the physical evidence. With each piece they found, the question was, was it important or not? If so, what did it mean? He and Jinx had gone over the room several times to examine or reexamine things he thought might be important. And he had talked to people Herschel had worked with at the Union.

He'd sat down with the reports Herschel had written for John and articles in the Union and learned a lot about the man's life in San Diego, but with all he'd learned he still didn't have any idea why Herschel was murdered or who did it.

The next logical step was talking to people in his past which was why Johnny was here. An exchange of telegrams had given him several names at the newspaper and at City Hall, and the next day he was on the train north. Soon he should know more about Herschel's life before they'd met.

He stopped inside the front door and adjusted his gun belt. He was still getting used to wearing it again, and he'd noticed people looking at him and then at the canted holster on his hip. In San Francisco not too many men wore pistols these days. Still and all, he felt comfortable with it already, and with what he was trying to do, he was glad it was there.

Roger Hammond was a silver-haired fellow who looked to be about fifty or so. When Johnny reached to shake hands, the man held up ink-stained hands. "Been changing a ribbon on my typewriter," he said with a grin.

"Oh yeah," replied Johnny. "I've been learning how to do that myself."

"You a reporter?"

"No, I'm a bookseller, but we use typewriters in the store. I'm also a special deputy from the Sheriff's office in San Diego, and I'm looking into the murder of Herschel Grieve."

"Right. Charlie told me you were coming. Yes, I worked with Herschel. He was murdered, you say?"

"Yes, I stopped by his place one morning to see him and found his body. We were friends, and since I knew him better than anyone else, the sheriff asked me to help with the investigation."

"I don't know how much I can help you, Johnny. I worked with the guy for a couple of years but never knew much about him." He shook his head. "He never talked about himself. I don't even know where he was from."

"Did he ever talk much about his time with Sunny Jim?"

"Well, we did work together on a couple of pieces about that bunch and what happened to them after they got chased out of town. That was right when he came to work here, and he was helping me learn who was who in the gang so I could write the story. Of course, that was after they were out of office and had already left town. I knew who he was before that, but we'd never talked. From what I know, he was Jim's right hand man for a couple of years."

"He ever talk about anyone special?"

"He never did. Although, I remember he mentioned one fellow who he said was a nasty piece o' work. Barry Presgraves. I remember him because a year or so later he ended up in the slammer for a while. Got into it with another guy and knifed him. He said it was self-defense, but I had my doubts about that. Last I heard he had gone south, somewhere around LA.

He shook his head. "It was pretty bad. I said I knifed him, but actually he stabbed the fellow with an ice pick. Blood all over the place. Seems he carries it in his boot."

Johnny had been making notes on a pad but at this he looked up sharply. The medical examiner had said Herschel had been stabbed with something small and thin. Something like an ice pick.

Johnny noticed the Mill Valley Horse Ranch had some new features when he drove the buggy into the yard. A new stable had been added behind the barn, with an exercise circle covered by a roof off the back. The fence around the exercise track and new fencing around various fields had been freshly painted, and there were a dozen horses grazing in several pastures in view. There also were several cats around the place, including one sitting in Handy's lap.

He saw another buggy and realized Hank Rose was here. Annaliese's old anatomy teacher had become a partner in the ranch after Johnny left and came up for a few days every couple months to do the books, talk about plans, and see how things were progressing. He was glad. He wanted to talk to someone about Herschel's wounds and who better than an anatomy professor?

Handy and Hank were sitting on the porch rocking and talking when Johnny handed the reins to Bits and joined them. After greetings and news of friends and family had been exchanged, Johnny said to Hank, "I'm glad you're here. I don't know if you've heard but Herschel Grieve was murdered last week."

They were both shocked and wanted to hear the details, so he told them. "Since the sheriff and his deputies are new at being lawmen with not much experience, he asked me to come on as a special deputy."

"Why you?" asked Hank. "You don't know anything about solving murders, do you?"

"No, but I found the body and looked over the room before I called him, and since I'm the only one down there who knew much about Herschel, he thought I could help."

He told them what he had found out, and about the startling revelation he had uncovered from the reporter at the paper.

"It does seem like an unusual weapon," said Hank. "Not the kind of thing that's commonly used in a fight or to stab someone. You say he was stabbed in the throat?" Johnny nodded and demonstrated where the three puncture wounds had pierced the neck just to one side of the windpipe.

Hank sat quiet, thinking for a minute. "From what you say about the wounds, I'll bet there was a lot of blood." When Johnny nodded again, he continued. "It sounds like someone knew exactly where the jugular vein was since two of three tries seemed to have hit it. From what you said all three wounds were close together and aimed for the one place it would do the most damage."

"I thought maybe that was the case. Maybe the murderer went into the room with the idea of killing him. They spent time together before he did it, talked, smoked, and had a drink. Maybe other things. It looked like they'd been in bed." He shook his head. "The problem is I don't know why. I guess maybe if I find out who did it I'll find out why."

"To inflict those wounds, I'd say the killer was taller than the victim, and stronger," said Hank. "To come up behind him, pull the victim's head back and expose the neck I'd think the killer would have to be strong to do something like that to another man but also would have to know he could do it."

"If that's true, it sounds like he might have done something like this before," said Johnny.

He sat quiet for a minute looking out at the forge. He could see someone working, could hear the hammer ringing on the anvil, smell the smoke from the fire. His mind wandered to the times when he'd worked in that forge and loved every minute of it. More than any other place it was where he could feel his father's presence, hear his voice. "When you've got a problem, think it out," Pa would say.

He jerked his mind back to his problem and began to review what he knew and didn't know.

"The one thing my mind keeps coming back to is the bed. It looked like two people had been in it. Of course, maybe he never made his bed but there was a cigar butt in a glass by the bed. Herschel didn't smoke, at least I never saw him smoke and this was a good cigar. Still had the band on it. It wasn't a cheap stogie."

"If he had a visitor there would be only one reason I can think of to be in bed," said Handy. "Can you think of a woman who could do that to Herschel?"

"Actually, I can think of one who could, but she wouldn't."

Handy chuckled. "I believe she could, at that. She probably wouldn't use an ice pick though."

"What are you two talking about?" asked Hank.

Handy grinned at him. "You've never met Woman, have you?"

"Let's not get off the subject. You can tell him that story after I leave," said Johnny. "I want to catch the afternoon train which means I need to catch the noon ferry. Show me what you've done around here since I left. We can talk while we're walking."

Hank left shortly to talk to Gray in the barn office and he and Handy stood leaning on a fence watching someone exercising a horse in the distance.

"I'd say since this Presgraves fellow has a history of using that kind of weapon you've got a good reason to think he might be the one," said Handy. "Now what?"

"I'd say I've got to find out if he was in the area when the crime was committed. So, I guess that's the next step. Then try to follow Herschel's footsteps, see if he might have seen the man and if he was there, figure out why he was in Herschel's room that night and find out why he was in the bed."

"Like I said, only one reason I can think of."

"Yeh. It's a little hard for me to see that happening. Doesn't seem natural."

"Might just depend on someone's nature."

Johnny was gathering up the reins of the buggy. "How's the head?"

"All healed. Hair's even grown out so you can't even see the scar anymore."

"Were you ever able to remember anything about those two days?"

Handy shook his head. "No, but as long as I got a cat to pet I seem to be OK. When I go down to the mansion for a visit, I leave them here and I feel OK without them. I guess I'm just getting used to having them around. Looking for a little black kitten but so far haven't seen one."

Chapter Twenty-Seven

Since John's offer to have the tutors teach Estelita had broken the logjam on the idea of her joining the practice things had moved along pretty quickly.

With Grace's OK they had moved a bed and some furniture into her room at the store and Este, as they all called her, was soon getting used to the routine of three days with Annaliese and the practice, and two days at school with Grace.

Quiet at first, she had quickly adapted and was soon studying hard, working hard and enjoying her new life. She and Grace became fast friends and at mealtimes were constantly chattering and laughing to each other and to others at the table. The usual partnerships were Grace working with Annaliese, and Este with Maggie and the Doctor, but occasionally they would work together or switch partners.

Though she didn't like the idea of homework, Annaliese encouraged their curiosity and always tasked them to look for answers when they had questions. Far from being jealous Grace was always ready to explain or instruct her friend. Este quickly became part of the practice, and no one missed a step.

The girl was quietly beautiful and anyone who saw her smile remembered it. To make things easier for all Lillie arranged a place for Este to sleep over whenever it was convenient and before long the only time Este was home with her family was on weekends.

Right away everyone noticed how good she was with children. Scared or nervous youngsters seemed attracted to her and were noticeably calmer and less agitated when she was in the room. This was especially true with Mexican children. She seemed to know everyone in Old Town and seemed to sense whether sympathy, support or humor would best help the patient relax with the idea of being in the doctor's office.

There were times when Annaliese let Grace teach Este new things while she watched over their shoulders. This seemed not only to move along Este's education but also boosted Grace's confidence and gave her a different point of view about what she was teaching.

When she was working with Grace, Annaliese had noticed when she taught the girl something new it reinforced her own view of the importance of that thing. Indeed, one reason she had taken the two of them on was that she felt it made her a better doctor when she was helping someone else learn something she thought was important.

Johnny caught the train that afternoon and on the long trip down the valley, he thought a lot about what he knew and what he didn't. He closed the notebook where he kept everything about the case and sat tapping it on the arm of the seat thinking about getting home. As much as he had gained from his trip north the one thing he missed was talking to his wife about things.

She listened to him when he needed to talk and usually had good things to say. He felt he needed her views on the problems he was dealing with. He wanted to lay it all out for her and get her views on what it meant. If there was one thing constant in his life it was how much the things he and his wife talked about influenced how he thought about things.

When he had a problem, they talked and he usually found the answers he was looking for. Not that she gave him advice or suggestions. No, she just guided him to solutions by asking questions so he could find solutions himself.

Thinking about Presgraves, he suddenly remembered something Herschel had said: "A lot of places in the state are getting cleaned up and the rats have to go somewhere." Los Angeles was the fastest growing city in the state. Maybe the rats had gone there? He wondered if it might be worth his time to drop off the train and spend a few hours at the local sheriff's office to see if anyone there knew anything about Presgraves.

Three hours later he swung onto the station platform, hailed a cab and arrived unannounced at the LA County Sheriff's office. As luck would have it the sheriff was out, but when he explained the situation to a deputy, he was given a name at one of the newspapers and shortly was having coffee with a man whose job was writing about crime in the city and the surrounding county.

"Yeah, I know Presgraves," the reporter said. His name was Ray Kidd and he'd been on the beat for several years. "He was a shoulder striker for Tom Haines up in Santa Barbara a while back. I believe he drifted down the coast and ended up here a couple years ago.

"He's a bully boy and he works right close to the edge of the law but so far has been smart enough not to cross the line most times, or at least not get caught if he does. He's smarter than most and has a gang of sorts he hangs out with. Some of them are in and out of trouble occasionally, but he manages to keep his hands clean, or at least they never catch him. He had a few girls working for him from time to time, but I don't think he's ever flush with cash. I think he spends it as fast as he gets it."

"Do you know anything about his history before he got here?"

"I know he almost went to jail for stabbing someone up the coast; don't know any details. You know, I knew Herschel, at least I met him and we exchanged letters a couple of times when we were both working on stories."

"Ever hear anything about Presgraves carrying an ice pick in his boot?"

"Now that you mention it, I did hear that, though I've never seen it." He took a sip of coffee and motioned for a refill. "Have you ever met him?"

"Not really. I saw him one night but there was a lot going on that night and he didn't impress me one way or another."

"He's a big fellow, built like a bull. Not too tall but broad though the shoulders and chest. Funny thing. He has a high-pitched voice. I've talked to him several times, and it's the first thing you notice about him. Sounds a little like a woman. It's kind of strange hearing it in a man who looks like a thug.

"I haven't heard anything about him lately, but if you'd like to find out more, I have a friend who's a bartender at a place he used to frequent. I've got something to take care of here, but I can tell you where it is and you can go talk to him. Maybe he can help you."

Johnny nodded and stood.

"You want to go now?" Kidd looked a little startled.

"Yes, if it wouldn't be a problem. I want to catch the evening train to San Diego, so I've only got a couple hours."

"Well, it's a place called Angel's and the bartender's name is Fred. Just mention my name and he might be able to help you."

Angel's was a dive located near the waterfront, and as he rode through the neighborhood in a cab he was glad he had the Colt on his hip. It was early in the afternoon and there were just a few customers sitting at tables scattered around a big room.

Johnny hadn't been in many saloons in his life, but this was one he'd remember. The windows were dirty and, with all the smoke, there wasn't much light in the place. The sawdust on the floor looked and smelled like it hadn't been changed in a while.

Fred was a big round-shouldered man with small beady eyes and an enormous mustache. He was eating a sandwich and reading a newspaper when Johnny came up to the bar.

"What can I get you?" he asked, brushing crumbs off his shirt.

"If you're Fred, Ray Kidd at the Daily Times told me you might be able to help me."

"Is that right?" He looked at Johnny and his eyes strayed to the holster on his hip. "I guess that would depend on what it is you want."

"I'm trying to find out what I can about one of your regular customers, a fellow named Barry Presgraves."

Fred looked at him in silence for a long moment. "Are you looking for him? Cause I ain't seen him in a while."

"No, just trying to get some information about him for now."

"What for?"

Johnny had wondered how he'd answer that question if it came up. "A fellow was killed a few days ago down in San Diego, murdered. Presgraves worked with him in San Francisco a few years back. I wanted to find out what he can tell me about him."

"You a lawman?"

"Not really. I'm just helping the Sheriff down there try to find out why a friend of mine was murdered, that's all."

"Like I said, I haven't seen him in a while. Someone told me he'd gone down south of the border. Some of the gang he used to hang with were from down around Tijuana."

"Hmm." Johnny pursed his lips and stood looking at himself in the cracked, dirty mirror behind the bar.

"A little advice, mister. He's not the kind of person who answers questions from any kind of lawman. He's a bad man to mess with. If I were you, I wouldn't try to find him. You might succeed."

Chapter Twenty-Eight

Grace was sitting in the treatment room when Wash came in supporting an older black man.

"Where's Annaliese?"

"She's upstairs. Maggie's here."

She was helping the seated patient remove his blood-stained shirt when Maggie hurried into the room. Most of the blood on the shirt had come from a wound inside his left shoulder blade but it had clotted.

The problem now seemed to be what was seeping down his face over his jawbone and into his long white beard. Maggie turned on a lamp and had Grace hold it while she washed the beard and cleaned the gash running from his cheek to the side of his nose.

"Grace, get me some of that new sterile gauze and some tape." She continued cleaning and began to lay out tools for stitching the wound. "We can almost see your cheek bone in there, Mister," she paused. "I'm sorry, I don't know your name."

"It's Nate, Miss. Nate Harrison. No, I don't reckon you would. I can't member the last time I seed a doctor."

"Well, what happened to you, Mr. Harrison?"

"A couple of young fellers with too much hooch in 'em were havin' a little fun and got carried away." His accent was deep south, soft and almost melodious.

"Having a little fun, my eye," said Wash. "They jumped on him for no reason. One from the back with a club, and the other with a hook of some kind in the face. Came close to putting his eye out." He took a deep breath and went on. "Willie Ray, one of the boys from the nursery took him to the hospital but they wouldn't do anything, told him to leave, so he brought him to Kate's. Woman and I were still there, and I brought him over here."

While Wash had been talking, Maggie tied off the stitches in Nate's cheek and taped the dressing over the wound. While she'd been stitching his skin back together, Nate's face had remained impassive.

Cleaned of the dried blood, the injury on his back seemed to have come from a blow with a club of some kind and trailed down the back, becoming less severe as it came down.

"It looks like you were moving away from him when he hit you."

"Oh, I was tryin' to get away, alright. Just wadn't quick enough."

Annaliese had come into the room, and at this she snorted and looked disgusted. "Were these men or boys?"

"Tell you the truth, I didn't really notice, Mam. They was swinging things and I was just trying to get outta the way."

She turned his head and looked at the dressing on his cheek. "We need to report this to the police."

"No," said the man on the table quickly. "It wouldn't do any good and just cause trouble." Annaliese noticed the accent had suddenly changed.

"You don't think they would do anything?"

"That's exactly what I think," he said. He looked at her intently for a moment. "You ever been in Escondido?"

She shook her head.

"It's what they call a 'sundown town.' He looked at her with a serious expression on his face. "That means if you're a negro and you're in town after sundown you'll probably get shot or hung."

Annaliese gaped open mouthed at him and turned to look at Wash, who nodded in agreement. "I've heard that, too."

"Los Angeles is almost as bad," Nate said.

She was sure about the accent now. The man sitting before her was speaking good English, easily understood. It was as though he had been wearing a mask before, speaking the way it was expected he should.

A quote from her past echoed in her head. "A soft answer turneth away wrath." Maybe his life was lived behind a façade he had erected because he felt that was necessary to survive in his world.

Maggie was writing in a chart. "Mr. Harrison, we need to keep you overnight in case you should start bleeding again and there could be other problems that will show up overnight." She looked at Grace. "Can you help get him settled in 'C'?"

"No." The refusal was flat. "You don't need that kind of trouble."

He looked at Annaliese with a sly smile and slipped behind the façade again. "Laws no, Miss, I can't afford no doctor bill. I'll just go on home and ma woman can watch me." He struggled off the table and moved unsteadily toward the door. Wash steadied him with a hand and turned back to Annaliese, trying to suppress a rueful smile, which made Annaliese realize he had seen it too. She was glad she wasn't losing her mind.

"So how was your first night at the hospital?" said Johnny. "I was a little startled when I came home this afternoon and you were taking a nap."

"We drew lots and Maggie got the short straw, and then Tom Hendricks, so this is my shift."

"So, what's the routine? How many nights are you on call until you hand it to someone else?"

"We decided on three nights at a time and then off for three weeks. Este will work with me and Grace with Maggie. At least that's the way we figure to start. There are ten of us in the rotation so it shouldn't be too bad.

"I figured a nap might help me to start. Maggie said it comes and goes sometimes it was almost too much to handle and yet one night she slept all night. If she had someone at home she'd probably feel differently, but I think she'll volunteer to cover for others if need be."

She had just finished unpacking her things in the on-call room when the tube whistled, and her first shift began with a young boy injured in a fall while learning to ride a horse and continued steadily the rest of the night.

Twice in the middle of the night she was called out of bed to handle patients and Tuesday morning two Mexicans came in having suffered injuries on a construction job site, and she had to stay and help Maggie get them taken care of.

On the way out she passed the new administrator's office and since she had something on her mind, decided to stop and talk to him about it. They had met several times, and he looked up with a smile when she appeared at the door of his office.

"Come in, Dr. Fry. How can I help you?"

"Well, Mr. Robinson, you can begin by calling me Annaliese."

"I will if you call me Mica."

When she was seated, she said, "We had something happen at the clinic the other night and I don't quite know what to think about it."

"Oh, what was that?"

She explained what had happened with Nate Harrison.

His face didn't change expression, but he sat looking at her and running his tongue over his lower lip. Then he opened a drawer and slid some papers across the desk.

The more she read, the more wrinkles appeared in her forehead.

"Are there any more letters like this?"

He handed her more letters and, after she had scanned these, a petition with three pages of signatures that protested the treatment of Mexicans, Chinese and Negros at the hospital.

"These are letters from some people in the community. I think you need to read them and see how some in town feel about this issue. Then we can talk about how we should deal with it."

She went back to reading and he continued. "Actually, I think most of them live in the county."

Each of the several letters was a complaint about the idea of treating Mexicans and Chinese at the hospital and usually included a demand that the hospital facilities should be reserved for white Americans or at least provide separate facilities to treat 'foreigners' and 'niggers'.

She looked at him and pursed her lips in thought. "How do you feel about this?"

"Annaliese, I grew up in a system where that kind of thing was the rule, so I realize it's possible, even feasible, but I trained and worked in places where it was unthinkable. A hospital should be a place where the only criteria for service is injury or illness. On the other hand, we're new and I don't think we can ignore the opinions of the community."

"Have you discussed this with any of the other doctors in the county?"

"No. To be perfectly honest, since I knew it would probably affect you and your patients more than the rest of them, I thought I'd bring it up with you first."

She leaned back in her chair and looked up at the ceiling for a moment while she gathered her thoughts, then she nodded at him.

"OK, Mica, my first reaction is to explode like a bomb but over the years I have learned to count to ten in a situation like this." She took a deep breath and looked up at the ceiling again.

"This is the kind of thing that needs some thought. If I indulge my impulse, it could have ramifications that might cause long term problems for the hospital and the people around me. Sooo," she drew the word out, "before I answer your question, I'm going to discuss it with those people to see what we all feel about it. How's that?"

He smiled. "That makes me feel better. This is the kind of thing that can cause real problems in a community, and we have enough of those as it is, just getting started and all. I think that's a good way to approach it and I appreciate that. I imagine this is the kind of thing where you will want to write something so your position is clear. If you could discuss it with me before it's made public, that will give me a chance to formulate hospital policy taking it into consideration."

On the way home with Este, she was quiet, and her mind was so full of the problem she drove right by the store and didn't even notice.

On the train ride home, Johnny's mind had been churning with all that he'd learned and about the warning he'd been given. He tried to think of some sort of plan on how to pull it together, but by the time he walked in the store he hadn't gotten very far.

He greeted Harriet, the new girl, and Roy behind the counter, scooped up Jinx and put him on his shoulder and climbed to his room up under the eaves to sit and think 'til his wife got home. He knew she was supposed to finish her first three-day shift at the hospital today and would be tired but hoped she could listen to him for a while. Of course, he might need to listen to her too.

The whistle from the tube startled him. They had recently installed speaking tubes in the store and the rest of the house. With all the stairs in the place it made sense, especially with him being on the third floor so much.

"Is this my darling wife?" he answered.

"Yes, it is, but I don't feel so darling at the moment."

"Hard day?"

"Actually, not too bad, but I got handed a big headache as I was ready to come home."

"Sounds like you need to talk too."

"Yes, but since it concerns everyone, I'm going to wait 'til they all get here."

"Well, I've got to talk to Roy, so whistle when you're ready."

Roy knocked on the door jamb as he was finishing. He handed Johnny the usual sheaf of papers and sat down. Johnny glanced through them, asked a few questions then brought up what was on his mind.

Roy was a good listener. He didn't interrupt and when he wrote something in answer he was inclined to think about it first. For years Johnny's listener had been Wash who approached problems the same way but since he had a job and a lady friend he wasn't around as much as he had been.

Johnny had typed three pages of details on the investigation and watched Roy read them before he spoke.

"I need to get my head organized about this thing. There are certain questions I need to have answered and then I've got to figure out how to use the things I learn. So read that again and put on your thinking cap tonight. We can talk in the morning."

Since everyone she wanted to talk to would be at dinner, Annaliese waited until they had finished eating before she tapped a glass. Sitting around the table were Johnny, Lemuel, the Doctor, Roy, Maggie, Grace, Este, the twins and Mrs. Keane.

After Mrs. Keane had taken the twins upstairs, Annaliese read from two of the letters and the petition. "The petition is signed by thirty residents of the county. Most of them live outside the city."

She looked at her new student. "Este, you're part of our family now, and while I realize this might be a little difficult for you to hear, it's something that we all need to discuss. If you have anything you want to say I want you to speak up.

"That goes for each of you," she said, looking around the table. "We need to hear from everyone here. One thing I'd like to say before we begin talking. We need to keep our tempers. This is the kind of thing that could throw ripples out a long way in all directions and we need to consider the problem carefully. Our response should be measured and thoughtful."

She looked at her father and he nodded.

"This is not something I've had to deal with much," he said. "The Mormons are Christians, and they would never turn away someone in need of medical help no matter who they were.

"The sad thing is, most if not all the people who signed the petition are likely Christians too. On the other hand, there were few negros in the state, and the few Chinese were in Salt Lake City. There were some Mexicans, but they tended to stay in their communities, and I don't recall many times when I had to treat one.

"I know there was a lot of this kind of thing at the diggings, and in San Francisco to some extent and I know some of it got into laws and local ordinances, so it's not unexpected. How do we approach it? We're not reformers and can't expect to dictate how others should treat their fellow man, but somehow it seems a hospital should be different." He looked at Lemuel.

"Since I'm only marginally involved in this I won't say much," said Lemuel. "Whatever is decided here I'll support." He looked at Maggie.

She had a determined look on her face when she said, "This is one time you don't have to worry about me making jokes. I, for one, believe the idea is unthinkable but if they decide against us what will we do? A lot of our patients live in Old Town. If the powers that be decide to let these bastards get away with this, how should we respond? Speaking for myself, I could never support it or be associated with it.

"One other thing. When I was in Chicago I opened and looked at the insides of many kinds of people. I found that once you get past the skin there's not a lot of difference. People are people."

They all looked at Roy. He wrote swiftly on his pad and handed it to Maggie to read. *"I'm with Lemuel. However, you decide I'm with you."*

Grace was next. "I think it's terrible and I agree with Maggie. I wouldn't want to work there. I don't know what my parents would say but I don't think they'd like it. Of course, Papa has to think about his business. I guess I'll need to ask him."

"If it comes to that, I'll talk to him, or Johnny can." Annaliese looked at him. "Or shouldn't I put you in that spot?"

Johnny looked around the table. "Like the rest of you, I don't like it much, but I can remember some of the things I've read that make me realize it can be an explosive issue. Violence is not unusual among these people if we aren't careful about it.

I agree with Will. We're not reformers, but in this circumstance, I believe we should take a stand. He's right, a hospital should be different. So, I'll bring it up tomorrow when I meet with John if you like."

She smiled at him. "Thank you." She turned to Este. "What do you think about this, Este?"

Este sat up straight, raised her chin and said, "My Papa and I talked about this before I became your student. He said it might become a problem. He told me I should trust you to do what's right, and I do."

Annaliese closed her eyes and took a deep breath. She could feel an emotional surge deep inside her and tears in her eyes. "I'll do my best to live up to that. One thing I want you to understand. Regardless of what happens about this, you must not feel it's your fault. It's not. Whether you were here or not, we would have had to face this problem."

Lemuel spoke up. "Este, I'd like to hear what else your Papa said about it. I'll bet he and your family, indeed the people of Old Town, likely have a different view of all this one that might help us decide what to do about it."

The more Este talked the more relaxed she seemed. "My Grandfather was from the valley north of Los Angeles," she said. "He worked on a ranch when my father was born. He said it's been like this since after the gold, when all the Anglos came in and took over the government.

"New laws came that took the land from us. One set of laws for us and another for them. It used to be worse but even now things can be bad, especially north of here, around San Francisco and at the gold camps. Papa and Mama sometimes talk about hangings and murders."

"A lot of people in the county are farmers who came out here from the south," said Johnny, "and in the old Confederate States there have been movements to push the former slaves into the back of things, and from what I've seen in the back issues of the papers in town, there seems to be some of that here.

"One thing about it. When it comes to this kind of problem it don't take much to stir some people up. And some Anglos won't object, even if they don't like it. Don't want to rock the boat or upset their neighbors. I guess they don't see how it affects them."

"So, what do I tell Mica when I see him?" asked Annaliese, looking around the table.

"Have you talked to any of the other doctors about this?" asked Maggie. "Seems to me we might want to find out how they feel."

"And what about some of the business leaders in town?" asked Lemuel. "Mexicans spend some of the money they need to keep their doors open."

Annaliese looked at her father. "So, is the next step to contact the doctors in town and see what they say? And do we take this to the community and mount an organized effort, or do we try to deal with it on our own hoping that they will follow our lead?"

Maggie spoke up. "I'd like to hear what the doctors have to say, and we can go from there."

Everyone in the room was nodding. "Should we have a meeting then?" More nods. "OK, I'll get a list together. If it's agreeable I'll assign some of you certain people to contact? And of course, we'll need to decide when and where."

Will spoke up. "I'd say the sooner the better. We need to deal with this issue before it goes too far."

Chapter Twenty-Nine

Two nights later she was sitting at the mirror brushing her hair when Johnny came in from the shower. He kissed her on the head as he walked by on the way to sit cross-legged on the bed with the cat.

He loved sitting like this watching her brush her long red hair, watching it shimmer in the muted light. He could see in the mirror the way light and shadows played across her body where her robe was open. She had shaded the electrics, and it cast a romantic glow on the room, but still gave her light to see herself in the mirror.

"Well," he said. "I know you've had a busy day and so have I, so we better get started or we'll be up all night."

She finished counting and looked at him in the mirror. She sat for a minute, then shook her head and took a deep breath. "I can believe I'm taking all this time dealing with something that should be self-evident."

She sighed and crossed the room to join him, sitting cross-legged on the bed. "I met with the doctors this morning. The Doctor was with me. We laid it out for them, and if we'd talked all day, we couldn't have agreed on anything. There are fourteen doctors in town and ten were there.

"Three of them, Dr. Carter, Dr. Bledsoe, and Dr. Green, don't see it as an issue worth taking a stand on. They think we'll lose and see no sense in stirring up trouble. One of the two who weren't there probably feels the same. So, we probably have ten in our camp; that includes Maggie. Of course, the question is, will they stay in our camp and what do the people in our camp feel ought to be done about it?

"After the three left, those of us who remained decided to appoint a committee to meet with the board. Then we can put something on paper so when we meet with them, we'll have a plan. We'll see where it goes from there.

"I'm on the committee as chair, with Carter James and Tom Hendricks. We have to remember not to mix the Carters up. We have a Carter James and a Robert Carter, both of them new graduates.

"Tomorrow, we meet with the board. Then we'll see where we stand." She shrugged and one of her nipples peeked out of her gown.

"Behave woman," he said, grinning at her. "Just because you've finished doesn't mean we can play. I need to talk a little.

She smiled demurely at him. "Why sir, I don't know what you mean." He reached over and tucked it back in.

"There, that makes it easier for me to concentrate. I've spent the last two days trying to find out where my murder suspect is. I think I've been in every saloon in the county all the way down to the border. Finally got a nibble at a foul dive right down near Tijuana. Ever hear of Tia Juana City? No? well you're not missing much. Couple bars and a store or two.

"Anyway, it seems like my man comes in occasionally. When I mentioned his name, you could just see everyone hunch their shoulders. Took a while to get anything out of the bartender, but he finally loosened up. Old Mexican fellow. He's Consuelo's mother's cousin or something, so he talked to me. It seems he knows some people in Tijuana who hang around with Presgraves. I got some information from him but not much."

He ran his tongue over his lips and shook his head. "A good part of my life I've avoided saloons. Always thought I'd have fewer problems if I stayed out of them. Now I seem to spend a lot of my time in them and apparently, I stick out like a sore thumb when I walk into one. Everyone seems to know exactly who I am and that I'm nothing but trouble for them.

"Also, it seems like this guy is considered dangerous although no one will talk too much about that. I'll be glad when I can put this whole thing behind me."

"Shouldn't you have someone working with you? I remember you like to have someone backing you up in something like that."

"Several times today I thought the same thing. I may have to see if Wash can help me out for a while, though I hate to ask Kate.

"Going back to your problem. You do understand that even with me in pursuit of a murderer, you're in the middle of something that could be much more dangerous?

"Bigots can be dangerous. Mobs can do a lot of damage. Be careful. There have been more than a few murders and lynchings back east and there has been violence around here a time or two."

The next day Kate was waiting on a customer when Johnny came in.

"Hi Kate, Wash around?"

"He's in the back room."

He found his friend cleaning some tools. "I don't know if this is possible, but I might need some help. Think Kate would give you a little time off?"

"This thing with Herschel?" When Johnny nodded, he continued. "I was wondering about some of the company you'd have to keep. You need someone to back you?"

Johnny nodded. "I need someone I can trust, and I don't know any of the deputies well enough. I'd rather have you there."

"Your suspect have a name?"

"Barry Presgraves. I think you know him."

"When I was out in the dark back home, I heard him talking to Herschel a few times. I don't think he's a very nice fellow."

"Well, from what I hear, he's gotten worse. I remember Herschel didn't like him, but he never talked about him."

"Let's go talk to Kate and see what she has to say."

"About what?" Kate had walked in while they were talking.

"I need to borrow this fellow for a little while." Her mouth dropped open and he went on. "I'm working as a special deputy on Herschel's murder, and I need someone to cover me as a partner. To watch my back when I need it. He's the one I trust."

"For how long?"

"All I can say is, for however long it takes, but if it looks like I'm not getting anywhere I'll turn him back to you."

"Well, I'll miss him. You two be careful. A fellow who knows he's going to hang if he gets caught might be dangerous."

"That's why I need him."

Chapter Thirty

Mica Robinson looked up when Annaliese and the two men came into the office. "Thank you. I was hoping we'd have a chance to talk before I meet with the board."

When all three were settled in chairs she began. "Mica, this is a difficult situation and the potential for a problem is very high. The first thing I want to do is to hear how they feel about it, and then we'll have to sit down and come up with a policy we can move forward with. If their attitudes are anything like what we had to deal with among the doctors, we may be hard put to come up with an acceptable solution."

Mica nodded. "Acceptable to who and how many is the question." he said. "How do you see the problem at this point?"

"We feel hospital services should be available to all who need them. Since we don't have the resources to create separate facilities that means we treat everyone who comes to the hospital who needs it."

Mica thought for a moment. "And if the board doesn't agree with that?"

"We would have to consider what our next step would be."

"And would that step be not supporting the hospital?"

She looked at him for a long moment, holding his gaze. "We would have to consider what our next step would be," she repeated slowly and distinctly.

She looked at her watch and stood. "I assume you'll want to talk to us after the board meets?" When he nodded, she continued. "Dr. Hendricks is on duty today, so he'll be here and if it's alright with you we'll just wait with him. Do you mind if I ask what your position is on the issue?"

He took off his glasses and sat sucking the earpiece for a moment. "Generally, I'd say I agree with you and will present your position favorably, but if they decide otherwise..." he smiled at her ironically, "then, I will have to carefully consider what my next step would be."

It took a few days to arrange a meeting with Presgraves but finally, at the appointed time, Johnny and Roy were standing outside the Mexican saloon watching Wash disappear into the darkness of the alley that ran between two of the three buildings in Tia Juana City.

Wash had looked the place over earlier and was enroute to a window where he could see and hear what happened in the saloon. He was carrying Johnny's seventeen shot Henry rifle.

Out of habit Johnny drew the Colt and spun the cylinder, holstered it then pushed open the batwing doors. He stood for a second allowing his eyes to adjust to the dimness of the large, gaslit interior.

The room was crowded. A piano was being played badly and loudly against the wall, and just to one side of it the man he had come to see was sitting at a table alone, both hands around a glass in front of him. Behind him Roy moved and jacked a shell into the chamber of a Winchester.

Barry Presgraves looked up and smiled. He gestured to a seat at the table and said, "Got a message you wanted to talk. Don't think we've actually met, but I remember seeing you one night in San Francisco..." he paused and looked around. "In a place much like this. If I remember right, seems to me you were carrying a big shotgun that night." He half-stood and extended his hand.

Johnny smiled and touched his hat brim. He carefully pulled out a chair with his right hand and sat down, half facing the long bar, left hand resting on his leg and clear of the table

Presgraves' smile broadened and he nodded and settled back in his chair. "How can I help you?" He was a big man, broad across the shoulders and chest with a thick, dark beard, but his voice was high pitched, a little hoarse and strangely feminine.

Johnny scanned the men standing at the bar. Something about three of them made him feel he knew why they were there. He also knew that Wash, standing watching and listening through the window behind the man, knew it too.

"A mutual acquaintance of ours, Herschel Grieve, was found dead last week, murdered, in fact. I know you worked with him in San Francisco for a while and wondered if you might be able to give me some idea about who would do such a thing."

"Murdered, you say?" he asked, as though it was a surprise, but his face didn't show any surprise. "So old Herschel cashed in his chips. Well, I didn't like the bastard anyway."

"I heard that was the case. According to the medical examiner he was stabbed three times with something like an ice pick. I wondered if you knew anyone that carried a weapon like that?"

"Come to think of it, I do." Slowly he reached to his boot, drew out an ice pick and stuck it into the table before him so hard it quivered when he released it. The saloon had gradually grown quiet as the tension around the two men became evident.

Several of the men at the bar left. They knew enough to be out of the line of fire if it came to it. Johnny smiled at the ones who remained, the ones he had expected to.

"I'll bet that makes me the chief suspect, doesn't it? Of course, you'll have to prove it. That might not be so easy. Besides, I spend most of my time in old Mexico these days, so I'm not so easy to find if you ever start to look."

"You know deputy," he paused, "you are a deputy, aren't you?" When Johnny nodded, he continued. "You know, if I go to the outhouse here, I'll be pissing across the border. If you were to die in here tonight, the man who killed you could just disappear over there, and they'd never find him." He shook his head. "Funny thing is no one in here would be able to remember much about him."

"I'd say that's probably true, but I'll bet you realize I'm smart enough to know that. I'd also bet you don't think I'd be stupid enough to come down here alone."

The noise of the Henry being cockled in the dark outside the window behind the man was loud in the quiet room, and when everyone's eyes went to the noise, Johnny drew the colt and swung it to cover the men at the bar.

"You know, Mr. Presgraves, the one thing that's certain in your life right now is that you'll be the first to die if anyone in this room makes any sudden moves that might startle that fellow outside. From there he couldn't miss and he's carrying a seventeen shot Henry."

The mocking grin on the man's face was gone, and he shrugged. "That wasn't a threat, Fry. Just a warning."

The men at the bar had frozen, everyone with his hand on his gun. A Mexican and a couple of pug-uglies. All were caught flat footed by his draw, and all knew Roy was behind them.

Johnny's Colt was centered on the man in the middle, on the middle of his chest. Johnny held his eye for a second and said quietly, "You first. If anyone in here starts anything you'll be the first one I shoot."

The saloon was a frozen tableau, the silence complete except for night noises coming in the open window.

"You know, I was of two minds when I came here tonight," said Johnny over his shoulder, "but you've convinced me. So I'm going to take you back, and we'll hold you until the judge gets here and see what he has to say. There's a wagon outside and we have lots of ammunition."

This last he addressed to the men in the room, then he turned back to Presgraves. "If we suspect anyone of trying to interdict your transport to the hoosegow in San Diego," he paused, "let's say it would be a dangerous undertaking. Fingers will be on triggers, and we'll be nervous. We've plenty of ammunition and will be shooting to kill." He smiled at Presgraves. "Under the circumstances you might not live through it."

Roy was driving with Johnny sitting beside him, face turned to the prisoner, whose wrists were tied in front. Wash was sitting in the bed of the wagon with the Henry centered on Presgraves's back less than two feet away. There were several people watching out the door of the saloon when they disappeared into the night, but no one came outside.

Chapter Thirty-One

Annaliese shook her head in exasperation. She was pacing back and forth in her small office, frustrated and angry. The letter from the hospital board was on her desk and she had no idea how to answer it.

Her reflex was to tell them to go to hell, that they would take care of their patients and the white people of the town could have their hospital for all the good it would do them with most of the doctors not practicing there.

On the other hand, she remembered her remarks to the family about keeping her temper and not going off half-cocked on issues that could have long-term effects on everyone in the county and their health care, indeed, on their future in San Diego.

"Well, it looks like you got your answer. Was it what you expected?" Maggie had come in and seated herself in her usual chair.

Annaliese handed her the letter and watched as she read it.

"So, they take two pages to tell you they don't know what to do?"

Her father had appeared in the doorway, and they watched him take his seat. "I tried, but they're afraid to make a decision," he said. "So, until they can, it's a de-facto no Mexicans." He looked at them. "What do we do?"

"Well, we can make a decision about how we handle it, but we also need to talk to the other doctors about it." She took a deep breath. "Was Kate there?"

"Oh yes and she raised Cain about it, but she's only one vote."

"Can't believe they all went against us," said Maggie.

"I don't think that's necessarily the case," said Will. "I don't believe most of them like it but they fear the consequences. Situations like this can get violent and that frightens them."

"John will be back in the next day or two and we can talk to him about it. Actually, Johnny said he'll talk to him. Where are the girls?"

"They're upstairs," said Maggie. "I think they're both worried about this."

"So am I," said Annaliese. She sighed deeply and raised her eyebrows. "We've committed to Este and to her family, indeed to the whole Mexican community, and now this comes up." She shook her head. "So, what do we do?"

She stopped for a moment and said in a very measured voice, "Do I write them a letter and say we refuse to be a part of this action, or lack of it, I should say? I mean, that's how we all feel isn't it?" She looked at them and they both nodded.

"Well then, I'll telephone Mica and let them know. The other doctors in town can join us or not. For some of them I think it will be a toss-up. For some reason I think it might be better if each practice sends Mica a letter laying out the reasons we stand where we do."

She turned to her father. "Papa, I heard Lemuel say something once that applies to this kind of thing. He said, 'These people are trying to take from us under threat of violence. If we can stop them, we need to try.' I know you put a lot of yourself into the hospital but I'm glad you see it our way."

"You've got it backwards," he said with a tired smile. "I'm glad you see it my way. We're all in this together."

She was brushing her hair that night when Johnny finally got home. He kissed her on the top of her head, put Jinx on the bed and began to undress.

"Look at my hands," he said. She did and was surprised to see them trembling. She looked up at him, a question on her face.

"He's in jail."

"That guy you think might have killed Herschel?"

"Yes, about an hour ago. It wasn't until right now I realized my back has been tight as a fiddle string for the last few hours. I think that's why my hands are shaking. I just took a deep breath and suddenly I feel better.

"Wash and I went down there this afternoon, and Roy came down about dark with the wagon. We checked the layout and made our plans. We saw him come in a little after dark.

"Wash went down the alley and the window he was looking in was right behind the table where Presgraves was sitting. Roy came inside, Winchester in hand and stood by the door where he could see and hear everything that went on.

"I went in to talk to him, and when he threatened me, Wash cocked the Henry and Roy cocked the Winchester. It was amazing how quiet it got. They covered me while I disarmed his bunch and herded them into a corner. After that it was a matter of getting him outside into the wagon, and us getting out of town.

"Annaliese, the whole time I felt like I was handling a rattler. He's a dangerous man. Wash sat in the back with him on the way back and I was turned watching him from the front seat. He was looking at me the whole time and I had this feeling something was crawling up my backbone all the way to the jail."

She sat for a minute then shook her head angrily. "Damn it, now I've forgotten the count." She flung the brush down and turned back to face him.

"You didn't have anyone else with you? Where was the sheriff?"

"I didn't know I was going to arrest him. I was just going down there to talk. But when we got there and I talked to him I realized I believed he did it and I didn't think I should just let him walk away. He was too close to the border, and we can't go down there and look for him."

"Well, are you through with it now? No more sheriff's deputy?"

"I'll still have to testify at the trial, and I think I need to keep looking around for information. They'll need all they can get at the trial."

"You think he's the one?"

"Yes, I do. I talked to the sheriff, and he feels I had enough to arrest him, and he threatened me, knowing I was a deputy. He'll try to talk his way around it, but he did. That's when I realized he was likely the one. Why threaten me unless he wanted me to stop looking, and why stop me from looking unless he thought I'd find something?"

"At least you got out of it in one piece."

"That remains to be seen. He has a gang, a bunch that hang around the border where they can disappear if they need to. They could be a problem. Ed's going to let me have a deputy when I think I need one, and Wash and Roy will be spending a lot of time with me."

"Roy? Why are you bringing him into it?"

"He asked me to. He wants to help and he's handling a gun well enough now he'd be good to have around."

She shook her head and rolled her eyes. "As if I didn't have enough to worry about." She sat still for a moment, thinking, then told him about her letter to the board and her talk with Mica.

"Have you heard from them yet?"

"No. If they behave like they have been I probably won't for a while. They can't seem to agree on anything, much less something like this. This has political ramifications that scare the hell out of them. John and Kate are the only ones who aren't afraid of the consequences. The rest seem to feel they could be creating big problems for themselves down the line."

"So, you wait 'til they make up their minds?"

"No. We can't let them decide by doing nothing. We need to sit down and plan what we're going to do and do it. If we don't, they'll feel they've won and the people who support us or are in the middle on it will probably throw up their hands and accept the way things are rather than make waves."

The next day she wrote a letter to the hospital board and asked Roy to deliver it. Mica had him wait and wrote her a note in response. *Please come to see me as soon as can be arranged.*

Since she wanted to have things settled and needed to know the reaction she could expect from her letter, she telephoned Maggie at the clinic, told her she'd be back before long and set off for the hospital.

"From your letter I'm assuming you intend to withdraw your practice from association with the hospital, is that correct?" Mica laid his finger across his lips waiting for her to answer.

She took her time and laid out what she thought the board needed to do to avoid that eventuality.

"From what I've learned since I've been here," he responded, speaking slowly, "your father, Kate Sessions and John Spreckels were the driving forces behind bringing the hospital into being. If the three of them and you and some of the other doctors withdraw your support, it would likely be a crippling blow to efforts to bring needed services to the city, indeed to its entire future. Are you sure you want to take such a drastic step?"

"No, not at all sure," she shrugged, "but what choice do we have? The board's failure to act puts us in a position where they're saying we must support a reprehensible policy simply because they can't make up their minds.

"The people they want to exclude are citizens and residents. They supported the building of the hospital, and they support the business community with their patronage. Besides that, they are our patients and our friends, and in one case, a member of our practice. The other night Este told me she and her family believed I'd do what was right. I'll not disappoint them." She paused and held his glance. "Or myself, for that matter."

He templed his fingers in front of his mouth and was quiet for a moment. Finally, he said, "I have a little different problem than you. If you take this stance and the board comes around to your position in a couple of weeks or months, then you can re-engage with the hospital and move forward together. If I support your position, which I agree with by the way and resign then I'll have to leave, and the future I envisioned for me and my family when we came here will be gone."

He looked at her for a moment, letting that sink in. "To avoid that situation, I have to be willing to put into place a policy I disagree with. Do you understand what I'm trying to say?"

She looked at him, letting what he said reach her understanding. "So, what you're saying is that it's your responsibility to support the board's policy, but if it changes, you'll still be here to support our policy if they do come around."

"Exactly; I can only advise. If they ignore my advice, I still must do my job which is to administer the hospital under the guidelines they set. It's that or leave and I don't want to do that, at least not yet."

She sat quiet for a while thinking about it, then nodded. "I see what you're saying, and it seems like it might be best if I don't let the board know what you just told me."

He smiled. "They probably already know it but let's say we don't want to remind them."

"How do you think they will react to the letter?"

"I'd say it will make them consider things very carefully, knowing they're walking very close to a precipice that could be dangerous to their future plans and the future of the hospital in the city."

She stood and held out her hand. "From here on, let's meet at my office when we need to talk. It might be best if we're not seen together too often. Do you agree?"

He shook her hand and said, "I was hoping you'd see it that way."

As she climbed into her carriage at the front door she stopped, sat looking up at what they had built, and realized she liked that man a lot.

Wash and Johnny were sitting on a large piece of driftwood watching Roy practice. The boy had gotten to where his movements were smooth and seemingly almost instinctive, and his accuracy was improving noticeably.

"You boys go through a lot of brass out here. How often do you do this?"

"We come down here about once a month. I know a fellow who lives north of town that reloads and rearms them for me, so it keeps the cost down some."

They sat quiet for a while watching. Roy was getting so good that a floating piece of wood was soon reduced to splinters. "What's going on with the case?"

Johnny exhaled noisily and grinned ruefully. "Tell you what, if I'd have known how much time it would take and how much trouble it would be, I don't think I'd have gotten into it. Even though he's in jail I have to talk to people, try to find new evidence, and help them organize what we do know to get ready for the trial.

"Then there's the problem with his gang. I have no idea how they'll react to this. Are they going to come after me? Do I need to take the possibility seriously?

"I've got you looking out for me, but you've got a job and a wife." He paused and grinned at his friend. "Sort of anyway, and I can't keep you to myself just because I've gotten into something I probably shouldn't have."

He motioned at Roy. "He wants to help me with it and I like

having him around. Only trouble with that is Annaliese thinks he's too young and she still sees him as her patient so she's not too happy with the whole idea."

"How old is he?"

"He's coming up on twenty-one. Of course, things are different now than they were even a few years ago and this isn't the wild west anymore. People don't carry guns around here the way they used to or use them, for that matter. Lawmen occasionally do and sometimes for good reason, such as now, in the situation I'm in."

He turned his palms up. "I know Presgraves is a dangerous man but does his arrest put me in danger from his associates?" He shrugged. "I'd say your guess is as good as mine. He doesn't seem to be the kind of man that inspires devotion in his followers. But that doesn't mean I don't have to watch myself. They might have reasons for loyalty I don't know about."

Roy came up to stand at the log while he reloaded. He stooped, emptied his pockets of brass casings and put them in a bag Johnny had sitting beside him, then looked at Johnny inquiringly and gestured toward the cabin.

"I guess we better," said Johnny. "She may send the sheriff if we're not back soon."

While Wash walked on back to the cabin, Johnny stopped, sat down on the rock and gestured to Roy to join him.

"I talked to the sheriff, and he said he wouldn't object if you were to become my partner. He doesn't have enough help as it is, so he's glad to have the extra hand."

Roy nodded. Looking into his eyes, Johnny remembered what Annaliese had said about them: "dark, still pools". Johnny could see questions in Roy's eyes and somehow felt that Roy believed he, Johnny, would have answers. For some reason he seemed to feel the questions in his friend's eyes as though something in Roy's mind was touching something in his.

Fanciful? Maybe, maybe not. Everyone in the house had noticed Roy was different since the accident and Johnny had talked with each of them about the differences.

Since they spent the week together in Los Angeles and brought home a new method of communicating, he could feel them steadily growing closer. Could they be creating a new pathway between themselves, something beyond what others could see or hear or even understand? What if Roy's loss of speech created a circumstance where something like that was possible?

He smiled. What would Annaliese or Lemuel say if he tried to explain something that was fanciful to them? He could imagine their reaction. Should he try? Or should it be something between himself and Roy and no one else? Maybe if he spoke of it to someone else it couldn't exist.

"Can you arrange things at the store so it won't be a problem? I don't know how much of your time it will take," he said.

Roy took a pad and a pencil from his pocket and wrote, *"The girls can handle it."*

"First of all, I want you to understand Annaliese and how she feels about this so it won't be a problem. She's not happy about it at all. She still sees you as her patient and she also sees you as Greta's husband. In both cases she feels responsible for you to a certain extent. Of course, I do too but I accept the fact that you've become a man, and I'll treat you like one.

"She, on the other hand, sees you as though you're still a boy and she worries about you. It's her mother's instinct. She had it with Greta. Try to remember she's like that because she cares for you, so don't let it bother you.

"Now, about us working together. I have no idea what to expect from this situation I'm in. But the one thing I do know is I'd be foolish if I'm not careful. That means you have to be careful too.

"Careful means we need to be alert and watchful and to communicate what we see and hear with each other." He grinned at Roy. "Considering the circumstances we need to spend time thinking about ways to do that. Do you agree?"

Roy nodded and he continued. "Recently life seems to have put us into an unusual, indeed almost unique position and I'm beginning to wonder if maybe I can understand some of your thoughts."

They looked at each other in silence for a moment and Johnny saw no reaction on Roy's face, no look of surprise or incongruity. His friend's face was blank. Then he wrote quickly on his pad and handed it to Johnny.

"Me too," was all it said.

Chapter Thirty-Two

"He's working with me on the case for a while."

He was answering the look of surprise on John's face when he sat down, and Roy was sitting where Herschel usually sat.

"So how is the case going? Getting anywhere?"

"We have someone in jail. I think he probably did it. Now we just have to prove it which is what I'll be trying to do until the trial. Roy will be with me when I'm working on the case and help me think about it. I figure he needs to know whatever I know so that's why he's here."

John nodded a greeting at Roy and then said, "I heard you had this guy in jail, so you must have some evidence he did it. Any idea why?"

"We're still trying to find enough evidence to prove he's guilty. While we're doing that, we may find out why."

John was quiet for a moment, apparently thinking. "I won't pry about it. I'm sure it will come out in the paper while the trial's going on. Let's talk about the situation at the hospital."

For the next few minutes, they talked about the events before the board and their inability to reach a decision.

"It's a puzzle," said John, shaking his head, "and I'm not sure there's an easy answer to it. The potential for violence is there and I'm sure you understand there is more than one way to look at this. Personally, I don't see it as a problem, but I also realize there are those who think that it is. Some of us have large long-term interests in the future of this place and a split over something like this in the community could jeopardize those interests."

"By the way," said Johnny, "Annaliese told me to tell you how much they appreciate your opening up your home to Este and letting her work with Grace's tutors. She also wants you to know she realizes you have to consider other factors on this issue, and they may affect your decisions. If we disagree on this, we hope it won't affect our relationship."

John smiled. "I can't imagine how it could." He turned to Roy and said, "I'm glad you're going to be meeting with us. Any time you have something to share please do so."

When they were on the ferry crossing the bay, Roy handed him a note. *"Nice fellow."*

"Yes, he is," responded Johnny, "but he has his own fish to fry. I hope his don't taste too much different from ours."

Johnny was sitting up under the eaves reading when the voice tube whistled. "There's a customer down here who would like to talk to you."

When he walked into the store Pauline, a new girl behind the counter, gestured to where a man was sitting glancing through a newspaper. When he folded the paper and laid it down, Johnny was looking into the face of Barry Presgraves, and the man was smiling at him.

"Thought I'd drop by and surprise you. Aren't you glad to see me?" He had stopped smiling and Johnny's left hand felt for the gun that wasn't there.

"Didn't think you needed it anymore with me in jail, did you?" he said, noticing Johnny's hand. When Johnny didn't answer he continued. "The judge said you didn't have enough evidence to hold me, so he made the sheriff let me out. Maybe you'd better put it back on." He stood, folded the paper slowly and deliberately, put it down and walked out of the store, closing the door behind him.

When Carlotta answered the door, Lemuel was standing there with a big smile. "Are they up yet?" he asked.

He followed the maid into Madame's San Diego 'cottage' and found the ladies finishing breakfast before a large window looking out at the ocean."

"Ladies," he said, removing his hat and taking an available chair. "You've been gone for a few days."

"We've been in Los Angeles for a while and got home late last night," said Sarah. "We were tired and decided to make an early night of it. We were just getting ready to telephone the store and invite everyone for dinner at the Del."

"I'm assuming you mean Kate too, so I'll let her know."

"Oh yes, and Wash and Woman if they'll come," said Madame. "They wouldn't last year when we were here."

"They may surprise you this year," he said. "They seem to have changed a bit. They came to dinner at the store a couple months ago, a first for them. I think this is home now and they're getting more comfortable."

He accepted a cup of coffee when Carlotta refilled theirs and they exchanged news. When they had covered everyone, Lemuel said, "Since you were here for the opening you might be interested in what's going on at the hospital." By the time he finished explaining it to them, the ladies were sitting open-mouthed with looks of amazement on their faces.

"But this is horrible," said Madame. "What are Annaliese and Will going to do?"

"They're still trying to figure that out. They can't accept what is being proposed but they haven't quite figured out what the next step is. Of course, they were planning to work at the hospital and admit and treat their patients there but since it doesn't seem like that's going to be possible, they're trying to come up with a plan to move forward."

Madame shook her head. "I can remember some pretty bad goings on a few years ago back home, especially around Sacramento and the diggings. Some of it in the city, too. I know there are laws on the books in some places. Of course, there are more Chinese up there. You don't have many Chinese down here, do you?"

"Not many, here it's Mexicans, Indians and anyone else who's not white apparently," he said. "We had a meeting at the house to talk, and I know Annaliese and the rest of them are upset about it. They do realize it's an explosive issue that can divide the city and could bring on violence but there's no question which side they'll come down on."

"Well, more than half her patients are Mexican, aren't they?" asked Sarah.

"More like three out of four," replied Lemuel. "And besides that, she has taken on another student. Consuelo's daughter, Estelida. If they don't want Mexican patients, what are they going to say about her working there?"

Though her mind was busy with the problem at the hospital, Annaliese felt a warmth sitting at the table with these people. These were her friends. She could talk to them and learn from them, knowing they were true, and this was one time she needed to find out what they thought.

"Talked to Lemuel this morning. He says you've got some trouble at the hospital," said Madame, leaning forward to talk around Sarah.

"That's right. I think we've decided where we want to go," replied Annaliese, "now we just need to decide how to go about it. We had so much pinned to the idea that we had accomplished something here and would move forward as a community. Now we're back where we started, trying to figure where we go from here."

"Why don't you talk to Lemuel about it? He had an interesting point of view about the issue when we talked this morning."

Annaliese looked at her in silence for a long moment then turned to the others at the table and tapped on her waterglass. When everyone had turned to look at her, she said, "Lemuel, talk to us."

He looked taken aback, then glanced at Madame, who nodded at him.

He took a few moments to gather his thoughts and said, "One thing I have at the warehouse is time to sit and think so lately I've been thinking about what's going on at the hospital." He paused and looked around. "One time, back east, I read of a fellow who wrote, 'It is a characteristic of wisdom not to do foolish things.' Now it seems to me we have to think about how we're going to handle this and make sure we don't do something foolish. We already know why they're acting the way they are. What we need to do is figure out the best way to handle it."

He took a drink of water and continued. "This looks like bigotry, plain and simple, and from what I've read bigots are passionate about what they believe. Usually we're talking about emotions; things like fear, hatred, anger, and the impulse to protect what you have. We need to be careful we don't oppose emotions with emotion because that way nobody wins; there's just more fear, hatred, and anger.

"I believe we should face this whole problem using wisdom and not do foolish things." He paused again to let that sink in.

"Let's say, instead of angrily opposing these people, we go back to what we wanted to do when we had the idea for the hospital in the first place. We wanted to make things better for the people who live here. We still want that.

"Unfortunately, there are people around here who believe only the favored few, white people, that is, should reap what we all have sown. If we oppose these people they're not going to listen. It will only make them more determined to pursue their bigotry, with violence if they believe it necessary.

"To win this fight and gain what we're aiming at, maybe we should just ignore the other side. Let them do what they want to do rather than waste time and energy trying to stop them or argue with them. Instead, let's work toward providing the benefits to the rest of the people, the ones denied those benefits by bigotry of this kind."

"There are enough people around here who stand with us. We can do this! But we can't do it if we act like they do, with anger and hatred. If we try that we'll end up with everyone shouting at one another and nobody will win."

He looked around the room, pausing at each of them, finally stopping at Annaliese. "Let's outsmart the bastards. Let them do foolish things." he said.

Johnny was sitting on the rock talking to Wash and Roy was listening.

"Suddenly, I could feel my heart beating when I saw him sitting there. Startled the hell out of me. Without even thinking I put my hand on my gun, but it wasn't there. The man is dangerous, and you can see it around him, almost like," he paused, searching for a word, "an aura or something."

Wash shook his head. "I don't like the sound of that. Did he threaten you?"

"No, there was no threat, but that's the problem. The threat was implied. He knows I must react simply because he's free, because he's out there walking around, because he might do something, but what? We have no idea. Will he plan and work toward revenge or just sit back and feel the satisfaction of knowing I'm looking over my shoulder every day of my life?"

He looked at Roy. "What do you think?"

Roy looked back, expressionless for a second, then shrugged. He sat looking at Johnny for a moment then closed his eyes and tapped his forehead.

Johnny chuckled. "Yeah, me too. I need to think about it." He shook his head. "And if that isn't enough, I have to tell Annaliese about it tonight."

"What are you going to tell her?" asked Wash.

"I'll just lay it out for her and see what she says." He looked at them. "What if it's all in my mind and he's just playing me for a fool?"

"Is that what you believe?"

Johnny was quiet for a moment, thinking. He shook his head. "No. I believe he'll want revenge and will do anything to get it."

Wash stood and patted him on the shoulder. "Keep thinking like that. It will likely help you stay alive."

He had been listening to her talk of the dinner and about Lemuel's idea of how to move the practice forward. He loved the way she was smiling at him in the mirror. He could see she was excited about the idea and the challenges of trying to make it work and he really hated what his story would do to her excitement.

When she finished and put the brush down, he took a deep breath and plunged. "You know, as we get older this sharing everything with one another gets harder."

She gave him a puzzled look. "What do you mean?"

"A little while ago I walked into the store, and he was sitting there smiling at me."

"Who?" She was looking at him and he could see her face change into a look of horror as she realized who he was talking about. "That guy you have in jail?"

"That's the problem. He isn't in jail anymore."

"What?! Why?

"The judge said we didn't have enough evidence to hold him." He gave an ironic chuckle. "Told Ed that, in the future, not to use amateurs. He said we'd jumped the gun arresting him and he let him out."

"What did he say?"

"Ed told him no one else had any better ideas about how to go about it. The judge said he was in his office and available anytime to answer any questions they had about things like that. If we'd have gone over the evidence with him, we wouldn't have made the mistake in the first place."

"I didn't mean the sheriff, what did the guy you had in jail say downstairs?"

"For future reference, his name is Presgraves. He didn't say much. When I reached for my gun, he noticed it wasn't there. He told me I might want to start carrying it again. Then he walked out the door."

"He wanted to scare you?"

"He wanted to get inside my head whether I want him there or not. Wash and Roy and I sat out at the rock and talked about it. Roy listened anyway and I've been thinking about it since he walked out the door."

"What are you going to do?"

He'd been standing at the window staring out while they talked. Now he turned toward her. "That's going to take some thinking. When I figure it out, you'll be the first to know."

"What did Wash say?"

"He pretty much said 'say your prayers and keep your powder dry'. In other words, he thinks it's a serious threat." After a moment of quiet he continued. "I tell you what I'm not going to do. I'm not going to let him change my life. That's what he wants me to do. Be scared. Jump at every sound. Be suspicious of strangers. I need to be myself and not become someone else because that's what he wants. Can't do what he wants cause then he'd win, even if he does nothing."

He turned to face her again. "I'll have to start wearing the Colt again and I think Roy will be carrying too. I won't go looking for it but if it comes, I need to be ready."

"I agree. You do what you feel will keep you safe."

"I don't know if he'll hire someone like his old boss did or try to do it himself, but I suspect the latter. I think it just might be a personal thing, something he wants to take care of himself."

Chapter Thirty-Three

Beginning the next day the practice came together, made their first plans based on Lemuel's idea, and began to move forward with them. Given that they had property at the office and the clinic, they decided to enlarge the office area to include several more rooms for treatments or overnight needs, a room for surgical procedures, and one for emergencies.

What they had learned about necessary equipment and costs for the hospital they could now put to good use. Remodeling the clinic downstairs for expanded patient care would still leave the upstairs available for Maggie as an apartment.

The Saints had built a house for the Doctor and his family, which included one of his wives and several of his children. Over the two and a half years since he arrived, the Mormon community had grown and combined with the Mexicans and a growing practice among the Anglos it looked like they would stay busy.

They talked with the other doctors in town and to John and Madame and other potential donors and began to feel realistic about their prospects for having some kind of facility that would allow them to provide the services needed for their patient population.

Ultimately, only three of the doctors in town fell in with them the rest deciding their patient's and the city's interests were best served in remaining associated with the hospital regardless of a policy they abhorred.

Soon the sound of saw and hammer resounded in the store again. They also contracted for additional parking space for carriages and an enlarged stable for horse traffic. The equipment they had ordered would give them a capability approaching that of the hospital. Meetings and discussions led them to consider the need for an administrator, but they decided to wait and see how things developed once the expansion and equipment were in place.

Several times the hospital board had approached them, but everyone on Annaliese's side seemed happy with the impending arrangements and weren't that interested in discussions about rejoining the hospital staff and giving up what was becoming an enticing future of their own.

As it was, Annaliese had taken on much of the paperwork and communication necessary to make things happen. She spent more time than she liked in her office with this stuff and one day a couple of weeks later she was growling to herself about it when her voce tube whistled.

Her husband's voice came over the tube. "Annaliese, are you busy?"

"No, just doing paperwork," she answered. "What do you need?"

"Fellow down here to see you. Shall I send him up?"

"Do," she replied and stood to greet him. She was surprised to see Mica Robinson, the hospital's administrator, open the door. She was glad to see him. She poured him coffee and asked, "So, to what do I owe this pleasure?"

"I just wanted to stop by and talk about things."

"What things?"

"Well, you are a competitor of sorts now and it behooves me to keep an eye on what you're about. So, what are you about?"

"First, tell me about the hospital. How are things? Are you staying busy?"

"Not so much. You know, of course, we built for our future needs rather than what was needed today, so it's not supporting itself, if that's what you're asking. There are days when it's eerily quiet in my office and there are never many inpatients as of yet. How are you and your people getting on?"

"We're busy enough and we have plans to grow."

"I can see that. Both here and at the clinic." "You've been over there?"

"Oh yes. The board has asked me to keep an eye on you and report back. I get the impression you don't have plans to rejoin us in the future."

"I don't believe so. We decided not to engage you on the issue. The idea is pretty much to ignore you and go about our business and I believe all of us are looking forward to a future as an independent organization that won't have problems with deciding who we treat. The more we think about it the better we like the idea."

"You know, I thought that might be the case. Will you be needing an administrator?"

She was startled by the question, and it showed in her face. "We've talked about it," she said slowly, "but we've decided not to at this point. Why? Are you looking for a job?"

"I don't know, at this time." He smiled at her, almost a grin. "The way things are over there, they're getting nervous about my salary, not to mention the other costs that are running up. It could be things will get so bad they won't be able to afford me, and I have a family to feed -- not large at present but my wife is expecting, so it's on my mind."

"I'm not sure we could afford you right now. Maybe later, but we don't even really know where we are at the moment."

"I don't want to press you right now. Just put a bug in your ear. Keep me in mind when you think about your future, will you?"

"What I will do is talk to the other doctors and see what they think. If something comes up, I'll drop you a note."

As he closed the door, she was thinking what a relief it would be to get all this paper in someone else's hands.

Johnny stood looking out the front door of the barn at the pouring rain and the dark, heavy-looking clouds that extended to the horizon north and west. Behind him he could hear the sounds of Roy disassembling his pistol and laying out the tools so they could clean their weapons.

This was the first time they'd had to practice indoors in a while. Lately they had been on the beach several times a week and Johnny's hand was getting calloused from handling the Colt again. With Barry Presgraves walking around, it seemed like it might be important. Though they were working inside they still had the habit of cleaning the Colts just because they needed oiling, even if they hadn't been fired.

Roy looked up at him and Johnny said, "No, I'll do mine, but thanks anyway." As he said this, he realized something. "You thought that didn't you?"

Roy was looking at him intently and nodded slowly.

"Did you try to do it?"

Again, the slow nod. Roy's dark pools had a speculative, maybe a questioning look in them.

"Is it all right?" Johnny could hear the words as though they were spoken but they hadn't been, couldn't have been.

"I guess it is," said Johnny. "I need to think about it. Never had anyone inside my mind before. Is that what's happening? Are you inside my mind?"

Roy nodded again. He picked up his pencil and began to write. *"I think so but not like I'm reading your mind. Nothing like that. Sometimes I can guess what you're going to say but I don't hear your thoughts if that's what you mean. I've found out that if I think about it hard, I can feel something connect between us, like I'm touching you just enough to get your attention. Then I think maybe you can hear some things I think about. Not all the time, but sometimes."*

Johnny let out a long breath. His eyes seemed to be locked in place, focused on Roy's eyes, not really staring, just hard to look away.

With an effort he finally turned away and looked out the open door at the rain. After a minute he said, "I don't know how I feel about that."

He took off his hat and ran his hand through his hair. "What say we sit down and try to figure out what it is and what it isn't. Define it a bit. Then maybe we can figure out how to use it, find what's possible and what's not." He paused. "For example, what if I'm in the house and you're out here? Can you still do it, or do you have to be looking at me or at least be close?"

He turned and said, "I doubt if we'll ever understand how or why it began, but if we experiment with it a bit we can learn what's possible."

Suddenly he heard the words, *"other people?"*

He smiled. He wasn't surprised or shocked this time when it happened. From here on it seemed he would recognize it for what it was. This voice in his head would become a part of his life, a strange new thing. How would it affect him? Would it change him? And what kind of special relationship would he have with the only person in the world who could think thoughts at him?

And of course, one big question about it was, should they tell anyone else? What if it disappeared if others knew about it? Was that something they should risk, or should they keep it to themselves and see how it affected their lives?

And yet, he didn't know if he could keep it from his wife. Their commitment to always sharing was a cornerstone of what they were. How would she feel if, down the road a bit, she found out he'd kept something this significant from her? Did he want to risk her hurt, maybe anger?

He turned back to look at the rain.

"This rain could be dangerous."

"Yes, it could be," he agreed. "I've seen the lakes behind those dams up in the hills. If one or more of those dams fail or are even overtopped, it could mean a disaster in the city. We would likely be all right here, up on the hill like we are, but there are places that would catch it full bore. It's like living in the mouth of a shotgun. If the trigger gets pulled the damage could be severe and widespread."

"What can we do?"

"We could warn everyone we talk to, especially family and friends. Maybe we should move the books out of the warehouse. That inventory would be hard to replace, and we have enough room to store it here."

He was quiet, thinking. "Could probably use the telephones, though they may not be working. Last time we had a rain like this they were out for a while, just like the electrics."

Before long they were skirting the pools of rainwater on the way to the house to begin warning people of the danger they faced if the rain continued.

John Spreckels was thinking along the same lines. Even better than Johnny, he recognized the amount of water pouring into the lakes backed up by the dams in the county for the danger it was. He had recognized the significance of water in his plans for the city, and one of Heschel Grieve's main responsibilities had been reporting back on any water related issues raised at city hall or in the county.

Their rides into the hills to look at dams and examine watersheds had been a monthly routine and he had assessed the machinery and capabilities of each of the completed dams and had monitored the progress of the one under construction.

He was sitting on the porch of the fifth-floor meeting room looking out over the city when his wife joined him with Grace in tow.

"How're my two favorite girls?" he asked, glad to have something to take his mind off the water pouring from the sky.

"Actually, two of my three favorite girls," he amended with a grin.

When they were seated and had ordered tea Lillie said, "Grace has some questions about how you feel about the situation at the hospital."

He looked at his daughter and sat waiting. She seemed to be a little reluctant at first but finally took a deep breath and said, "Papa, I know you have supported the hospital from the beginning and that this problem with the Mexicans and all has put you in a spot."

He nodded. "Yes, it has. I have a lot of business interests in the city and there are people among them who have come down on both sides of the issue, which means I have to take a careful approach to the whole thing. On the other hand, what I do will affect what many of them choose to do."

"I understand," she said. "Mama and I have talked about it, and she explained it to me. That's why I haven't said anything to you about it. But now I need to know if you can help us at the clinic."

He sat waiting for her to go on. He could see she was struggling with what she wanted to say.

"When it all started, we had a meeting and Este, and I were there. We all agreed we were not going to fight against those people but instead were going to try to put together a way to give the Mexican and Chinese people of the city what they were being shut out of at the hospital."

"Everyone at the practice has put in some money and so have others in town but we need more help. Because they don't want to put you in an uncomfortable place, they won't ask, but I want to know if you can help us make it work." She clearly had rehearsed what she wanted to say and was visibly relieved she had been able to get it out. Now she sat back in her chair, holding her mother's hand and waiting for him to respond.

"I don't see that it's a problem to support both sides of the issue, but I can't let myself get drawn into the controversy behind it. As much as I disagree with them, it's not my place to dictate to anyone what to believe." He paused and looked at her meaningfully.

"Sometimes disagreements with these kinds of people can lead to violence. Where they grew up and lived their lives before they came here, this is a perfectly normal thing to advocate, and they see it as a threat to themselves and their families.

"What I can do is assure Annaliese and Johnny that I will help them provide medical care to the Mexican community in the county. You can tell Annaliese so and have her send me a letter with the details of what they need. I'll see what I can do."

"Oh, thank you Papa."

He held up his hand. "Don't think I'm doing this just because of you. It's the right thing to do, and if you weren't involved with them, I would still try to contribute. Also, if the rest of her community is anything like Este, I can see it will be money well spent."

"Since we got that settled, I want to change the subject," said Lillie, and she leaned forward, concern on her face. "Are you worried about all this rain?"

"I am," he replied. One of his secretaries came onto the porch as he said this and said, "Sir, Johnny Fry is calling for you."

He nodded, rose, and said, "I'll be back."

They could hear him talking into the receiver and within a few moments he was back. "That was Johnny," he said. "He's worried about the dams and says we need to spread the word as best we can to warn people about the danger involved." He turned to the steward. "Let Harold know I want to meet all department chiefs in my office as soon as it can be arranged." He took Grace's hand. "I think it might be best for you and Este to be where you can help if you're needed. It's nice that the place sits on the hill like that. It should be out of danger up there."

She came to hug him. "Thank you again, Papa."

"That smile is all the thanks I need," he said. "Now you two get out of here so I can get to work. It looks like it's going to be a long day."

Chapter Thirty-Four

Woman was soaked to the skin, and even though they were both wet, tired, and muddy, Wash really couldn't help grinning.

"You know, your nipples look like they're going to punch a hole in that shirt."

"I'm cold," she said. She reached out, touched him, pulled him close to her, chest pressed into his. "How does that feel?" she whispered, not really caring if anyone else noticed her.

His arms circled her, pulled her tight and held her. "Gives me another reason to get home and take off these wet, dirty clothes."

Outside the rain continued. They had come up on the porch to catch their breath before plunging back into the fray, a fight to keep as much of Kate's life as possible away from the rising water.

The proximity of the canal to the nursery had been a big reason for its success over the years and Kate had been the first to use concrete and rock walls to retard erosion along both sides. Others, including the city, had followed her lead until the water flow throughout the city had been tightly constrained for miles and thus did not behave as it had before man had stepped in to 'tame it'. Now the unrestrained current had forced the rising water out of its banks, and already it was swirling around their legs in places.

They were trying to move as many young trees and plants as possible, and wagon after wagon had headed for higher ground. Everything that could be moved was being loaded onto wagons while men and women working frantically along the edge of the rising water were being forced steadily back through what they were trying to save until they too would have to abandon the fight and seek higher ground.

Kate joined them on the porch. Like everyone else, she was soaked through and muddy from top to bottom. "Looks like it's time to quit and get out. Have we decided where we're going from here?" she asked Wash.

"We've been taking the trees and stuff up to your place and some over to the store, but you don't have room for all of us. If I thought we could make it we'd head home, but I don't think the bridge over the Otay is open, even if it's still there." He looked at Woman. "Should we go to The BookSeller?" She nodded.

"We'll get this last load unloaded and then head over there," said Wash. He looked at Kate. "Are you going to stay there or go somewhere else?"

"I may go with you. Once we get to my place, we can make sure everything's as safe as possible, then we can see what's happening in the rest of the city. They'll probably know what's going on. We can see if we can help somewhere. Because it's on high ground it should be safe."

The water had already begun to climb inexorably up the steps below where they were standing when finally, Wash led them out the front door into the pouring rain.

The store was already crowded when they got there. Whole families were sitting together on the floor in the store itself, and the house was surrounded by many of the trees from the nursery. Every square inch in any shed or building was filled with plants or books.

Annaliese, Maggie, and the girls had joined Will at the clinic.

Because the store was filling up with refugees from the low parts of the city, the clinic had become the intake area for any medical problems.

Johnny was sitting at Annaliese's desk talking with Roy and Lemuel when the refugees from the nursery arrived. Lemuel shared with them what he knew of what was happening in the city.

"Much of the lower part of the city has been evacuated," he said, "and I think the hospital might be flooding as we speak. When we were coming up here you could see the water headed that way. I don't think it will be the last area in town to flood. A lot of New Town will be underwater if it keeps up."

"What about the dams?" asked Kate. "Have you heard anything about them?"

"No," said Johnny. "I talked to John Spreckels before the telephones went out and he said several of the roads up into the hills are washed out and he's had no way to find out anything."

"Do you think they'll hold?" asked Kate.

Johnny shook his head. "There's an awful lot of water behind Sweetwater Dam and it will only hold so much. Even if the dam holds, the water might top over and could wash out some of the supporting walls. If that happens it won't just be rising water. It might be rushing water. A lot of it, and all at once."

They all looked at him in silence. "What about the Otay dam?" asked Wash. "They were close to finishing it weren't they?"

"John Henderson is downstairs with his family," said Lemuel. "He told me the lower bridge over the Otay River is closed. Said he wouldn't be surprised if they lost it. It's wood and it's not built for something like this. About the dam itself, I've not heard anything."

"I guess that means we're stuck in town for a while," said Wash. "Don't have any idea what will happen if that one goes. That creek that runs by our place comes out of a spring up in the hills. It didn't flood the last time we had a big rain but this one looks to be a lot different."

"It seems like all we can do now is wait and see what's left when it stops raining," said Johnny.

It was dark when Johnny left the clinic. He had come to let them know about the flooding of the hospital and stayed to talk about what they could expect as a result. With no way to let people know where they were and what they provided, they began a word-of-mouth campaign with everyone telling as many people as they could about the clinic. Maggie had opened her apartment upstairs as a place for the staff to rest and eat, and they had stocked all the food, water, and medical supplies they could carry up the narrow stairs.

As dark as it was and with all the water collected in puddles in the streets, it was difficult to navigate the familiar route back to the store. He was about halfway there and had stopped to catch his breath and comfort Black when he heard a sound like a locomotive passing through a tunnel. It was the sound of rushing water, a lot of rushing water, below them.

It seemed to come from north and east of him, but in the pouring rain and dense darkness he could see nothing beyond ten feet, so he had only his imagination to tell him what was happening in the city below him.

Men have been building dams from time immemorial. The purpose of a dam is to control water. Water storage, flood control, water diversion for canals, industry, and irrigation, and in our own time, the production of electricity. But wherever water is dammed there is always the danger of water doing what water eventually does; that is, change things.

The great river valleys and many canyons and gorges of the nation are all testament to what water can do over time. Once in a great while, however, the changing energy of a body of water is released suddenly and with great force.

The water in a beautiful lake formed when a river is dammed is potential energy. When it rains, the dam stores that energy and is designed to release it under controlled conditions that protect and enrich people and their livelihoods situated downstream.

If some natural or man-made event triggers the release of that water suddenly, or the water rises high enough to 'top over' the dam, then man's plans go out the window and the energy of that water will be applied to the area downstream, suddenly and with sometimes catastrophic effects.

Johnny was up under the eaves when dawn began to reveal what the city looked like the morning after. For years now he had spent hours each day sitting at this desk watching a prosperous, beautiful city slowly grow up around him. His view was north and west, and this morning there wasn't much he recognized. Some of what he did recognize wasn't in the same place it had been the day before.

What he could see of the bay was clogged with flotsam; lumber, whole houses, wagons, trees, and there were bodies, more livestock than human, but still too many of each. The river and the canal were still out of their banks, and much of New Town was in ruins or standing in two or three feet of water. Though he couldn't see the hospital, he knew it was flooded.

So, what did that mean to Annaliese and the practice? In the short term, they would probably be inundated with injuries and illness. He knew that among the people who needed the clinic's help would be some of those who had stirred up the problems at the hospital.

How would they react to having to come into Old Town, among the Mexicans, bringing their loved ones to be helped and healed by people they wanted to exclude from that same help and healing?

Long term it would probably help. Years before, he'd read that prejudice was to judge without knowledge; in essence, to judge before you knew what you were judging. That sounded about right to him, so maybe they would get to know each other and solve what, before it started to rain, was a big deal. This morning it didn't really seem very important anymore. The most important thing about this day was that it was still raining.

Johnny had been right; they were inundated. Annaliese looked across the body lying on the table between them and said, "That's three so far tonight and it's just beginning. You know that's more tonight than I've had to pronounce this year."

Grace shook her head. "There'll be more, won't there?" Tears were in her eyes. The little boy had blond hair and looked to be the same age as her youngest brother. They hadn't been able to stop the bleeding from his face and neck where he'd been struck with something, something heavy and jagged and moving rapidly in the water.

"Now I must tell his mother, though she won't be surprised. I could see it in her eyes when they brought him in." She looked at Grace. "I'd give you a hug, but I don't have time." A weak smile peeked through the tears she could see as she led the way from the room.

There were four rooms on the first floor of the clinic and two of them were crowded with people. Men, women, children, and even a cat were lying on the floor, leaning against walls and sitting on every flat surface. The air was warm and moist throughout because everyone was wet, and the floors were muddy with an occasional puddle. An earthy smell permeated, and they could hear crying and moaning as they began to examine a woman who seemed only partly conscious.

After talking to the parents of the child who had died, she and Grace followed two men carrying the woman into the treatment room on a stretcher. On the way they passed several other doctors and nurses working among the people. There were five doctors and a dozen nurses and orderlies who had responded to the flood, and everyone was working steadily in the face of a crisis. Indeed, that was all they could do; work steadily and keep working steadily until it had passed.

She could see dawn out the window, and in the distance the

wreckage of their beautiful city. Around her the strange glow and smell of kerosine lamps felt unreal. They had gotten used to the electrics, but they had flickered and died hours ago. Besides Maggie, herself, and the Doctor, three of the doctors associated with them had found their way to the clinic at different times of the night. Even so the front rooms were filled with the injured and dying.

Most of the injuries seemed to be from being struck with flotsam of one kind or another. Trees, boards, wagons and even a water tower. There were rails and rail cars at unusual places around the city, some a good distance away from any tracks.

There were bales of barbed wire that had washed out of a hardware store. Strung out by the force of the water, it had wrapped itself around whatever it came into contact with. There was plenty of glass, small pieces of metal, and nails in the flood, so gashes and punctures were common. Anything moving at the speed of this current could injure or destroy.

She had been surprised when Mica Robinson showed up with his family. "My wife and I can help down here if the children can stay upstairs," he said with a hopeful smile. She was amazed at how helpful he had been, and his lovely wife Helen had been an extra pair of hands wherever they seemed to need one.

Mica was an administrator with all that entailed, including the movement of what was needed and the disposal of what was not. So far, their efforts had been enough to keep them ahead of their needs, but if they ran out of things, the flood had badly compromised their ability to replace them. Especially medical supplies: they must be careful with what they had.

The telegraph and telephone had disappeared with the poles that were floating in the bay, scattered around the landscape, or in one case, poking through the window of a house turned over on its side. The switching yard was damaged, and part of the repair shop was missing.

With the bridges washed out, a train couldn't come within several miles of them and had to back out of the city after it unloaded because there was no place for it to turn around.

There were also no roads and few wagons to transport things, so what the train brought had to sit where it was offloaded across the river from where they were. The river was not passable until the water receded, or a new bridge was built.

She knew there had been floods in the city before, but this was different. The dam was the difference. In years before, the water from winter rains had passed out to sea, sometimes in a flood, but not like this. She had no idea what had happened at the dam, but she was seeing the results of whatever it was.

Her father and Maggie came into the room followed by Tom Hendricks and Homer Place, two of the doctors who had supported their move away from the hospital. "I know you're busy, but we need to talk for a bit," said Will. "These two fellows can relieve you and let us take a short break."

Doctor Place's wife Gen had followed them into the room, and she smiled at Annaliese and stood by to help. Their two-year-old was upstairs with the other children freeing her to be here helping with patients.

All around them boxes and crates of medical supplies were stacked, many of them taken from the hospital when its eventual flooding became evident. Mica had been checking and moving some of these supplies and he joined them in the kitchen at Will's invitation.

A pot of coffee was on the stove and when they were all served Will began. "Since we're cut off from the city offices, we need to begin to think about organizing ourselves so we can help people on this side of the river do what must be done about getting food and clean water to them.

"With all the water around us it's easy to forget we can't drink any of it so we'll need to find a source of clean water. If this river water stands for long, we could also have trouble with disease. We need to get information out to keep people from drinking water that isn't safe. Diseases like typhoid and cholera could complicate things and make a bad situation much worse."

He turned to Mica. "Some of this stuff looks to be right up your alley."

"I was thinking the same thing. Why don't we get a list together of things that need doing, decide who can do them and move forward from there."

"Annaliese, if you and Maggie continue to man the clinic and deal with what's necessary, we'll begin to handle these things. Now that we can get over to the store, we can get Johnny to help. Don't think there's anyone on this side of the river who knows the city and how it works better than he does."

As they were headed back down the stairs to the clinic Maggie said, "We've had so much to deal with I hadn't thought about all that stuff. It's all public health. If we can get people working on handling those problems now, we can save ourselves a lot of headaches down the road."

As they hurried through the rooms downstairs, Annaliese was struck by how many of the people helping them were from Old Town. In addition to the ones taking care of patients, others were cleaning, changing beds, washing clothes, and helping wherever they could. She didn't remember hiring anyone. Because they lived on higher ground, there were fewer patients among them. They hadn't been hit so much by the force of the flood, but that didn't keep them from being here when and where they were needed.

Chapter Thirty-Five

Johnny was working up under the eaves when he heard a voice. *"Lemuel wants you. Kate's here. Some other fellow too."* He looked around but saw no one. He and Roy had been experimenting with their new form of communication. This was the first time he had been able to hear when Roy was obviously downstairs.

When he walked into the store, the first thing he did was look at Roy, who smiled faintly and nodded.

"These two want to talk to us about something I'd call logistics if I was still in the Army," said Lemuel. He was sitting in the reading area with Kate and Mica Robinson. "Mica has just come from the clinic. Things are under control over there, at least for now, and they think we need to look to other things that need doing."

Since Johnny rarely saw one without the other, he asked Kate, "Where's Woman?"

"She and Wash are stabling the animals. I talked to John Spreckels, and he is organizing the people at the Del to work with the city people in Coronado to see what they need to do. I thought I'd come over here to help. Hard to get over there with so much stuff floating in the Bay."

Johnny nodded a greeting at Mica who said, "We're working on getting organized to feed and house the people who are going to need it, and figured you'd be able to help us."

When Johnny didn't respond, he went on. "Food and clean water seem to be first on the list, then shelter and probably warm clothing."

"How are they doing over there?" Lemuel asked.

"It seems like the worst is over," said Mica, "if it ever stops raining, that is. There are six doctors there now and a lot of nurses and I think half of the Mexican community is helping out or standing by to see if they're needed."

"We have all sorts of people in the kitchen," said Johnny, "cooking and helping around the house. We still have some room left, but we're filling up fast. Mostly families with children and older people. We're out of places to sleep but still have space on the floor. Better than being out in the rain. Is it still raining hard?"

"It seems to have slowed down a bit," said Kate, "but it still looks like it's going to last for a while yet. There's a lot of water standing in places, even up here on the hills, though we were able to get through alright."

While he listened to them talk and plan, Johnny was staring out the window. Even with the rain still coming down they had already begun planning for tomorrow; how to get what people needed, how to clean up, and how to build the town back up again.

Wash and Woman were the first people to use the temporary Otay River ferry three days after it stopped raining. As Wash was cranking the ferry across the now-shrunken river, Woman asked, "Are you nervous about what we'll find?"

He guided the ferry into its berth before he turned to answer her. "Yes," he said. "No news is not really good news at a time like this. Looking around the cabin, it's easy to see where it flooded before, and..." he gestured at the town across the river, "if this is any marker, it will likely be flooded again."

Looking around them, they could see the signs of the river's passage the last few days. "The same thing seems to have happened at the Otay dam that did at the Sweetwater Dam. Too much rain, and it topped over. They had built an outflow pipe to pass the river through while they worked on the dam, but with this rain, there was more water than the pipe could handle. On top of that, trees and all sorts of things tried to go through the pipe and clogged it. Didn't take long for the water to rise above what they built.

"It wasn't as bad as the Sweetwater, though. There the dam held, but the water topped over and some of the supporting wall on either side collapsed. That's why that big rush of water came through downtown and did so much damage."

"The river won't affect us, will it?" she asked.

"No, but with all this rain running into the creek off the rocks east of us, it might be pretty bad. Not much place for it to soak in so most of it will run downhill and end up in the ocean right at our place. All we can do now is enjoy a nice ride on a nice day. We'll see it soon enough."

She grinned at him. "Nothing bothers you, does it? I don't believe you know how to worry." She leaned over and kissed him, horses humping one another.

"Can't pick cotton that ain't in the bowl," he said.

They turned their horses away from the river and began to pick their way carefully across the path damaged by the flood. In less than a half mile they came to a hill that had thwarted the water and suddenly it looked like every other day they had ridden the road.

They could see some results of the storm, though. There were places where rivulets had become small streams, and small streams rushing rivers. Mud had brought along some trees sliding down to the road. Things were still muddy in places, and there was a lot of standing water, but nothing they couldn't handle.

"You know, I've never felt about a place like I do about the cabin," he said. They had paused to let the horses drink and were looking at the ocean. "Most of my life I've been happy when I was movin' on but for the first time this feels like home.

"So yes, I worry. Do I think it will be as bad as back there? No, I don't, but don't fool yourself. It could be we'll have to build again and I'd want to. I want to fix everything back and live there again, cause it's home." When they were back on the road he said, "Sure do hope the rock is still there, though."

It was, but the cabin was pretty bad. At first glance it seemed alright, but as they got closer, they could see that the whole thing had shifted and to the rear a small cliff had undermined the rear corner. The whole structure was sagging with several feet hanging over where a small cave had been carved out beneath it. The other end of the house had a tree through the roof directly over their bedroom.

They sat and looked at it for a while. "Well," he said, "I guess the first thing is to decide if it's safe inside."

They dismounted and carefully climbed the steps. On the porch it looked normal, but when they opened the door, they could see it wasn't. The side closest to the creek was slanted, so that end of the cabin was going downhill. The fireplace looked to be intact and fortunately the kitchen area had been on the other end of the room. In the bedroom, the floor of the loft had several tree branches through it, and the bed and the room were full of wet things: tree branches and pine needles.

They tied a rope across the cabin and stayed to one side of it while they began to clean and dry what belongings they could salvage.

Back at the nursery the loading dock was intact, although most of the rest of the office and shop was gone or damaged beyond repair. Kate had set up a table on the dock and several people were drinking coffee and talking when Wash and Woman arrived.

"Any problems out there?" asked Lemuel. Several of the nursery workers were with him and they made room for Wash to sit down. Woman stood looking at the damage and said, "It's worse here."

They all looked at Wash. "The creek got to the cabin. The southeast corner of the house is undercut and sagging. A tree went through the roof and down into the loft. We're going to sleep in the big room until we decide what we're going to do. The Outhouse and barn are gone."

"You want me to come out and look it over?" asked Lemuel.

"I'd appreciate it," said Wash. Got to figure out the best way to go forward. Do we want to repair or tear it down? Didn't have any foundation. Probably best to just start over and come out of the ground with it."

Kate said, "Well, I'm so sorry about the cabin but glad to hear you're thinking along those lines. If I can help, let me know."

Wash grinned around the circle. "At least the rock's still there."

The next day Lemuel and Wash spent several hours examining the cabin and deciding what the next move should be.

"I was a little surprised you were so quick to think about rebuilding," said Lemuel. "I would have thought you'd just go traveling for a while."

"Didn't even come to mind," said Wash. "Truth be told, for the first time in my life someplace seems like home." He was quiet for a moment. "With Woman and y'all here I got good reasons to stay, and we both feel like Kate's family. I reckon maybe it's time I settled down."

"Well, I know Kate feels the same way," said Lemuel. "We all do." He got up and brushed off his pants, grasped Wash's hand and pulled him out of the rocking chair. "Let's get back. I've got work to do at the warehouse and I know Kate needs you."

"That's another reason to stay. It's nice to feel needed for the first time in my life. Guess I've felt that way since I met Johnny but didn't recognize the feeling 'til now." There was a mischievous smile on his face when he continued. "Seems you know a lot about what Kate's thinking these days. Are you going anywhere with that?"

"She's a good friend," said Lemuel. "We spend a lot of time together. Who knows. One day, maybe more."

"Can't think of anything that would make me happier," said Wash, big smile on his face.

The next day they began tearing down the cabin and making plans to build another one.

They started by emptying the damaged half of the cabin and walling it off from what was stable and usable, then pulling down the damaged side, leaving the remaining part to be used as shelter while they were building the new one. It would be a little north and east and completely clear of the original site. Friends from the nursery came and went, providing labor and expertise, and they all worked under Lemuel's direction.

Before long they had the work laid out and out of the ground. The roughhewn, occasionally crooked logs of the old cabin were replaced with trees picked for size and shape so as to fit tightly along the walls and at the corners. The idea was to slope the roof toward the creek, and Woman wanted a new floor, tightly fitted and proof against the bugs and small critters that had been a problem before.

It was a project that progressed in fits and starts as everyone also had to work for a living as well as help put the nursery and the city back together, but they could see steady progress. Much of the lumber had to be hauled out from the city. The remaining section of the old cabin was large enough to live in and either Wash or Lemuel was there as the work progressed.

More than a few weekends were spent with friends from the nursery and various farms in the area helping and a state of mind similar to a barn raising prevailed with people working together to build the cabin. Women provided food and drink and towels soaked in cool water from the creek as needed, and everyone seemed to have a good time. It reminded Wash of watching the Mormons work together to help one another.

Johnny was lying on the bed, Jinx purring on his chest,

watching Annaliese brush her hair and trying to figure out how to go about telling her something he knew she wouldn't believe.

"If you could figure out a way to get paid for doing that you'd be rich," he said. "Sure like the way it makes your hair look, though." With sudden resolve he moved the cat and swung his feet off the bed facing her. "I need to tell you something, and I want you to listen to me until I finish what I have to say."

She was looking at him in the mirror, a question on her face.

"I know this sounds crazy, but I seem to be able to hear what Roy's thinking." He stopped and let the statement sink in. "We found out about it just before the rain started last week, and we've been trying to figure out how it works and what we can do with it."

She put down the brush and turned to look at him. She opened her mouth to speak but he held up a finger and she didn't.

"It's not like I'm hearing everything he thinks about, but when he's trying to, I can hear him as clear as I hear you. I know it sounds impossible, and I've never heard of anything like it but it's a fact. When he wants to get my attention, he can send me his thoughts, and I can hear them.

"We've been experimenting. The other day I was up under the eaves, and he was downstairs in the store, and I could hear him like he was standing next to me. Same when he's in the store and I'm outside or in the barn."

He stopped and sat staring at her. She started to say something, then stopped and with her face in a puzzled frown said, "You're saying you two can talk without talking?" When he nodded, she said, "Can he hear you thinking?"

"No." He shook his head. "It only seems to work one way. When he wants to tell me something he can, but I need to speak for him to hear me."

She patted the seat beside her and moved over so they could sit and look at each other in the mirror. She was quiet for a while, looking at him with a thoughtful expression. "I want to make sure I understand what you're saying. When Roy wants to tell you something he can focus on you and then send you a thought that you can hear. Is that right?"

He nodded.

"And you can hear it as though he's speaking?"

He nodded again.

She went back to thinking, sucking her bottom lip, looking at him but not really seeing him. Finally, she asked, "What do you think about it? I know you well enough to know you've had to be thinking about it, probably a lot."

He took a deep breath and blew it out before he answered. "Yeah, I have. We've learned some of what we can and can't do with it, but I have no idea what to make of it, what to do with it, how important it is.

"It doesn't change things much. When you come right down to it, it just means Roy won't have to type messages to me. It seems like it ought to be more important than that but for the life of me, I can't think of any reason it would be."

In the mirror she saw the question on his face. "Well, I've never heard of anything like it," she said. "But other than giving you something to wonder about, why would it be important?"

"I don't know," he replied. He took another deep breath. "I just hope I don't go crazy trying to find a reason it is."

"Have you told anyone else?"

"No. Not sure who to tell. Not sure if I want to tell anyone."

"What does Roy think about it?"

"I'm not sure he's thought about it much. He just seems to accept it. He doesn't seem to worry about it. To him it's just a part of what he is."

"Can he do it with anyone else?"

"Not that I know of. We haven't talked much about it. I seem to be his connection to the world. I don't know if he's tried or even if he really wants to see if it works with other people."

"You know, that doesn't surprise me. Since the accident and Greta's death the two of you have become very close. He doesn't communicate much with the rest of the world anyway."

"I know. I think he believes people look at him as strange because he can't talk. I remember when he was recovering from the accident you asked me to think about ways to help him. That's where the idea for the typewriters came from. When we went to the class together, that began it."

"Well Johnny, just remember it takes the both of you to do this..." she shook her head, "whatever it is you do. He can send his thoughts but you're the one that hears them. No one else does."

Chapter Thirty-Six

Jinx jumped on the desk and butted Johnny to get his attention. He picked up the cat and leaned back in his chair thinking, Jinx on his chest purring. A lot to think about right now. The store sat on a hill and from his perch up under the eaves he could watch as the city began to pull itself back together.

Everywhere he looked, people were busy, and even around the house he could hear the noises of construction and see homes and buildings going up or being repaired. Below him workmen were coming and going around the house to where Lemuel was building additional space for the anticipated needs of the clinic.

Many of the businesses in New Town were open while they were cleaning up and rebuilding and people were moving around trying to put their lives together again. Ferries were operating across some of the local rivers and creeks and construction on several new bridges promised a return to normal soon.

With Jinx on his shoulder, he descended to Annaliese's office and found her doing some of the paperwork she detested.

"Good morning, Sweetheart," he said and kissed her on the top of her head.

"You were up and gone early this morning," she replied. "Where'd you go?"

"Roy and I met John for breakfast at the Del early, and he wants us to ride up to the dams with him this morning, so I came home to tell you and pick up some things we need. We've been planning it for a couple of days. We're going to ride up on mules. Wash is supposed to meet us here and he's going with us."

He cocked his head in a way she'd come to recognize, and she watched as he listened to Roy for a moment. Then he smiled at her.

"Wash and John are downstairs so I'll see you when we get back." He grinned. "Can't remember the last time I rode a mule. Should be fun."

"Will you have any problems with the roads and trails going up?"

"Hope not. That's why we're taking mules. Wash says they handle problems climbing in the mud better than horses. John's had some men scouting them all the way up and he seems to think we'll make it alright. Probably won't be back for a few days. So don't worry."

When he was a boy working with his Pa in the livery stable, Johnny had learned about special shoes for horses in mud and snow. When John had first brought up the idea of inspecting the dams, he and Wash had decided to shoe several mules in this manner and use them to negotiate the trails up into the hills.

When they came out of the store Johnny was surprised to see other men waiting with John. Several were associated with water in the city, and he could understand their interest. It was easier to feel the potential danger of those dams today than it might have been a couple of weeks ago.

As they began to rise into the hills, the narrowing trail still allowed them to ride two abreast and naturally Wash and Johnny rode side by side so they could talk. Roy was riding behind them.

"Still got Presgraves on your mind?" Wash asked.

"Yeh," Johnny replied. "Although not so much since it started raining."

"That's gonna be a problem for you. Any ideas on how to solve it?"

They rode in silence for a while. Finally, Johnny shook his head. "Not a one," he finally answered. "I tell myself not to worry about it or think about it, but that doesn't do any good. He's in my head whether I want him there or not, which is what he wanted."

Another silence. "You got any?" Johnny asked finally.

"Every idea I can think of has a Sharps .50 caliber bullet somewhere in it."

"Me too, except mine's a .44 caliber."

They had crested a ridge and Sweetwater Lake was below them noticeably lower. They paused to look across the water which had been much on everyone's mind the last few days.

"You'll probably have to kill him."

"I think so too," he said, answering the thought he heard. Wash looked at him strangely, but Johnny just smiled and rode on.

To their right the trail led to the dam, and they turned to follow it. They had been told what they would see but they were still surprised. The road that had led to the top of the dam was being repaired and to get to the dam itself they had to scramble across the place where it had been. In the middle of the wash-out was a small stream that cascaded down over a wall that had been eaten away by the water.

Ahead of them, across the dam they could see a similar wash-out on the other side with a small waterfall falling over the edge. Obviously, water was still draining from the lake and would be until they could move enough rock and pour enough concrete to fill the gaps and move aside enough debris to open the spillway.

The arrival of the party had drawn a group of workers, and all stood and listened as the foreman talked about the damage the storm had done and pointed out what was being done to correct it.

While he was listening, Wash glanced up and saw that Johnny and Roy, who he thought were behind him were still on the other side of the washout and had moved along the rim of the canyon wall to where they could look down and see the whole structure, what was there and what wasn't.

"Wow," said Johnny. "Looks like if it would have kept raining, the whole thing would have gone." They stood looking at the dam and where a good third of it, from the top, stood with no connection to the canyon walls on either side.

He sat for a moment, mesmerized, and then turned to Roy. "You know, if we don't tell Wash about this and keep doing it when he's around, he's going to think we're crazy."

"Tell him."

They left the Sweetwater dam early the next morning and took a trail that led to the new Otay River Dam. The group now was Wash, John, Roy and Johnny. The rest had stayed behind to get some more time with the problems of the Sweetwater Dam and the water behind it.

"So, what do you think about the dam?" John asked.

"I think they need to come up with something to anchor it to the canyon walls more securely," said Johnny. "If they don't this will probably happen every few years when we have a bad storm. In addition to providing water to the county, the dam's supposed to help control the river's flow and protect us from the effects of bad storms. It didn't. I think the question should be, what will it take to make it do what we want it to do?

"Of course, that's a question for someone who knows how to design and build dams. It seems to me we need to let the engineers know what we need, and they need to build something that will do it."

"Hard to argue with that," replied John. "The question is, can these fellows do the job?"

"Maybe you need to bring someone in to look over their shoulder and put together a plan that will give us dams that don't fail when we have one of our 'every few years' deluges."

"Sounds like a good idea."

After supper that evening, they were sitting around a campfire when Johnny said, "Something is happening between Roy and I and we think we need to talk to y'all about it so you'll know what it is." He explained their new method of communication and watched as their friends sat quietly for a moment and thought about it.

"You mean you can communicate with one another without talking?" asked John, with a puzzled frown on his face.

"Not quite," replied Johnny. "He can think something, and I can hear it. He can't hear me think."

"That's a new one on me," said John. "Never heard of anything like that." He looked at Wash. "You?"

Wash, looking amazed, shook his head and then suddenly pointed a finger at Johnny. "That's what happened today. I wondered what you were talking about. When you said, 'I think so, too' earlier, you were answering something he was thinking, weren't you?"

Johnny nodded and Roy smiled when both men looked at him.

"Since it looks like he and I are going to continue to use this..." he paused, "*thing*, I don't know what to call it then either the people around us have to know about it or they'll think I'm crazy and talking to myself."

They all laughed, and John said, "What if we think you're crazy because you think you can hear what he's thinking?"

More laughter.

"That wouldn't surprise me. I know it sounds strange, but it's a fact. We've tested it. He can think and I hear it."

John frowned again. "How far apart?" he asked.

"Don't know, really. I hear him when he's outside and I'm in the store, or when I'm under the eaves and he's somewhere else in the house. Haven't tried it beyond that."

"And you say it doesn't go the other way?" asked Wash.

"So far it doesn't. Who knows where it will go."

"Does anyone else know?" asked John.

"Only Annaliese. I told her the other night. I've been thinking about how it could have happened and why and it's no good. Have no idea."

"What does Roy think about it?"

"He wrote me a note about that. As far as he's concerned, it doesn't matter why or how. It is and we should spend our time learning how to use it and not waste time wondering how or why. And he's right. We're never going to figure out where it comes from or why, so why waste time trying?"

They were quiet for a while digesting that. "Besides," he continued, "maybe in the midst of learning about it we'll find all that out." Again, a pause and a shrug. "And maybe we won't."

They all went to sleep thinking about it.

The whole time they had been dealing with the flood, their plans for the clinic were on Annaliese's mind, drifting around in her thoughts and occasionally demanding attention even in the midst of hurrying from one crisis to another. Now that she could sit down and catch a breath, she was consumed with them again. She and Maggie were sitting in her office talking to Grace when her voice tube whistled.

"Mica Robinson is here and would like to speak to you."

"Send him up."

She stood to greet him and when he was seated said, "Do you need to see me alone?"

He shook his head. "Not necessary. These ladies know what things are like right now." He accepted a hot drink and stirred in some sugar. "It seems like the hospital won't be able to pay me until they reopen."

He looked around at all of them, eyebrows raised. "But they want me to help them out and keep working until that time, apparently gratis. With a family I can't afford to do that, so I guess I'm looking for a job."

Annaliese smiled at him. "We've been discussing our needs

since things calmed down and it might just be we can work something out. The problem is we can't pay you what you deserve with your experience and education right now, so we're not much better off than the hospital in that sense. Of course, since we get paid in kind with food a lot, we can probably feed you if you like Mexican food, that is."

"I was wondering about that. Of course, I see your immediate future as somewhat better than the hospital's at this point. Even when they are able to reopen, I don't see them prospering what with the issues that we were dealing with before the flood and then being underwater on top of everything else.

"People will get used to turning to your facility for their needs and that will make it much harder for them to get going again, even when they're able to."

"I've been thinking along the same lines," said Annaliese. "By the time they're up and running again we should have gotten our operation to a point where we will be a good alternative to what they can offer the city. If you can have a little patience until we get on our feet, maybe we'll have a future together."

She made some notes on a pad on her desk and said, "I'll need to talk to the Doctor and some of the others we're working with. We'll see if we can make you an offer you can live with."

He sat back in his chair and seemed to relax. "I was hoping you'd feel that way. I'd say it won't be long before your operation can use the skills I can bring to bear, don't you agree?"

"Yes, I do, but we'll need to decide what we can afford. I know you need a certain amount to support your family and pay your bills and we have to see what we have available, what with the damage we've sustained from the flood and all. I'll talk to some of the others and I'll try to get back to you soon. I know you'll need an answer before long."

When he'd gone, they talked about what the idea of an administrator meant to their plans for the future.

Annaliese sat for a minute looking out the window and tapping a pencil on the desk. "What with the plans and ideas we have about where we're going it seems we could probably use him, but before we jump into a commitment, we need to be careful. It's not just the money.

"I think we can afford him, and we can surely use the experience he has. But the question is, what is our future and where are we heading and where is the hospital heading? If we take most of their personnel, how will they see us in the future? We don't want to make an enemy."

"Well, with the attitude they seemed to have before it started raining, what else would you call them?" asked Maggie. "We're working against them in the city and the people who created the problems that divided us are still around. How are they going to feel when the place is ready to open again and we've taken most of their staff and patients and they can't find what they need to keep their doors open?"

"I'm going to telephone some of our people and get together for a meeting," said Annaliese. "We need to discuss this and our future." She paused. "I think we need to assess their future too. What happens to the doctors and nurses in the city will affect us too.

"I'd rather have waited a bit, but it seems Mica can't afford to wait long so we might be forced to make up our minds sooner than we thought."

Chapter Thirty-Seven

Johnny could see the light under the bathroom door, so he knocked.

"Who's there?" Her sing-song voice told him she knew damn well who was there.

Slipping into a seductive whisper he replied, "It is I, Don Giovanni, come to transport you to paradise."

"Oh please, do come in," she said breathlessly, and he opened the door.

"Hi, when'd you get home?"

The room was steamy, and she was inside the circle of the shower curtain. All he could see was her hair piled on the top of her head.

"Just got here." He began to undress with designs on joining her. When he pulled open the curtain she squealed.

"Johnny, it's cold! Close that!"

He slipped inside and pulled it closed. There was just enough room for the two of them to stand but they were touching in so many interesting places neither wanted to move.

"If you're thinking about what I think you are, you ought to know I was just getting ready to get out. The water will be getting cold before long."

He embraced her, kissed her, and began to run his hands over her wet body.

"Johnny," she squealed, "it's getting cold."

"If you really loved me it wouldn't matter," he said, holding her tightly.

"Johnny!" she screamed. "If we fall and hurt ourselves, I'm going to kill you."

"Well, if you're going to be that way about it." He reached behind her and turned off the water. They climbed carefully out of the tub, and he wrapped her in a large towel, kissed her and held her tightly, until she stopped squirming.

"There," he said. "Is that better? They were pressed together and getting warmer by the minute. "Now who's this Don Giovanni fellow you were inviting into the shower?"

Afterwards he got a damp towel and gently patted her face and forehead.

"It's always more fun when I've been gone for a while."

She looked at him with raised eyebrows. "Johnny, you've been gone for two days."

"Well, it seemed longer. So, what have you been up to while I've been away?"

"More than you'd ever believe." She shook her head. "We now have an administrator."

"Really! Who?"

"Mica Robinson. It seems the hospital couldn't afford to pay him but wanted him to help them get back on their feet anyway. With a family to feed he couldn't afford that, so he came looking for a job. After a quick meeting we decided to hire him.

"We all saw how useful he was during the flood and decided if we're going to grow, we would eventually need him so we jumped. It was that or have him leave town and later we'd have to find someone anyway."

"I'm wondering if it will ever re-open," Johnny said. "Most of the people they have on that board don't seem to really know anything about running a hospital and unless they raise some money pretty quick, they'll just sit there with a building and nothing to put in it."

"You're probably right. All the people who moved the project along are with us. They don't have any of the pushers over there."

He was quiet for a minute, and she could tell he was thinking. "Along with what Lemuel said at the meeting make sure you take that into account. There may come a time in the near future when you might need a place to grow into. What better place than one built as a hospital? So, it would seem to me you'd want to make sure you didn't create any ill will with them. Make it as easy as you can for them to join you and not be angry at being pushed out."

"What about the issue that caused the split in the first place?"

"The clinic will be what you people make it. If they want to join you, they can't force you to accept anything you don't want to."

He started to kiss her again, but she laid a finger across his lips. "If we start that we'll keep going, and I've got things that need doing. Let's save it for later."

"Promise?"

"Promise."

While they were getting dressed, she said, "It will be so nice to have someone else to give all this paperwork to."

"When will he start?"

"Tomorrow's Sunday so he'll be here Monday."

"I was thinking. You've been so busy keeping things running from day to day since the flood, you haven't worked on the business side of things. Since you're the only real medical clinic for many miles, you're going to be busy; probably very busy. It seems to me you need to get ready for that." He looked at her and smiled.

She looked back, mouth open, seemingly puzzled. "I guess I knew that, but there's been so much to do, I kept putting off thinking about it. You're right; we can't keep putting it off. "

"I thought that might be the case. I propose that Will and I sit down with Mica and a lawyer and see what ideas we come up with. We might want to include Lemuel in the discussion, too. He's pretty savvy about such things."

"Hmm," she said. She sat and looked at him for a long moment. "Then what would you do?"

"We'd bring what we find to you with some suggestions about how to go about setting them up. You, Will, Maggie and the other doctors could then see what you like and what you don't."

She sat still, looking at him but not really seeing him. "I see what you mean. One thing, though. See if you can get Kate to sit in with you. I like the way she gets things done."

"Good idea."

"When would you start this process?"

"Can't see any reason to put it off. When we meet with John Monday, I'll bring it up. It seems like a good idea to let him know about something like this. The newspaper got flooded and with all that's going on with the flood and rebuilding, I doubt if he'd want to be directly involved, but he knows a lot about business and might have some good suggestions."

He did have some good ones, and when Johnny and Roy sat down with the others he had mentioned, on Sunday afternoon a week later, he had a plan to put on the table for moving things forward. Not only that but he had been discussing it with Roy and Annaliese and had laid out a first draft for the direction he wanted the meeting to take.

"I don't want to seem pushy, but I've been thinking about this a lot, so I've got some ideas I'd like to share as a way to begin." He looked around and they were all nodding.

He handed everyone several pieces of paper. "I've put together a list of things we need to think about. I need you to listen while I read it then we can go over the list and work on each point. Then we can go around the circle and see what everyone has to say.

"Before we do that 1 need to know something. Exactly how do the people at the clinic see the future?" asked Kate. "That will give us a goal to work toward."

"Annaliese and I have talked about that a lot this week," said Johnny. "The flood has forced them to change their ideas somewhat. When they began, the idea was to function as an alternative for medical services for a part of the city. Now suddenly, we'll probably have the whole city on their hands, at least for the near future. So, the first question is, where will we get the help we need to handle the job?"

"Are you speaking about the staffing needs or funding?"

"Probably both, eventually, but right now mainly staffing. Many of the people we hire will come from the hospital and we need to think how to deal with that. What happens if the hospital gets ready to open and we've got all the help, and they have none?

"Going back to what Lemuel said before, we don't want to have a war with these people. Wouldn't it be better to reach out to find common solutions instead? We'd be bargaining from a position of strength, so we could pretty much decide what we want and see if they want to join us. If not, then we go our own way, but let's give them a chance."

"So, we feel that any long-term decisions about the clinic and its future should be after we talk to representatives of the hospital."

Johnny was listening when Will told Annaliese about the meeting.

"Other than that, we talked about how to put together a plan to deal with the patients we have. Mica will be a big part of organizing the business and supply parts of things.

He's already contacted all of the suppliers we'll need and has begun to put together the set of books we'll need to keep track of everything. I think for a while he'll be the most important asset we have as far as knowing what comes in and what goes out."

"That takes a load off my mind already. I was pulling my hair out trying to figure out what was what. Nice to be able to see patients again." Annaliese was quiet, thinking for a moment. "So, what ideas do you have about dealing with the hospital board?"

"Kate and Johnny are going to approach the board and see what comes from it. If you'd like to join them that's fine."

"No, I don't think so. I've got enough to do around here, and those people bring out the worst in me."

Johnny leaned forward and spoke. "Decision comes from this room. You three decide. We go and talk and come back, and the people in this room decide what we do and where we go from here. We're just the messengers."

"OK, that's fine. So did you come up with a name?"

"Yes, we did. *The San Diego Clinic and Dispensary*. But we all know that's probably temporary until we see where they stand."

"Will you talk about the Mexican problem with the board?"

"Don't see how we can avoid it. But we will stand firm on the idea that in our facility we will provide healthcare to everyone who needs it. No exceptions." Johnny looked at all of them and everyone was nodding emphatically.

"Let's take the next step so we can know where we go from here."

"So," said Lemuel. "I guess what they say is true. It's an ill flood that flows nobody good. It looks like the flood and its aftermath will be good for the future of the clinic."

Johnny was feeling good. The challenge of working to help his wife and his friends cope successfully with the flood and its aftermath was stimulating and rewarding. As an added benefit, he was able to get his mind away from the violence he had felt looming over him since the night Barry Presgraves had come into The BookSeller.

He glanced at an envelope lying on his desk, picked it up and sat thinking. He didn't recognize the handwriting.

He tore it open absently, thinking about his meeting the next day with the hospital board.

"We need to settle this."

He turned the paper over and there was nothing else. With his forehead furrowed, a puzzled expression on his face, he began to refocus his thoughts on the letter, no longer pondering his immediate future, thinking only of the strange message. Slowly he realized what it meant. Suddenly the violence was back.

He could feel his heart beating, almost hear it thumping in his ears. He knew this was what his enemy wanted; for him to react, to feel fear, anger, whatever emotions one would feel knowing someone he knew to be a dangerous man was stalking him, wanting to kill him.

He picked up the envelope and turned it over. Nothing. No return address. How would he respond to this? How could he? The man could be anywhere and apparently, he didn't want Johnny to know where. An image passed over his mind of a stalking animal, a big cat who would watch and wait and then decide when and where to leap.

So, what would be the next step? Another message and one day suddenly he'd be facing the whole thing? Johnny didn't like the idea that he could do nothing but wait while someone else set the rules of the game.

Another image flashed across his mind. His wife's face when he showed her the letter. He closed his eyes and took a deep breath. He really, really didn't want to tell her but he had no choice. He couldn't hide this little five-word message from her, a message that might just turn their lives upside down. He shook his head. He had no thoughts on how to handle the problem that didn't lead to gunfire, or maybe an ice pick.

"Where'd you get to this evening?" She looked at him in the mirror where she sat brushing her hair.

"Roy and I rode out to the cabin. Needed to talk to Wash."

She smiled. "Did you sit on the rock?"

"No. Just sat on the porch and talked for a while."

"What about?"

He handed her the envelope. For the second time that day his heart felt like it was going to jump out of his chest. He watched as her face went through the same expressions of puzzlement, realization and then horror he had as she gradually realized what it meant.

She looked at him, mouth open in horror. "What does he mean?"

"Well, I don't think he's inviting me to a picnic."

"Johnny! It's not funny!"

"I agree, but I have no more of an idea about what it means than you do other than to say it's not good."

"What are you going to do?"

"I thought about it all the way out to the cabin and talked to Wash, Woman and Roy about it and thought about it all the way home and I'll tell you," he paused, "I have no idea."

"What did Wash say about it?"

"He thinks the same way I do. Presgraves will want to fight and likely with weapons."

"You mean guns?"

"I sure ain't going to fight him with my fists. The guy outweighs me by forty pounds, and he carries an ice pick in his boot. So yeah, I figure it will be with guns."

"Can't the sheriff do something?"

"In case you didn't notice, he didn't sign it so how's he going to arrest him? We know who it is. So will the sheriff, for that matter but he can't prove it. And we've seen what the judge will do. If we put him in jail, he'd probably let him out again." Johnny shook his head. "Besides, he's likely in Mexico. Can't arrest him there anyway.

"I should leave it to Woman. She wants to stalk him and put a bullet in his brain. I think Wash is thinking along the same lines."

"You can't let them do that."

"I know, and they wouldn't. But when you're grousing you say things you don't mean."

She turned back to the mirror and threw the brush down. "Well, that sure made me lose count. So, what are you going to do?"

"I guess all I can do is play the hand I'm dealt. If he wants a fight, not much I can do but defend myself."

"Another gunfight! Johnny! No!"

"What else do you suggest? If he comes after me, it's probably going to happen."

She gave a long sigh and tears began to fall. "All this because of Herschel."

"No," he said. "No. I was doing what I thought was right. Besides, nothing can change that, so the 'why' doesn't matter." He reached out and pulled her into a fierce hug.

"I'm scared, Johnny. From what you've said he's dangerous."

He ran his hand down her hair and pulled away, looking into her eyes. "I'm pretty dangerous myself, you know," he said quietly. "If he pushes me into a gunfight, I might just make it out alive."

"Can you trust him to fight fair?"

"No, and I'd be a fool if I did." He turned away from her and stood looking out the window.

"Annaliese, in a gunfight, fair is not really a part of it. If you can get an edge, you take it or you're liable to end up dead." He kissed her and said, "I have a lot of reasons to want to stay alive."

Chapter Thirty-Eight

Lemuel was in the store when Johnny came downstairs the next morning.

"Hear we got a new problem," he said from where he was drinking a cup of coffee in the reading room.

"You musta talked to Wash this morning."

"I did. I was over at Kate's, and we all talked about it. What are you going to do?"

"Don't know. Just have to wait and see what happens. It's his game at this point. All I can do is wait for the next letter or he may show up here. He's a talker, I know that about him."

"You know," said Lemuel, "between the bunch of us we carry a lot of firepower. If you need some help, I'm here, and if Handy hears about it he'll come running."

"I appreciate it, but no, this is my problem. You've got the twins to worry about. No, if I need help I've got Roy, and Wash and Woman for that matter. When I had a problem in Tucson she backed me with the Henry, and she almost cut an Apache in half with that Bowie she carries."

"Roy? He's just a boy."

"Lemuel, by the time I was his age I'd killed two men. He's quick and he shoots straight."

He grinned at his friend. "Besides, I'd hate to see Kate disappointed. She'd never forgive me if I let you get yourself shot full of holes."

"Well, there's that," he said, smiling sheepishly. "You know, it's nice to have something to look forward to again."

"In my case I just hope I have something to look back on."

A couple of weeks later Annaliese was sitting at her desk writing in a chart when Johnny walked in, quietly took a seat and sat waiting for her attention. When she finished writing she laid the chart on her desk.

"What did the board decide?" she asked. "Are we going to work together going forward or not?"

"There's still some hemming and hawing, but I think they're getting there. There's not another path for them that makes any sense."

"Not sure they have any sense. I don't think their decision to support those people showed much sense or courage, for that matter. If they hadn't given in to them, we'd already be working hard at putting the hospital back together and getting it open."

She turned and gazed out the window. The sun was out, and they were having San Diego weather again. When she watched people in the city pulling together, reaching a hand to help each other when there was need, and even when there wasn't, it was difficult to have much patience with timidity in the face of a disaster.

"Johnny, we can't just wait for them to make up their minds. We can't! We've made our plans, and we need to move toward realizing our goals. If and when they finally decide to join us, then they'll have to do so under the conditions we set. The building will still be there, but it doesn't seem they're going to get it open again any time soon. The longer they wait the less inclined I'll be to consider giving in to any changes or conditions they'd propose."

"I agree. How's Mica doing? Are you glad you hired him?"

"Johnny, I think we're riding on his back right now. I don't think I'd be able to practice medicine without him here. I never realized how much there was to do on the business and supply side of a clinic, especially one like we're proposing that's liable to grow the way it could.

"Fortunately, the Doctor has some experience with it, and between him and Mica, they're getting it done." She sat up and gave him a silly smile. "Which means I don't have to."

He cocked his head to one side, and she recognized Roy was speaking to him. They had decided to keep knowledge of the phenomenon in their circle of friends. They were all becoming comfortable with it and all recognized the signs when it was happening. There didn't seem to be any reason to tell anyone else.

The shocked look on his face reminded her of him saying, 'throwing a bucket of cold water in someone's face,' and by the time he'd refocused his eyes on her she realized what he had heard.

"It's another letter, isn't it?" She put her hand to her mouth. "Oh my God."

"Roy's with a customer so I'll go down and get it."

By the time he returned her heart had slowed a bit. She watched him open and read it.

"Well, what does it say?"

He handed it to her and watched as she read what was there.

"Soon."

She looked puzzled. "What does it mean?"

"You know as much as I do about it. I'm damned if I know what it means."

She sat looking at him in a shocked silence.

He ran his finger along his lips and shook his head. "I believe he wants to rattle me, get me upset and distracted. It's easy to say, 'don't let it bother you', but it's much harder to do. Remember when we had that meeting before the storm and Lemuel said, 'It's a characteristic of wisdom not to do foolish things'?

She nodded.

"Well, I've got to make sure he doesn't push me into doing something foolish. This is not a place where I want to make mistakes. It would cost me too much."

Roy was behind the counter adding some figures when the man came in. Roy remembered the time he had appeared before, fresh out of jail and surprised Johnny. He closed his eyes and thought about Johnny, felt him listening. *"He's here."*

Messages he sent in this fashion had to be short. It took effort for him to send his thoughts, and he was learning to get ideas across with as few words as possible. He was sure Johnny would understand this one.

Within a minute Johnny was downstairs. The man had already taken a seat in the reading room and opened a magazine when Johnny stopped at the entrance, stood looking at him, nodded and said, "What can I do for you?"

"I thought you'd look more frazzled than you do," he said, smiling. His eyes went to the canted holster at Johnny's hip. "Be a little upset or maybe nervous looking." The smile was cold; so were the eyes. "Is that because of me?" he asked, nodding at the holster.

"Yeah," Johnny replied, nodding slowly.

"So how are we going to go about settling this matter between us?" He was still smiling.

"I'm not sure there's anything to settle. I was doing a job and things I learned pointed me toward the idea that you were the one I was after. There was nothing personal. What's there to settle?"

"You know, somehow, I knew you'd say that, but I look at it a little differently. I take it personally cause I want to. I choose to take offense."

"In other words, you're looking for a fight?"

The man nodded slowly.

"Why?"

He was quiet for a moment, taking his time. "I don't like you.

That's reason enough."

"Since it seems like it's going to come down to a fight, I want you to know something. You'll never put a hand on me. If you try, I'll kill you."

Neither of them said anything for a moment, and then Johnny said, "If you come looking for me or mine, bring a gun, cause that's what I'll have."

"A gun?" he said.

Johnny smiled. "I don't like ice picks."

The man's lips were twitching into a reluctant smile and then a grin almost in spite of himself.

"I can see why you wouldn't. You know, Herschel never liked them very much either." He nodded at Roy standing behind Johnny. "He's your bodyguard?"

"If I decide I need one, he's it."

"Doesn't look like much. You might need more."

"If need be, I'll have what I need."

Johnny cocked his head. *"You should kill him now."*

Johnny smiled and said, "Probably have to, but not tonight."

The man was puzzled. "What? What did you say?"

Johnny looked at him steadily for a moment. "I wasn't talking to you."

They stared at one another, neither willing to look away.

"Send your friend away. I want to talk to you alone."

Johnny cocked his head. *"Leave?"*

"Go ahead."

He heard Roy come from behind the counter and move into the next room.

"I can still see you."

"Good."

The man's eyes narrowed, and he looked puzzled again for a moment. Then he said, "Do you really think I killed him?"

"Yeah, I do."

"You're not a deputy anymore, so if I tell you I did, what would you do about it?"

"Not much I could do now; maybe later."

"That's the reason we need to settle this, because I did, and sooner or later you're going to decide to do something about it."

Once again Johnny felt that aura around the man as though some evil inside him was dimly glowing. The smile now seemed somehow malignant, diseased.

"I hear you're pretty good with that thing." He nodded at the canted holster.

Johnny didn't answer, just nodded slowly.

"I'm not bad myself. Maybe that's the answer. A gunfight. We meet somewhere and shoot it out. Like they used to do in Kansas. Of course, I like the ice pick better."

"I'm from Kansas."

"I know you are. Herschel told me. In fact, we talked about you a lot that night."

"The night you killed him?"

"Yeah, I had lost him, and I was jealous."

Johnny was startled. "What?"

"Didn't you know? Oh, he was in love with you. That's why he moved down here. To be around you. I don't think he had any idea about doing anything about it, but he was fascinated by you."

Johnny's mouth had fallen open, and he was staring.

"You ever see him with a woman? You wouldn't. He liked men. We were together for a while and then we weren't, and there got to be some bad blood between us. I came down to see him, to see if we could put things back together.

"We talked but all he talked about was you. I got mad and... well, you know what happened. Sometimes when I get mad, I go a little crazy. Don't even remember it, but there he was, dead on the floor."

"A little crazy? Sounds like more than a little."

"And he just got up and walked out?" said Annaliese, open-mouthed in amazement.

"He did say we'd meet again." Johnny shook his head. "Don't ask me what it means or what I'm gonna do. I have no idea. I know I'll think about it a lot, and I guess that bothers me most of all. He's playing with me, like a cat with a mouse. He wants to get inside my brain." He grimaced in disgust. "And he's there, whether I want him or not."

"Do you really believe what he said about Herschel?"

"That he was in love with me?" She nodded. "When I think about it, probably. I don't know much about that kind of thing, but he's right. I never saw Herschel with a woman or heard him talk about one. He sure seemed to be devoted to our friendship so it might be true. If so, he never said or did anything about it."

He stood and pulled her into an embrace. "Herschel was my friend, and I trusted him. That's all that counts for me. Now, I'm going to get my horse and take a ride. Maybe that will help me figure out how to go about this." On the way out the door he scooped Jinx up and onto his shoulder.

"I think better when he's with me," he said over his shoulder.

Woman and Wash were entertaining friends on their newly finished front porch when Johnny and Jinx rode onto the yard.

"You look like a man with something on his mind," said Wash.

"Good guess. How do you figure that out?" said Johnny, swinging down. Jinx went in to explore the half-finished house.

"I'm good at reading sign," replied Wash. "Come up and join us. We're just enjoying the evening."

"What have you been up to?" asked Kate from the dark at the end of the porch where she was perched on the railing.

"I'll bet I can guess what he's got on his mind. From the look on your face, I'd say you've heard from him again," said Lemuel.

"Good guess," Johnny said again. "In fact, he came into the store today and we talked for a while."

The faces he could see registered the same shocked expression.

"No!" said Kate, disbelieving.

He recounted the meeting, and they all sat in silence for a long moment.

"Sounds like he should be in the booby hatch or someplace close," said Kate. "That's crazy."

"Yes, it is, but the fact is he's not, and he's walking around with a killing grudge against me."

"Where's Roy?" asked Lemuel. "Getting used to seeing the two of you together all the time."

"He had something to do at the store. I miss him. Feels like I've got a cold draft on my back when he's not with me."

"I'd be like a cat on hot bricks after something like that but you're not. You seem pretty calm," said Wash.

Johnny shrugged. "I haven't thought about anything else since he closed the door behind him. Haven't come up with any ideas, but I do have some thoughts about it."

"We're listening," said Lemuel.

Johnny leaned forward, elbows on his knees so he could see all of them. "I don't think he'll lay for me in an ambush. Nothing like that. The whole thing is strange but so is he. I think he wants to do it in some kind of ritual. Have no idea why he would, but it fits what he seems to be."

"What he seems to be? What do you mean?" asked Kate.

"Don't know if I can tell you what I mean. He's an evil man. I sense that about him, but there's something more. Herschel was stabbed in the jugular vein with an ice pick. You have to know what you're doing to do that. It was as though it had to be done a certain way. I think that's the way he sees this thing with me. It will have to be done a certain way."

They were all quiet for a minute, thinking.

Finally, Johnny said, "Of course I doubt I can trust him to be fair and honest so when we meet, I can't let him set the scene but so much."

"I'm glad you don't expect him to be fair, cause he won't be," said Lemuel. "Likely he'll try to stack the deck when you meet, have someone hiding out."

"I don't think he'll give me an even break if that's what you mean. No, I'm not such a fool as that. I'll have someone to cover my back when we do meet."

He gave Wash a questioning look and his friend nodded. "I'll be there," he said.

"As will I," said Lemuel.

"No. I don't want you there," said Johnny sharply. "If something happens to me, you'll need to stand by Annaliese. And you have the twins to consider," he smiled slightly. "And maybe someone else too," he said, looking down the porch at Kate.

Chapter Thirty-Nine

Maggie was washing instruments when Annaliese walked into the clinic.

"Are you busy?" When Maggie shook her head, Annaliese continued. "Let's take a ride. I've got so much swirling about my brain I need to get away for a bit so I can think straight."

A half hour later they were sitting in the buggy looking at one of their favorite views of the Bay. They sat quiet for a while, Annaliese wrapped in her own thoughts and Maggie waiting.

Finally, Maggie said, "What's on your mind?"

Annaliese looked at her friend and shook her head. "Maggie, if I told you all that's on my mind we'd still be sitting here 'til tomorrow." She was quiet again and finally said, "A crazy man is after my husband. With all I have on my mind with the board, and the clinic, and the haters, that's what it all comes back to. He's being stalked by some kind of wild animal who wants to kill him because he likes to kill.

"On top of that, I'm trying to set up a system to provide healthcare to the city and am being opposed to hatred, bigotry and maybe even violence, before it's all over."

"It seems to me I remember when Johnny was threatened in San Francisco, he confronted the man and told him to leave or fight. Why doesn't he do that now?"

"I asked him that. He said the man wouldn't fight. He'd turn his back and dare Johnny to shoot.

"Maggie, I'm used to solving people's problems. As a doctor and as a nurse before that, it's what I've done all my life. I can't think of anything that's ever been a more dangerous threat to my life and happiness than what's going on in my life right now, and I can do nothing about it."

She turned to face the water again and tears were running down her face. "Nothing!" she said in an anguished moan.

There are times when the best thing to say is nothing and Maggie sensed this was one of those times. She just hugged her friend and waited.

Finally, after a deep sigh, Annaliese said, "Well, in that case I better get to work."

"Doing what?"

"What I can do. Helping you and the Doctor take care of our patients, helping Mica set up a working clinic, helping my city get back on its feet, working with the board to see where we go from here and with who. None of these problems are going away, and even if they're not my biggest problems right now, they still have to be solved." She looked at her friend. "The other problem is for Johnny to solve. But if you see me staring off into space the next little while, say something funny. That always helps."

Roy let Johnny know when she came into the store, and he walked into the office from upstairs just as she sat down at her desk.

"So did the two of you solve any problems?"

"Not really, just inventoried the ones I have. But I decided I can't let it keep me from doing what I need to do around here."

"Like what?"

"The Doctor and I need to talk before the next meeting with the hospital board. That's tomorrow afternoon. I think we have to tell them we won't wait for their decision on the future of the place. The building's still in decent shape now that they've cleaned it out, but most of the people they need to operate it now work for us.

Most of their equipment was moved upstairs, so while they have the makings of a hospital, they don't have the people they need to run it."

"So, the idea is to move forward with your plans and handle the future if and when they decide whether they want to join you?"

"Yes. I'm determined not to let them make decisions for us by not deciding. So, we go without them."

"I thought you said you weren't going to meet with them again."

"I decided to go with the doctor and lay it all out on the table. If nothing else, I can let them know what I think about them."

"Well, there's things that need doing around town so I'm going to begin there. If you need me for something let me know." He paused for a minute. "Tell you what. I'm going down to Kate's place. Tell Roy to call me. I want to see how far this thing can reach."

He reached for her, and she was in his arms.

"Johnny, I'm scared." Her voice was muffled against his chest. "How are we going to get through this?"

"I'm working on it," he said and hugged her tighter.

Wash was at the pump, washing off the day's dirt when Kate called from the porch.

She waved him over. "Let's talk a bit."

Woman joined them and they sat for a moment, looking at all they'd accomplished since the flood.

"I'd say it won't be long 'til we're back to normal around here." The hard work of rebuilding the store and unloading wagon after wagon from the sanctuaries where their trees and plants had weathered the flood was done. Now everything had to be arranged as before, and then they would have to replace with new stock what had been lost.

"Are you going to rebuild the gazebo?" asked Woman.

"Once we get everything else done. Then we can sit out there and enjoy what we have again."

"So, what have you and Johnny decided?" asked Kate after a moment. "Have you figured out a way out of this mess?"

"He's thinking a lot about it. When he gets to a place where he's ready he'll come talk to me and we'll work out a plan."

"Any ideas?"

"Oh yeah. But he has to come to the point where he'll accept my advice. He knows what I'll say but it goes against his grain."

She sat waiting for him to go on, but he didn't. "Are you going to tell me or not?"

"Not now. Maybe later."

Kate rolled her eyes with an exasperated look. She looked at Woman. "How do you put up with him?"

"It's not so hard," said Woman. "You just have to be patient. He'll tell you when he's ready."

Johnny walked out to the rock and waited for Wash to join him. When he needed to think he did it best around his friend, and right now he really needed to think. He was in a place where he could see no path that led him out of danger. His enemy was stalking him and playing with him, manipulating him by forcing him to become someone he didn't like, someone constantly looking over his shoulder, consumed with the threat hanging over him.

Wash came up behind and stood looking at him in silence. Johnny was so deep in thought he didn't hear him or notice he was there until he spoke.

"When I was trying to figure out what to do about Schweder, I decided not to go by the rules because it was too important. This was a man who had killed for money and would continue to if I didn't stop him. I wasn't going to allow ideas of fair play to keep me from doing what I felt I needed to do.

"So, I climbed up a tree and put a bullet through his knees and he can no longer kill people for a living. No way I could have done that if I'd braced him and given him an even break. If I had, I'd probably be dead, and he'd still be killing people for a living."

He paused and let Johnny think about that for a while, then continued. "This fellow's the one who's thrown the rules out the window, not you. If you try to play fair with him, it gives him all the advantages. He don't know what it means to play fair. I think you're too smart to let him do that to you, Johnny.

"You need to end this thing and the only way for you to come out of it in one piece is to face him, force a fight and if he won't fight, shoot him anyway, and I'm not talking about in the knee. Put a couple of bullets in his chest. You'd be doing the world a favor."

"You mean ambush him?"

"No, Johnny. I did that because it was the only way I could solve my problem and come out of it in one piece. No, I think you should go into the saloon where he hangs out, brace him, and if he won't fight, put a bullet in him."

He let Johnny consider that for a moment. "He's playing this game with you cause he thinks you won't do that. People like him always think of people like us as suckers because we play by the rules. Don't play by his rules."

"What about the law?"

Wash shrugged. "If it's across the border, just stay out of Mexico in the future. You know more about the law around here than I do, but with the threats he's made, I don't believe it will be a problem. When it comes to the law, I know things aren't like they used to be, but I can't believe any jury would convict you. I doubt you'd even be arrested. Besides, Roy and I will be there to be witnesses if need be."

"If I decide to do this, how would I find him?"

"I'll find him. I doubt if it will be too hard. Kate will understand."

"What will Woman say about you going off on such an errand?"

"She always understands."

As usual, Kate was watering some plants in front of the nursery when they rode up.

"Bout time you came to work," she said to Wash.

"Let's sit and talk," said Johnny. He led the way to the porch where he knew the coffee was and when they were seated said, "I need to borrow Wash again for a while."

Her eyes narrowed and she looked at him. "What is it this time? That same man again?" When Johnny nodded, she continued. "Have you decided what to do about it?"

"Yes," he said. "I think we may finally have a plan to deal with him and put an end to it, and I need Wash along to make it work."

Woman had come up behind where Wash was sitting and he reached to take her hand over his shoulder.

"Can you tell me about it?" asked Kate.

"Not right now, later probably. It may take a while, but I think we can put an end to it, and I can go back to being Johnny again."

After they left, she sat for a while, nursing a cold cup of coffee, staring into the distance. She didn't believe Johnny would be back to being Johnny when this was over.

Behind her she heard the sounds of a buggy and Lemuel walked in. "Good morning, Kate. You look marvelous this morning."

Actually, she had been helping with some irrigation problems. She was splattered with mud, including a smear on her forehead where she had pushed her hair back with a muddy hand and she looked a mess, but she grinned at his banter.

"Sounds like you kissed the stone this morning," she said. "You're not Irish, are you?"

"Scot actually, but my people came over from Belfast. I think it's in the air thereabouts."

He reached across the table and took her hand. "You know this is getting to be the best part of my day; coming over here to see you and drinking your coffee and saying, 'Good morning, Kate'."

She took his other hand. "Mine too," she said.

He followed her back onto the porch, and when they were both sipping coffee, looked at her and said, "You know, everyone is asking me what's going on between us. What do you think I should tell them?"

To hide her smile, she covered her mouth with her hand. "What do you think is going on between us?"

"Well actually I think there might be a little spark, and even if it's just a little one, I think we should blow on it, make a big fire."

She chuckled. "That's what I love about you, Lemuel. You've been around long enough to know how to charm a woman." He reached across the table and took her hand.

"That sounds good," she said. "Let's make a big fire." She took his other hand, "You know, it's been a long time. Harold has been dead for ten years. I think one of the reasons I stay so busy is so I won't have to remember." They sat looking at one another.

"It's nice to feel this way again." She leaned toward him, and he met her in the middle of the table. She heard someone come up behind her, and figuring it was Woman, waved her away without stopping what she was doing.

After a minute they separated and sat back smiling at one another.

"I hate to break up such a wonderful moment, but this thing with Johnny worries me," she said. "I just talked to Wash. He thinks Johnny is having trouble dealing with it. Wash thought he'd eventually come to him, and they'd talk, but I swear, I don't see what they can do. It sounds like he's a crazy man. How do you handle someone like that?"

"Well, if it was me, I'd just shoot him." He sat back in his chair. "On the way down here in the wagon, some fellows stopped us and one of them threatened to see me down the road. I blew his head off with a shotgun because it was the only way I could figure to keep him from shooting me from behind a rock somewhere."

Kate's mouth dropped open. "You really did that?"

"Yes, I did. I figured staying alive was more important than playing by his rules. Told the sheriff in the next town and paid to have him buried. He didn't have a problem with it. Seems like there had been some instances of robberies and such, and this guy was the leader of a gang."

They sat quiet for a long moment, looking at one another.

"So, you're saying Johnny should just shoot him down like some kind of mad dog?"

Lemuel shrugged and nodded his head. "Yep, and I think he'll come to see it the same way before it's over. It seems like the only way to solve the problem. So, just like I did when I pulled the trigger on that guy, Johnny will be doing the world a favor."

"I'm glad I'm finding these things out about you before things go too far," she said. She looked at him for a long moment. "The problem is I think they already have."

Kisses like that are very sweet and even more so when you're a little older.

Grace was writing in her diary when Este came into the bedroom drying her hair.

"I'll never get over the differences between your family and mine," said Este. "I never see your brothers or sister. Oh, we talk at meals and things, but you never do anything with them. At home I can't get away from mine."

"We spend time together, but it's usually on trips, and since I began at the clinic, I'm not home very much. When Papa traveled for business, we'd usually go along, and we were together most of the time then. Since we've lived here, we all seem to go our own way. We're all growing up and interested in different things. Because Papa's rich we can do pretty much what we want, so we do.

"Since we don't go to a regular school, Mama thinks we should do things to help us learn about other people. That's one of the reasons she and Papa were so happy about me working with Annaliese."

"At my house everyone is usually busy doing chores, working, or playing outside and the house is empty most of the time, which is good because it's so small. Here it's like a different world."

When she came back from the dressing room she was smiling.

"What are you smiling about now?" asked Grace.

"I was just thinking about having a place to get dressed. We all get dressed around each other at home and no one thinks anything about it. I've seen every backside in the house and probably the neighborhood too when we go swimming, and the closets here are so big. We have one closet in the house, and it ends up being full of things we don't know what to do with."

She sat down on her bed and began to brush her hair.

"I'd like to visit you at home sometime," said Grace. "After three years at the clinic, I know all your family and most of the people in Old Town, for that matter."

"Really? Why? You've been there many times."

"I'm usually with Annaliese and we're..." she paused and looked thoughtful. "We're being doctors, I guess. Taking care of people. It's not like visiting. I know people are different when a doctor's there. It would be nice to see them when there's no doctor around and everybody's just being themselves."

"I'll ask Mama and maybe you can come home with me next week and stay. We'll be going to church Sunday morning. Will that be OK?"

"Will Juan be there?"

"After work. He works with Papa at The Del. Why?"

"Well, I might have to find someplace private to dress. I won't mind the younger children but he's almost as old as I am."

"Yes. I understand." She looked thoughtful. "It might be a problem." She was quiet for a moment, thinking. "We could hang a curtain in my bedroom. It's just me and my two sisters there most of the time. You'd have to sleep with me and Nina."

Later, after they finished their schoolwork, Este said, "You're always writing in that diary. Is it just from the clinic or do you put other things in there too?"

"It's mostly about the clinic and what happens there. When I started with Annaliese, Papa told me I should keep a diary, so I have. I've been here three years now and I'm just beginning my fourth."

"Really? Would you mind if I read some of it?"

Grace took her time answering. "I guess not. No one's ever read it before. Most of it is just stuff from work. But once in a while I write about other things in it. Like right now. There's some kind of crazy man after Johnny and Annaliese is really upset about it.

Sometimes I think she just needs to talk, and since I'm the only one around she talks to me. I probably shouldn't write that kind of thing down, but it's a diary, so I guess it's all right."

She sat quietly for a while pondering, and finally said, "It would probably be a good thing for you to use as a way to learn. That's what I wrote it for, especially when I first started. Sometimes things would be happening so fast, I'd have to write everything down before bed at night because I didn't want to forget it. I don't write so much now because I'm used to things and there's not so much that's new."

As they were getting ready to leave Este asked, "Do you ever talk to Roy?"

"Once in a while, I guess. Not very often. It seems strange to talk to someone who doesn't talk back."

"He looks at me," Este said.

"Este, I think you should get used to the idea that men are going to look at you. The way you look, it would be strange if they didn't."

"No, it's not like that. I don't know, it's like he…" she paused. "He wants me to know he's there. Sometimes it's hard for me to look away from him. It takes effort."

"What do you mean?"

Este thought for a moment. "Unless I make myself stop, I'd look at him as long as I'm in the store. Have you ever noticed his eyes?"

It was Grace's turn to think. "Well, he is good looking, but I know what you mean about his eyes."

Este rolled her eyes in exasperation. "He's not that good

looking." She shrugged. "Although I think that's part of the problem. For some reason, I like looking at him too."

"Isn't he a bit old for you?"

"He's twenty-one and I'm fourteen. Some of my friends are married already, one of them to a man older than that." She laughed. "I'm not going to marry him." She stopped and smiled. "Well, maybe I am, but I have other things I want to do first. I don't want to get married right now. Once I become a doctor there'll be time for that."

Grace grinned at her. "Oh, so you're going to be a doctor. You've already decided that?"

"Of course. I can't think of anything else I ever wanted to be. I want to be like Annaliese and Maggie." She paused and smiled at her friend. "And you."

That night they had just turned the lights off when Este said, "I wonder what it would be like to be married to someone who couldn't talk?"

Chapter Forty

Sarah was packing things for their annual move to San Diego when Rebecca came into the room.

"Getting ready to leave?" she asked and sat down on the bed.

"I was, but she had to do something here, so we're not leaving 'til next week. We'll catch the Monday morning train."

"Good. I want to ask you something. Is Madame here?"

"Yeah, I think she's in the library with Nate, her lawyer. We're going to lunch, so she'll let me know when she's ready. What did you want to ask me?"

"The men at the ranch have come up with an idea. They have things running real smooth up there, so Handy suggested each one of them take off for a while each year. They decided to try it and drew lots to decide which would be the first to go. Handy won, so we'll be moving down to San Diego for the winter. The plan is for each one to take off for three months and then decide if they want to continue to work that way at the end of a year. They figure to take a month between each one to get ready for the time off."

"Sounds like a great idea."

"They'll try it, each of them for three months and then see. But the thing is, we can rent a place for the winter, or we could stay with you at Madame's place. We don't want to push in, but you'd get to see Bobby a lot more that way, and we'd get to spend more time together doing things."

"I know what she'll say. You're family, come and go as you like."

"I know but I feel better if I ask."

"When are you leaving?"

"We can be ready by Monday, so why don't we go together? Is Carlota taking Geppetto?"

"She's already down there with him, opening up the house. Tony and Mrs. Jensen are going down with us."

"She's the new cook?"

"She's been training here and she's going to go down with us every year. At least that's the plan." She shrugged. "Who knows. I can still cook if it comes to it."

Monday morning saw them all settled in a first-class compartment headed south. Bobby was glued to the window watching the world go by while the rest of them talked. After a few miles, Handy put his small black kitten on Rebecca's lap and drew out a letter.

"I got this the other day. This is the reason I came up with the idea at the ranch. It's from Roy. Seems Johnny's got his tail in a crack over this investigation into Herschel's murder. There's a fellow who was involved with the bad guys we threw out of City Hall up here who's threatening to kill him.

"Roy thought I ought to know. Looks like Johnny didn't want me dodging bullets with him again so he didn't let me know this time."

"What are you going to do?" asked Sarah.

"I guess that depends on what I find when I get there. It may be over, and it may not be, so what I'll do depends on what I find. But if Johnny needs me I'll be there."

"What do you think about that?" Sarah asked Rebecca.

"I don't like it much but all we can do is wait 'til we get there and cross the bridge if that's what's there. If he feels it's important then he needs to do what he feels is right."

Madame gestured at the shotgun leaning against the seat by the door. "Is that the ten-gauge I've heard so much about?"

Handy nodded. "I've only fired that thing one time in anger. Nearly cut an Apache in half and that was just one barrel. That thing's a cannon. When it's around, people suddenly check their hole card. It tends to defuse unpleasant situations."

When Handy came into the store he petted Jinx hello, but the cat was only interested in what was on Handy's shoulder. The little black kitten sitting there seemed to feel the same way about Jinx, but before they had a chance to examine one another Handy was climbing the stairs on the way up to Johnny's room under the eaves.

"It doesn't look like Jinx likes My Boy," he said when he walked in.

Johnny looked up and smiled. "Hey Handy," he said standing to greet his friend. "What's your boy's name?"

"My Boy."

"He looks like Jinx when he was a kitten," said Johnny. He shook his friend's hand and reached the other up to scratch the kitten's ears. "I didn't know you were coming down. When'd you get in?"

"A little while ago. Rebecca's at the cottage unpacking but I wanted to see you. Got a letter that said you might need me. It was typed."

"That'd be Roy. He likes his typewriter." Johnny leaned back and laced his fingers on top of his head. "Did he tell you what it's about?"

"Something about one of the henchmen from the City Hall gang."

It took Johnny about ten minutes to lay the whole story out for his friend. While he was at it Jinx came carefully into the room, hopped on Johnny's desk, and began to watch the kitten closely. By the time he had finished explaining the whole thing to Handy, Johnny was smiling. He pointed at the cats and Handy turned to watch.

Jinx was sitting on the desk disdainfully watching the kitten, who was trying his best to climb up Handy's pant leg. By the time he got up to the knee, Jinx had jumped down and was examining his bed where the kitten had been lying when he came in. When the kitten regained the floor he bounced up to Jinx wanting to play. All he got for his trouble was boxed ears which, predictably, had no effect on him and Jinx had to do it again, after which he walked stiff legged to Johnny and stood to be picked up.

Johnny grinned at his friend. "How old is he?"

"About four months. I got about six running around the place. Soon have more cats than horses. He's the only black male. For some reason I just took to him." Jinx hopped in his lap and Handy sat petting the cat.

"Any problems with the head since you got back?"

"No, with all of them around, I've always got one to pick up when I need one."

"So, it looks like it's not just Jinx that helps your head?"

"Well, that or time has solved the problem. At any rate, I enjoy having them around and most of them earn their keep. And this one," he picked up the kitten and sat him on his lap. "This one's special, though. He's my boy." Handy paused. "So, what's Wash think about all this?" he asked.

"He thinks I should just blow his head off. He's let me think about it for a while, see if I come up with any answers on my own. He thinks that's what it will come down to."

Johnny sat for a moment gathering his thoughts and continued. "I haven't told you this but when he first got down here, he ran across the man who shot Jed and Lemuel. Couldn't figure what to do about it. Couldn't take it to the law because he couldn't prove it.

"Found out enough to believe he was the one and finally ambushed him. Shot him through the knees. He figured a man who couldn't walk couldn't do what it takes to keep killing for a living. Now he sits on his porch and watches his orange trees grow. I think he wants me to do something along that line to this guy or maybe let him do it."

"How do you feel about that?"

"The more I think on it, the more sense it makes."

"Sounds like this guy thinks he's got you backed into a corner."

"Not quite, but he believes I won't just up and shoot him, so he keeps pushing and trying to keep me on edge. Well, he's got me on edge all right and I don't like it. It looks like Wash's way might be the only way. That's what Lemuel says anyway."

"When do you plan on doing something?"

"We have to find him first. Wash is looking and he doesn't think it will be too hard. He hangs out in Tijuana a lot. If I brace him down there, I won't have so much trouble with the law up here."

"Well, let me know when and I'll be there."

Johnny shook his head, "I don't want you involved in this one."

Handy sat quiet for a moment with a puzzled look on his face. "Why not?"

"It's not like it was before. When we went on the trip in the desert, we didn't really expect things to play out the way they did, and before that you weren't married with a son."

"And another one on the way."

"Congratulations. That's one more reason for you to stay out of it. It's not fair to your family. Roy will be with us if we need help."

"What about Lemuel?"

"You probably haven't heard, but Lemuel and Kate are becoming serious about a future together. With all the grief he's had, I don't want to put him in the way of a bullet. No, Roy will be with me, and Wash."

"I brought the ten-gauge with me."

"Good. With Wash holding that thing it should keep any bystanders cautious enough to stay out of it."

Handy sat rubbing his nose for a minute. "It will seem funny not being there to back you, but I think you're probably right. Need to think of them first, and with Wash and Roy there you probably won't need me anyway. You should be OK."

Johnny was lying on the bed with Jinx on his chest enjoying being petted while he watched his wife brushing her hair, thinking how much he enjoyed it.

"I got a note from Rebecca," she said, looking at him in the mirror. "She told me about the arrangement they have at the ranch now, so they'll be here for three months this time. I know you're glad to have Handy here right now."

"Yeah. He came by and we talked." He sat quiet for a moment and when he didn't elaborate, she asked, "What'd you talk about?"

"I told him I didn't want him involved in this thing that's going on now."

She turned to face him, still brushing. "Why would you say that?"

"He's got Rebecca and Bobby to worry about, and by the way, it seems Rebecca's pregnant again. That's one more reason for him not to be in it. So, Roy and Wash will be with me, and I think that's enough."

"Be with you to do what?"

"I've decided what I'm going to do to end this situation."

She carefully put the brush in its place by the mirror, turned to face him and asked. "So, are you going to tell me?"

"Yes, but I don't want to. You'll worry, get upset and cry. I don't like it when you do that."

She shook her head and closed her eyes. "But you are going to tell me?"

"I've decided to brace him, and if he won't fight, I'll shoot him anyway."

She looked at him, mouth open, eyes wide. "Johnny, isn't that murder?"

"I'm hoping when I make it clear to him how it is, he'll draw instead of just letting me shoot him, but even if he doesn't, I'm going to kill him. Besides, it looks like it will be in Mexico, which means as long as no one stops us I shouldn't have to worry about the law."

They sat quiet looking at one another. "When is all this happening?"

"Wash has found out where he spends most of his time. A little place on the other side of Tijuana. He lives upstairs over a cantina. He usually eats there and has a few drinks most evenings. I think we'll be leaving tomorrow night. I'll be away the night."

"So, you and Wash."

"And Roy."

"You know how I feel about that."

"He's a man and he wants to be there. He'll watch my back and Wash will have the ten-gauge to keep anyone from interfering. We'll spend the night at the cabin, and I'll be home the next morning."

"If you make it home."

"Annaliese, it looks like it's the only way to get past it."

They were sitting on their horses under a tree looking across the main street of a little Mexican village at the front door of a small cantina. They sat quiet for a while and finally Johnny said, "I swear, it seems like every time I go into one of these places I'm walking into a fight."

"Don't drink much that way."

"There's that."

"I assume you're talking to him," said Wash. "I can't tell in the dark."

"Sorry," replied Johnny. "He said I don't drink much that way."

"That's true."

Johnny nudged Black and the horse began to move out of the shadows. The others followed. "Let's get started," he said. "I want to get this behind me, and we can't finish what we don't start."

They tied their horses at the side of the cantina and picked their way through scattered refuse and trash to where they could see through a dirty window. Inside it was dim and smokey but they could see Presgraves sitting at a table with three other men, all in Mexican attire.

Johnny looked at his companions, took a deep breath and nodded. "Let's go," he said and led the way through the front door.

When three strangers walk into a cantina at night in a small town in Mexico it suddenly gets silent. When the strangers are two Gringos and a black man carrying a big shotgun, the silence is deafening. Even the guitar player stopped playing.

Presgraves looked up when he came through the door and Johnny could tell he was startled, surprised to see him there.

Johnny glanced around the room. Not so crowded. A quiet night about to be disturbed. He got the impression everyone in the room knew who he was and why he was there. The man's three companions turned to look when Johnny came in, and two of them slowly got up and moved away from the table. The other repositioned his chair so he was facing Johnny.

He stopped a few feet from the table and stood quiet, eyes locked on Presgraves.

"Didn't expect you to show up here," the man said. "How'd you find me?"

In the bar mirror Johnny could see Roy standing to one side of the door and Wash, ten-gauge cocked, at port arms on the other.

"Wasn't too hard. You're a famous man among these people. Crazy white men do stand out south of the border."

"I should take offense at that, but I'll let it pass. So, what do you want?"

"Well, I've decided I don't like the situation I find myself in, what with you threatening to kill me and all, so I've decided to put an end to it."

"If you've come here looking for a fight, I'm afraid you'll be disappointed. I won't fight you."

"You misunderstand me. I didn't come here to fight you. I came here to kill you."

His eyes narrowed, "You mean if I don't draw, you'll still shoot me?"

Johnny smiled and nodded slowly. "Right in the middle of your chest. You see, I've decided it's the only way I can put a stop to this game you're playing with me. I think you're betting I won't do something like this. You know what? You lost the bet."

Johnny's eyes were locked on his and even in the dim light he could see something in them; not fear, maybe uncertainty. It wasn't supposed to be like this.

Johnny took a coin from his vest pocket. "I'm going toss this in the air, and when it hits the table, we draw. If you decide not to, it doesn't matter. I'm going to and once I start there's no stopping."

The man stood so suddenly the chair fell over and Johnny tossed the coin. When it topped out and began to fall, Presgraves started to draw. He never had a chance. Johnny's two shots struck him in the chest before the coin ever hit the table.

His companion pushed back from the table so fast his chair went over, and he came up grabbing at his holster. He was facing Johnny, and Roy's bullet to the man's shoulder knocked him sideways into the wall behind him where he slid down to sit, holding his shoulder with blood running through his fingers.

At the door Wash had swung the ten-gauge around so that it covered the room and everyone looking at those barrels knew what destruction would occur if he pulled the triggers.

"No one else needs to get hurt here tonight," he said in that slow, deep, gravelly voice. "But that's not up to me, is it?" He smiled at them. "In case you wondered, it's loaded with buckshot." Not one of the men standing before him had any doubt he would pull both triggers if need be to protect his friends.

"Let's go Johnny," he said.

Johnny was standing still staring at the man sitting on the floor in front of him. His gun was still centered on the man's chest where the .44 caliber slugs fired from three yards away had left two slightly smoking holes in his shirt. He was dead and his eyes were open, looking at Johnny, seeing nothing. There was a ghost of a smile on his lips.

With the smoking Colt in hand, he stood looking at the man who had been so much in his thoughts for so long and realized he would continue to be for a while yet, maybe forever. He stepped closer, squatted on his heels, and reached to close the eyes.

Finally, Johnny holstered the Colt and turned to face the room. "Sorry about the mess," he said and tossed several coins on the bar. "This ought to bury him." With Roy following, he walked out the door.

Wash stopped at the door, shotgun ready. He looked around the room and said, "We're leaving now." He smiled. "I hope none decide to follow." He backed out the door and followed Johnny and Roy to where the horses were tied.

Within a minute they were mounted, and when they rode by the front of the cantina, no one was looking out.

Chapter Forty-One

A couple hours later they rode into the clearing where the cabin was being built. None of them had said a word since they'd crossed the border. They tied their horses and followed Wash up the steps to where Woman was sitting, waiting for them.

When Johnny was seated in a chair on the porch, he finally said, "You know, between the two of you, I had a lot of time to think about what just happened back there."

Wash chuckled. "With one of us who doesn't talk much and one who doesn't talk at all, that's liable to be the case." Even in the dark he could see Johnny cock his head, listening.

"What did he say?"

"He asked how I felt about what happened back there."

When Johnny didn't continue Wash asked, "So, how *do* you feel about it?"

Johnny sat with his chin in his hand for a long moment. "I tell you what, I don't know what life has in store for me tomorrow, but it's got to be better than today."

They sat quiet for a moment, thinking about that.

"Can you tell me what happened?" asked Woman.

Between Johnny and Wash they did, and then Johnny began to talk. "You know, every time I've had to draw my gun on someone, I felt I had no choice. It was that or die." He looked at Roy. "You don't know much about the first one, do you?"

"A little."

"When Handy and I were coming out here from Kansas a drunk cowpuncher in Julesburg, Colorado got mad, drew his gun and tried to shoot me." He paused, gave a grim chuckle. "He was trying to get on Black and I grabbed his belt and pulled. He landed in some horse shit. I guess because everyone was laughing at him he got angry, but whatever the reason, he reached for his gun.

"I remember standing there looking at him afterwards. He was lying half on the boardwalk and half on the ground with blood all over his shirt and in the dust where he lay. His hat landed five feet away from him and I remember looking at it thinking, "How did this happen?" Another dry chuckle and he shook his head. "Still don't know. It happened so fast I never even had time to think.

"You know about what happened in Carson City and San Francisco," he said and shook his head. "How many more times will something like this happen to me?

"You know, by any definition, I committed murder tonight. To use a legal term I've read about, I walked into that place with 'malice aforethought.' I know he drew his gun first, but I would have killed him even if he hadn't, because that's what I went in there to do."

"What choice did you have?" asked Wash. "Were there any other options that would have solved the problem? He pushed you into a corner. I can see why your mind's in a whirl, but it will calm down," said Wash. "He was a man asking for someone to do what you did. I'm amazed he lived as long as he did. You just saved someone else the trouble of doing it, so I'd say don't lose any sleep over it.

"Besides, didn't you say he admitted to you he killed Herschel?" When Johnny nodded, he continued. "No one would have ever been able to prove that, so you just made sure he paid the price for what he did." He paused and sat quiet for a moment. "I did something like that one time, and it still bothers me, so I know a little of what's going on in your head."

Johnny was quiet again for a while. "I wonder what price I'll have to pay," he finally said.

The next morning, he and Roy rode back to the city early. Johnny was quiet most of the way but when they stopped to water the horses at a creek that ran into the ocean Johnny looked at his friend.

"That's the kind of thing you should try to stay out of in the future," he said.

Roy didn't react for a while and then, *"It made my stomach feel strange."* Quiet for a while, then, *"You think he'll die?"*

"Probably not, but under the circumstances, it wasn't really our concern. If you keep bad company these things happen. Don't worry about it. You were doing what you needed to do, and I appreciate it, even if he doesn't."

They were quiet for a while, horses cropping grass in the shade.

"Can I ask you something?"

"Anything."

"It's about something at the store." He took a deep breath, closed his eyes for a moment, then let it out and said, *"I'm going to speak to her family about Este. I wanted you and Annaliese to know before I did."*

Johnny smiled. "I'd say it would be a good idea to tell Annaliese. What do you think her parents will say?"

Roy sat for a moment with his eyes closed. Johnny remembered the effort it took, the rest he needed before he could do it again.

"Not until she finishes school."

"I imagine she feels the same way."

Roy nodded.

"I think it's great, but it's how *they* think that counts. And Annaliese. You might have more trouble with her than Consuelo."

Roy looked rueful and rolled his eyes.

He was lying on the bed, cat on his chest, staring at the ceiling when she came in. All day, no matter what she was doing her mind kept coming back to Johnny and what he was going to do. But she was busy, so she had to wait until she saw him (if she saw him) to find out.

He had called her at the clinic when he returned, and knowing he was safe, she had stayed busy at the clinic all day and was now seeing him for the first time since it happened.

As much as she wanted to talk, she was also reluctant to hear what he'd say. She knew somehow this confrontation would change her husband. He wouldn't be the same person he was before and knowing that gave her a strange feeling down deep in her stomach, as though she was afraid of what he might have become.

Johnny was at that place in his life where he was leaving what he had been and becoming what he would be, stepping over a line into his future, so to speak. He still had much of the boyishness that drew her to him, eagerness to live every day, a sense of right and wrong, and a thirst for learning that comes with being young and knowing there's so much to learn. How much of that would be lost after what he had done the night before? She was a little afraid to find out.

When, freshly showered and in her bath robe, she sat down to brush her hair, she could see him in the mirror, sitting on the edge of the bed looking at her.

They sat quiet for a while looking at each other. Finally, she said, "Tell me."

He shrugged. "It went pretty much like we thought it would," he said. "Looking back, I'm amazed we were in and out of the place in less than five minutes. He was surprised to see me there and when I told him why I could see he was even more so.

"Wash was right. He believed I'd play by his rules, and when I didn't, he didn't know what to do. To this point he was the one who had controlled the game. Me standing in front of him with a gun on my hip wasn't in his plan. For the first time I was running the show."

"Did you kill him?"

He nodded, looking in the mirror, into her eyes, wondering what he'd see there when he said it. They sat quiet while she finished brushing her hair, then came to sit beside him and lay her head on his shoulder.

"Are you still my Johnny?" she asked in a whisper.

He took a deep breath. "I want to be. We'll just have to wait and see how it plays out. This was a tough one. All that went on in my head while he was playing with me is still there. Am I always going to have it in my mind wondering if I did the right thing? I have no idea how long it will take to fade away, or if it ever will." He ran his hand over her hair and said, "Tomorrow I'm going to talk to the sheriff about it and see where I stand with the law."

"What do you think he'll say?"

"Wash and Lemuel seem to think he'll just let it pass. I'll let him know what's happened, so he won't be surprised. He'll probably talk to the judge and then do whatever he tells him."

"Do you think he'll arrest you?"

"I don't see how he could, but I don't know how things work across the border. I guess I'll find out before long."

He stretched out on the bed again and she lay beside him, her arm across his chest.

When she awoke, he was asleep, and she lay looking at him for a long time.

Their first morning back in town, Madame and Sarah had breakfast with Kate on the terrace at the Horton House.

"I had to remember to call Lemuel last night to tell him we were meeting. He said to tell you 'Hello'. He wanted to come but I told him it was just for us girls."

They chatted through breakfast and after. With tea before them, Sarah said, "So I hear you have a fellow."

Kate grinned. "Where'd you hear that?"

"A little bird told me."

"So," said Madame, hitching her chair a little closer. "Tell us about it. Leaving out no details, of course."

"We've been seeing a lot of one another lately and talking about things, getting to know each other."

"Has he asked you yet?"

"Not in so many words, but yes, he probably will. I know he wants to and I feel the same way, so why not. Neither of us need anyone's permission."

With both of them looking at her with knowing smiles, she could feel herself blushing for the first time in many years.

"I remember when we were doing the militia thing, Greta told us he was born in 1830. That'd make him sixty-five," said Madame.

"You'd never know it. To use an expression I've read somewhere, he's pursuing me and wooing me."

"That sounds like fun," said Madame. "I always thought he had it in him. Just needed the right someone to bring it out."

"I hope I am. I had a 'marriage of convenience' with Harold. He was the only boy around the ranch where I was raised. We were always doing things together and it was just expected we'd get married. He was never in good health and was sick for three years before he died, so it's been thirteen years since I've had a man in my bed."

"You never had any children?" asked Madame.

"We wanted to, but I lost one and for some reason we stopped trying."

"Well, at that age, he may not want to start."

Kate grinned again. "Oh, he wants to start alright. He kissed me yesterday morning and I could tell that."

They all laughed. "How do you feel about that?" asked Sarah.

"I was thinking about it last night. It never was important to me before, but now for some reason I feel excited about the idea." She shook her head. "Listen to me. I sound like a schoolgirl."

"Could be because that's what you feel like," said Madame. "As long as you're healthy, it's never too late."

"He's going up to Los Angeles with me tomorrow. I've got to see a supplier and he has several bookstores he wants to visit."

Madame leaned forward and said in a stage whisper, "Sounds like it might just be an interesting trip."

She had been thinking about that and felt herself blushing again.

"I'll see you back here at one o'clock."

They were standing in front of the hotel, each ready to go their own way for the morning.

She held on to his hand when he tried to leave and said, "I enjoyed dinner last night."

"Me too. And candlelight was just the right touch." He pulled her to him and kissed her firmly on the lips, his mouth open just enough so she could feel the tip of his tongue.

"Makes me remember how much I like looking at you," he said when they finally parted.

She looked at him for a moment. "I can't believe I just did that in front of the nicest hotel in Los Angeles. And you know what? I don't really care who saw it."

She walked away. When she got to the corner, she turned and saw him still standing there watching her. *Maybe that's the way it should be,* she thought. *When you kiss someone you love, the rest of the world should cease to exist, not be important compared to what you're doing, what you're feeling.*

Chapter Forty-Two

Lemuel had a productive morning, adding two new accounts to his ledgers and taking orders for dozens of books he would put on the train as soon as he got home. When he returned to his room, he opened the window and stood feeling the breeze.

He closed his eyes and thought about Kate, how much he liked her smile, her eyes, and just about everything else he had seen since this whole thing began. Thinking about what he hadn't seen excited him even more.

At his age, ten years away from a woman's touch, from touching a woman, it made him feel a little anxious. Or maybe excited. He didn't think his stomach could tell the difference.

They had rented separate rooms with a small sitting room between them, and she came in just as he opened the door from his side. This time the kiss was long and tender, then passionate. When they separated, she said, "I've never felt like this before. What are you doing to me?"

He leaned forward and whispered, "Only what you want me to."

She held his hand and looked at him for a long moment. "It's been such a long time, I think maybe we should practice at least once before we get married," she said seriously. "What do you think?"

"You know damn well what I think," he said. He took her in his arms. "The only way I'm going to let you go is to help you take off your clothes."

"Your room or mine?" she asked breathlessly, not really caring which.

"Or somewhere in between."

So, they began on the couch and moved to one room, then the other, and after, lay looking at each other, touching each other every place they could think of that might feel good.

She thought of Harold once when they began, and then she was only thinking of what was happening to her.

His kisses sent a warmth rushing into her stomach then beyond, all through her body and some places he touched brought her surging off the bed, crying out with pleasure. Things happened to her that she'd read about, heard of, but never really believed existed. In the end she lay beneath him, eyes closed, catching her breath, and felt herself floating away to somewhere she knew she'd never been.

When she opened her eyes, he was propped up on his elbow looking at her.

"What are you looking at?"

"I'm trying to decide which part of you I like best." He pulled the covers off her breasts and bent to kiss one. "This spot right here, this freckle. I like this best." He moved up to her neck. "Or maybe this spot." He kissed and began to suck lightly. Then he kissed her on the lips and said, "Actually, I think I like all of you, every last little bit."

He looked into her eyes and said, "Now that you've had your way with me, what do we do now?"

She burst out laughing. "Well," she said, a mischievous sparkle in her eyes. "We could do it again."

He grinned at her and raised a finger. "Give me a few minutes and there's nothing I'd like better."

He lay back and closed his eyes, felt her move on the bed, and when he opened them she was sitting up on her knees looking down at him.

"This changes things, doesn't it?" she asked. He nodded, smiling, and she continued. "We're a couple now. From here on, most of the time, when I want to do something, I'll have to think about how it will affect you and us. Haven't had to do that for a while."

She sat quiet, thoughtful.

"Would you like to get married?" she asked.

He looked at her, fighting a smile. "Why buy the cow when you get the milk for nothing?"

She pounced on him, and they wrestled until he came out on top. "Why'd you do this to me?" she asked. "I was perfectly happy with my trees and my flowers and now look at me. In love! Ha!"

He was trying to keep a straight face and failing. "So, you admit it. You love me."

"How could I help it? You're so charming," she said. She made a face at him and then smiled.

He kissed her, but with them both smiling it wasn't much of a kiss. Then it became one, and one thing led to another.

In the morning, she was helping him dry himself after a shower when she said, "How did you get so many scars?" She pointed to his shoulder.

"That happened at Yellow Tavern, Virginia when I was with Sheridan. That's the fight where Jeb Stuart was killed, and I was wounded with a saber."

She shuddered. "And that one?" she asked, pointing to his thigh.

"Actually, I've been shot in that spot twice. Once by some bandits on the way to San Francisco, and again when Jed was killed. The first one was not quite healed when that one happened. Took a long time to get back to myself after the second one."

He finished dressing and was watching her when he said, "That last one is the reason I use a cane sometimes. There are days when I can hardly walk. Especially when it's wet. That's another reason I'm glad we moved down here. Of course, you're the main reason I'm glad."

She moved close to him and muttered, "You're a tough old bird, aren't you?"

"Not so old, I reckon."

She embraced him and kissed him. "No, not so old," she murmured.

Later that morning they breakfasted in the sitting room, and she sat quiet, thinking about how different her life would be from now on.

"Should I get the room for another night?" he asked, holding her hand across the table.

"We both have things to do at home, and if we stay everyone in town will know why." She slid her glasses down her nose and looked at him over the top. "With all your charm I know you could talk me into it but please don't. I have a business to run and, as good as Woman is, there are certain things only I can do." She grinned at him across the table. "Besides, we don't want to use it all up so soon."

He raised her hand to his lips and kissed it lightly. "It would take a lifetime to use it all up," he said.

"Hey Johnny, come on in and have a seat," said the sheriff. He was one of those really tall men who always looked like he was worried about bumping his head on a doorway. He usually sat sideways because his legs were too long to fit under his desk. He was the only man Johnny had ever seen who was taller than Handy but unlike Handy he was rail thin with a head of thick, white hair that made him look older than he was.

"Are you ever going to get a new desk?"

Ed grunted, "Took 'em six weeks to find this one after the flood. I take what I can get. What can I do for you?"

"I thought you should know I killed Barry Presgraves a couple of nights ago down in Mexico."

"In Mexico? What were you doing down there?"

"Looking for him. Wash found out he hung out at a cantina down there.

"You went down there to kill him?"

Johnny nodded.

"What do you mean, kill him?"

"He let me know when he got out of jail that he planned to get even with me. I got tired of waiting. He told me he wouldn't draw against me, so I told him if he didn't, I'd shoot him anyway. He drew, I shot him. He's dead."

Ed leaned back in his chair. "Why are you telling me this?"

"I didn't know if the authorities down there would get in touch with you or not. I figured you ought to know in case they did."

"You think he killed Herschel Grieve, don't you?"

"I know he did. He told me so. The problem was we were alone when he told me. With no witnesses he knew we couldn't prove it."

Ed sat pulling at his chin, looking thoughtful for a moment. "I don't usually hear much from down there. I think they're like us, got enough to do without worrying about something like this. I'd say you don't have much to worry about. I'd stay north of the border for a while, just in case, although I doubt if they'll cry any tears over him. He was a strange hombre, and they'll know he was probably living down there because of something he did up here.

"You wouldn't be interested in coming back as a deputy, would you? Just for while? I could surely use you since the flood."

"Ed, if I did, I'd be sleeping on the couch for a year. No, I like selling books and reading the newspaper." He smiled at the sheriff. "And being happily married, which I might not be if I took the job. John's been after me to take Herschel's old job, but I stay busy enough as it is.

"Well, I just wanted to let you know. If something comes up, you know where to find me."

After he'd gone a deputy stuck his head in the open door. "Is he going to come back?"

"No, but I sure wish he would. Damn that judge." He hadn't known Johnny long, but he could tell he had something on his mind.

"Will you be at the store tomorrow?" Este asked while Roy was preparing to mount his horse. He nodded and smiled at her. She touched his hand and smiled, looking into his eyes. She had heard Annaliese say they were like dark pools, and she felt that mystery whenever she looked at him, could feel her mind trying to touch his, to know what he was thinking.

"I'm glad," she said and kissed him on the cheek.

He touched the spot and smiled a slow smile at her, then mounted his horse and rode out of the stable yard.

After he was out of sight, she stood quiet for a while, looking after him and out at the bay in the distance. Behind her she heard Grace close the door and knew her friend had left her alone to think her thoughts, to ponder how to solve this problem that seemed to have no answer.

Roy was a good listener, which made sense since he couldn't talk and when he listened to her his eyes were always focused on hers, on her face, on her mouth and she sometimes felt lost in them.

When she talked to him about her life and where she wanted to go he seemed to understand how important it was to her, but did he really? Could he wait four years for her to reach out for her destiny, give her a chance to be what she knew she could become?

And could she wait to learn what he could teach her about love and life? She thought about how it made her feel when he was close and wondered if she could wait. Was there a path through this maze of emotions to where they could both be happy?

Since she had begun working with Annaliese, her ideas about what her life could become had grown and become important to her. What she was learning led her to feel that she had a chance to become someone far different from her family and the friends she had grown up with.

Sometimes the idea of living cut off from what she'd grown up with frightened her a little, but she was steadily coming to accept the possibility that with the help of Annaliese and Grace, it might become real.

Could she and Roy wait for her future or not? Maybe not. Maybe one or the other would have to be disappointed, to feel the agony and sleepless nights of love denied. Who would have to make the choice, if a choice it became?

In the time she had known him she had already learned to read his face, his eyes, the energy in his body and already they communicated much better than she would have believed. She knew he recognized the ways her emotions were pulling her.

She sighed, shook her head, and followed Grace into the house "Do you see any answers out there?"

She was almost startled by Grace's voice and realized she'd been standing looking out the window at nothing for a while.

She sat on the bed, took a deep breath, and said, "No! No answers, just questions. What am I going to do?" She shook her head and looked at Grace. "I have dreams and hopes about what I want to do and yet he's a special person, maybe unique, and I want to be with him. But is it an either/or situation? If I want to be a doctor, does that mean I can't have him? And what will he do if I tell him he has to wait until I finish school? How many years will that be?" There was a question on her face when she looked at her friend.

Later when Grace came into the bedroom, only one light was on, and Este was lying in shadow on her bed. She brushed her hair for a while in silence and finally asked, "Are you awake?"

"Yes."

"Want to talk about it?"

"What?"

Grace rolled her eyes. "Your appendix, what else?" she said with exasperation. "Roy, of course."

After a moment's silence Este sat up and shook her head. "A year ago, my mother asked Annaliese if I could go to work for her and since then I've been living in a fairytale. A mansion on the beach, a shower every day, nothing to do but learn and help people that need it, surrounded by people who want me to succeed, who'll do anything they can to make it happen.

"I want to be a doctor, to follow you and Annaliese into a world where I never dreamed I'd be. And I can. You'll all help me every step of the way, and before it's over, I'll be a doctor and be able to come back here and help people live better, help them change their lives."

She was quiet for a long moment and Grace said, drawing the word out. "But..."

Este sighed deeply. "But, what about Roy?" she said resignedly.

"He's special. I'll never meet someone like him the rest of my life and yet can I ask him to wait to be married, to put off living together as man and wife for *four years?*"

She sat up and looked at Grace. "Having a baby would destroy any chance of that future and I can't see getting married without having a baby. Right now, being together is hard because we both want to find the closest place to lie down."

"Have you talked to Annaliese about it?"

"No. But she knows. I think she's waiting for me to bring it up, but you know how she is. She won't interfere."

"What does Roy say?"

Este sat quiet. "One thing I love about Roy is that he has to write everything, so he thinks about what he wants to tell me. He wrote me the most beautiful note." She paused and took a deep breath, her emotions near the surface. "He said he'll be there whenever I'm ready."

Grace stood, reached out for her, and they stood holding each other for a long time.

"Sounds like that's the only answer. You've got to try to make it work, because if you, one way or another, you'll regret it the rest of your life."

Chapter Forty-Three

Will stood, leaned on the long table in front of him and looked slowly around at the hospital board.

"Based on our past problems, there seems to be one significant issue that led us to go our separate ways." Out of the corner of his eye he could see his daughter fidgeting in the chair beside him.

She was clearly uncomfortable being there. Her level of patience dealing with these men who seemed to be loath to take a position that would lead to criticism and possibly from some of the community, was at an end; and to be honest, she didn't give a damn what they thought about the clinic's plans for the future.

"Unless we come to a meeting of the minds on this we may be permanently sundered and the building and organization we have jointly worked to create will become a thing of the past and of no use to the community at large."

Unable to sit quiet any longer, Annaliese spoke up. "Do you still take the position that the Mexican people of the city, American citizens all, will not be allowed to receive treatment at the hospital if we join with you in working to reopen it?"

The chairman of the board sighed deeply. "That has never been our position. We merely feel that separate facilities should be developed so that the various races can be treated separately. There are a number of ways this can be done and we have sought a plan to do so."

She took her time and made eye contact with every member. Slowly and distinctly, she said, "I speak for everyone associated with the clinic when I say we will not compromise on this issue. Any person, regardless of where they come from or what they look like, will receive care at our facility, no exceptions, no qualifications.

"We have discussed this among ourselves and beginning tomorrow, we will move forward with it as a basis for our future as an institution. If and when you decide to join us under those conditions, we will discuss it. Until then I see no use in continuing this meeting."

No one on the other side of the table could have been surprised to hear this but they acted as though they were. "Is this your position Dr. Crawford?" the chairman asked.

"It is and it is also the position of every doctor who works with us. We will treat people who need it not just those who fit into a category created by you or anyone else." With that he put on his hat and followed his daughter out of the room.

A few minutes later he stopped the carriage in front of the store and Annaliese said, "Any future meetings we have with those fools will be here in the meeting room of The BookSeller. I'll not dignify them by going there again."

"Agreed. Let's sit down with Mica tomorrow and talk about what's next."

When she walked into the store, Roy nodded hello and pointed toward the ceiling, so she knew Johnny was upstairs.

"Tell him I'm here, will you please?" When he nodded, she said, "Thanks."

He met her in the office. They embraced and stood for a while holding each other. When they were seated, she asked, "Did you talk to the sheriff?"

He nodded. "Pretty much what I thought. He doesn't think it will be a problem. He'll let me know."

"Is it over now?"

To answer her he walked to the hat rack standing in the corner, unbuckled his gun belt and hung it on a vacant peg. "I hope so," he said. "I surely do hope so."

There were tears welling into her eyes, and as she closed them she could feel the wet on her cheeks. They embraced again, holding each other tight and when they separated, he said, "No one needs either of us for a while, so let's go for a ride and talk."

When they were in the buggy he asked, "Any place you want to see?"

"Let's go out to the rock at Wash's place. We can see how the cabin is coming along and sit and talk for a while." She leaned her head on his shoulder and continued. "And who knows what else we'll get into, seeing as how we'll probably be alone."

"It will take a while to get there."

She shrugged. "Maggie and the Doctor are minding the store. I'm not doing anything the rest of the day, and neither are you."

It was a beautiful day for a ride. "We don't do this as much as we should," he said. They had just forded a creek and stopped to let the horse drink. A small herd of elk were drinking upstream, and they sat watching them for a while. On the road again they talked of things not serious and arrived at the cabin excited about being away from the rest of the world for a while.

Wash and Woman were working so the cabin was empty. Wash was doing the finishing up work on the cabin himself, a little at a time and it was still a bit rough. What was to be the guest room wasn't really livable, but they knew what they were going to do when they walked up on the porch, and the couch would do just fine.

As soon as he closed the screen door they were in each other's arms, and within a few minutes she lay nude on the sofa, feeling the breeze through the open door watching him undress and welcoming him when he joined her. This was what she needed, a reconnection, a time when she could just be excited when he knelt between her legs, not caring what had happened yesterday or what would happen tomorrow, only what was happening then.

"What do we do if they come home? I really don't feel like moving," she said in a lazy voice.

"They'll see the buggy, so they'll know we're here. If they walk in, just say 'hello'."

She giggled and stretched like a cat awakening from a nap. They embraced again and lay in each other's arms for a while, feeling heart beats, listening to sounds of breathing in an otherwise silent world.

Finally, he sat up and said, "Do you want to go out to the rock, or just lie here and see what happens?"

She giggled again. "We should go." She leaned up and kissed him. "Thank you. I didn't realize how much I needed that."

She was sitting on the ground in front of the rock, eyes closed, his hands stroking her hair, listening to the ocean. "Tell me what you're thinking," she said.

"I'm thinking how nice it is when we do something like this every so often. It reminds me of that hotel room in Los Angeles that time."

"It does, doesn't it? Same kind of thing; a new place makes it special." She reached her hand up toward him and he took it and kissed it.

"We both have had some not very pleasant things going on lately," she said, "and not much time for each other."

"Well, mine's in the past now and I just have to be patient and let it bleed out of me, like the air going slowly out of a balloon. How is yours doing?

"I told the Doctor it was the last time any of us would go to the board's place to meet. Tomorrow, we meet with Mica and decide what to do next. If they want to join us, they'll have to come to us."

"You think they will?"

"Don't even have to think about that; no, they won't. For a number of reasons, but mainly they're still afraid of what the haters will do."

"The haters?"

"You know who I mean. The people who signed the petition."

"Do they have a leader?"

"If they do, I've never met him."

They sat quiet for a minute and finally Johnny said, "I have a suggestion. Why don't I spend some time and effort to find out who they are and what they are, and sort of assess the situation. If these people are going to create problems in our lives, I think we should find out as much about them as we can and see if we think they're dangerous."

"Do you think they might be?"

"There have been some pretty nasty incidents up north, near the diggings, and I'm sure you remember Chinatown in San Francisco. And there have been problems back East in some of the old Confederate states; lynchings and such.

"I don't know if I ever told you, but when we first met Wash they wouldn't let him eat in a restaurant in Casper, Wyoming. He sat at our table, but someone objected, and he left. He joined us on the trail the next night."

"They didn't do things like that in Salt Lake."

"No, but by now I know you realize how different that place was. That's one thing I can say about the Mormons. They seem to live what they say they believe better than most folks."

"How will you go about it?"

"Just do what I always do. Read newspapers and talk to people. I'm seeing John in the morning, so I'll probably start there. The newspapers, the library, city hall, the county courthouse; I'll make the rounds. Shouldn't take long."

"Johnny, you really should go into politics. You know everyone in town and probably half the county."

He stood and offered his hand. "We need to get going if we're going to be home before dark."

They were walking toward the buggy holding hands when she said, "Well, aren't you going to answer me? Can you see yourself as a politician?"

As he was handing her into the buggy he said, "Let me think about that a while before I answer. Ask me again next week about this time."

Johnny was up under the eaves typing a note to Roy when he heard steps on the stairs he didn't recognize. That was unusual, so he swung his chair around and saw his father-in-law pause on the top step for a breather.

Will grinned and took a deep breath. "Boy, that takes the wind out of you."

"It helps me stay in condition. I'm up and down them all the time. You should have had Roy call me, I'd have come down."

"That's alright. This leg of mine makes it a little harder but I wanted to talk to you and I wanted it to be private. Besides, I've never been up here and wanted to see why you like it so much."

He sat in the wing chair Johnny kept for visitors and they gazed out at the city in silence for a while.

Finally, Johnny said. "So, what can I do for you?"

"Actually, I guess I should take this to Annaliese before I talk to you about it but I need to know what you think first." He reached into an inner pocket and brought out an envelope. "I know you've been working on finding out as much as you can about the people who signed that petition that caused so much trouble. Have you had any luck?"

"I have. Been nosing around the last couple o' weeks and found out enough that I want to keep an eye on them."

Will handed Johnny the envelope.

"That was in our box this morning."

The letter was typed, and it looked like someone didn't know how to change a ribbon. He had to squint but when he looked up at Will he had gotten the gist of it.

"I recognize the name. He owns a ranch out northeast in the county. I think he's from down south somewhere. I've never met him, but I've talked to some people who know him. Haven't heard much good."

"From this note, it seems like he's working up to threatening us. Are these people dangerous Johnny? What can we do if they are?"

"First question, probably. From what I've heard, they fussed a lot about the issue before the flood and got themselves all worked up about it. Now that things are getting back to normal, I'm not surprised to hear from them.

"From what I've been able to gather, there's some heat among them, especially the leaders. There seem to be about half a dozen who've made it their business to stir things up. The leaders look like the kind of people who have no problems using violence if they can't get what they want any other way.

"There are some women in it too. They're the ones who talked to the board. Seems like they believe women put a better face on it, talking about the kids and all, and give them someone to hide behind."

Will was nodding his head. "Mica told me about the women, and we talked about the meetings they've had with the board. From what I've seen of the board, they're worried about the same thing we are. How far will they go to get their way?"

"I wish I could tell you. I think they need to feel on top of the heap, to be a part of those who rule. I don't mean holding office or being in politics. I mean they like being white and having white men make the rules. That puts them on top and they like that.

"We've seen it before. When California became part of the country, they wanted it to be a slave state and were never happy about the compromise that made it free instead. Since whites arrived, they have worked toward pushing the natives down taking away from them the very things they claim for themselves. They formed a government that allows them to do that, and they've learned how to use it.

"Of course, we're not in the same position we were at the hospital. We're an up and running business, and a private one to boot. If they don't want to use our services, that's fine, but I think them telling us we have to change would put them in a different position than when they were dealing with the hospital.

"The only way they could put pressure on us would be to try to use the city or the county to pass an ordinance requiring us to separate people, and they may succeed, and they may try to use violence or the threat of it. We need to face these possibilities and decide, before anything happens, how we'll deal with them."

"So, we need to take steps to either block them or counter them at city hall. Is that what you're saying? Can we do that?"

"It probably won't be easy. We'll need help. I know a lot of people but on an issue like this you don't know how they'll come down. One problem we'll have is the fact that many people who agree with us aren't necessarily willing to face the problems that might come from standing with us.

"When you come right down to the nub of it, will they see it as something they want to take a stand on? Will it be worth the cost? I don't think we'll know that until the time comes."

They sat quiet for a while, gazing out at the city.

"The violence?"

"We need to sit and talk about that possibility. It's a little late to plan for something like that after it's already happened."

Finally, Will took a deep breath and asked, "What's the next step?"

"I think there are certain people at city hall and the courthouse I need to talk to. I need to see where they stand and see if they have any ideas about how to deal with the problem. What I find I'll bring back to the three of you and see what you want to do."

Chapter Forty-Four

Annaliese was washing her hands when Grace and Este came in behind her. Today had been her first turn at the clinic since they'd begun a new system to cover the changing patient load and she was tired. Not for the first time she blessed her decision to bring the girls into the practice.

In addition to helping her with patients, they were both learning so fast it amazed her, and they always seemed to be ready for more. Este was especially good with patients from Old Town. It seemed like every other patient was related to her one way or another and she was good at putting them at ease in a place where they didn't usually feel that way.

When they were seated in the office she looked at one and then the other. "So, what are we going to do with them?"

They looked at each other and shrugged.

"That's exactly the way I feel." They were talking about two children who seemed to have fallen into her lap. Their mother had died the month before, and their father had left them with his cousin in Old Town and departed on the next train with no plans to return and no forwarding address.

"Elana is nice, but she has three of her own," replied Grace. "She and Pepe can't feed two more children."

She looked at Este who was shaking her head. "With things like they are right now, I don't know of anyone who can. Everyone is just getting over the flood."

That was the problem. Even though the waters hadn't damaged most of the homes in Old Town, crops had been destroyed, and with them many jobs had been lost, at least temporarily, leaving locals leaning on each other to feed their families. Two more mouths would strain the resources of most of their patients.

"Well, at least they can sleep here until we decide where they're going to end up."

"You never did tell me how you felt about becoming a politician." She was brushing her hair, and he was lying on the bed with Jinx on his chest, and even across the room she could hear the cat purring.

"I've thought about it. Talked to Lemuel about it. He thinks it's a good idea. Of course, it's a little difficult to get him talking these days. He sits around smiling most of the time."

Annaliese chuckled. "Yeah. Love'll do that to ya." She patted the seat. He joined her and they sat looking at each other in the mirror. "Remember when Dr. Clark left here—he was going to England with his daughter and her husband. You know, she wasn't really his daughter."

"Seems to me she and her brother were orphaned, weren't they? He was going to care for them until they found a home, but they never did, so he raised them."

She looked at him meaningfully in the mirror and it gradually dawned on him where they were going with the conversation. "You mean we've got an orphan on our hands?"

She held up two fingers.

"Oh Lord." He closed his eyes and shook his head slightly. "Are you saying they come with the job?"

"Looks like they might. Their mother died last month, and their Papa left town one night, not telling anyone where he was headed."

They sat staring at each other, him digesting what he had heard and her waiting to see what he'd say next.

"Girls or boys?"

"One of each. She's six and he's four."

"Mexican?"

She nodded.

"Where are they?"

"They're at Elena's house right now, but we'll have to make up our minds soon."

"Well, I was hoping to be a father one day but didn't expect it to be so sudden."

He looked at her in silence for a moment. "Will we be taking in every homeless child that pops up around here?"

"Of course not, though this does show the need for a way to deal with the ones that do. Right now, there's no solution for this type of problem. As a result, there are orphans on the streets. Not a lot, but some. We need to talk to someone at City Hall about it."

"So will this be a permanent thing, or will we be..." he paused. "I think the word is *in loco parentis*?"

"What does that mean?"

"I think it means we're responsible in the absence of parents, implying, of course, that there will be parents in the future."

"What do you think?"

"Since you've thrown a bucket of cold water in my face, at least give me time to dry off and think about it."

She grinned at him. "I guess it was kind of like that, wasn't it? I'm sorry to spring it on you like that but what do you think?"

"Taking it a step at a time, I'd say I'd like to meet them first and then we can talk again."

Later when they were lying in bed he said, "I don't know much about raising kids; do you?"

"Nope, but I guess we can learn. I hope so anyway. Besides,

with Maria and Consuelo around, we'll have someone to correct our mistakes."

Johnny was smiling. He was watching a beautiful little dark-eyed girl looking through a book of pictures and explaining them to her little brother. The boy sat listening to her, reaching out to touch the figures in the book and haltingly reciting the words. They both had big, dark eyes and black hair, and it was easy to see she would grow up to be a beauty.

It seemed his wife had drawn a line in their lives, and if they stepped across it henceforth everything would be different. He knew she wanted to do this so he understood it would happen. Now he needed to decide how it would fit into his life, how he would relate to the children. He was sure it would change his relationship with Annaliese, and he wondered how.

He squatted down in front of them and said, "Hi, my name is Johnny, what's yours?" He could see curiosity in the way she looked at him and he could tell she didn't understand. That was interesting. It looked like he might not only be teaching someone to speak English but having to learn Spanish in the bargain. He was looking at the girl and suddenly he could see understanding in her eyes.

She pointed at him and asked, "Johnny?" When he nodded at her, she pointed at herself and said, "Teressa."

Johnny looked at the boy and again she understood. "Manuel," she said.

This would be interesting.

Annaliese was sitting at her desk writing a letter for Roy to type when Este stuck her head in the door.

"Need you right away. New patient came in. Eight-year-old boy. Looks like he has a broken leg. The bone is sticking out the side of his leg just above his ankle."

Annaliese followed her to the treatment room. The boy was lying on the table moaning and crying. "You wash up and clean the wound," she said to Este. "I'll talk to his mother and then examine him to see what we'll need."

The child's mother and an older woman were standing by the door looking pale and worried.

"Is he going to be alright?" asked the older woman, probably the grandmother.

"When did this happen?"

"He jumped out of a tree and landed on a rock. His leg just snapped."

"How long ago?"

The woman looked at her companion. "Maybe a half-hour, forty-five minutes ago. We were in the house and heard him scream."

"You might want to wait outside." She looked at the younger woman. "Setting the leg will be painful and we need to clean the wound really well to avoid infection. I can give him something for the pain, but it will still hurt and setting that leg will not be pretty to watch."

"I'll stay."

Este was cleaning the wound carefully, but she had worked her magic, and the boy had stopped crying and was watching her. He winced. "It hurts when you do that."

"We need to clean it good, or germs might get in there and make you sick."

"Can the doctor fix it?" he asked.

Este looked up and smiled at him. "I've seen her fix broken legs before. She's pretty good at it."

"What's your name?" Annaliese asked when she joined them.

"Johnny."

"Oh, that's my husband's name. Well Johnny, we're going to have to set your leg. That means we'll have to put the bone back where it belongs and put a cast on your leg so it can grow back together and won't get dirty and let germs in.

"Because it's going to hurt some, I'm going to give you a shot of morphine, so it won't hurt so much."

"A shot? You mean with a needle?"

Annaliese nodded.

"Will it hurt?"

"It will be a little hurt but what's in it will help with the big hurt in your leg."

He looked at his mother then at Este who smiled at him and reached out to take his hand and then at Annaliese.

He had a half-determined, half-afraid look on his face, but he said, "O.K."

She nodded at Este who got a sheet and draped it across the boy's legs. When Annaliese approached the table with the hypodermic needle, Este took the boy's hand and squeezed it.

Once the morphine began to take effect, Annaliese went to work. She explained what she was doing as she was doing it. Getting the bone back into the leg meant trimming some skin around the wound and then carefully aligning the bone so it could begin to knit naturally.

By the time she was finished both she and the boy were sweating profusely, but he had managed to endure it without moving his leg, though he had moved everything else. Tears were streaming down his face and there had been some moaning and crying.

The women watched intently, sometimes closing their eyes or wincing, but soon it was over, and Este was bandaging the leg while Annaliese gathered the materials necessary to cast it.

"We'll keep him in bed here for a day or two while I get him some crutches. It won't be long before you'll have to sit on him to keep him down."

Annaliese was sitting at her desk writing some notes. "You'll forgive me, but I like to write about something right away if I can. Easier to remember that way." She finished writing and looked up.

"I think he should stay here at least two days so we can see how he's doing and get him a set of crutches that will fit." She smiled at them. "I'm sorry, in all the commotion I didn't get your names.

The older woman looked at her keenly. "I'm Madeline

Housden. This is my daughter Dolly Madden."

"I'm Dr. Fry. Here is a card with my telephone number. Call me anytime and we'll let you know how he's doing."

"How long has the young girl been with you?"

"Coming up on a year. I have two girls working with me. They want to be doctors, and their parents asked me if they could work with me to see how they like it."

"She's Mexican, isn't she?" asked the daughter.

"Yes, she is. If she realizes her ambition, she'll be the first Mexican woman doctor in the state, as far as I know. She and Grace make my life so much easier and they're going to be fine doctors one day."

They were quiet for a moment and then Mrs. Housden said, "I signed that petition about the hospital not treating Mexicans."

Annaliese smiled. "Though I recognized the name. Well, I'm glad we could help you. Looks like the hospital's out of business for a while so we stay pretty busy."

"I'm surprised. You don't seem to harbor any bad feelings about the whole thing."

"You needed help. I doubt if your son ever thought about it. He seemed to like Este well enough. She's very good with the young ones."

"Yes, I see that."

Annaliese stopped on the steps outside Johnny's office and listened to the voices coming from inside. She could see Teressa and her brother sitting on Johnny's desk, and he in his chair facing them. To one side Consuelo, their housekeeper, was sitting, listening intently.

Jinx was in his lap and Johnny said to the children, "This is my cat. His name is Jinx." Consuelo, in Spanish, slowly repeated the words to Teressa. She then did so in English. Teressa repeated the words in halting English, then looked at Johnny and in Spanish asked. "Can I pet your cat?" Once again it was translated into

English and Johnny replied, "Si, but gently."

"Gently", Consuelo translated for the girl, and tentatively she reached out and ran her hand down his back, then sat back and watched her brother feel the silky black coat.

Annaliese hated to interrupt what she could see was something special, but she had a meeting and needed to talk to Johnny.

She kissed him on the cheek and smiled at the children. "I'm glad to see this happening, but I need to talk to you for a few minutes before I go to the meeting." She looked at Consuelo and continued. "It won't take long, they can come back when we're through."

"Actually, we were about through," said Johnny. He picked them up, kissed each on the forehead, and set them on the floor. "I'll see you at dinner tonight." They took Consuelo's hands, and as she went out the door Teressa looked back over her shoulder and smiled at him.

"I think she already thinks you're special. It looks like you've got a good start on being a father. I'm so glad."

"Well, it seemed like the most important thing we need to do is understand each other, so Consuelo and I cooked up this idea. I'm going to spend time talking to them every evening and then learn some words every night before I go to bed.

"She's going to do the same thing with them, and she and I are going to speak Spanish at dinner or whenever we see each other in the house. I've heard that speaking it is the best way to learn a new language.

"So, what did you need to talk about?"

"I had a patient this morning named Johnny Madden. He fell out of a tree and broke his leg. He's downstairs in one of our rooms. I wanted to ask you what you know about his grandmother.

He looked puzzled and she continued. "Her name is Madeline Housden."

He raised his eyebrows, and his mouth formed an O. "Well, I've never met her, but I definitely know who she is. Her husband's Max Housden. They live on a big farm in the northeast part of the county.

They have a daughter who married a friend of Ed's, George Madden. He runs a grain store here in town. They live out east of town and he has a small farm. Grows feed and stuff he sells at the store."

"You mean Ed, the sheriff?"

"That's right. Ed tells me there's no love lost between the son-in-law and the old man. They had a falling out over money, but I think he's just a cranky old son of bitch so if it wasn't that it would be something else."

"She told me she had signed the petition and seemed to expect me to react."

"And you said?"

"I didn't say anything about that. Talked about the boy and what they needed to do for him the next couple of days."

Johnny leaned back in his chair, hands behind his head and stared at the ceiling for a moment.

"Hmm," he muttered. "Who knows. Could be a pebble in the pond. Ripples might go out a long way."

Chapter Forty-Five

Johnny had friends all over town, but he didn't recognize the young Mexican who handed him a message in the store one afternoon. It was from Freddie, a bartender at one of the seedier places in town saying he needed to talk to Johnny right away, before he opened for business that day if possible.

When Johnny knocked on the saloon door a few minutes later, his friend opened it immediately, stood aside for Johnny to enter, then looked up and down the street before following Johnny into the dim, musty room and closing the door carefully behind him. Freddie already had a cup of coffee on the table, and the cook brought Johnny one and disappeared into the kitchen.

"So, what's up?" asked Johnny.

Freddie looked around the room again then leaned forward and said in a low tone, "I've been hearing about some of the boys from out in the county. They are getting together to cause some trouble in Old Town. Something about Mexicans being treated the same as whites at your clinic."

"What kind of trouble?"

"Burning a cross, maybe torching some houses, beating up some people."

"Is this something new? We've had some contention at the hospital, but violence? That's new."

"No, it isn't. They've been doing some of that stuff for a while, especially out in the country, but in small groups. I hear there's even been a murder or two. The law doesn't pay much attention to it, because Mexicans don't go to the law. They don't believe they'll get fair treatment, and it will just cause trouble, so they don't bother."

"What's changed? Why suddenly are they going to try this with us?"

"From what I hear they've been recruiting new members and feel strong enough to push the issue in town now. Some people have been complaining you're too friendly with the Mexicans and Chinese."

Johnny sat back in his chair, a thoughtful expression on his face. "Any idea when? How many are we talking about?" he asked.

"Sounded like tomorrow night, and it seems like there'll be a bunch; maybe as many as twenty or twenty-five."

"Where'd you hear this, Freddie?"

"Actually, Pedro overheard it when he was cleaning and told me, but I've been hearing bits and pieces for a while. Men get drunk and they talk, you know. Pedro and I've been working together for a lot of years. He's good people and there's a lot of good people in Old Town. I don't like bullies beating up on good people so I decided to let you know."

When Johnny sat quiet for a while thinking, the bartender asked, "What are you going to do?"

"Have to think on that a bit. Doesn't sound like we have much time to get ready. I'll have to get some of my friends together and also warn the people in Old Town and probably other places about the possibility." He stood and shook hands with his friend. "I better get going. Thanks Freddie, I owe you one. Anytime I can return the favor let me know."

"Sheriff in?"

The deputy looked up. "Hi Johnny. He's upstairs talking to the judge. Said he'd be back in a few minutes. You can wait in the office."

"Hey Johnny," the sheriff said when he came in the door. He sat behind his desk and listened as Johnny explained the reason for his visit. He sat in silence for a minute, a look of concentration on his face.

"I don't know, Johnny. Might just be drunks being drunks. You had any other warnings about this kind of thing?" When Johnny shook his head, he continued. "I don't have anyone to spare to send over to your place right now."

"I think we can probably handle it. The chances are they'll try it at the clinic, and we can be ready for them. I just wanted you to know we're going to take it seriously and be ready so if you hear some racket at our place try to get some people over there right quick, O.K.? We may need to defend ourselves and the clinic and someone might get hurt."

Ed scratched the back of his neck. "You know, there's people around here that agree with them on this thing. Might be more people there than you think. Make sure you can handle things before you start something."

"Ed, you know me. I don't go looking for trouble, but if someone pushes, I tend to push back kinda hard. If they attack the clinic, that's not a political problem. They'll be breaking the law. If you're not there, someone could get hurt because we're not going to just lie down for them. If they push, we plan to push back."

"All I'm saying is, be careful."

Johnny sat outside the courthouse for a moment trying to decide his next move. He needed to talk to Wash and Lemuel and yet he turned toward the store first, and when he walked in immediately went to find the cook and housekeeper.

He explained the problem and within minutes the two women were on their way home to alert the gossip network that was a critical part of life in Old Town. Then he called Lemuel and directed him to

Kate's so they could meet and talk to Wash and Woman.

When he tied up his horse at the nursery, he could see a group waiting for him at the table on the dock, not just his friends but some of Kate's other workers.

"So, what's going to happen and when?" asked Lemuel. "This sounds serious."

Johnny shrugged. "I had a bartender in a saloon tell me that one of his people heard some drunks talking. Supposedly they want to cause some problems. What if we get all excited about it and it turns out to be nothing?" He looked at Wash. "What do you think?"

Everyone sat quiet waiting for him to answer. Finally Wash said, "Can you afford not to take it seriously?" He cocked his head and looked at Johnny. "The question is not whether or not to do something. It's what to do and when."

Lemuel nodded his head. "I agree. If you dismiss it out of hand and it happens it could be a disaster."

Johnny glanced at the three nurserymen standing listening to the conversation. They were nodding in agreement "I've already sent Maria and Consuelo to alert everyone in Old Town. It would seem to me since the reason they're upset is the clinic, so that's where any attack would likely be focused.

"If we set up to wait at the clinic and they go elsewhere in Old Town, at least we'll be placed to move to the problem quickly and they should be alert in any case."

"Doesn't sound like the law will be there if we need 'em, so I'd say we need to be ready to handle it ourselves," said Lemuel when Johnny told him about the conversation with the sheriff.

So, they laid their plans.

As soon as she closed the front door, Consuelo reached for the telephone. Since Annaliese had installed it she had used it rarely because it was for medical things, but now she called her daughter at the Spreckels.

She had to wait while the girl was called from her classroom.

"Este, I need you to come home right away. There is going to be trouble, and I'll need help."

There was a shocked silence at the other end of the line and then her daughter said, "What about school? What should I tell them?"

"Tell them your mama needs you."

After she hung up, she stood thinking for a moment, then called to the children playing in the yard. When they trooped in and were standing around her, she said, "I want you to go to every door in town and tell everyone they need to come here as soon as they can. Tell them it's important." She clapped her hands and sent them scooting out the doors, watched them organize and start off in different directions, running.

No sooner had the children gone than Maria and Estela arrived and others, men and women, began to stream into the yard. They stood quiet, murmuring to one another and when she could see the flood slowing, she stepped onto the porch and began.

"Tomorrow night some men, mostly Anglos from out in the country are planning to attack the clinic, maybe with torches. I don't know what or when, but we need to find out and get everyone we can to help them defend it. I will find out what I can and let you know."

"We would need guns," someone said.

"Yes, we would, but we don't have many. Bring what you have as weapons. The idea is to make them believe they can't win. If we all show up, then they might just decide to go home.

"If they don't? What do we do?" someone shouted.

"We fight," said a man. "These people care for our children. They help us every day. We need to help them now, and besides, we'll be helping ourselves." There was a rumble of agreement and as others began to arrive, more began to talk. When Este arrived, Consuelo arranged for her to be the contact with the clinic, and they began to plan.

She was brushing her hair again and he sat quietly, Jinx on his lap, watching until she finished and turned toward him, her eyes large and solemn.

"How can you just sit there with this going on?"

He gave her a bleak smile. "Hanging around with Wash over the years I've learned to think and act in a more deliberate manner. It's like he says, 'You can't pick cotton that's not in the bowl yet.' The only thing I can do tonight is try and get some sleep. I've done all I can to this point, and the rest will have to wait until tomorrow."

"Will you be able to sleep?"

"I hope so. That's another trick I picked up from Wash. Sleep when you get a chance."

She turned out the light and joined him on the bed. "Johnny I'm afraid about this. What will happen?"

"The plan is to meet them with more force than they expect and discourage them from the beginning."

"Will it work?"

He shrugged. "Should. These aren't exactly the men who charged up Cemetery Ridge. I doubt if they'll be inclined to die for the cause, so I'd say we've got a good chance to get out of it with a whole skin."

She kissed him and he felt her breast on his arm. "Don't think I can concentrate enough for that. Let's wait 'til it's over."

He was quiet for a minute then said, "Consuelo says everyone in Old Town will help, so that could tilt the odds considerably in our favor, but it only takes one damn fool to make it explode. Some of those people are damn fools or they wouldn't be here."

He was quiet for a moment. "All we can do is do what we can and hope it's enough."

"I guess this is one of the drawbacks of being in love," said Kate.

"Yes, it is," said Sarah. "Pity poor Annaliese; this is the third time she's had to sit waiting to see if Johnny's coming home."

The three women were sitting in the breakfast nook and while

Sarah and Madame were eating their normal breakfast Kate was only able to handle coffee.

"What did Lemuel say about it?" asked Madame.

"He thought they had it set up well enough that there wouldn't be any trouble but it's like Johnny said, 'It wouldn't take but one fool to start something and then people could die.' Kate took a sip of coffee, and the saucer rattled when she put the cup down. "Look at me. I'm shaking so much I can't even drink a cup of coffee."

"Are the people of Old Town going to help?"

"Supposedly, but what does that mean and how much could they help? When push comes to shove, will they stand when they have to?"

"Johnny seems to think they will, doesn't he?"

"If he's wrong about that it might leave them out on a limb that could get sawed off. There's five of them against God only knows how many."

"What time is this thing supposed to get under way?"

"They don't really know. Lemuel said they're going to be ready once it gets dark, but it could be anytime during the night. And if Johnny's information is wrong, they could sit there all night for nothing."

Kate was quiet for a minute then said, "I can shoot a rifle good enough to hit something. Why do women have to sit at home and wait?"

"Someone has to take care of them after the battle," said Sarah.

Roy stretched his legs and looked up at the first quarter moon high above him. By its pale light he could just make out the time. Two AM. He was sitting by a window in the apartment above the clinic watching, and suddenly he saw the shadows of two men moving on the street by the old mission across from the clinic. One man appeared to be carrying something, and when they stopped, he began to dig in the center of the street.

Downstairs the clinic was dark. Johnny was talking to Wash

when he suddenly cocked his head.

"They're here." Everyone waiting with him knew what had just happened and when Johnny stood up, they all did.

"Are they here?" asked Lemuel.

Johnny nodded and said, "I'll be back in a minute." He left the room, and they heard him climbing the stairs.

Standing beside Roy he watched the men digging and saw several others approach carrying something. Several of the men positioned what he could now see was a cross in the hole, while the man with the shovel filled in the hole and tamped it down.

"They're noisy."

"Yes, they are. Do you have your rifle?" When Roy nodded," Johnny said, "The signal will be when Wash fires the Sharp's."

He stood, squeezed Roy's shoulder and went quickly down the stairs to where the others waited in the dark.

"Everyone ready?" They all nodded, and Johnny and Lemuel left through a side door. Wash and Woman took positions at windows, Wash with his Sharp's, and Woman with Johnny's Henry. Under the porch that ran around the building and wearing dark clothes, they moved unseen and were standing side by side in front of the building when the cross erected in the street burst into flame.

Before them a group of men, heads covered with hoods in which eye and mouth holes had been cut were spread out in a rough line in front of the cross. No feature was visible with the burning cross behind them, but the shapes were visible as targets if necessary.

For a moment, the only sound was the noise from the kerosine soaked cross burning and illuminating the front of the clinic. Then a figure in the center of the line spoke. "We don't think you should mix the races. Take care of white people, not Greasers and Chinese. Or Niggers either, for that matter. Let them find their own."

"And if we refuse to accede to your demands?" asked Lemuel calmly.

"We'll burn the place down and maybe the rest of the town too."

Johnny spoke just loud enough for the man to hear him. "Since you're doing the talking, I'm going to assume you're the head of this outfit and I think there's something you should know. There's a Sharp's fifty centered on your chest and if anyone starts anything," he let that hang in the air for a few heartbeats, then continued, "well, he never misses."

From the alley beside the clinic came the noise of a match striking and a torch flared, illuminating a crowd of people, the people of Old Town. Then another torch was lit by a building down the street and another on the other side of the clinic, each revealing many people. In the light from the torches, sharpened steel glittered, sickles, axes, hatchets and machetes and a few guns.

Considering how many people were there, it was amazingly quiet for a while, everyone just standing looking across the street at each other, the only noise from the burning cross.

Finally, Lemuel said, "You were saying something about who we could treat. It really doesn't look like you've got what you need to make that stick. What do you think?" From the windows behind and above them came the sounds of rifles being levered.

The man in the center cleared his throat and said, "You better listen to what I said." He was trying to sound threatening, but his voice was anything but steady.

Johnny stepped forward and lifted the ten gauge. "You fellows standing next to the cross, you better move away from it a little?" When they did, he aimed at the cross piece and pulled both triggers, one at a time.

There was a tremendous roar and the cross disintegrated, flew in all directions, and the men in the line began ducking and covering their heads as fiery chunks rained down on them. Several hoods caught fire, and the men tore them off and stomped on them.

Johnny calmly broke open the gun, removed and replaced the cartridges and flipped it closed.

"Well gentlemen, we've enjoyed your visit but it's late and we need to get in bed. Good night," said Lemuel. The ten-gauge was pointed at one of the two groups separated by the burning remnant still sticking out of the ground while Lemuel's twelve-gauge was covering the other.

Some of the men began to drift away and then most of them were gone and horses could be heard riding away. The man in the middle, the leader maybe, still stood in place with a few of his cohorts and finally Lemuel said, "You know, you people have threatened us and our friends and our homes and no one would blame us for blowing your goddamn heads off. Go! We won't tell you again."

"How many people were there from Old Town?" asked Kate.

"Looked like almost everyone. Couple hundred I'd say. It was the damnedest thing. They never said a word when it was over. Just left and went home."

Everyone sat quiet for a moment, then Wash said, "I think a threat to the clinic is probably the only thing that would have brought them all together."

It was the morning after and he, Kate, Lemuel, and Woman were sitting at the nursery drinking coffee. Lemuel repositioned his chair and sat looking around at the others. "We should have pushed things last night, made them mad and started a fight." He looked at Wash meaningfully.

"We're going to hear from that bunch again, I guarantee it. If we'd have shot a half dozen or so, especially the leader, it would have made it less likely to happen again."

Kate was looking at Lemuel in horror. "You mean just shoot them down?"

"No, but we could have provoked them and when they attacked we could have wiped them out."

"Lemuel, you are so bloodthirsty sometimes. Some from our side could have been killed or hurt. Did you ever think about that?"

"You mark my words. Some of the people that helped us tonight are going to die at the hands of some of those we let ride away last night." He looked at Wash. "Do you agree?"

Wash looked at him steadily for a moment then nodded. "I'd say it's likely."

"Really?"

"I'd bet money on it," Lemuel replied. "This kind of thing is like a disease in a community. It spreads. It's like a cancer. You have to cut it out and hope the patient survives.

Chapter Forty-Six

Johnny stepped out on the porch of Madam's cottage in Coronado and stood looking at the ocean a hundred yards away. The ladies from up north were inside talking to the ladies from here abouts pretty much non-stop, and he needed some fresh air. Suddenly he heard, *"Needed to get out of there."* and Roy appeared at his side.

"It does get overpowering when they're all talking like that."

They stood in silence for a minute, then Johnny said, "I'll bet a nickel Jonas will be out here before long. He was looking ready for some fresh air when I left."

Jonas Burke had come with Sarah for a visit and would be there for a couple weeks. They had been dating for years but seemed to be content to be companions without needing to take the step into marriage.

"I'd love to stay longer," he had said, "but I need to keep an eye on things back home." This was the first time he'd been able to get away from business back in San Francisco.

He owned a fleet of wagons that hauled things for people and businesses up and down the peninsula south of the city. In addition, he was a city councilman and in charge of the police and parks in the city. He had recently opened a yard building wagons, both for himself and for anyone else who wanted to buy one.

A few years before, when the rascals in city hall were thrown out by a good-government movement Madame and Lemuel had organized he was chosen to fill one of the vacancies and in the intervening years had become an important man in the operation of one of the largest cities in the country.

Sure enough, they had just settled into rocking chairs when Jonas pushed open the screen door.

"Wondered where you two got to," he said. He positioned a rocker so they could talk, and he could see the ocean.

"It's good to see you," he said to Johnny. He nodded at Roy. "I remember you when you began working in the store back home. Sorry to hear about Greta."

Roy nodded. "He doesn't talk," said Johnny. "He was injured in the same accident."

"That's what Sarah said. She also told me you two have an unusual way of communicating. Something like reading his mind?"

"Not quite that." Johnny explained the phenomenon. "We don't do it often. It takes a lot of effort on his part so we don't have long conversations although it does seem like it's getting easier the more he does it. We have typewriters at the store, and we sit together a couple times a day and read what we've written. Mostly stuff about the store."

"Any idea how it works?"

"No idea. Been doing some reading about such things but haven't learned anything that would explain it."

"It seems to me we have a school in San Francisco that teaches sign language to deaf-mutes."

"We've talked about that, but he likes the way we do things. The thing is if he learns that, then someone else would have to learn it too. Maybe it would be useful to him around others who couldn't hear but around here he doesn't need it. Maybe one day he'll decide to learn it, but not yet."

"Changing the subject, Sarah tells me you spend a lot of your time here just learning about the city."

"That's right. Sometimes I sit in a newspaper office and read back editions for a whole day. Annaliese thinks I'm crazy."

"How come?"

Johnny looked thoughtful for a moment. Finally, he shrugged and said, "Once we got the store up and running here, I didn't have much to do, so I decided to focus on learning about the city. I mean, it looks like this is where we'll be living for a while, so it seemed to make sense. Read all the books we had in stock about the city and county, then all they had in the library. The more I read, the more interested I became.

"All the newspapers in town have back copies so I've made sort of a hobby of reading them. Also, I spend time at city hall and the county courthouse asking questions, talking to people, and listening to trials and public meetings."

"So, do you have any plans for using all this stuff you're finding out?"

"Before Herschel was killed, he and I met with John Spreckels once a week and talked about things that were happening in the city and county. Herschel worked for him at the newspaper and kept him up on what he found out poking around town. I've never worked for John, but I learned a lot about what's going on in the city from them. I usually stop and see him every week and we talk the same way.

"Do you remember Herschel from city hall back home?"

"Oh yeah. When he was a reporter, he used to come in my office pretty regular."

"He was a reporter at the Union down here and worked for John. He was murdered a few months ago." He looked out at the ocean for a moment then said. "Annaliese says I should be running for some office or other. I think she just wants me out from under her feet. Lemuel and I have talked about it, and he thinks Kate would be a good manager for a campaign."

"I was going to suggest the same thing. You could do good

things for the city or county down here. One of the things I learned back home is how important it is to have someone around who really knows how things work and knows the people pulling the levers. Someone like that is important to any local government. Hell, you could say they're essential. Sun Li at the BookSeller back home is a gold mine for me. She's been a big help over the years."

Johnny looked at Roy and said, "He sounds like you." Roy grinned and nodded.

"Lemuel and I have talked about it," said Johnny. "There's a seat on the city council opening up in a couple of months. Herb Pennock is moving back east, and everybody says I should run for it."

"Who's everybody?"

Johnny nodded at the house. "Everyone in there. John D thinks it's a good idea. The sheriff and a couple of people on the council have encouraged me to run, and I know Kate would love it."

"You mean the Kate I met yesterday?"

Johnny nodded. "She's a lot like Madame up there. Feels like this is her city and she looks out for it. She was pretty deep with the hospital they wanted to build."

"I thought they built it."

"They did but about the time it was opened it was flooded out and they've never been able to re-open. Now our clinic is the only large medical practice in the county."

Behind them the door opened, and Lemuel joined them.

"Speak of the devil," said Johnny. "When'd you get here?"

"Just walked in. Left Kate inside with the ladies." He nodded at Jonas. "Heard you were coming down."

They shook hands. "Just talking to Johnny about getting involved in city government."

"You and everyone else," said Lemuel. "Kate wants to know when you'll be ready to talk about getting your campaign going."

"I've been thinking about it. I've got some ideas about things I'd like to see happen in this city. I guess the only way to make them happen is to push them myself. I could do it from outside the system, but I'd have more power to get things done from inside."

"Well Kate and I will help you anyway we can and I imagine John D feels the same way."

Since they had moved most of their life into the store, Annaliese had found the time she enjoyed most was dinner. With all the people who live there plus assorted visitors, the long table was usually full, or nearly so and since most of the others at the table were close friends or family members there was usually good conversation and laughter.

Since the children had joined them, she enjoyed watching them talking to Este and Grace and had noticed Teressa watching others at the table when they spoke. The girl was more outgoing than her brother but he'd likely grow out of that. Many boys were shy at that age.

Every once in a while, Teressa would look at her and smile shyly then go back to watching the others. At those times she would see curiosity in those dark eyes and wonder how much of what was being said she could grasp.

Of course, Este was her favorite, both because they could talk and because she was Este. With the children a part of the family now she was even more grateful for what her two pupils brought into her life, not just in the clinic but everywhere. The idea of the two children growing up surrounded by all the good things in this house, into the life they had built since they arrived here, gave her a warm feeling whenever she thought about it.

"So, I hear you've decided to become a mother," said Sarah.

Annaliese rolled her eyes at the ceiling. "Yes, I

think so. You've heard the story, I take it?" Sarah nodded. "She's six and he's four. We've moved them into the house and given Consuelo a raise. She's going to be helping Mrs. Keane. Since they're about the same age as the twins, it will be a lot of work. It will be nice when Bobby and Geppetto are here. They'll make up quite a bunch for the ladies to handle and they should have fun together."

"What's Johnny thinking about it?" asked Rebecca.

"You know Johnny. He likes to keep life interesting. We talked about it, and he understands it's for the long haul. He's met them already. For some reason I'll bet he ends up spending more time with them than he thinks he will."

Johnny was thinking the same thing. He and Handy were riding out to visit Wash and Woman and sit and talk for a while, and as far as he was concerned the thing he wanted to talk about was becoming a father. He realized he should be thinking about his dive into local politics or the problems with the clinic but for some reason, images of a little girl and little boy looking at a book of pictures were constantly popping up in his mind's eye.

They drew up at a creek to water the horses and Handy said, "Supposedly we were going to talk but you haven't said a word since we left town."

"Let's let them graze a bit, come on," said Johnny dismounting. He led Handy to an overlook above where the creek ran out to join the blue Pacific. He and Roy had found it once when they were walking on the beach and Johnny loved to stand and look at the headlands in the distance and take the ocean air deep into his lungs.

"What's the best thing about being a father?"

Handy thought for a moment. "Seeing his face when he's happy or excited, I guess. That always makes me feel good."

"What's the worst thing about it?"

Handy didn't even have to think about that one. "Worry," he said. "You worry when he's sick or when he hurts himself. That can get you right in here." He put his hand on his heart. "I have a feeling that's a thing you never lose. As long as they're alive you'll have it. I've got it for the new one and Rebecca's not even showing yet."

"Ever worry you're doing the right thing?"

"My God yes, constantly. But Sarah told Rebecca that's

something else you always have. I think it's a part of the job."

"Well, it looks like I'm going to have a lot to learn. I guess I better get moving on it. The trouble is I still have other things to do but it seems like I've got a couple of new things on my list of what's really important in my life." He looked at his friend, took a deep breath and said, "And knowing my wife they'll need to be right up top."

Chapter Forty-Seven

Lemuel sat in his office finishing the paperwork for the new accounts added on the trip to Los Angeles. They had saved most of the inventory and equipment during the flood by moving it to the clinic and The BookSeller and with the city recovering, business was good. Not only that but his trip to Los Angeles had opened up a new market and he was determined to take advantage of the opportunity.

Of course, whenever he thought about that trip he thought about Kate and that made him smile. It seemed as though he might just get married again. He was not a person who spent much time looking over his shoulder at the past, but the loss of Greta was too recent not to hurt. The idea that he could find love so soon after that terrible time amazed him.

He realized it had been coming on for a long time, since the day he had arrived in San Diego actually. That day she'd been standing in front of the nursery holding a watering can and with a smudge of dirt on her cheek and a warm smile of welcome. He could remember it when he closed his eyes. He just never really expected things to happen the way they had.

As much as he missed his daughter, he felt he was much too old to spend time in the limbo of grief. He believed his love for Kate could help him move forward, be a balm for his pain, as it were, and felt no guilt about feeling happy so soon after her death. His memory of Greta was vivid, and he knew she'd want him to be happy again, the sooner the better.

There was a rap on the office door; he opened it and saw Johnny standing there.

"Got time to talk?"

Lemuel motioned him in and said, "Come on in and have a seat. Just sitting here thinking."

Johnny was grinning when he sat down. "I'll bet a dollar I can guess what you're thinking about."

"I guess it shows. I have trouble keeping my mind on anything else lately."

"According to my wife, that's the way people behave when they're in love."

"What'd you want to talk about?"

"A couple things. First, I think I'm ready to begin getting organized to contest for Herb Pennock's seat on the council."

"Great. What made you decide to pull the trigger on it? Just yesterday you were still on the fence."

"Annaliese thinks I'd be good at it and everyone I know is urging me on, so just to shut them up, as much as anything, I decided it was time. What's the first thing we need to do?"

"Talk to Kate. We can bring some ideas to the meeting, and she can take them and lay out a plan. You know it takes money. Maybe you should talk to John D first thing."

"I've got enough to start with."

"Ok, I'll see her tonight, and we can plan to meet. I would say the first thing is to take care of the necessary paperwork down at City Hall. Before we meet her let's sit and talk about what obvious steps we need to take. That way when we talk with her we'll have some direction and maybe some goals to work toward."

He paused and smiled ruefully. "We may have a disagreement

or two among us before it's all over, so in the name of diplomacy and my future happiness, I'll let you handle those."

"I'm seeing John D. tomorrow, and I know we'll talk about the campaign." Johnny shook his head. "It will feel strange asking him for money."

"I'd be surprised if he doesn't bring it up first. I'm sure he's used to it. He's been in the game for a long time, and I bet anyone who's run for office in this part of the state has solicited him at one time or another."

"I know he's in my corner and between him and Kate we should learn how to go about it right quick. I imagine Ed will be a big help too."

"Any idea who else is trying for the seat?"

"Haven't heard of anyone yet, but I imagine there'll be a few."

"What else is on your mind?"

"I'm trying to get ahead of the problem at the clinic. I've been poking around about the people who put their names on that petition. With the problem we had it seems there's the potential for more so I've been talking to friends at city hall. It looks like they may have problems if they try to use the levers of government to help them."

"Oh yeah. I remember you said you were going to try to find out as much as you could."

"I've found out a lot, but something happened last week that might have an effect on the whole problem." and he told his partner about the boy with the broken leg.

"Humm," said Lemuel. "I wonder how much influence the grandmother has with her husband. Might just take one person on the other side to create a change."

"From what I've learned, he sounds like a hard nut. He's one of the leaders of the group; in fact, he might have been the man in the middle that night at the clinic and he seems to be a bit of a bully. Has a reputation as a brawler and a drunk. Ed tells me he's had him in jail a time or two for it."

"Anything I can do to help?"

"Drop by Madden's store and get to know George a little. I hear he's a decent fellow and wants no part of pushing the Mexicans around. They do a lot of business with him, and I'll bet he doesn't want to get into something that could hurt the store."

"I can do that. Anything else on your mind?"

Johnny had to fight to keep from smiling.

"You might say so. I'm going to be a father."

"Kate told me. You'll do alright. Just be honest with them and realize one day they might be taking care of you." He grinned at Johnny and slapped him on the back. "You'll do fine, Papa," he said.

John Spreckels looked up from some paperwork on his desk.

"Where are you ladies off to today?" he asked.

His wife came behind the desk and kissed him on the forehead. "I'm taking these girls downtown to do some shopping. Then we're meeting Annaliese and Maggie at The Del and having lunch there."

"Isn't that a coincidence? I'm meeting Johnny and Lemuel in the Crown Room for lunch." He glanced at his watch. "I've got to be going, or I'll be late." He tucked the watch back in his vest pocket, walked them to the front door and watched them climb into the carriage.

Johnny and Lemuel were already seated when he walked into the dining room.

"Well," he said. "This is a little different than our usual meetings. Do you have anything important for me? Anything going on I should know about?"

While they ate they talked about events and people in town.

"Any new problems at the clinic?" asked John.

"No, no new problems, but after what happened there the other night, I decided I wanted to be in a position to wield some power if that kind of thing became a problem in the future. So I'm thinking about running for a seat on the City Council and I'd like to have your support if I do," said Johnny.

John grinned. "I can't think of anyone I'd rather see run. What seat are you running for?"

"Well, it looks like Herb Pennock is moving back East and will be stepping down so there'll be a special election next month to fill his seat. It seemed like a good time to make a move in that direction."

"Will you still come by every week to sit and talk like we usually do?"

"I can't see any reason not to."

"Then I'm all for it. If you need contributions, I'm more than willing to help out."

While they ate, they talked about the city and what Johnny could expect if he won his race. Since he'd begun to consider the move, he'd been thinking about what the city needed and how he might go about helping them get it.

John tossed his napkin on the table and stood. "I've got some people I need to meet, but before I go I want to tell you how glad I am that Grace is working with Annaliese. She's become a young lady before our eyes, and she seems to love working at the clinic."

Johnny smiled. "I know how Annaliese feels about her and Este. She says they make her life easier and help her keep up with things. She told me the other night that finding answers to their questions has made her a better doctor, helped her learn things she probably never would have if they weren't around."

Annaliese and Maggie were sitting in Annaliese's office talking about things not related to being doctors, which was unusual.

"You know, you've changed a lot since you came to San Diego." They had been talking about some of the new entertainment that had come to town. "As pretty as you are, I'm surprised I've never seen you with a man. With all the new things in town I'd think you'd want to see some of them"

Maggie's face twisted into a frown. "I'm still married," she said, "even if Charlie doesn't think so. I need to do something about that, but for some reason it hasn't seemed very important lately. Of course, that's true of most things since I got here. The only thing I really pay attention to is work."

"You don't seem like the same person you were in school. You laugh and smile less and less as time goes by."

"Don't have much to laugh about." She stopped for a moment. "You know, that's not true. Being a part of life around here is special. I guess maybe I need to look at what's happening around me instead of looking over my shoulder so much."

Lemuel was standing at the railing on the ferry when Johnny joined him. "It seems like everyone wants you to run."

"Well, I'm not really surprised about John. Having Grace in the clinic has brought us closer and I spent a lot of time talking with him and Herschel. I'm not sure how that will affect my being a councilman.

"He has a lot of interests in the city and county, owns a lot of property. If he supports me, I hope he understands that to do the job right I need the freedom to use my own judgment."

"You know him much better than I do but I don't get the feeling he'd lean on you. I think you'll agree much more than disagree."

"I hope you're right. But sometimes when people start thinking about money and power they'll surprise you."

No matter what she tried to do or think about at present, Kate couldn't stop thinking about Lemuel and the weekend they had together. This wasn't like her and she wasn't sure she liked it. She was the kind of person who worked steadily and doggedly toward a goal and achieved it.

After her husband died, she had struck out on her own and made a success of it. She had always been focused on her future, on her plans and goals, on how to make the city what she thought it should be. Now suddenly she was focused on something else and was not sure how to feel about it.

Since the weekend in Los Angeles, whenever she sat at her desk trying to concentrate, visions of the day in the hotel room would float lazily through her mind. She remembered how he looked in the dim romantic light, the excitement she felt when he came to her in the bed, what it was like afterwards when she lay, eyes closed, and drifted dreamily into another world.

She was brought back to the present with a jerk when she looked up and saw Woman standing in the doorway.

"How long have you been standing there?" she asked.

Woman smiled her slow smile. "Long enough to wonder what you're thinking about," she said.

Kate sighed and rolled her eyes. "I don't know what I'm doing here. I'm just sitting here like a bump on a log not getting anything done."

Woman walked past her, opened the drawer to a filing cabinet, took some papers out and as she was going back through the door said over her shoulder, "Lemuel just came in. He said he'd be in the gazebo if you're not busy." She turned and raised her eyebrows. "You don't look busy."

Kate stuck out her tongue at her friend and stepped to the window. She could see Lemuel standing at the railing in the gazebo leaning on his cane looking out toward the bay.

She kissed him on the cheek and sat down across the table from where he was standing. He looked at her, a puzzled look on his face then took a chair facing her.

"Did I do something wrong?"

She shook her head. "It's just that I'm not sure what's going on between us, and until we decide I don't quite know how to handle the whole thing. When I look at the situation, we're in I have no idea what to do next."

"What do you mean?"

"The other night we found out we love each other, but at our age what does that mean? What's the next step?

"We both have businesses to run that are important to us. We each have a house, and you have a family in yours, two orphaned grandchildren who need you. I'm not sure we can fit the feelings we have for each other into our lives the way they are.

"Do we want to change our lives? That will happen if we keep on like this. We need to decide where and how we can make it all fit with what we are. Until we figure that out, I don't want to take this any farther." Her voice faltered and he could see her emotions clearly written on her face.

He looked at her in silence for a moment, saw the tears forming in her eyes, and finally said, "What we had the other night was special and I'll never forget it, but I can see what you're saying is true. Where do we take it from here?" He sat looking at her, fists on his cheeks for a long minute.

"Do you have any interest in a love affair, something where we love each other when we can and live our lives until we figure out what's next?"

"When you say, 'love affair', you mean sleeping together?"

He nodded his head and waited for her to speak again.

"When I was young," she said, "I would have given anything to have this, to feel this. But I'm not young anymore, and I can see how this could change my whole life. I need to be sure where it's going before I make any decisions about it. There's too much in the pot.

"I love you Lemuel but at our age and with our lives, I'm not sure love is enough."

Again, he looked at her in silence for a while. Finally, he took a deep breath and smiled. "The first time I saw you there was something about you that made me want to look again, and then again. Since then, I've spent a lot of time thinking about you and wondering if we would ever have the kind of thing we had the other night."

His smile widened. "From my reading I think they call those fantasies. I believe we can have that kind of thing again, and I don't just mean the lovemaking. We were happy and excited that night and all the next day in a way we could be every day for the rest of our lives. Being in love does that to you, gives you something to look forward to every day."

He picked up her hand, kissed it and continued. "And every night too, for that matter. I believe we can find a way forward together." He winked at her.

"Now, this is not the reason I came to see you. Johnny has decided to run, and we need to set up a meeting where we can lay out a plan. With all this going on in our lives, can we still work together to help our friend?

"Under the circumstances, I can see you might need a little time to decide if you still want to run the campaign. But he needs to get started and we'd like to do some planning. We're going to City Hall today to file the papers. About 4:30 tomorrow afternoon we're going to meet in Johnny's office in the BookSeller and, with Roy, we'll begin. I hope you'll be there."

She was smiling as she watched him walk away and tears on her cheeks.

Chapter Forty-Eight

Johnny was lying on the bed playing with Jinx when she came in from her shower and sat down to brush her hair.

"Anything going on at the clinic tonight?"

"Had a woman who fell off a stepladder and broke her hip. She'll be off her feet for a while. Other than that, nothing special. What about you?"

"It seems I already have a campaign manager and a financial backer, plus Lemuel will be lending a hand."

"So, you've decided to do it." She looked at him thoughtfully. "I imagine John D is the backer. Who's the campaign manager?"

"Kate."

"Kate Sessions?"

"How many Kates do we know?"

"Never heard of a woman campaign manager before. Come to think of it, I never knew a man campaign manager either, for that matter."

"I don't really know anything about it myself but Lemuel, Roy and I talked today and came up with some ideas on getting started. We're going to meet Kate tomorrow to set up our organization and put together a plan to move forward.

"Lemuel and I went down to City Hall today and did all the paperwork. John D says he's with me, and Ed told me the other day he's on board and, of course Roy will be with me a lot. I don't think we'll need anybody else. Of course, if we do, I know some people."

"What about the store?"

"We've got a good staff and Roy and I can handle the office stuff, plus Lemuel can help out if we need him."

He sat down on the bench and looked at her in the mirror.

"Does the idea of having a famous politician for a husband excite you? I mean, does it make you want to drag me into the bedroom?"

She grinned at him. "Johnny, we're already in the bedroom."

He stood and pulled her into an embrace. "Then you don't have far to drag me, do ya."

"Is this because you love me or are you just excited by all the power you'll have if you win?"

He kissed her and looked into her eyes for a moment. "Yes," he said and pushed her down on the bed.

Madame was drinking coffee and reading the paper when Sarah came into the breakfast room.

"Good morning, dear," she said as Sarah leaned over, kissed her cheek, and settled into the chair on the other side of the coffee service. When Madame bought the cottage, she had immediately remodeled it to include a bay window on the second floor that looked out over the ocean where they could breakfast each morning. They also had meals on the adjacent porch when the weather was nice, which in San Diego it was most of the time.

"Is that a beard rash I see?"

Sarah rolled her eyes and heaved a deep sigh. She patted her face. "He shaves every morning, but he's Irish with the black hair and everything that goes with it, so yes it's probably a beard rash."

She opened the newspaper. "Is this yesterday's Call?" she asked in amazement.

"Yes, they put it on the train first thing. We usually have it by midafternoon. The Union's right here too."

They sat for a while, the only sound the rustling of newspaper pages being turned.

"Does it bother you that I slept with Jonas last night?" asked Sarah.

"No, as long as you don't get too noisy and keep me awake. Why? Should it?

"I don't know. It felt a little strange knowing you were in the next room, maybe listening."

"You mean it inhibited you?"

Sarah didn't answer right away. "Actually, I think it excited me a little bit," she said thoughtfully.

"Just a little?"

"Well, maybe more than a little."

"Guilty pleasure you reckon?"

"Hadn't thought about it that way, but probably."

"Did it bother you when Woman and I spent the night together?"

"If I remember right, I'd say yes it probably did. I didn't think about it that way at the time, but it might have been that I was excited." She laid the paper in her lap and grinned at Madame. "All right, what do you think it means?"

"I think it means it doesn't take much to get you excited and I must say that's something I love about you." She returned the grin. "I like it when you get excited, and I don't really care how it happens." She reached out and took Sarah's hand.

Sarah looked out the window thoughtfully for a long moment. "If you'd have told me ten years ago that one day I'd have both a man and a woman as lovers, I'd have said you'd lost your mind. But here I am and loving every minute of it."

"And you seem to like it more as time goes by."

Carlota's knock on the door heralded Jonas' entrance and the conversation took a different turn.

"Morning ladies," he said, smiling and taking a seat. "Thank you, Carlota," he said, and sipped the coffee she had poured him. He spied the newspaper. "Just like home."

"The food's a little different but we try," said Madame. "Any plans for the day?"

"Sarah said she was going to show me the town. Are you going to join us?"

"No, I've some plans of my own, but I'll see you at dinner."

Jonas was standing at the rail for the ferry ride across the bay. He looked at Sarah and said, "You look beautiful this morning."

"You always say that."

"It's always true."

"Did you talk to Johnny yesterday about running?"

He nodded. "He's been thinking about it for a while. What's Madame up to today?"

"She and Woman are going on a picnic."

"You expect me to believe that?" He grinned at her. "Are they lovers?"

She wagged her finger at him. "Ask me no questions."

It was a picnic but the basket they had brought was standing unopened. In a clearing near the rock Woman was lying nude on a blanket and Madame was sitting on her knees looking down at her.

"I've missed you." Madame reached out and lightly touched Woman's breast and let her finger slide down to the nipple. Woman's eyes said much the same.

"Were you ever going to tell me about Sarah?" she asked.

"I knew you'd ask one day, then I'd tell you." Madame took a deep breath. "I can only say I'm lucky to have two such warm, wonderful friends as lovers, or lovers as friends. Don't know which it is."

Woman lay staring up at her. "Do you love her the same way you love me?" she finally asked.

"No, and I don't love you the way I love her. I love you both and you're different, so I love you differently, love different things about each of you."

She stretched out on the blanket, and they lay looking up at the clouds.

"Do you love me the way you love Wash?"

Woman turned over and leaned on her elbow, looking down. She slowly shook her head and smiled her slow smile. "No," she said.

Suddenly she scrambled to her feet and pulled her friend up. "Let's eat this lunch I worked so hard over, and you can tell me what's happened back home."

"Should we put our clothes on?"

"Are you cold?" When Madame shook her head, Woman said "No reason to. Wash is the only one around and he won't bother us. Unless we want him to, that is."

The clock chiming brought Kate back to the present. Two o'clock. She was late for lunch with Madame and Sarah. When she disembarked from the ferry in Coronado a carriage was waiting to take her to the cottage.

The ladies were seated at the window talking over cups of tea when she arrived. After she was seated and served, Madame smiled a knowing smile at her.

"Well, how was your trip?"

Kate shook her head and said, "I haven't been able to get it off my mind since we got back, but for the life of me I can't decide what to do next."

"Was it bad?" asked Sarah.

Madame was looking at Kate carefully. "I don't think that's what she means," she said slowly. "I think it was very good, maybe even wonderful and that's the problem," said Madame. "Am I right?" She continued looking at Kate.

Kate closed her eyes tightly, then her lips and nodded. "How did you know?"

"I know you both pretty well and knew how you felt about each other. It was easy to predict fireworks and all the rest when it finally happened."

"So, what's the problem?" asked Sarah.

Kate took a deep breath. "The problem is it's all I can think about, and I've got other things I need to think about. I'm going to be managing Johnny's campaign for City Council, I've got a business to run, and people who depend on me. And I can't get him off my mind. It's not like I'm a young maiden looking for a husband, for God's sake. I've got a life to live."

"I think they call that 'having too much of a good thing,'" said Madame. "Want to talk about it?"

"If I don't, I'll go crazy. If this is what they call a bittersweet experience, I don't like it at all." She was smiling and crying. "He's wonderful. He's charming and educated and funny and attractive and I think I love him so why am I crying so much?"

"Did he ask you to marry him?"

"Actually, I asked him."

"What did he say?"

Trying to suppress a smile she replied, "He said 'Why buy the cow when you get the milk for nothing?'"

Shocked silence followed by loud hilarity.

"I love a man who's a scoundrel at heart," announced Madame when they had stopped laughing.

"It sounds like you've got a problem similar to the one I had back home a while ago," said Sarah.

Kate looked at her inquiringly.

"Jonas. He asked me to marry him a few years ago. He was all you say about Lemuel and more but ultimately I told him 'no'. I didn't want to give up the life I had."

"That's it, exactly!" exclaimed Kate. "So what did you tell him?"

"Basically, I told him I'd rather be his mistress than his wife."

Kate was on the edge of her seat. "What did he say?"

"He laughed fit to bust."

"Lemuel suggested that. He asked me if I was interested in loving each other when we could and living our lives the way we have been until we figure out where it's going."

"How do you feel about that kind of arrangement?" asked Madame.

"It's not the way I was taught that things should be between a man and a woman. On the other hand, with my life right now, it seems like a good way to 'have my cake and eat it too', as my mother used to say."

"So, what's the problem?"

Kate was quiet for a long moment, staring out the window at the ocean in the distance. She was thinking about the way her stomach felt when he was around and the warmth that spread from between her legs to the rest of her body when she thought about that night.

"I guess maybe I'm afraid," she said. She looked at them in silence for a moment. "Afraid of losing who I am. Afraid of losing something I value. My independence, I guess. The freedom to choose what I want to do with my time and my life without consulting someone or worrying about what someone else wants. I'm not sure I want to be an 'us', if you know what I mean."

She looked at Sarah. "Is that how you felt?"

Sarah nodded. "Yes. But remember I had a family to consider. That's not in the picture with you."

"That's one of the reasons I always liked sailors," said Madame. "They come and go but never stay so I never feel a threat to my freedom. I think maybe you're worried about what your mother would say about the life you'd be living if you slept with a man out of wedlock.

At your age and in this day and time you don't need anyone's permission to do that, especially with someone you love. Love's more important than what the world thinks. None of your friends will care."

"So, you believe I should take the chance?"

They both nodded at her. "This might be something special, and if you pass it up for the wrong reasons, you'll probably never get the chance for something like it again," said Sarah.

Madame smiled at her. "So, start thinking about how it's going to fit into your life instead of worrying how it might change it. Next year at this time you'll probably find it's been worth it."

Wash was unloading some fruit tree saplings in the barn at Schweder's Grove, and as he handed the last one to the man on the ground, Enrique walked through the door.

"Hey Wash!" said the foreman. "If I remember right, you're good at fixing things."

"I guess that's right. What needs fixin?" He jumped down from the wagon brushing his hands on his pants. He looked around the well-kept barn but saw nothing that looked broken.

"It's the boss's wheelchair. One of the wheels is locked up. Can't get it to turn right."

Wash stood looking at the man in silence so long that Enrique asked, "Anything the matter?"

"No, no," said Wash. "Just thinking. Kate wants me back as soon as I can make it."

"It won't take long, and the boss will appreciate it."

He followed the man up on the porch and around to the front of the house where Schweder was sitting, looking out over his groves and toward the rugged hills rising in the distance.

He turned and smiled at Wash. "I've heard you can fix anything." He gestured at the wheelchair sitting beside him. "See what you can do with that."

With the chair laying on its side, he could see the axle was the problem.

"Looks like the axle's bent. Did you run over something?" He turned the wheel with some effort and could see where it was binding the bracket that held it to the chair.

"Is it worth fixing or should I get a new one?" His strong accent made it a little difficult for Wash to understand him.

Wash took his time answering. "I could just repair it, but if you want, I can make it better. I can make it stronger so that kind of thing wouldn't be so likely to happen."

"What would you charge?"

"It's hard to say," replied Wash. "I'd need to get some material, and I don't know how long it would take. I can take it with me and do the work down at the shop. When I bring it back out, I'll bring you a bill."

The man looked at him appraisingly for a moment. "You've been working for Kate a few years now, haven't you?"

Wash nodded. "My lady works there too."

"Well, if she trusts you, I do. The sooner you can get it done the better. I can't get around much without it."

When he was walking back to the barn with Enrique, the foreman said, "I hope it doesn't take long to fix. He's used to being out in the middle of things. He'll go crazy just sitting there."

"He takes this chair out into the groves?"

"No, but Tomas puts it in the wagon and drives him around. It's how he keeps up with what's going on. He likes to see for himself. I think that's how the axle got bent."

Kate was standing on the dock when Wash drove into the yard.

"What are you doing with that thing? Isn't that Ger's wheelchair?" She watched him lower the gate and lift the chair up onto the dock.

"He asked me to see if I can fix it."

"Can you?"

"I think so. It looks like the axle's bent. Shouldn't be too hard. I think I can reinforce the undercarriage and use a larger axle. That should keep it from happening again."

"That thing looks pretty banged up. What's he do with it?"

"Enrique says he goes out into the groves in a wagon, so it gets bounced around a lot and I don't think he lubes it much."

"Looks like you might end up with a side business," said Kate. "Fixing things for some of our customers. You ought to advertise. If you want to set up a shop in the back, have at it."

He was taking the wheels off the chair when he looked up and saw Woman standing watching him.

"Is that his chair?"

He nodded and looked at her meaningfully.

"How do you feel about that?"

He shook his head and smiled ruefully at her. "Lot of stuff going around in my head right now. I figured I'd wait and talk to you about it after dinner tonight."

She looked at him in silence for a moment. "I understand," she said.

"You always do"

Chapter Forty-Nine

He was sitting on the rock running his hand over her hair the way she loved and pondering the turmoil churning in his head. Since he had seen Schweder sitting on the porch that afternoon, the thoughts and visions wouldn't stop. When he closed his eyes he could still see the empty pant leg, pinned up and folded back along the remaining part of the man's thigh.

He wondered at the guilt he felt and remembered how the Sharpe's had jumped against his shoulder when he'd fired the bullet that put that man where he was; dependent on two wheels and a strong man to do things Wash took for granted.

His rational mind told him the man was guilty, was a murderer, probably many times over and he shouldn't feel guilty about what he'd done but he couldn't control the tightening in his gut that came on him once in a while. When he thought about why he'd done it there were always doubts.

What if he'd been wrong? Though he felt the evidence pointed to the man's guilt, nagging doubts remained and he knew for the rest of his life he'd probably continue to wake in the night feeling panic and wondering if he'd been wrong.

"We came out here to talk but you haven't said a word," she

said. "What are you thinking about?"

"I'm thinking the same things I've thought about since I did it, so talking probably won't help much." He sat quiet staring out at the darkness, seeing nothing.

Three days later he was unloading the chair in front of the house when Tomas came out the front door.

"He'll be glad to see that thing. He's been hard to live with waiting for it." He peered at the chair and said, "It looks different. What did you do to it?"

"New axle. A lot thicker, and the brackets are much stronger. I fixed a rubber tire around each wheel that will make it easier to roll on the ground, and I widened the stance a bit so it's more stable." He swung it up on the porch. "Also, I made some changes to the arm rests. Now they come off so it will be easier for him to get in and out."

From inside the house Schweder called, "Bring it in here. I want to see what you did."

The boss sat looking at it as Wash explained what he had done and why. Finally, he shook his head. "If you ever need a job," he paused, frowning. "I don't believe I know your name."

"It's Wash; short for Washington."

"Well Wash if you ever need a job let me know. With all the new machines we're getting around here we'd keep you busy."

"Kate says I can do any work you need done at the shop so just bring anything down, or need be, I can come out here."

"Sounds like she wants to start a new business."

"With Kate, nothing would surprise me."

All the way back into town he thought about seeing that man on a regular basis, and it was a good thing the horse knew where he was going because he hadn't noticed.

The sheriff's office was part of his weekly rounds and Johnny was standing talking to a deputy when Ed came in. The sheriff waved him into the office, and when they were seated, said, "Looks like you've got someone running against you."

Johnny looked a question at him.

"Max Housden."

"I thought he lived in the county."

"Well, his farm is in the county, but he owns the house his daughter lives in and he says that's his legal residence."

"Woo!" Johnny let out his breath in a rush. "That could make this council thing a bit more interesting."

"That's one way to put it," said Ed with a grin. "Max is a bit of a rough customer. I've heard he was with that bunch that was over at your place with the cross that night. I've had a couple of problems with him, but he's a friend of the judge's. I think they knew each other back east and that plus a few other people around have helped him stay out of jail. He's not your run of the mill council candidate."

"He was the leader of the bunch that caused the problem at the hospital."

Ed nodded. "He and his wife. She lives in town with her daughter now, I think. Max doesn't get along with his son-in-law too well, so he spends most of this time at the farm.

"Is he really running or just talking about it?"

"Seems like he is. I hear Arkie Lambert is going to be running his campaign."

"I don't know him."

"He was a cotton farmer back east. From the name, probably from Arkansas. He and Max go back a long way. He was probably in on that problem you had at the clinic too."

Johnny was on his way back to The BookSeller when a strange man hailed him from across the street.

"Hey Fry, hold up a minute. I want to talk to you."

Johnny stopped and watched the man, and two others cross the street. He looked to be in his forties and was tall and powerfully built through the shoulders, but a paunch was visible below. Something about the way he walked made him appear slightly drunk.

"I understand you're running for City Councilman, that right?" It sounded almost like a challenge and Johnny was suddenly leery but still wasn't prepared when the man's fist crashed into his head snapping it backward and throwing him against a post he'd been standing beside. He bounced forward into a punch that landed just below his heart, and he lost consciousness.

He began to come back when he felt hands lifting him into a wagon and heard someone say, "Let's get him over to the clinic. They'll take care of him." Then he passed out again.

When he awoke, he couldn't see and felt a sudden panic, but his hand touched what seemed to be a damp cloth over his eyes and when he moved it a bright light startled him.

"He's awake, Doctor," said a familiar voice. He recognized the voice as Grace's and relaxed, knowing he was in the clinic. A hand lifted the cloth, and he was looking into his wife's shadowed face, the light above her creating a halo around her head.

"How do you feel?" she asked.

He thought about that for a minute. "Like I was kicked. What happened?"

"It seems like someone punched you, from the looks of it, probably twice. You got a bruise coming up on your head and a red mark on your chest that looks like it was made by a fist with a ring on it. You must have ducked a little and what was intended to break your nose hit you on the forehead. Ed's outside and he wants to talk to you when you feel up to it."

Johnny took a deep breath and struggled to sit up, but Annaliese's hand on his chest held him in place. "He can come in here and talk. Lie still."

He closed his eyes and fell into a doze. When he heard the door open, he looked up and saw Este leading Roy in to see him.

"Are you OK?"

"Tell you the truth, I don't know but it's nice to know it didn't affect what we do." He looked at Este. "You know what I'm talking about, don't you?"

She nodded. "Roy told me about it. Well, he didn't really tell me but…"

"I know what you mean."

The door opened again, and the sheriff stood there, hat in hand. "Feeling good enough to talk?" he asked. "I can come back if need be."

"I think I'm OK. Head hurts a little. Chest hurts more, but the doctor tells me nothing's broken. So, who hit me?"

"Max Housden, your opponent in the Council race. He got a little drunk. He likes to scrap when he's drunk."

"He sure is a big fellow."

"He's a loudmouth bully. I can see why his wife stays in town most times." He paused. "Do you want to press charges? I can pick him up and hold him 'til the judge gets back."

"Let me think about it. I should be on my feet tomorrow, so I'll stop in and see you."

When the sheriff closed the door he glanced at Roy.

"I like him."

"Me too. I need to think about this though." He looked at Este. "Are you hanging around with this fellow now?"

She reached out and touched Roy's hand, smiled and nodded. "Yes. Whenever I can."

"Does your Mama know?"

Again, she nodded.

"Well. I'm glad."

"Me too."

When he opened his eyes again, Annaliese and Grace were there. "Swing your legs around. I want to see if you can stand up," she said.

When he was standing, she asked, "Feel dizzy at all?"

"No. I think I'm fine. Just a little sore."

"Why don't you go sit in my office? I'll be there shortly, and we can talk."

He was sitting at her desk reading a magazine when she came

in.

She sat down in one of the chairs for visitors and asked, "What happened? Ed said Max Housden just walked up and hit you. Have you ever met him?"

"Wouldn't have known him from Adam before today. I imagine I'll recognize him from now on."

"Do you suppose it was because of the Council Seat?"

"Can't think of any other reason."

"What are you going to do?"

"As much as you don't want to hear it, I guess I'm going to put the Colt back on."

"Oh, Johnny! Must you?"

"Annaliese, the guy outweighs me by forty pounds, and he likes to get drunk and pick fights."

"You're not going to kill him, are you?"

"No, but I have to let him know if he tries that again I'll do whatever it takes to stop him."

"Do you think he will?"

"From what I hear that'll probably depend on how much he's had to drink the next time he sees me."

"I hear you've had an interesting day so far." Lemuel was sitting in a chair looking out the window at the city and the bay in the distance.

Climbing up the steps to his office had winded Johnny, and feeling a little weak, he stopped and leaned on the doorway.

"Let's say the campaign has begun," he said.

"I see you're wearing the Colt again. What'd she say about that?"

"She understands. The guy's a brute. I don't plan to be his punching bag again if I can help it."

Kate knocked on the door jamb and when she came in bent and kissed Lemuel before she sat down.

"Now how in the world am I supposed to concentrate after

that?" He rolled his eyes at Johnny.

"You're right," she said, trying to keep from smiling at him. "We need to keep things on a professional level when we're around here."

For the next couple of hours, they did just that. Housden's attack and the aftermath began the discussion, but eventually they put it aside, so by the time the meeting was over they had the beginnings of a plan. Afterwards, Kate and Lemuel disappeared holding hands and Johnny went in to dinner.

He sat down next to his wife, and in answer to the unspoken question on her face, said, "I'm fine."

"Did you decide whether to press charges?"

"We talked about it. Lemuel thinks I should just put it behind me. The fact that he's running against me changes things a little. If he ends up in jail, he'll get his picture in the paper. Won't do us any good to help make him famous."

Annaliese was looking thoughtful. "So that's going to be part of our lives from now on, is it?" When he looked at her curiously, she continued. "From now on whatever happens to us we have to think about how it will affect the campaign. Hmm. That's going to make life interesting."

"Hadn't thought about it quite like that but I guess it's true. And probably beyond that. One of the reasons I decided to run was because I have ideas about the city that will affect people's lives. For the better I hope, but to accomplish those things will likely mean convincing some of those people to support me. Since things I do in my life will help people to decide whether or not to give me their support, then yes, it looks like it's going to be a part of our lives from here on out."

He looked at her meaningfully. "I think that's what they call politics. I guess that makes you a politician's wife."

"Can I drop you somewhere?"

They were standing in front of The BookSeller.

"I was thinking about having dinner," said Kate. "Will you join me at the Horton House? I'm buying." She looked at him solemnly.

"I accept," he said, and followed her to the hotel. She waited while he tied his horse and shortly, they were seated in the ornate dining room.

"I've gotten so used to the Del, I'd forgotten how nice it is here," she said as they were being seated.

"If it's alright with you, I'm going to look at you instead of the dining room," said Lemuel. He wasn't staring, but he was looking at her as though he wanted to memorize every line and feature of her face.

She looked at her lap for a moment, took a deep breath then looked up and said, "So where do we go from here? What's the next move?" She took his hand. "I love you and have decided to accept the future we can have together. So, any ideas you want to talk about?"

He was having a hard time not laughing at her solemn dignity but somehow knew that wouldn't be the right thing for this particular time. "How about if I kiss you? Would that be a good start?"

Trying to keep from smiling, she nodded and leaned forward, eyes closed, felt his finger on her chin, and then a brief tender kiss. When she opened her eyes, he was smiling at her.

"There, that seemed just right. Now let's get practical; where do you want to live? The twins have Mrs. Keane and Consuelo, but I do need to show my face at meals occasionally."

"I assume we will be sleeping together once in a while?" she said.

"How do you feel about that?" His voice was low, just above a whisper. "At our ages, most couples don't. I think it will be more romantic if we make it an occasional thing. That way it would always be special. And it would help us to see if we want to take it any further."

"I'm going to leave the romance stuff to you, cause you're so good at it. I've never seen your rooms at the house. Do the children sleep close by?"

"We can have all the privacy we want."

Their food arrived and they talked while they ate and looked at each other a lot.

"Of course, there's always a trip to Los Angeles," he said. "I know of a hotel there that has some special memories."

She grinned at him. "Where do you come up with this stuff? You're different from any man I've ever heard of."

"I slept alone for many years after Mary died, and I read a lot of novels. I thought about romance many of those nights, and you're the first woman I've had a chance to practice on."

"Are those the fantasies you mentioned?" When he nodded she said, "You'll have to tell me about them sometime."

"How about tonight?"

Chapter Fifty

Lemuel, Roy and Johnny were waiting for coffee in a small café near the courthouse and talking about the meeting they had just left. They were also waiting for Kate, who had stopped to talk to the owner of the cafe. It was the first time Johnny had ever been to a meeting where everything was about him. All the people there wanted to hear him speak and wanted him to know they were on his side.

"Lots of people there."

He looked at Roy. "Yes, lots of good feelings in that room today."

"It looks like we're off to a good start," said Lemuel.

Kate sat down and said, "Just got us a couple of votes, maybe three. It's amazing how many people you know around here."

"It's something I try to do. I think one time or another I've talked to most of the business owners in town. Just stop in to get to know them. Maybe I've had this idea in the back of my mind for a while."

"Naw, I think you're just naturally nosey, a busybody of sorts. Like to stick your nose in everybody's business," said Lemuel grinning.

They talked for a while, making plans, and talking about what were the best ways to go about what they were trying to accomplish. After a while Johnny noticed Roy looking intently out the front window.

"Housden."

Johnny glanced at three men on the porch of the general store across the street and then looked again. "I do believe those gentlemen might be waiting for me," he said and got to his feet.

"That one sitting down looks like Max Housden," said Kate. "I don't know the other two."

"I do," said Johnny. "They were with him when he punched me the other day."

"What do you want me to do?" asked Lemuel.

"Stay in here with Kate." He looked at Roy and they pushed back their chairs and stood. "We've been expecting something like this."

Kate watched open-mouthed as they went out the door.

"What are they going to do?" she asked Lemuel.

"I'd say that depends on what Housden and his friends do, but I trust you noticed that both Johnny and Roy had their guns on."

"He's not going to shoot him?!"

"Well, I'll say this. Johnny won't let Housden do again what he did the last time."

Through the screen door they heard Housden call across the street. "Wondered if you were ever going to come out of that place."

Johnny stood by the door of the café and waited.

"Have you decided to get out of the race, or do I have to persuade you some more?"

Johnny answered, speaking distinctly. "No, I haven't but I think there's something you should know."

"What's that," sneered Housden. He was standing now and his two friends had moved off the porch and were standing by the hitch rail in front of the store.

"I won't let you put your hands on me again."

"Is that why you're wearing that gun?"

Johnny didn't answer, just stood waiting for what he knew was probably coming.

Grace was cleaning the examining room when three men came in carrying a stretcher with a very large man on it. His pants leg had been cut away and his thigh was covered with a bloody bandage.

She grabbed the voice tube, said "Injured patient!" and hung up. She was washing her hands when Annaliese and Este hurried into the room.

Annaliese lifted the patient's leg and seeing a large bruise but no wound on the back, realized the bullet hadn't come out.

"Get Maggie! She's upstairs," she snapped at Este.

In the time it took Maggie to get there they had removed the bandage, washed the wound and the back of the leg where a large dark bruise had formed. With Maggie and Este helping, they managed to turn the patient over. Then they all stood and watched Maggie examine the wound.

"It feels like it's just under the skin here. It probably hit the bone, which is why it didn't go through. He's going to bleed a lot when I go in after that bullet so put a tourniquet here." She pointed to the groin near the crotch. She cleaned the skin with alcohol, and instead of working on the front where the wound was, made an incision below the bruise on the back of the leg and using forceps, began to probe for the bullet.

Within a minute she held it up, then dropped it into a bowl. Then she cleaned and packed the wound with gauze, put a dressing on it, and secured it with adhesive tape. She motioned for help turning him over, then with a long pair of tweezers and the light as close as she could get it, began to look closely at the wound in the thigh.

"She's looking for bits of cloth or anything that might have gone in with the bullet," Annaliese whispered to the girls. "Things like that left in a wound can cause an infection."

They watched as she pulled small, bloody bits and pieces of

things from the wound. Heat from the overhead light had made the room stifling already, so Grace folded a cloth and used it to wipe perspiration from Maggie's forehead.

She finally stood and said, "I got all I could see. Lots of blood in there, even with this on." After she had dressed the incision on the front of the thigh, she released the tourniquet and stood looking closely at the dressing. "Looks like the bleeding stopped. It's a good thing he's unconscious. That would have been a lot harder if he'd have been awake."

It didn't take long for them to clean the man up and get him in bed. While Grace and Este cleaned the treatment room, Maggie sat in the office with Annaliese writing up the procedure when there was a knock on the door. Annaliese looked up and found herself looking into the face of Madeline Housden.

"That's my husband you got lying in that bed back there," she said.

"Really?" asked Annaliese. "Well, Mrs. Housden this is Dr. Maggie Kramer. She's the one who took the bullet out of his leg. She'll be taking care of him."

"That may be, Dr. Fry but your husband is the one who shot him in the first place."

Annaliese sat back in the chair and looked at the woman thoughtfully. "You know, I wondered if that might be the case."

"Have you anything to say about it?"

"You know I had my husband on that same table the other day because your husband beat him up," Annaliese said. "So, there's a couple of things I'll say. First, I know Johnny well enough to know he wouldn't have shot him without warning him first and second, Johnny told me he wouldn't let your husband put a hand on him again, so the chances are that's what he tried to do. Johnny told me he wasn't going to be your husband's punching bag again."

She stopped and waited for the woman to speak. When she didn't, he continued, "Under the circumstances, all I can tell you is we'll take care of your husband and do our best to help him make a complete recovery. But if he tries to do it again, Johnny will likely shoot him again, probably in the other leg."

"It seems like you're being mighty flippant about it."

"And it seems to me that your husband is a drunk and a bully and I'm surprised someone hasn't done it before now."

They looked at each other in silence for a long moment; then the woman suddenly seemed to deflate. She closed her eyes and shook her head. "To tell you the truth, I am too," she said. "He's been getting away with doing this kind of thing for years."

"Maybe this will teach him a lesson."

The woman shook her head again. "I doubt it. He's kind of hardheaded."

"Mrs. Housden, he's probably going to have a bad limp for quite a while, maybe for the rest of his life. He might even get an infection and lose his leg. That might be a good reminder for him."

When he saw Lemuel and Johnny walk in the front door Ed waved them into his office. When they were seated Johnny said, "Do you ever get tired of hearing my problems?"

"Actually, it keeps my life interesting," replied Ed. "Who'd you shoot this time?"

"Max Housden."

Ed grinned. "I don't blame you. I've been hoping someone would. It might have been better if he was not running against you." When Johnny didn't react, Ed cocked his head and frowned. "You're not joking. Are you?"

"Unfortunately, no I'm not."

"Was he armed?"

"No but he raised his hand to hit me, and he outweighs me by forty pounds. After what happened the other day, I warned him not to do anything like that again, but he was going to anyway, so I shot him in the leg."

"Jesus! Johnny." Ed's mouth was hanging open. "Where is he?"

"I think his friends took him to the clinic. I tried to help him, but he didn't want me to touch him. His friends were there so I figured I'd come over here and give you something new to worry about."

Ed ran his fingers through his hair and took a deep breath. "I think we're going to have to take this before the judge."

"Are you going to lock him up?" asked Lemuel.

"I need to go talk to Max and see what he says. Ed stood up. "Are you going to the store?"

Johnny nodded and stood. "I'll be there."

"I'll need your gun, Johnny," said Ed. "Just until the hearing."

Johnny looked at him steadily for a moment, then unbuckled his gun belt and handed it to the sheriff.

They were quiet on the ride to the store and were seated in Johnny's office under the eaves before either of them spoke.

"What do you think the judge will say?" asked Lemuel.

"You know he and Max are friends, don't you?" said Johnny.

"Seems to me I'd heard that somewhere. I don't see any jury in this part of the country convicting you. You were defending yourself. Hell, I don't think they can find anyone in the county who doesn't know you."

"Did you notice the first thing Ed asked me?"

"I know he wasn't armed, but what about him attacking you without warning at that time and threatening you again…" His voice trailed off. "Under the circumstances I'd have shot him too. I think most men would have."

They were talking about the campaign when Kate knocked on the door jamb. "I thought maybe I'd find you up here. So what happened with Ed?" She kissed Lemuel and sat down.

"He's going to come by here after he talks to Max, or maybe his friends, so I'm glad you're here. We can use another witness." Lemuel smiled at her. "Of course, that's not the only reason I'm glad you're here."

She rolled her eyes at Johnny. "Isn't he the most charming thing?"

"Tell you the truth, I never noticed," answered Johnny with a grin. They all laughed.

She joined their conversation about the campaign and was telling them some of her ideas when Johnny cocked his head.

"The sheriff is here."

"Send him up," said Johnny into the voice tube and within a minute they could hear him on the steps.

"This is the first time I've been up here." The sheriff stood looking out the window. "What a view," he said. After a moment he moved a chair into position to join the conversation.

"What did Housden have to say?" asked Lemuel.

"He wants Johnny in jail. Wants to swear out a warrant. As I was leaving Jim Wilde from the Union showed up. I'll bet he won't be the only one."

"Well, it's a good story. I know Jim. He's a pretty straight fellow. He'll probably be here next."

"Johnny, the way I'm supposed to do this is to hold you until the Judge can set bail. Unfortunately, the Judge is on circuit and won't be back for a week or so. That puts me in a spot, but I know you aren't going to run off, so I'm going to ask you to post a bond against showing up when he holds the hearing, and you can't leave town until then."

"Thanks, Ed. I'll abide by whatever you say."

Lemuel was trying to keep a straight face. "You can rely on us Ed. We'll make sure he doesn't run off."

"How much of a bond?" asked Johnny.

"Tell you what. I don't think the judge is going to say much, so we'll just make it fifty dollars. Is that OK?"

"Whatever you say."

Chapter Fifty-One

Kate was behind the counter a few weeks later smiling to herself when a young Mexican came in the store and handed her a note with 'Wash' written on the back. When he came back from a job planting some trees she handed it to him.

He read it and looked up. "Looks like they need me to fix something again."

"Schweder?" asked Kate.

Wash nodded. "I put a tool kit together after you said something about doing repairs on equipment for customers. If you don't need me, I'll get it and head out there."

Woman had overheard the conversation and was standing on the dock when he put his tool kit in the wagon. "Be careful. I've got a bad feeling about this."

He shook his head. "Every time I go out there I feel like I'm walking in a minefield."

"Why do you say that?" Kate had come out on the porch and heard something she probably shouldn't have.

Wash looked at her in silence for a long moment. He shrugged. "I don't know. Just a feeling I have."

When he drove into the yard one of the workers called to him.

"He wants to see you. He's on the porch."

Wash waved his hand in acknowledgment and after he'd tied the horse to the hitch rail found Schweder sitting on the front porch talking to Enrique. He dismissed the foreman and gestured to a rocking chair.

"The chair is working fine. I really like being able to take the arms loose. I just leave them off mostly."

"Did you have something else that needed fixing?"

"Yes, but before we get to that I need to talk to you about something else."

The man's accent was such that Wash almost had to interpret parts of his conversations and when Schweder said, "You're good friends with Johnny Fry, aren't you?" it took him a moment to realize what he'd said.

He nodded, his stomach suddenly full of butterflies. Schweder was looking out at his orange and lemon trees. "You moved down here from up north with him and he and his partner had a bookstore in San Francisco, true?" When Wash nodded again, he continued. "Enrique told me he saw a Sharp's fifty in your wagon one day. Is that yours?" Wash nodded again.

Schweder was looking at him now. "These things lead me to a conclusion I don't know what to do about."

The silence was one Wash didn't want to break. Schweder's gaze had returned to the grove, and nothing was said for a long moment.

Finally, he said, "It seems I have two choices what to do about this situation. Either act on what I know and suspect, or let the sleeping dog lie, as they say. What do you think I should do?" He had turned back and now his eyes were boring into Wash's. They sat like that for a long time.

"He's very good with a gun, isn't he?"

Again, Wash nodded.

"So, one of my choices could lead me to doing things that would change my life forever and might even end it." This was a statement not a question. "The other would allow me to continue a life I enjoy, a productive life with no one the wiser. Except you and your friends that is." He smiled a strange smile at Wash. "What path would you choose?"

Wash took a long time to answer.

"I'd say the second choice makes more sense."

After a moment Schweder said, "I think I agree." He smiled at Wash. "We have a watering machine we pull through the groves that stopped working on us. Enrique thinks maybe the gears are the problem. See what you can do with it, will you?"

As Wash got up to leave, Schweder said, "From what I've heard, your lady friend might even be more dangerous than Fry."

Wash paused on the steps of the porch and was fighting a smile when he said, "I think you might be right about that."

When Mica began working at the practice, they had created an office for him in the store which is what they all called the building where they lived, worked, ate, and slept. With Annaliese having an office there the proximity would allow them to interact with each other more efficiently. With the hospital no longer functioning, the clinic was beginning to feel the pressure to expand.

Mica, Maggie and Will were waiting in her office when Annaliese came in.

"So, what ideas do you have for more space?" she asked when she was seated. "It's just getting too crowded around here."

The building they had inherited with the practice had needed an upgrade and eventually they had gradually moved all the other tenants out, remodeled to create treatment facilities, and almost doubled functional space downstairs. Upstairs was Maggie's apartment and three medium sized rooms, one for storage and two set-up for rest for people on call at the clinic.

The store itself was becoming crowded, and soon they would be looking at moving some of their operations out to make more room for the residence.

Will spoke first. "We have enough land to build on around the store, but the question is, how much of it do we want to use for the clinic?"

"What about the hospital building?" asked Mica. "Granted it would be quite a task to take on the burden of purchasing the entire facility, but maybe we could work out some kind of lease with the board for a part of or all the building. Surely that's the best place. It was, after all, designed to be exactly what we need."

Annaliese smiled at him. "And you could get your old office back."

Mica grinned at her in return. "Yes, there's that."

"I don't know if that's going to work. It would be a complicated arrangement," said Will. "Let's explore it and hold it in reserve. I don't like the idea of putting everything else on hold while we try to work something out with them. I think we should move ahead with our own plans the way we have been. We can adapt as things develop."

"Agreed," said Mica. He looked at Maggie then at Annaliese and both nodded.

Annaliese stood and reached for her umbrella. "I need to get over to the clinic. I have an appointment coming in. Are you coming?" she said to Maggie.

"Tom's there with the girls, isn't he?" asked Maggie. When Annaliese nodded, she said, "I have a luncheon engagement, so I'll be over later."

As Will and Mica went through the door ahead of her, Annaliese paused and asked in a low voice, "With a man?"

Maggie grinned. "Never you mind. I'll tell you about it later."

As she was getting out of the carriage, she saw her appointment approaching. Like any boy his age, Johnny Madden had turned learning how to use his crutches into a game, and his mother was having a hard time keeping up with him.

Annaliese met them at the door and led them into the treatment room where she boosted Johnny onto the examination table, pulled his pants leg up and examined the cast on the lower part of his leg and the foot sticking out the bottom. Color in the foot indicated a good amount of blood was flowing there and the cast looked to be intact, though dirty and covered with signatures and drawings.

Este came into the room and Johnny's face lit up. "I'm learning to do all sorts of things on my crutches."

"Does it ever cause you any pain?" asked Annaliese.

"If I bump it against something; and once in a while I wake up at night cause it's hurting. It itches me like crazy sometimes, and Mama made me a scratcher for when it gets bad."

"It hasn't slowed him down much, if at all," said his mother. Este and Johnny went in search of some candy they kept hidden in the next room and Annaliese led his mother into her office.

"It looks like he's doing fine. We'll leave him in the cast for another month. By then he should be able to begin walking on it."

She made some notes, and while she was writing the woman said, "I hear your husband met my father again yesterday."

Annaliese looked up. "Can I call you Dolly?" she asked. When the woman nodded, she continued. "Well Dolly, it seems so. Yesterday your father was lying on that same table your Johnny was just on, and my partner was doctoring him. She took a bullet out of his leg, actually and it seems my husband put it there. Have you seen him?

"He's at our house in the back bedroom. Mama is sitting with him. With the medicine you gave him he sleeps most of the time."

"Well, tomorrow Maggie will try to get over to change the dressing and check on how he's doing. Try to keep him in bed, and for God's sake, tell him not to take another swing at my husband. He's only got two legs."

"When Pa gets to drinking you never know what he's going to do. It was bad when I was at home, but it seems to be getting worse as he gets older. That's why my mother spends most of her time in town with me and George and Johnny."

"I think he's running against Johnny for a seat on the City Council."

"I think that's part of the reason. The way Pa thinks that makes them enemies. He can get carried away about something like that when he's drinking."

"I hope it doesn't happen again."

"So, do I. A part of the reason he's running is he's still upset about y'all treating the Mexicans. Where he comes from, they don't allow that kind of thing."

"How do you feel about that?"

Dolly shook her head. She was getting ready to answer when her son Johnny came in with Este. She took a deep breath and said, "I think we don't live there anymore. We have a new life out here, and he should leave that kind of thing back in Arkansas."

"Ma, Grace said I could come and visit them at home one day when they're not working," said Johnny, obviously excited about the idea.

"We'll see," said his mother. As she was leaving, she looked back and said, "We're not like Pa. None of us."

That night she was brushing her hair and Johnny was lying in bed reading a book about the city.

"I could write a better book about San Diego than this."

"Why don't you? You keep talking about writing something but never do more than talk."

"Well, I am kind of busy at the moment, but when this is over, win or lose, I think I'll take a shot at it and see what I can do."

"I read somewhere that a fellow approached Victor Hugo, the French writer and said he had a great idea for a book. Supposedly Hugo replied, 'Congratulations. All you need now is a hundred thousand words.' Why don't you set a goal of, say ten pages and see what you've got? That shouldn't take long. Then you can decide if you want to keep going. That way you could either have a good start toward something or maybe you'll get it out of your system."

"Sounds like a good idea." He got up, stood behind her and kissed the top of her head. "How'd you get so smart?"

She smiled at him in the mirror. "I think about things." Her face assumed a somber expression and said, "Max Housden's daughter and her son were in today."

"How did that go?"

"She says her father is sleeping a lot and they take turns sitting with him."

"How's the boy's leg?"

"It's fine. Healing. They bounce pretty well at that age."

"I hope Housden realizes I won't allow him to take a poke at me whenever he has a couple of beers."

"I think he'll have a reminder about that for a while."

She was quiet for a moment brushing her hair.

"Something else I've been thinking a lot about lately is the children." She scooted over and patted the seat beside her.

He settled down beside her and she continued. "With Consuelo and Mrs. Keane, we don't have to worry about them as far as doing many of the things most parents have to do. I usually see one or the other of them and we talk about the children and how they're doing, but that's not the same."

She turned to face him. "I was really glad to see you working with Consuelo, trying to teach them how to understand us. We need to be a part of their lives as parents, not just someone paying the bills. I know we've both got busy lives and it's not something we're used to, but I don't want them to be an afterthought. Please remind me of that when you see I need it."

She put her hand on his knee. "Let's try to plan so that they're a part of what we're doing every day. I like what you're doing, learning the language and all. I may join y'all when you work on it. I could surely use the practice."

"What did your mother say when you told her about Roy?"

Este looked up from where she was writing in her diary. She had started one because Grace had one, and found she really enjoyed recording things about her time working with the doctors. Lately, though, there have been more personal entries about her first real boyfriend and the new feelings and thoughts that crowded her mind because of it.

"She wasn't surprised. I've been talking about him for a month."

"What did she say?"

"She likes Roy, but she reminded me that getting married or getting pregnant right now could ruin any future idea of medical school. So, if that's what's important to me I should make sure I always think about that whenever I get too excited about a future with him."

"I remember that time you wondered what it would be like being married to someone who couldn't talk. Remember that?"

"Yes. I think about it a lot."

"So, do you have any answers to that yet?"

"When we spend time together, we seem to do all right. There are times when I believe he's thinking to me the way he does with Johnny."

"Really?!!

"No, not really, I guess, but he looks at me and it feels like I understand what he wants me to know. Usually, we talk with notes. He types very fast, but sometimes we're not near his typewriter and he has to write." She smiled to herself. "I feel I know him even though he never says a word.

"I guess one of the things I like about him is how much he thinks. He has to. Everything he wants to say he has to put on paper so he has to think about it before he gives me a note. You've seen how much he reads."

"What does he think about your future and what you want to do?"

"We've talked about it. I think he believes it's a good idea and he understands how I feel about it. I don't think he's very happy that it will be three or four years before I'm through, but somehow, I just believe he'll be with me when I finish.

"We talked about him moving to San Francisco if that's where I'll be studying. There's a sign language school there. He thinks if we both learn how to use it, it will be better after we get married."

"Are you going to marry him?"

"I think so. I think I love him." She shrugged. "Of course, I'm not really sure I know what love is, but I know he's special. I'm sure it's because he can't talk. He thinks a lot about things. You wouldn't believe the different things he reads. Sometimes he picks a book off the shelf and reads it just because it's there and he hasn't read it before. I asked him about that, and he said he learns something new from every book he reads."

"It's lucky he works in a bookstore. Has he ever talked about Greta?"

"We've talked about the accident. Nothing else."

"Before you started here, Annaliese told me I wouldn't be unique anymore with you around, which was true. If things work out as you plan, you'll be unique. A Mexican woman doctor married to a man who can't speak; that would really have to be one of a kind."

Chapter Fifty-Two

"What do you think the judge will do?" Kate was unbuttoning her blouse, and under the circumstances, what the judge would do was the farthest thing from Lemuel's mind.

"Huh?" he said distractedly. "Oh, with all the friends Johnny has around here, he'll probably get run out of town if he does anything at all. People know what Max Housden is and they know what Johnny is. Now come here and kiss me."

He was lying on the bed, and he reached a hand out to her. She stood by the bed holding his hand and looking down at him. "I thought this was supposed to be an occasional thing so it would be more exciting. This is three nights in a row."

"I'm still excited about it. How about you?" he asked.

Trying to keep from smiling she said, "Sick and tired. Sick and tired, that is, of having to take all these clothes off every night and then put them back on in the morning." She knelt on the bed and continued. "Why don't we just stay in bed tomorrow, so we don't have to get dressed?"

He pulled her into the bed and when she was lying beside him, he leaned on his elbow, stared down at her nakedness and ran his hand lightly across her body.

She smiled up at him. "Tell me about that fantasy again. The one with the three women?"

So, he did.

The next morning when he awoke, she was leaning on her elbow looking at him.

"Good morning," he said. "You look beautiful."

"Of course I do," she said, grinning at him. "Haven't touched my hair or my face. I'm sure it looks like I slept in a haystack." She kissed him and looked at him lying there in silence.

"This is probably not an appropriate topic for a romantic morning after, but I overheard Wash say something to Woman yesterday and I can't get it off my mind."

"Tell me."

"He was talking about going out to Schweder's Grove to fix something for them. Woman said she had a bad feeling about it, and he said, 'every time I go out there, I feel like I'm walking in a minefield.' Why would he say that?"

He looked at her in silence for a long moment.

"What's the matter?" she asked when he continued to stare at her.

"I'm debating whether to answer that question or not."

"So, you know why he said it?" He nodded. "But you're not going to tell me." He shrugged. "Why not?"

"If I tell you why, I might as well answer your question."

"Why wouldn't you tell me?"

"Because it would probably change the way you feel about someone, you're close to; maybe more than one someone."

"Wash?"

He nodded. "And others."

She shook her head. "I can't imagine anything you could tell me about Wash that would change the way I feel about him."

"If I tell you, I'm going to be breaking a confidence, and I don't like to do that, but since it's you..."

He came around to her side of the bed, pulled back the covers and held out his hand. "It's a long story, so let's get dressed and go for some breakfast. That will give me time to think about how to go about telling you." He kissed her. "You look beautiful, in case I've never told you."

She rolled her eyes and disappeared into the bathroom.

An hour later they were sitting in the dining room at The Horton House, coffee before them, and she said, "So tell me."

"OK, but I want you to promise me you'll never repeat what I'm going to tell you. To anyone, and that includes Wash and Woman." She hesitated, then nodded and he began.

"A few years ago, when we were running the bookstore in San Francisco, someone fired a bullet meant for me that killed Jed, my son-in-law, instead. The shot came from a second story window across the street, and Johnny got off a couple of shots in return.

"Investigation found that it was likely an assassin paid by someone who wanted revenge against me and evidence seemed to show that one of the bullets Johnny fired scored, leaving a distinctive wound on the side of the killer's face.

"Not long after Wash went to work for you, he saw a man come into the store who had a scar that looked like it might have been caused by that bullet. He investigated and found evidence pointing to the man as the killer.

"So, what could he do about it? Couldn't go to the law. They'd take the side of the local businessman. He couldn't call the man out because he'd probably get shot. Felt he needed to stop him before he did it to someone else."

"So, he's the one who shot Ger in the leg?!" Kate's mouth was open, and her face was a study in shock."

Lemuel nodded slowly. She sat staring at him, hand over her mouth.

"And Woman knows about this?"

He nodded. "I don't know the details, but I imagine she helped him."

"Why? Why did he do it?"

"I think there were several reasons. He felt it was payment for what this man did to a friend. Also, he believed if he waited and Schweder got another job, someone else would die. He couldn't go to the law. Johnny was three hundred miles away, so he decided to do what he felt had to be done.

"As far as deciding to ambush him, he knew if he tried to face him, he'd probably end up dead and the killing would go on. It's like Wash said, 'I'm not a magician with a six gun like Johnny'. It seemed like the only answer."

They sat staring at each other until Lemuel said, "Close your mouth. You look funny sitting there with it open."

She closed it with a snap, then took a deep breath and shook her head. "I don't know what to say. How do you feel about it?"

"I'd probably have blown his head off with a shotgun. He murdered my son-in-law on the day he found out he was to be a father, and almost destroyed my daughter's life, not to mention putting a bullet into my leg."

"He can't take the law into his own hands like that."

"To him it looked like the right choice. It was that or murder him. With the way things were, he felt it was the only way to handle it."

"I just have trouble seeing Ger as a murderer, an assassin. He's a good farmer and all his people like him. He's one of my best customers and he's a nice man."

"It's hard to see inside someone. Maybe that's how he got the money to buy the land and maybe he just got in the habit of killing for cash. It doesn't seem to be hard work as long as you can live with yourself."

Wash was unloading a wagon in the yard when Woman called, "Wash, someone here to see you."

"Tell them five minutes and I'll be finished here." When he came inside, he was surprised to find Nate Harrison waiting for him. After greeting him Wash said, "Good to see you again. Let's go out to the gazebo and talk."

He could see the scar across the man's face had healed. It was similar to the scar on his own face, and he wondered idly whether he had scars on his back too. Most men who were slaves did and more than a few women. For a slave it was hard to go through life without coming under the whip.

When they were seated Wash said, "It's good to see you all healed up."

"The lady doctor did a fine job on it. Healed with no problems." Wash noticed he was speaking without the exaggerated accent and seemed to be relaxed.

"This is nice out here. How does your boss feel about you sitting out here during work hours?"

"She's not my boss, she's my friend. I don't have a boss."

Nat looked at him, a grin slowly spreading across his face. "That's the way it is for me. I don't have a boss, but I got to live up on the mountain to get away with it."

"What can I do for you?"

"Nothing really. It's the first time I've been in town since that night those boys jumped me. Thought I'd drop in and see how you were. Say thanks for helping me out that night."

"I'm fine. You heard about our set-to with the 'crackers' didn't you?"

"I heard you run 'em off . Anybody hurt?"

"No. The whole of Old Town turned out and they didn't like the odds."

Nate looked at him keenly for a moment. "Must be special people around there for that to happen."

Wash smiled. "They are. I think everyone in Old Town has been a patient at the clinic one time or another and a lot of their children."

"You know they won't forget what happened, don't you?"

"That's what Lemuel says. He believes we should have provoked them and then wiped them out."

"What do you think?"

Wash ran his finger down his nose and thought about that for a moment. "He thinks we'll have trouble with them again and I think he's probably right. He sees them as a disease. Says it will spread."

"Sounds to me like he knows what's what." He paused. "Are you doing anything about it? Strikes me you need to be watching out."

"We've talked about it, and we have a plan, but we all got to live our lives and it's just doctors and such there most of the time. We hung a triangle iron by the door, and if they need help, they'll jangle it and we'll come running. And of course, the people in Old Town will respond too. Tell you the truth, the other night when they saw all the blades those people were carrying, that's when they skedaddled.

"Do they ever bother you at your place?"

"Naw. They too damn lazy to climb the mountain to get me, I reckon. I live with my lady up on Palomar Mountain. Mostly my neighbors are Indians, and we get along. We help each other as needed and share food and water when we're hungry or thirsty. I been up there a long time and those 'crackers' don't know the mountain good enough to bother me."

They sat and talked for a while, finding out they both came from South Carolina, though Nate had come out before the War and after his owner died, was freed.

"When I come down for supplies and such, I try to be on the way home before dark. That last time I stopped to see an old friend and stayed late." He fingered the scar on his face. "Doubt if I'll do that again."

"Speaking of that I'd best get going. Like to get home before dark and it takes about four hours. Come up and see me sometime. It's the only road up the mountain."

As he mounted his mule he looked down at Wash and said, "Don't think this thing is over. Your friend is right. It's like a disease and it's right bad around here. Problem is there's no real cure. People either grow out of it or they don't."

He turned the mule and, with a wave, rode away down the road. Wash stood watching him out of sight.

Kate came up beside him and after a moment asked, "Was that Nate Harrison?" Wash nodded. "First time I've seen him for a while."

"Where's Palomar Mountain?" he asked.

She shaded her eyes and pointed. "See that peak sticking up there? It's just beyond that. It's up north and a little east of Escondido." She returned to the counter and when she turned, he was still standing there, looking out toward the mountain.

Chapter Fifty-Three

Johnny pulled his shirt collar out with his finger and stretched his neck. He didn't often wear a high-collar shirt and he liked it that way. But then he didn't often go to New Year's celebrations, especially at the dawn of a new century.

However, his wife had insisted, and since he rarely argued with his wife, here he was, 'dressed to the nines' and acting as one of the hosts at the ball the city gentry were holding to celebrate the beginning of the twentieth century.

Annaliese was looking at him in the mirror. "You look very handsome tonight."

He stretched his neck again and replied, "Well, that's something I guess, but I'm not sure it's worth it. This thing's heavy," he said, referring to the tuxedo he was wearing, "and the collar makes me keep my chin up. Feels like I'm looking down my nose at everyone. Handy won't even be able to talk to people without bending at the waist."

She turned on the bench at her dresser and held out her hands. He took them, pulled her to her feet and started to kiss her but she held up her hand. "Don't muss me. It took me two hours to get everything just right."

"You'd rather look impeccable at a once in a hundred-year celebration than kiss your husband?"

She touched him on the nose. "Just this once. When we get home you can muss me up all you want."

"Oh, Mama, you look beautiful." The children had come into the room and Teressa held out her hands to her mother.

"I'll bet all young daughters say that to their mamas the night of the ball," said Annaliese with a smile.

The girl turned and dropped a tentative curtsy to Johnny. He bowed in return, and she said, "You too, Papa."

"I look beautiful?"

"Oh, you know what I mean. Well, handsome then."

Manny was standing quietly, holding hands with Annaliese.

"Where did you learn to curtsy like that?" asked Annaliese.

"She and Este have been practicing all week," said Manny. "It looked silly."

"I wish I could go with you tonight," said Teressa. "Why can't we go?"

"It's just for grown-ups," said Annaliese. "Your time will come. Consuelo tells me y'all are having a party tonight."

"Yes, the twins will be there and Bobby and Gepp and some of our friends from school."

"Bobby's looking for you," said Handy to the girl from where he stood in the doorway. He stood aside for the children and watched them walk down the hall.

"Johnny boy, not long before you're going to be beating the boys off with a stick. She's a perfect little lady," Handy said, holding out his hand. "Happy New Year, Johnny." He nodded at Annaliese. "You too, doctor lady." He bent so she could kiss him on the cheek.

"Where's Rebecca?" asked Johnny.

"Right here," said Rebecca from behind him. "He's such a big oaf you can't see around him."

She pushed her husband out of the way and gave Johnny a hug. She was one of those women who never seemed to look older, and though she was dressed in hoopskirt finery, it was easy to see her Indian heritage, fancy dress or not.

"We'll be meeting Lemuel and Kate there."

'There' was an elegant ballroom at the Hotel Del Coronado and Lemuel was standing by the front door surveying the arrivals when they walked in. At one of the tables Kate was talking to Lillie Spreckels.

Managing Johnny's campaign had been Kate's first foray into politics and she never left, joining Johnny on the Council two years ago. She was probably the only one in the city who knew as many people as he did.

The room was huge. John Spreckels had knocked down a wall and spent a fair amount getting the place ready and it showed. Two hundred invitations had been sent, and it looked like everyone had shown up.

For the better part of an hour, he and Kate and the other commissioners stood greeting a steady stream of guests. By the time everyone was seated, his hand was a little sore from being shaken so many times.

Since the occasion was festive and most people had glasses in their hands there was much laughter, and greetings were heard on all sides. When members of the city council walked out on the stage and one at a time began to speak, the crowd became quiet, listening politely as they did to most politicians, especially ones who paid the salaries of many people in the room.

Not comfortable with speaking in public, Johnny had begged off and now sat beside his wife and thought about the coming 20th Century. He felt a little light-headed due to the unaccustomed champagne and his mind wandered away from what was being said. He would be thirty-four and fifteen years married in this new year and felt pretty good about that.

He counted his fall from a horse in a canyon outside of Salt Lake City and the breaking of several bones as the luckiest moment of his life. It had led him to marry the woman sitting beside him. He vividly remembered the night she kissed him for the first time and dated most of the good things in his life from that moment.

For him, their first ten years together had been ones of seeking and learning and trying new things, but with his election to the city council he seemed to have found the path to his future. He loved his position helping to shape the city he loved and couldn't imagine anything more enjoyable than getting to know the people he served.

Unless it was being married, that is. With her long, lustrous red hair, bright green eyes, and a generous spray of freckles across her cheeks, he felt she was as desirable now as she had been when he first opened his eyes in the hospital bed in Salt Lake and saw her looking down at him. If she had a few extra pounds and inches here and there, he loved every inch just as he always had.

When he looked around the room he saw most of his friends, the exceptions being Wash and Woman and they all joined him in toasting the New Year and gathering in the dark to watch the fireworks afterwards. It was an enjoyable evening, and Johnny came home tipsy for the first time in his life.

When Annaliese came out of the shower in her robe she held out her hand to him. "Will you join me on the porch for a final glass of champagne to celebrate the dawning of a new century?"

He and Lemuel had planned and built a porch onto their bedroom the year before and they loved sitting there at night after she had finished brushing her hair, looking out at the city and the bay, and enjoying the weather.

"How much champagne did you drink tonight? I get the impression you're a little drunk."

"Never having been drunk before, I'll just say I feel different. Kinda fuzzy around the ears." He grinned a silly grin. "And a little dizzy, especially when you sit next to me in a bathrobe with this hanging out." He reached to cradle her breast in his hand then bent his head to kiss it.

"Let's finish our drink and then..." she smiled at him and

adjusted her bathrobe "we'll play. In the meantime, let's talk."

"About what?"

"About the new year and the old one. How about that?"

He sipped. "I was thinking tonight about being thirty-four this year."

She took a deep breath. "Yes, and I'm forty-three. We seem to be doing alright, don't we?"

He nodded. "We've always known you were going to be a doctor, but what do you think about me becoming a politician?"

"I'm proud of you, Johnny. Usually, to call someone a politician is an insult, but not with you. You and Kate are really making a difference in the city, and I believe you'll keep doing it."

She took a sip. "You know, you're a natural leader and I'm glad to see you're using that talent. It's wonderful to see how the city is growing and changing since you and Kate have gotten into the system. When we came here, we said we wanted to grow up with the city and I think we have. You had a lot to do with that, you know."

They sat quiet for a moment. "Do you ever think of running for another office, maybe the legislature or congress?"

"People have mentioned it, so I've thought about it. Of course, the main thing is I wouldn't want to leave you to go to Sacramento or Washington. The roots we've put down here are deep and getting deeper. I can't think of anything that would tempt me enough to leave. Besides, I still have a lot I want to do here, and then there's your practice. They're your people and I don't think that'll ever change. I'd never ask you to leave them."

"You wouldn't have to move away. From what I know of the job, it's a couple of months once a year unless there's a special session. You've been away before."

"I've decided not to do that again. The first time I almost lost my hair."

"Johnny, there aren't too many wild Indians in Sacramento these days, although I have heard they get a little rowdy up there at times."

"I like what I'm doing around here. If that bug ever bites me, I'll let you know.

"Speaking of leaving home, I saw you talking to Este and Grace tonight. How are the budding doctors doing?"

"Este and Roy are getting settled into their respective schools, she in med school and he in sign language school. Apparently, he's going to teach her while he's learning. He's also going to try to get into the university up there. She said he doesn't know what he wants to study. Apparently, he'll figure that out later. He's getting used to the store up there again.

"Grace graduates in June in Los Angeles and she and her fellow, his name is Miles Gardner, are still trying to decide what to do next. It seems his family wants him home in Portland and she wants to come back here for a while, at least until she decides what's next."

Johnny chuckled. "Doesn't sound like a recipe for a happy marriage. Not like ours anyway."

"Are you still glad you married this old woman?" she asked. "I always wonder if you wish you'd waited and not married the first girl who ever kissed you."

He stood and pulled her to her feet, slid his hands inside her robe and ran them along her back down to her buttocks, then pulled her firmly against him.

"You're all I could ever want in a woman, and I was lucky enough to get you on the first try."

He led her to the bed and pushed the robe off her shoulders. The moonlight created shadows in interesting places on her body, and he just naturally wanted to examine them more closely. So, he did.

Woman and Wash were sitting in rocking chairs on the front porch of the cabin that same evening, talking.

"You never talk about when you were a Buffalo Soldier. How come?"

The day before an old soldier comrade from his days in the 10th

Cavalry had come into the store and they had left for a while to sit over coffee and talk about the old days fighting Indians on the Great Plains.

He was quiet for a while, pondering the question as he always did.

"I was with them for five years, and when I left, I was ready to go. I'd had my fill of soldiering.

"When I was freed the most natural thing to do was to join the army. I wanted to help the people who'd freed me win the war. Besides that, there were so many freed slaves that it was hard for everyone to find work to feed their families, let alone a young freedman five hundred miles from home. The army made sense if you wanted to eat every day.

"When the war was over it was the same. I went back to the plantation, but it had been burned. My family was gone and there were freed men trying to farm what was left. I didn't really want any part of that, so I joined up again.

"They used us on the plains fighting Indians and such. I had learned smithing on the plantation, so I just naturally started fixing things and ended up as a regimental armorer and blacksmith. It was boring and hot and dusty most of the time, but I liked most of the people and, all in all, it wasn't bad. Like most things in life, I guess, some good and some bad."

He reached for her hand. "Since we've been down here it's been mostly good. This seems to me what I've been living my life to find; being with you and living in this place, working for Kate and being around my friends."

They sat looking at each other in silence for a while.

"The only fly in my ointment right now is Schweder." He sat back in his chair and stared out at the darkness. "Whenever I go out there, I get this feeling in my stomach, like I'm standing on the edge of a cliff looking down. I'm never comfortable when I'm there. It's like I'm expecting something to happen, something bad." He took a deep breath. "Something dangerous."

"What could happen?"

"I don't know but I know he thinks about it. Sometimes I'll be working on something out there and I look up and see him watching me. He couldn't not think about it every time he sees me. I keep wondering if one day he'll decide to do something about it to, find some way to avenge what I did to him."

"How long has he known about it?"

"About six years, if I remember right."

"Didn't you say he had decided not to do anything about it because he didn't want to deal with the problems it would cause?"

"That's what he said, but why would I believe him?"

"What can you do about it?"

He sat rubbing his chin thoughtfully. After a while he shook his head. "I can't think of a single thing except maybe not going out there anymore. Of course, then I'd have to tell Kate why."

"You could finish the job."

He continued to look out at the moonlit landscape for a while. When he turned his head to look at her he could see she hadn't been joking.

He went back to looking into the dark again for a while, then said, "No I can't do that." He smiled at her. "I never told you what he said about you, did I?" She shook her head. "He said he thought you'd be more dangerous than Johnny."

"What did you say?"

"I told him he was probably right."

They had just returned from the New Year's ball and Sarah was sitting at her dressing table when she noticed a letter on the floor under her feet. She was reading it when Madame came into the room.

Suddenly she said, "Oh."

"Bad news?"

Sarah looked at her friend in the mirror with a look of surprise on her face. "I don't know. I guess."

"Who's it from?"

"Jonas. He says he's decided to get married."

"What?! That's kind of sudden, isn't it? Has he ever mentioned something like that before?" When Sarah shook her head she continued, "Does he say to who?"

"He says I don't know her. He met her when he was back east. Her name is Caroline. She's from New York." She handed Madame the letter.

When she finished reading it, she looked up. "Well at least he says he'll always love you. That's something, I guess. Maybe he just got tired of waiting."

They sat in silence for a while, each continuing to get ready for bed.

Finally, Madame held out her hand and said, "Why don't we go sit at the window in the dark and talk." When they were seated looking out at a beautifully moonlit ocean Madame asked, "So, how do you feel about it?"

Sarah shrugged. "Surprised, I guess, but I shouldn't be. We've been doing this for fifteen years. I guess it was just a matter of time. He's an attractive man. He's rich and apparently, he was available."

"Do you wish you'd married him?"

Sarah sat quiet for a moment. "No, I don't," she finally said. "He quit asking me a few years ago, and I thought he'd either decided to accept what we had or maybe begin looking, but to tell you the truth, I haven't thought much about it for a while."

"So, I guess you'll just have to hang around and take care of this old lady as she gets older."

The chairs weren't close enough to touch so she stood and held out her hands so she could pull Sarah to her feet and into a warm embrace. After a long moment she stepped back, loosed her dressing gown and did the same to Sarah's. The embrace now was ardent and the kiss passionate.

"Let's go to bed and do some wonderful things to one another. Maybe you can forget all about it," she whispered in her lover's ear and led her to the bed.

"So, it seems like we've had a pretty good year. Any interesting plans for next year?" Lemuel was standing in the doorway of her bedroom in a bathrobe.

"Do you want to get married this year?" she replied after a moment's thought. "

It was a question one or the other asked every New Year, but so far, they weren't married. He kissed her and gave the accepted response.

"Why ruin a good thing?"

"I'm sorry, but with a new century you need to come up with a better answer."

He kissed her on the nose and thought for a moment. "How about 'Yes'?"

She was taken aback, looked astounded. "Yes?"

"I've been thinking it would be a good way to start the new year, but I promise you I won't change anything." He took her into his arms and kissed her. "I like things too much the way they are."

Kate had liked Johnny's new porch so much he'd gotten Lemuel to build her one, and she took his hand and led him to it. They sat quiet for a while looking out at the Bay under a full moon.

"I've been thinking about bringing Woman and Wash in as partners in the nursery."

"Why's that?"

"I'm so involved with the city now I'm not even there much anymore. Between the two of them they pretty much run the place and I just think it would be the right thing to do."

"I think it would be great." He reached out and took her hand. "I can always count on you to do the right thing.

"Do you ever think about Wash and the shooting I told you about?" he asked. "I remember you said it wouldn't affect the way you looked at him. Has it?"

"I think the only time it comes to mind is when Ger comes in the store, and he doesn't do that much anymore. I thought about it a lot after you told me and finally decided I trusted his judgement. If the man was guilty, and Wash seemed to think he was, then he was probably right to do what he did.

"So no, I don't think about it much anymore. I trust them, always have, always will."

"What do you think about my idea about getting married?"

"Well, it took me by surprise, but I can't imagine saying 'no'. On the other hand, it gives me something else to think about."

"You mean a wedding?"

"Well, that's usually what happens when you get married. You have a wedding."

"Kate dear, if we have a regular wedding and invite all our friends, we'd need a room the size of the one we were in tonight to hold the reception. The whole town would be there, not to mention others from around the state."

"What do you suggest?"

"Let's elope!"

She burst out laughing. "I can just see you climbing a ladder to my bedroom window. We'd break our necks. Be a fine way to spend a honeymoon; in the hospital."

He grinned slyly. "Let's go on the honeymoon first and get married when we get where we're going. And besides, we don't have to tell anyone." He held up a finger and said "Wait here. I'll be right back."

When he returned, he knelt by her chair and offered her a small box. "You won't have to tell anyone. When they see you wearing this they'll know."

She looked at the box for a long moment, then opened it and smiled at the ring inside. "It's beautiful." His face was in shadow, but she could see him grinning. "Where do you want to go?"

"Right now, let's go to bed. We can figure out where we're going later." He stood for a moment looking at her. "You know, you've given me back my life, given me a chance to live out all those fantasies I had. Now they're memories. Thank you."

She leaned over and kissed him, "Come to bed and let's make another one."

They shrugged off their robes and embraced. She reached to take him in her hand. "You realize we're getting old. How much longer do you think we'll be able to do this?"

He urged her onto the bed and whispered to her. "Until we can't." he said and kissed her. "And I've read that the more you do it the more you can."

As he slid inside her, he looked into her eyes. "Does that feel old?" he asked.

She closed her eyes and said a little breathlessly, "Let's talk about it later."

"Johnny, are you down here?" In the light from the hall Annaliese could see his shadow in one of the chairs in the reading room. "Oh, there you are," she said. "I wondered what happened to you. Are you all right?"

He turned and she could see his face, see what looked like pain. He was crying. "Jinx is dead. He must have died while we were at the ball."

She stepped forward and took his hand. "Oh Johnny, I'm so sorry." She knelt beside him, hugged him, and looked around. "Where was he?"

"Wasn't in his bed so I called him and when he didn't come, I think I knew it then. I found him behind the counter." He shrugged. "I shouldn't be surprised. He spent a lot of time in his bed lately. It's been a couple weeks since we went anywhere together.

"When you came in, I was remembering the first time I really looked at him. He was a scrawny little thing. I was feeding him with a rag I had dipped in milk, and he was lying in my arms looking up at me with those big green eyes." He began to sob, and she sat quiet, hugging him. "From that time to this he's been a big part of my life. It's going to feel strange knowing he's gone."

"He lived longer than any cat I ever heard of," she said. "How old was he?"

"I've been counting back, and I make it seventeen this coming summer, half my life. I've never done that before, counted the years. I guess maybe I didn't want to know."

He wiped his eyes and stood, helping her to her feet. "Where is the body?" she asked, looking around.

"I wrapped it in a towel." He gestured at the counter, "and put it in his bed on a shelf behind the counter. When it gets light, I'm going to bury it in the garden out back. I think I'd like to put up a stone of some kind."

Two days later he knelt and fitted a gravestone in the ground at the head of a small mound of earth. After a moment he stood, brushed the dirt off his hands and pants, stood for a moment and read the inscription, remembering.

Jinx
A little black cat who loved me
1884-1901

"Goodbye little Buddy," he said. He took his wife's hand, turned and walked away.